PILOT PERFECT

The tape continued to play as they watched in awe. What happened next, happened in a heartbeat. One moment, the F-22 was closing behind the tiny, black-hulled aircraft, lining up for a missile shot. In a blur, the mystery craft darted to the right at an incredibly sharp angle and dropped altitude several thousand feet. Before the F-22 even started to turn around, the black aircraft was already just a few hundred yards behind it. Then the tape turned to static.

"Good Lord!" Tim said. "I've never seen anything like that. How could the pilot take that kind of G-force punishment?"

Jenny shook her head. "I don't think anyone could."

"What?"

Jenny hesitated. "That thing . . . That black jet is an un-manned vehicle." She paused. "There may not be a human inside, but it does have a pilot."

Tim frowned, finally comprehending what it meant.

"Are you trying to tell me that your father's creation can actually *replace* a human being?"

She nodded. "Yep."

VORTEX
ONE

J. A. LAYTON

JOVE BOOKS, NEW YORK

VORTEX ONE

A Jove Book / published by arrangement with
the author

PRINTING HISTORY
Jove edition / December 2001

For information address: The Berkley Publishing Group,
a division of Penguin Putnam Inc.,
375 Hudson Street, New York, New York 10014.

Visit our website at
www.penguinputnam.com

ISBN: 0-515-13204-7

A JOVE BOOK®
Jove Books are published by The Berkley Publishing Group,
a division of Penguin Putnam Inc.,
375 Hudson Street, New York, New York 10014.
JOVE and the "J" design
are trademarks belonging to Penguin Putnam Inc.

PRINTED IN THE UNITED STATES OF AMERICA

10 9 8 7 6 5 4 3 2 1

This novel is dedicated to my mother,
Audrey Elizabeth Layton.

"China sleeps; when she wakes, she will shake the world."

Napoleon Bonaparte

CONTENTS

PROLOGUE EXTRA CREDIT

"They're starting to bring it out now," Jimmy said. The seventeen-year-old was lying prone on the flat rock surface. His right eye was glued to the night vision scope.

"You can see it?" asked David. He was sitting next to Jimmy, half in, half out of his down-filled sleeping bag.

"Yeah. They opened the door. It's just sitting there . . . with its lights on."

"All right!"

Jimmy turned away from the NV scope, eyeing his partner. "Can't you get that thing to work?"

"I'm replacing the batteries. I think that's the problem." David cradled the radio scanner in his lap. It was about the size of a hardback novel. From one end, a stainless steel wire antenna extended upward about a foot. He slipped in the fourth size D copper-top Duracell and flipped the switch. The digital readout blinked on and then a screech of static blasted from the speaker. He backed off the volume. "It's working now."

"Good. Better check your camera. Something's happening."

David turned and peered through the eyepiece of the mini-cam. Like Jimmy's telescope, the video camera was mounted on a tripod and was also equipped with low-light optics. The lens was set to maximum zoom. Although the image in the viewfinder was grainy, with a bluish-green tint, the target was clearly visibly.

"Wow," David announced, "look at that sucker!" He then took a few seconds to study the image. "What is that?"

"I don't know. I've never seen one like it before." Jimmy paused and then asked: "You recording it yet?"

"I am now." David reached up with his right thumb and clicked a red button on the video camera. A sharp electronic *beep beep* broadcast from the housing and the REC icon flashed on inside the viewfinder.

Jimmy remained fused to his NV scope. "I think we hit the jackpot tonight," he finally said, barely able to suppress his awe. His heart thundered away like a racing locomotive.

"No kidding!" David replied, still studying the video image. A moment later he turned, now facing his buddy. "You know, Jimmy, Mr. Carlson's going to shit a brick when we show this tape to the class. He's going to have to give us an A for sure!"

"A-plus!" countered Jimmy.

The high school seniors had been hiding out for almost a day, nestled in between the rock outcrops at the crest of the ridgeline. They had hiked in the previous evening, arriving a few hours before sunrise. They managed to avoid detection by taking a new route, one that skirted the sensors.

The teenagers from Bakersfield had told their parents they were going to Yosemite for the weekend. They lied.

The night air was cooler than expected. Jimmy and David wore everything they had, including their sleeping bags. A fire would have been welcome, but that was impossible. It would have given their presence away.

From their elevated perch atop the Nevada butte, they had a commanding view of the dried-out lake bed. During the day, there had been little activity. A 737 landed at half past seven in the morning. It took off eight hours later. Other than the jetliner, and the occasional pickup truck driving between the buildings, they had observed nothing of interest. But that all changed when the sun finally dipped behind the Sierra Nevada.

The valley floor was soon awash with light. Everything was illuminated: the huge hangars, the massive office-laboratory complex, the army of parabolic dishes aimed skyward, the airport runway that seemed to extend to infinity. Even from miles away, the covert military base looked like downtown Las Vegas.

Just after sunset, the helicopters took off. There were two of the black-hulled Apaches. They were flying Dobermans.

About the same time the helos launched, half a dozen Jeep Cherokees streamed out of a parking lot near one of the buildings. Like their airborne companions, the occupants of the unmarked snow-white four-wheel-drive vehicles had carte blanche when it came to the use of deadly force.

Several hours after the night security forces were deployed, the four-story-tall doors on one of the hangars were rolled back. That's what Jimmy and David had been waiting for.

"What do you think they're going to do with it?" asked David.

"I don't know—maybe they're going to run some kind of test."

"Could we be that lucky? I mean, we've got a perfect shot from up here, and the lighting's real good for my camera."

"Yeah. I think we really lucked out tonight."

"Vortex One, Control."

"Control, Vortex One. Go."

"Vortex One, you are authorized to activate MERLIN for phase one test. I say again, you are authorized to activate unit for phase one test. Over."

"Roger, Control. MERLIN's on line and I'm rolling."

"Look at that thing!" David said. **"It's moving on its own now."**

"I know," Jimmy answered, still peering through the starlight-enhanced telescope. "You getting it on tape?" he asked.

"Yep, coming in real good."

Jimmy turned away from the scope, glancing at the radio scanner. The digital readout continued to blink as it cycled from one channel to another, hunting for an active transmission. But it found nothing. The RF signals that were currently being broadcast from the base were on an ultrahigh band, far beyond the scanner's range. They were also encrypted.

Jimmy returned to the telescope. *Holy shit, look at that!*

* * *

"Control, phase one is complete. All systems are in the green. MERLIN's right on the money."

"Roger that. You are cleared for phase two. Execute Program Delta. Your ceiling limit is seventy thousand. Over."

"I copy. Execute Delta. Cap at Angels seven zero."

"Where'd it go?" David asked. He was now on his knees, head bent back, looking upward into the star-studded heavens.

Jimmy was standing, also scanning the sky. "I don't know. I've never seen anything move like that before." He glanced down at David. "Did you record it?"

"Most of it, until its running lights faded out."

"Good."

David continued to search the blackness for a long moment before again addressing his partner. "Damn thing sure was noisy."

"Yeah, it didn't sound like anything I've heard before. Kind of like it was continuously backfiring, or maybe pulsing somehow."

"Right. Thud! . . . thud! . . . thud! One after another."

Several minutes passed. Both teenagers were now standing, still eyeing the night sky. "How'd they do that?" Jimmy asked. "Making all those crazy turns and then shooting up like that . . . there's nothing flying that I know about that can do that."

"I know. But we just saw it . . . so it's real, whatever it is."

"The pilot must have really pulled some heavy G's."

"Yeah. Those turns. Shit, I'd puke my guts out for sure if it was me in that thing."

"Me too."

"Control, Vortex One. I'm now in phase two cruise."

"Roger that. How's the ride?"

"She's really pushing my limit. Peaked at thirteen point five. I almost locked." A slight pause. "After that last run the thrust vector vibration started up again. Something's haywire with the controller."

"Can you dampen it?"

"Negative. It's cycling just like before. Those changes did nothing. I think . . . wait one. I've got a new problem here."

"Vortex One, state your problem. Over."

"Something new just happened. She's sluggish as hell, like I've lost some power. I'm okay but she sure feels weird."

"Disengage MERLIN and return to the base."

"Roger."

The two teenagers were now sitting cross-legged on top of their sleeping bags, looking down at the top secret U.S. government complex. They were too excited to notice the cold.

"Where do you think it went?" asked David, a mistlike plume of breath discharging from his mouth.

"Maybe it's heading to Nellis," Jimmy guessed.

"Yeah, I bet you're right. They could probably land there and nobody would see it."

"Right."

"Vortex One, you're losing altitude too fast. Slow up."

"I'm trying but the damn controls aren't responding correctly, or I'm not working them right."

"Have you disengaged MERLIN?"

"I think so but I can't . . . damn, what the hell is . . ."

"Vortex One, you're off course. Do you have control? Over."

"I'm supposed to be on manual but she still doesn't feel right."

"Do you want to abort?"

"No. It's manageable and I'm getting close." A short pause. "I just turned on my landing lights. Can you see me now?"

"Roger. We've got a visual on you."

"Hey, look at that!" shouted David. He was pointing with his outstretched right arm.

Jimmy tracked the glaring light. It eclipsed the inky sky with its brilliance—like a hundred-carat diamond on a bed of black velvet. "What the hell is that?" Jimmy finally asked.

"Whatever it is, it's coming this way."
"Do you think it's one of those choppers?"
"Damn, I hope not."

"Control, I'm still having trouble maintaining my heading."
"You're ten point six miles downrange. Can you make it back to the base? Over."
"I'm not sure. There's definitely a fault in the MERLIN interlink. I still don't have complete manual control."
"Copy that. Just set her down on the lake bed where you can and we'll come and get you. Over."
"Okay. That sounds . . . oh, shit!"
"Vortex One! You're descending too fast! Slow up!"
No response.
"Vortex One, come in."
No response.
"Vortex One, Eject! Eject! Eject!"

The two teenagers were now standing at the edge of the precipice, looking downslope. A fire burned about a mile away. The flames lit up the surrounding terrain. Aided by the NV optics in the telescope and video camera, they could see the wreckage—metal fragments littered the landscape around the impact point.
"Do you really think anyone was in it?" David asked, turning away from his camera.
Jimmy shook his head. "I sure hope not . . . what a way to go."
Neither boy wanted to think that they had just witnessed death.
"Maybe he bailed out," offered David.
"Did you see a chute?" Jimmy asked, now facing his buddy.
"No."
"Neither did I." Jimmy paused. "But maybe it was remote controlled. It was kind of small for a regular-sized one, you know."
David nodded. "Right. Those guys down at Groom Lake were probably flying it from their desks."

"Yeah, that's—"

Jimmy stopped in midsentence, interrupted. The radio scanner had finally come alive. It had locked on to one of the base's emergency frequencies. The signal was not encrypted.

"Base to patrol units. We've got an event in sector eight. I say again, we've got an event in sector eight. Execute plan Able."

Jimmy looked down at the scanner. A chill surged up his spine. "I think we better get going, Dave. They'll be crawling all over this place in no time."

"Yeah, let's go."

Jimmy and David had managed to hike for over three hours before one of the Apaches spotted them. The gunship's infrared camera picked up their body heat. In the open, no longer hidden by rock outcrops, they stood out like neon billboards.

They started running, fearing capture. They both remembered what the boundary marker sign had said about trespassing on the government reservation: a minimum of one year imprisonment, without a trial, and a $5,000 fine. They didn't want to think about the other part of the warning.

The helo made one high-speed pass, confirming the sighting. It then returned, hovering fifty feet over the teenagers.

Jimmy and David continued to run, trying to escape. But it was hopeless. The Apache's rotor wash sandblasted them while the Night Sun searchlight ignited the landscape. And then a mechanical voice barked from the heavens: "Stop, you're under arrest!"

Repelled by the specter of jail time, the honor students ignored the warning. Jimmy's Ford Ranger was just a few hundred yards away. They could make it!

As the boys fled, an encrypted radio message was sent from the helicopter. It was answered thirty seconds later. The decision was made.

Jimmy and David would have eventually graduated if they had just stopped and sat down. Eighteen months is what they would have served, the videotape adding another half year to their compulsory sentences.

The Apache didn't bother landing to inspect the kill. It just left them where they lay, shredded by chain gunfire. One of the 4×4s would collect the corpses later in the morning.

DAY 1

FLOOD TIDE

1 THE TEST BED

The sun had long disappeared but it was still in the low eighties. Earlier it had broken a hundred.

The dog days of August rarely hit the Pacific Northwest with such ferocity. But for the past week, the Puget Sound basin had been simmering under the cloudless skies. The uncommon heat was welcome after the drizzly July and the thoroughly wet June.

The half moon hung low in the sky, broadcasting its chalky radiance across the enormous building. The side of the ten-story structure appeared to stretch on forever.

The four-lane highway that paralleled the building was all but deserted. Just a lonely car raced past now and then.

The perimeter of the Boeing Company's Everett Assembly Building was dimly lit. About half of the floodlights that normally bathed the world's largest building by volume had been switched off. The Air Force Security Police found the illumination too bright. They preferred to remain in the shadows.

There were several armed guards monitoring the southeast corner of the Boeing factory this night. They were all business. No one got inside the security zone without a detailed ID check.

The two men that had just exited the building door near the corner had already been cleared. The short, stocky one used his handheld radio to alert the guards that he and his companion were coming out for a smoke break. They stood by themselves a few feet away from the building's sheer face. Like all of the other military personnel on duty tonight, they wore civilian clothing. Had they been in their uniforms, the squat one would have had silver eagles on his shoulder epaulets; his taller companion would have worn a pair of double silver bars.

The colonel was smoking; his aide just watched. The red

glow of the cigarette marked their position as they stood in the building's moon shadow. The colonel had been a smoker for nearly twenty-five years now. During his last fitness report it had been strongly suggested that, if he ever wanted to get his first star, he'd better give up tobacco. The Air Force was on a campaign to weed out smokers from its officer corps.

The senior officer took another drag and, after exhaling, turned to face his subordinate. "That last change seemed to help. The bird was a lot more stable during the landing, don't you think?"

"Yes, sir," replied the thirty-year-old engineering officer. He had been assigned to the colonel's project just a week earlier. So far, it had been a whirlwind indoctrination. Every day there was something new. "It sure learns quick, damn quick. I didn't feel nearly as much vibration this time." He paused. "We'll know for sure tomorrow when the data analysis is finished."

The colonel nodded, now looking out toward the highway. "I think we've finally got a chance at making the thing work right, at least for the dual control tests."

"I agree, Colonel, but it'd be a lot easier if we had the prototype to compare with."

"Absolutely. But who knows when we'll get it back."

The two men stood silent for nearly a minute and then the colonel reached up with his left hand and swiped away a bead of sweat from his brow. He turned back to face his aide. "You know, Bill, I had no idea it could get so hot up here. I'd swear I was back at Nellis."

"This is pretty unusual, all right. It hardly ever gets this hot. I can only remember a couple of times like this. Usually it stays in the seventies—real nice."

"You grew up near here?"

"Close by. Tacoma. About fifty miles south of here."

"Hmmm," the colonel acknowledged. He then took in another deep drag and glanced down at his wristwatch. It was 12:09 A.M. "Well," he said, now exhaling, "I wonder how General Mathews and the others made out this evening."

"They're interviewing Richmond tonight, too?"

"Yeah, the general called me a few minutes before our test. Said the whole team was sticking around for another round of questioning."

"I bet she didn't like that."

"Probably."

"Did the general say if they're making any progress with her?"

"Not much. She still refuses to cooperate, claiming she wasn't in on the breakthrough, and that she had nothing to do with the development work."

"But we know she has the skills—besides her engineering degrees she's heavily into robotics software and device physics."

"Yeah, you don't have to convince me. No doubt about it, she's one smart cookie." The colonel hesitated. "But I'm now beginning to think she's deliberately pulling our chain on this whole thing."

"You mean like what her dad did, all that trouble with patent rights and royalties?"

"Kind of." The colonel sucked in another lungful from the Camel. After exhausting, he continued, "But I think it goes beyond that. She's no doubt still pissed about what happened to him."

"But that wasn't our fault. The FBI was supposed to be watching him."

"True enough, but there's plenty of blame to go around. For starters, we should have never agreed to do the prototype testing up here." The senior officer swept his right hand outward, gesturing toward the adjacent highway. "These are wonderful facilities and Boeing's been cooperative as hell, but it's too goddamn public around here. We should be doing this whole thing back at Dreamland, right along with the rest of the replicate testing program."

"I agree, sir. But there's no way Dr. Richmond would agree to it. The terms of his contract were explicit: all testing with *his* prototype unit must be done at Boeing."

"Yeah, I know. The turkey just didn't trust us with the original. But all the same, if someone spots the sucker, then the crap's really going to hit the fan. No way we'll be able to keep it under wraps."

"It's a little risky. But as long as the tests are conducted over the Cascades, at night, no one's going to know."

"But eventually we're going to have to get real with it, just like the Nellis group is doing. And that'll mean total autonomous testing. I don't see that working out up here—too damn many people around. I'd still prefer doing this whole thing in Nevada—much more private."

"When do you think we'll be able to make our first solo flight?"

"Not until we get the prototype back. Until then we can only run fully monitored tests."

"Can't we try it solo with one of the replicate units—like the one we used tonight? It should work fine."

"Mathews won't allow it, at least not right away. His people still haven't completely solved the replicate stability problem. That's why they want Richmond's original unit. They need it to make a direct comparison between it and the replicates that he provided us."

"But I thought the Nellis group was already running autonomous tests on the backup Vortex—with the CPU he made for us?"

"They are and they've made a lot of progress since Major Collins augered in V-One. But just the same, until it's a hundred percent the general doesn't want our bird going solo." The colonel took another long drag. "It's one thing to drop a test bird into the middle of the Nellis range, but a triple seven going down around here . . ." He shook his head. "It'll raise a huge stink for sure. We'd have to deal with the crew problem, somehow get around the FAA and NTSB, and then fight off the press hounds. We're just not ready for that kind of exposure."

"They still think Major Collins screwed up?"

The colonel nodded. "Yeah, we're pretty sure now. Somehow he managed to accidentally shut down part of it without regaining full manual control. We think he was badly disoriented from the evasion test run."

"G-lock?"

"Everything points to that. It was just too much." The colonel took a deep breath. "Hell, there's no way I could take those kinds of turns without scrambling my brains."

"What a damn shame."

"I know. Mark was a hell of a test pilot."

"Are they running any flights down there with observers?"

"No. Not anymore. After we lost Mark, Mathews ordered all test flights unmanned. He even had 'em remove the cockpit, adding another fuel tank in its place." The colonel hesitated for a moment. "It was time anyway. From day one, the damn thing was never set up right for manual control. MERLIN's just too quick for a pilot at full power."

"How many of Richmond's replicates do we have left?"

"The two of ours, plus four more; two down at Dreamland, two back at the DARPA labs."

"Are any of those filtered?"

"DARPA has one of 'em, the rest are unrestricted."

"So we'll be the only group testing the filtered units."

"Yep—part of our deal with Richmond. They all have to be tested up here."

The junior officer took a long moment to mull over the facts. There were two prototype testing programs under way: combat operations, run out of Nevada, and civilian applications, based in Everett. The captain had been assigned to the latter. The combat test team used full power—unrestricted units; his group worked with a muted version, deliberately toned down for security purposes.

"When do you think we'll be able to make our own units?" asked the captain.

"Hard to say. DARPA's had some success with their own replicates but they're nowhere near as effective as the ones Dr. Richmond made, especially those for the Vortex program."

"So we've got to get the original back?"

"That's what they tell me . . . or at least figure out what Richmond was doing when he made his replicates."

"Do you think she knows where her dad's records are hidden?"

"I hope so . . . or everything we've been working on is

going to end up in the dumper. If we can't reproduce the damn thing, it'll be pretty much useless."

The junior officer just grunted. And then, about a minute later, just after the colonel field-stripped the spent butt, the captain asked a question that had been gnawing at him all night: "Sir, is it really true that Dr. Richmond made the breakthrough after a lightning strike?"

"Yeah. It happened a couple of years ago. He was testing it when the building was hit. There was some kind of grounding problem with his lab equipment. Anyway, that jolt created a hellish power surge in his equipment. Part of it even caught on fire. Afterward, when he was running a diagnostic test on the unit, he stumbled onto the phenomenon. It all happened by accident."

"That's just astonishing . . . it's so hard to believe."

"I know. But the damn thing works. And that's what counts."

The two men talked for a few more minutes before returning to the building. Unlike the exterior, the assembly building's interior was ablaze with illumination. It was as bright as the noonday sun. And mammoth. Ten NFL stadiums could fit inside.

The southeastern corner of the gigantic plant was partitioned off from the rest of the ninety-eight-acre building. The other bays were filled with dozens of Boeing 747s, 767s, and 777s, all in various phases of construction.

The segregated bay contained only one aircraft: a brand-new twin engine 777. The wide-body jet's green-tinted aluminum fuselage had not yet been painted. It would eventually be sold to an airline, but for the present the U.S. Air Force leased it.

The jet was surrounded by four guards, each armed with an assault rifle. Besides the sentries, there were just a handful of civilians in the restricted hangar. Everyone had a Top Secret security clearance.

From the exterior, the $140 million jetliner appeared normal. And inside the twenty-foot-diameter hull, every one of the 375 passenger seats had been installed, along with the galley and nearly a dozen lavatories. The only modifications were located in the cockpit.

The Air Force officers were now aboard the 777, standing at the aft end of the flight deck. The colonel still flew F-15s for practice; he was addicted to the Eagle's speed and agility. The captain was an electronics engineer; he was married to a desktop computer. Despite their differences, they were both awestruck at what they were viewing.

The pilot's control station had been gutted; there was no left-hand seat with its companion steering column and rudder pedals. Instead, an innocuous stainless steel box, about two-thirds the size of a washing machine, was bolted to the floor beams. To the immediate right was the copilot's station. Untouched, it remained 100 percent operational.

"Talk about your black box magic," the colonel said, gesturing toward what had been the pilot's station.

"I know, sir. Richmond sure knew what he was doing when he selected this bird. It's a perfect test bed for MERLIN. Everything's already wired up. All he had to do was plug her in to AIMS and see what happens."

The 777's Aircraft Information Management System was the fly-by-wire computer brain that controlled and/or monitored nearly every electronic and mechanical system onboard the Boeing jetliner. And with 150 separate computers scattered throughout the 210-foot-long ship, AIMS was state-of-the-art technology. Yet it was of Stone Age vintage when compared to what now occupied the former left-hand seat.

The colonel was shaking his head, equally astonished and appalled. "You know, Bill, if this all works out like I think it's going to, we're going to be in for some pretty big changes."

"I know, Colonel. It's a little scary when you think about it."

The colonel didn't reply, now consumed with his own thoughts: *How will I ever compete? This damn MERLIN thing could put me out of business overnight. . . . I'll be extinct, just like the frigging dinosaurs!*

2 A RUDE AWAKENING

Six of them came from the north. Outfitted in dark combat fatigues, they were nothing more than hazy shadows in the dim moonlight.

A helicopter had deposited the team onto a mountain meadow a few minutes before sunset. They used night vision devices and a handheld GPS receiver to find their way over the rugged terrain and through the dense forest. It took them three hours to hike the five miles to their destination.

When the men reached the target, they split into two units. The four-man primary took up position near the main entrance. The reserves guarded the rear.

The grounds surrounding the target were well illuminated, making a direct assault chancy. Even though the safe house was miles from the nearest neighbor, the FBI agents manning it this night didn't take security measures lightly. They were prepared.

After a minute of surveillance, the intruders located the guards. A man with an M-16 assault rifle was sitting on the porch of the sprawling two-story log cabin. Concealed by shadow and outfitted in camouflage, he would have been invisible without the NVDs.

The second sentry was out back, behind the building. He sat beside the trunk of a ten-story-tall Douglas fir, just beyond the dirt road that led up to the cabin. Like the first guard, he was also armed with an M-16. However, mounted above the breech of his automatic weapon was an electro-optical Javelin Model 223 night vision sight.

About fifty feet beyond the FBI sniper's position, almost at the end of the dirt road, was a four-wheel-drive vehicle. The Ford Expedition was parked next to the kitchen door. It had been turned around in the road, as if ready to race down the steep hillside.

Besides the exterior lookouts, the intruders spotted two

additional federal agents inside the mountainside cabin. The
men were sitting around a television set, watching a movie.

The assault team waited until a quarter of three and then
attacked. The FBI sniper was the first hit—a single round to
the forehead from another sniper-type weapon. The bullet
was .22 caliber and the end of the barrel through which it
passed was equipped with a suppressor. The resulting "zap"
was barely audible in the still night air.

The FBI agent on the porch was a more challenging target.
Because he was sitting down, the wooden guardrail that lined
the edge of the porch didn't allow for a clear head shot.
Consequently, the shooter assigned to neutralize the guard
was forced to move closer to the cabin, right to the edge of
the building's perimeter light cone. Had the assassin made
his shot right away, instead of taking his time to aim as if
he were at the rifle range, he would have succeeded. Instead,
the delay cost him his life.

Agent Audrey Jordan despised witness protection assign-
ments. Boring didn't even begin to describe the work. The
isolation was the worst part of it. The rural safe houses were
invariably located in some remote spot, with nothing around
but miles of trees and pastures. And they were so quiet that
Audrey actually found herself missing the amalgam of street
and traffic noises that, after decades of urban living, were
now programmed into her subconscious.

A New York City native, Audrey had been with the FBI
for over seventeen years. Four months earlier she had been
assigned to the Seattle field office, transferring from Quantico, Virginia, where she had spent two years as an academy
instructor. Normally, she would have been too senior to draw
the mundane guard detail. However, because of summer vacation schedules, she ended up running the detail that was
now guarding the special "guest."

Audrey had been asleep when her full bladder woke her
up. After returning from the bathroom, she happened to look
out the window from her second-story room. That's when

she spotted the trespasser. The gunman wasn't one of hers, that she was certain of.

The black-clad figure was near the outer edge of one of the floodlights. He had just knelt down on one knee and was in the process of aiming his weapon.

My God! He's going to shoot Manny!

Audrey's reactions were automatic. There was no time to radio the alarm or to order the assassin to drop his weapon. Instead, she grabbed the 9 mm Beretta—it was on the nightstand next to the bed—and aimed downward, gripping it with both hands. An instant later she fired, right through the double-pane glass window.

The target was about sixty feet away. It was a difficult shot at best—especially with the window glass to penetrate. But Audrey was an expert markswoman. She pulled the trigger twice, just as she had been trained. The first bullet shattered the window. It then plowed into the dirt just beyond the intruder, its trajectory deflected by the glass panes. The second round, now free of obstructions, found its mark. It burrowed into the man two inches under his right armpit, ripping through both lungs. He flopped to the ground, spilling into the light cone.

The report from Audrey's gunshot, although muffled by the walls of her bedroom, echoed through the otherwise tranquil air. Almost instantly, a barrage of suppressed automatic weapons fire peppered her room, shattering the remaining windows.

"Dammit!" shouted Audrey as she dropped to the floor, her ears ringing from her own pistol shot. "There must be a frigging army out there."

She waited a few seconds for the blitz to cease. She then crawled to the nightstand and grabbed the portable radio transceiver that had been parked on it. Before she could key the microphone, another flurry of gunfire erupted—this time from the cabin's defenders.

Good going, boys, she thought, *nail their butts!*

Audrey triggered the mike. "Cobra Three, One. Where are they?"

No response.

Audrey repeated the call, trying to raise the rest of her people. Again, no answer. The gunfire continued, both outgoing and incoming.

We gotta get out of here, Audrey finally decided. She began slithering along the floor, heading toward the door.

Jennifer Evelyn Richmond bolted upright in her bed when the first shot went off.

After another grueling day of interrogation, and then an evening of additional Q & A, she had finally retired to her bedroom, exhausted. As she climbed into bed, the eight-member interrogation team, Air Force officers and DOD analysts, became airborne, heading back to Boeing Field.

Jenny was in maximum REM when World War III erupted. Her dream world evaporated the instant Audrey triggered the Beretta.

The din of gunfire was bad enough, but the sound of bullets ripping through the walls and bursting glass, passing just inches from her bed, was outright terrifying. Instinctively she rolled off the bed and hugged the floor. She could smell the polish of the hardwood flooring. *What's happening?*

Audrey pounded on Jenny's door. It was locked from inside. "Miss Richmond," she yelled. "Open the door. We've got to get you out of here."

Jenny opened it. The FBI agent was on all fours, the heavy Beretta gripped in her right hand, the radio receiver dangling from her neck, suspended by its carrying strap. Forever cold, and because the nights in the Cascade Range could be chilly, Audrey wore a pair of white cotton long johns to bed. They were extra large yet barely fit her six-foot-one, 205-pound frame.

Agent Jordan's appearance would have been comical if there hadn't been a war going on downstairs. "Come on, Jenny," she said, "follow me and do exactly what I say."

Jenny hesitated. Tiny compared to Audrey, she was half naked, wearing only a cotton T-shirt and a pair of panties. "Wait a sec," she said.

"No!" commanded Audrey, "we've got . . ."

Jenny ignored the order. Instead, she crawled back a few

feet into the room and grabbed a pair of blue jeans and her tennis shoes, both sitting on a chair near the door.

"Okay," Jenny said as she hobbled back to the doorway, the jeans and shoes tucked under one arm, "let's go."

Audrey and Jenny headed down the long, dark hall. The gunfire from downstairs continued. But the battle was about over.

Before he was cut down, the FBI agent on the porch wounded one of the intruders who had been advancing on the cabin. The other two FBI men, inside the cabin on the first floor, managed to contain the attack. But it had cost them. They were almost out of ammunition. The agent with the Mosberg shotgun had exhausted his supply and was now using his pistol. The other man had just one extra thirty-round mag for his MP5 SF.

Audrey and Jenny were now on the first floor, at the base of the stairway. Jenny had just managed to slip on the jeans over her long, slim legs. Both women were kneeling, peering into the blacked-out living room.

Audrey spotted one of her charges. "Johnny," she called out, "how many?"

The agent with the MP5 was about twenty feet away. He had barricaded himself behind a heavy oak desk that had been turned on its side. He was peering through one of the shattered windows. It was pewter black outside. The attackers had shot out all of the perimeter lighting, blasted the power pole next to the cabin, and then disabled the backup/emergency generating plant.

"I think there are four or five of them. There's one down just outside and possibly another." The agent hesitated, now looking toward Audrey. "Manny caught one—out on the porch. It's bad . . . real bad. I think he's gone."

"You sure?"

"Yeah. Last time I was able to check, he wasn't moving."

"Dear God," Audrey muttered, shaking her head. She then continued, "What's it like out back?"

"Don't know. I just sent Carl to take a look. We haven't heard a word from Fred." A second later, another barrage of lead ripped into the living room. Jenny and Audrey flopped onto the floor. The agent behind the table squeezed off two rounds, aiming at the distant muzzle flashes. "Those fuckers must know we're getting low on ammo. I think they're going to wait us out."

"Did you get the call off?" Audrey was referring to the cabin's cellular phone. Even though the cabin was miles from civilization, it was still within the outer fringe of the local cell net.

"Yeah, they're mobing a chopper from McChord right now, but who knows how long it'll take 'em."

Audrey checked her wristwatch—it was 2:53 A.M. *Shit, we'll be chopped liver before they get here.* "We can't wait. I'm going to implement plan B—you okay with that?"

"I don't know. There could be more of 'em out there, just waiting. If we sit tight here, go easy on the ammo, we might be able to wait 'em out until the cavalry arrives."

Audrey shook her head. Her instincts told her otherwise. *These pricks are sophisticated. They'll anticipate the call for help. The rescue chopper will be a prime target.* "I can't risk that, Johnny," she said. "I've got to get Jenny out of here right now. We're going. You give us about ten minutes, and then take off."

Audrey was about to leave when another FBI agent crawled back into the living room from the kitchen. The African American was holding his right shoulder. Blood stained his white shirt. Somehow he still managed to hold the pistol in his right hand.

"There's more out back. One of 'em winged me."

Audrey moved forward to examine the wound. The bleeding had slowed to a dribble. "Doesn't look too bad," she said, trying to reassure the man. "We need to get it bandaged up."

"I'm all right—don't worry about me. But I think you and Ms. Richmond ought to take off. No way we're going to hold out against these bastards."

"What about Fred?" asked Audrey.

The agent shook his head. "They must have got him."

Dammit to hell, Audrey thought. Two agents down—both

probably dead—and another wounded. The safe house was surrounded with an unknown number of heavily armed assailants and there was no hope of a quick rescue. The operation was on the verge of disaster.

"Okay, guys," Audrey said, "I've got to get Jenny out of here, like right now. You know what to do."

The wounded black man smiled as he said, "Semper Fi!"

"We'll hold down the fort, boss," replied the other agent. He then turned back to face the window wall. An instant later another silent torrent of lead raked the room. He answered with two blasts of his own. "We're still here, you pricks!" he shouted.

Audrey turned to face Jenny. "Come on, follow me."

Both women then began wiggling along the floor like a pair of snakes, heading for the furnace room.

Half a minute later they were inside the ten-by-ten-foot room, door closed. Audrey switched on the flashlight. It had been mounted beside the door for such use. Most of the compartment was filled with the bulk of an oil-fired furnace. But behind the furnace, hidden under a throw rug, was a trapdoor. It led directly to the crawl space under the cabin. And linked to the crawl space, at the rear of the cabin, was the escape tunnel.

The tunnel, actually a thirty-six-inch-diameter corrugated metal pipe, was eighty feet long. It terminated behind the cabin, well into the trees and brush. The ten-foot-tall vertical riser at the end of the tunnel had steel handholds welded to the casing. The steel lid on top was hidden inside a thick tangle of blackberry bushes.

The emergency escape route had been designed into the safe house from its conception. All Audrey had to do was get Jenny down the tunnel, up the manhole, and into the woods. The final component of the escape plan was waiting about fifty yards away. Another Ford Expedition was parked inside a dilapidated wood garage, fifty feet off the dirt service road.

It took Audrey and Jenny only five minutes to reach the garage. The worst part of the ordeal was fighting the blackberries. When Audrey pushed open the hatch, she was instantly entangled by the prickly vines. She swore to herself as she pushed her way through the waist-high vegetation. Jenny struggled, too. By the time they emerged from the brush, their hands were covered with dozens of tiny cuts. Audrey was in worse shape. There hadn't been time for her to find any shoes. As a result, her feet were a bloody mess. Nevertheless, she ignored the pain. What seemed liked gallons of adrenaline flooded through her body.

Audrey pulled open the twin doors to the garage. The Ford was waiting. She then began searching the right corner of the building. It was so dark that she had to do everything by feel. She could have turned on the flashlight—she had switched it off once they climbed out of the tunnel—but she couldn't risk it. The bad guys were still close by.

It took Audrey half a minute to find the keys. They were resting on top of a two-by-twelve cross brace.

Audrey and Jenny were now inside the Expedition. The engine fired up instantly. They were ready to go—except for one problem. Audrey couldn't see ten feet in front of the hood. *Damn! If I don't turn on the lights we're going to run into a tree.*

Audrey didn't have a second to spare. *Screw it!* She flipped on the lights and pounced on the accelerator.

The gunman securing the rear of the cabin didn't hear the Ford start up, but he spotted the headlights.

"They're getting away," he said to himself. Without further comment, he moved into the roadway and began running downhill.

Audrey turned onto the service road and headed down. She smiled to herself. *Got it made now.*

The gunman watched in horror as the Ford turned and then sped down the steep grade. He had to do something. But he couldn't just hose the four-by-four. The target might be inside.

He pulled up his submachine gun, planting the metal stock in the pit of his shoulder. He squeezed off three quick rounds.

The gunman was aiming for the rear tires, partially illuminated by the red taillamps. But his aim was a little high and the Expedition was dropping downgrade fast. The nine-millimeter rounds slammed into the rear door. Two of the projectiles embedded themselves in the door's locking mechanism. The third slug, however, punched through sheet metal, both sets of seats, and then burrowed into agent Jordan's right side, just above her waist.

"Oh, God, I'm hit," Audrey called out, her voice shrill.

Jenny turned. "Where?"

Audrey reached down with her right hand. Already her long johns were warm and sticky. She held her hand up. It was blood wet.

"Stop the car and let me help you," commanded Jenny.

"No way, honey. Not until I get you to safety."

"But you're bleeding—badly."

"It isn't too bad," Audrey lied. "I'll be okay."

Jenny didn't reply. It was obvious the agent was badly injured. There was far too much blood to be otherwise.

The Expedition raced down the steep incline. The dirt roadway was miserable, full of potholes and ruts. Both women would have been catapulted into the ceiling if they hadn't worn seat belts. The jolting ride was especially grueling for Audrey. She was barely able to keep the 4×4 on the road.

After smashing through a gate and pulling onto the paved county road, the ride smoothed out. But Audrey was now failing—fast. She was light-headed and her lower right abdomen was numb, as if pumped full of Novocain. *Shit, this isn't good,* she thought. She reached down with her right hand and probed for the wound. A few seconds later she found the hole, a small penetration in the back of her right side. Gooey clotted blood oozed from the opening. She stuck her index finger into the hole, temporarily damming the flow. It didn't really hurt—but that would soon change.

Gotta keep going, Audrey told herself repeatedly. She was now fighting off stomach-churning waves of shock-induced nausea.

3 A CALL FOR HELP

Jenny pulled into the emergency entrance of the hospital and raced to the end of the lane. She slammed on the brakes and hit the horn, signaling she needed help. She then turned to her right.

Agent Audrey Jordan was slumped to the side, resting against the passenger door. Her face was deathly pale. She had lost a third of her blood supply.

Audrey managed to remain conscious for twenty minutes, until she drove onto the westbound lanes of I-90. Not trusting herself any longer, she pulled over and let Jenny drive. She had just pulled herself into the passenger seat when she finally passed out.

The on-call night duty nurse passed through the automatic sliding door and raced to the side of the Expedition. Jenny was already outside, standing by the open passenger door. She was trying to unsnap Audrey's seat belt.

"What's the problem here?" called out the nurse. He was dressed in tan trousers with the standard white medical jacket.

"She's been shot—in the back, lower right."

The nurse moved closer. Jordan's right side was saturated with blood. So was the seat.

"Okay, just stay put a second. I'll get some help."

Ten minutes later Jenny was in the deserted hallway of the hospital's waiting room. She was standing next to a bank of pay phones. Confused and scared, the attack on the safe house dominated her thoughts. Never in her thirty-three years had she ever been around any real violence. But in the past sixty minutes she had lived a dozen lifetimes' worth. The bullets slicing inches from her head, the appalling racket of automatic gunfire, the mad-dash race down the mountain roadway, and then Audrey's horrific wound. It was all too much.

What do I do? Should I call the police? No, the hospital will do that! It must be automatic for any gunshot victim.

She wondered if she should call the FBI in Seattle and tell them what happened. But then she remembered how they had virtually taken her away without any warning and held her against her will—all in the name of protecting her. *The hell with that! After tonight's fiasco, I'm better off on my own.*

I'll call Chris—he'll come and get me. Jenny had just picked up one of the telephone handsets, ready to call her fiancé, when a new thought occurred: *Wait a minute! If I get Chris involved and those guys are looking for me . . . No, I can't do that. . . . I don't want Chris sucked into this mess.*

But what should I do? And then Jenny had another idea. *Of course, he'll know what to do.*

The phone rang six times before it was finally answered.

"Hello," said the groggy man as he struggled to focus on the digital clock next to the bed. It read 4:11 A.M.

He was barely conscious.

"Tim, is that you?"

His brain finally snapped on. "Jenny?" he said.

"Yeah."

"Where are you?"

"I'm in a hospital near North Bend, just off I-90."

"Hospital! Are you hurt?"

"No, but the FBI agent guarding me has been shot, and they just took her into surgery."

"What happened?"

For the next two minutes, Jenny recited the past hour of terror. By the time she had finished, he was fully awake. It was time to take charge.

"Have the police or any FBI agents shown up yet?"

"No. I don't see anyone like that here."

"Is there someplace nearby that you can hide out until I get there? It's not safe to stay at the hospital."

"There's one of those twenty-four-hour truck stops just off the freeway exit. I remember seeing it. I could meet you there."

"How will you get there?"

"Audrey's Expedition. I've still got the keys. It's red with white trim."

"Perfect. Drive there right now but stay in the rig. And don't talk to anyone. It'll take me forty-five minutes to get there."

"Okay."

Tim Carpenter made it in thirty-eight minutes, pumping up his Porsche 911 to 95-plus miles an hour after passing the Issaquah exit on I-90.

"Was there any warning at all?" Tim asked.

"No, at least I don't think so," Jenny said. "I was asleep and then all of a sudden there was this shooting and then Agent Jordan came into my room and told me I had to leave."

"What happened to the other agents guarding you?"

"I don't know. I think two were killed. At least that's what one of the guys in the house said. When we left, there were just two inside and one of them had been shot." Jenny paused. "I just hope they made it out in time."

Tim Carpenter shook his head in anger. "Damn! That should have never, ever happened. You're lucky they didn't kill all of you."

Jenny didn't respond. She stared out the windshield, looking blankly at the scenery. The sun had just risen. It would be a warm, clear day.

They were in Tim's sports car, now heading west on I-90, near Lake Sammamish. Twenty minutes earlier, Tim had whisked Jenny from the truck stop. When they drove past the hospital Tim spotted three State Patrol vehicles at the emergency entrance. Word about the wounded FBI agent was now flooding the police airways.

Tim switched lanes, moving into the far left lane. He was running eight miles per hour over the speed limit. *What the hell should I do now?* he wondered.

Tim turned to check his passenger.

Jenny's T-shirt was smeared with blood—Agent Jordan's. She had lifted her legs, pulling her knees to her chest. Her lovely face was expressionless, but the solitary tear rolling down her freckled cheek told him everything.

"It was pretty horrible, wasn't it?"

"Yes. I've never been so scared in my life." She hesitated. "I just hope Audrey makes it. She saved my life."

Tim echoed Jenny's sentiment; he was moved by the female agent's courage and tenacity.

Yet Tim remained puzzled. The FBI was the nation's premier law enforcement agency. It wrote the book on protecting witnesses and designing safe houses, but something had gone terribly wrong. The carefully orchestrated operation to sequester Jennifer Richmond had been totally compromised.

It must have been a leak, he finally concluded. Someone on the inside tipped off the bad guys.

Tim turned to his right for a brief moment, once again eyeing Jenny. "Besides the FBI agents, who else has been up to that cabin?"

"General Mathews and some others were there till about eleven o'clock last night, before flying off in their helicopter."

"General Mathews?"

"Yeah, a one-star. Air Force. There was also a colonel and a couple majors plus three civilians. I don't remember their names."

"What did they want?"

"Some basic questions about my education and then my position at LorTech." She hesitated. "But most of their questions centered on Dad's work. They kept making inferences that I was working with him on MERLIN. They seemed desperate to get his original research papers. They accused me of hiding them."

"They know about the video?"

"No. I didn't say a word about it."

"So they're still in the dark about his will and the other documents that attorney gave you."

"Yes . . . at least they gave no hint of knowing about them. Never once did any of them ask anything about Dad's will, let alone the videotape. I don't think they have a clue that he made the tape."

"Good."

Half a minute passed and then Tim turned to face Jenny for just an instant. "You ever figure out what your dad was referring to in the tape . . . you know, the part about the riddle?"

"Yeah, I think so. It finally came to me yesterday. It's got to be when we moved all of that stuff out of my grandma's house."

"What stuff?"

"Some furniture, boxes of financial records, antiques, things like that. After Grandma died and Dad sold her house, he didn't want to get rid of them, but he didn't have any extra room at home. So he ended up renting a locker in one of those self-storage places. I helped him move the stuff in."

"Hmmm," Tim said. "Who else knows about that?"

"No one. Just Dad and me."

Tim knew the rest. Jenny's mother died when she was a baby. Her father never remarried, and he had been an only child too.

Poor kid, Tim thought, *now she's really all alone.* Tim again turned toward Jennifer. "You know where this storage locker is?"

"Sure," she said, and told him.

The helicopter landed just at sunrise. The men scrambled out of the Blackhawk, each carrying an assault rifle. There were a dozen, all dressed in black jumpsuits with Kevlar helmets. Each man wore a flak vest with the letters *FBI* stenciled in fluorescent orange tape on the back.

The SWAT team was too late. There were no survivors. Nor any sign of the bad guys.

Special Agent in Charge Ricardo Molina got the bad news at a quarter to six. He was in his car when his cellular phone rang.

"Molina here," he answered.

"Rick, Vicky."

"What's the situation?"

"Not good."

"Shit, did they get her?"

"We don't know for sure. I just got a radio call from the rescue team leader. Four down, no survivors."

Oh, God! thought Rick. His worst nightmare was playing out in real time. He had been awakened forty minutes earlier at his home. He was now heading for downtown Seattle. After initiating a series of emergency procedures, the FBI night operations officer finally called the head of the Seattle field office to inform him of the safe house's emergency call. It had shaken Rick to the core.

"What about Audrey?" he asked.

"Again, we don't know. They couldn't find any trace of her or the Richmond woman. They're definitely not in or around the cabin."

Attagirl, Rick thought. He let out a tiny sigh of relief. He and Audrey Jordan went back a long way. She was a trusted friend and one of the best agents in the bureau. If anyone had a chance of saving Jennifer Richmond, she was the one. "Tell them to check on the backup vehicle. Audrey may have tried to get her out that way."

"Yeah, okay, I'll do . . ." Special Agent Victoria Kwan's voice trailed off for a moment. "Just a sec, Rick, something's coming in." She picked up the conversation a few seconds later. "Hey, Rick, we just got a call from the State Patrol. Audrey's in the emergency room of a hospital near North Bend. Apparently she's been badly wounded, but she's alive!"

"Is Richmond with her?"

"They don't know."

"Shit, get someone there, right now!"

"We're working on it. I'll get back to you in a few minutes."

Rick hung up. He said a quick prayer for Audrey and then pounced on the accelerator.

As his government-issued Ford Crown Victoria raced down the freeway, he kept asking himself the same questions: *What the hell went wrong? How did they find out?*

* * *

The man watched from the driver's seat of the Chevy Sub-urban as the gray-hulled helo flared up for the landing. Thirty seconds later the Bell 205 was on the grass, forty yards away. Dirt kicked up from the pasture sandblasted the Chevy's windshield.

The observer stepped out of the four-by-four. A solid six-footer, he was imposing for his race. By now the helo's screaming turbine had spun down to a soft hiss and the mini tornado generated by its whirling rotors had dissolved into a gentle freshet. It barely ruffled his jet black hair. He took another look around. The secluded Snohomish County meadow remained deserted.

Nearly a minute passed before a side door on the Huey slid open. One of the passengers climbed out. His build was compact, like a fireplug. His right hand was encased in white; blood had soaked through the field dressing.

Trouble! was the observer's instant thought.

Two minutes later, the helicopter was empty. Of the six who had started out, only two were unscathed. The corpse was already sealed up inside a body bag; it now rested on the ground next to the helo's starboard skid.

The observer approached the team leader.

Despite the wound to his hand, the warrior had managed to light up a cigarette.

"Major, what about the woman?" the observer asked, addressing the team leader in their native tongue.

The commando vented a cloud of spent smoke while simultaneously shaking his head. "She got away."

4   SILICON TREASURE

"So, this is where your dad was talking about," Tim Carpenter said.

"Yep," Jenny replied. "This has got to be the place he was hinting at in the video."

Tim and Jennifer were in a private storage facility south

of the University of Washington campus. Even though it was short-sleeve warm, Jenny wore Tim's nylon windbreaker—it concealed her blood-painted T-shirt.

They were alone. The six-by-eight-foot locker was on the third floor of the building. It was filled with memorabilia from the estate of Jenny's grandmother.

It took a few minutes of rummaging through the locker before Jenny discovered it.

"This thing still work?" Tim asked, admiring the hand-crafted woodwork of the ancient RCA. The huge console radio occupied the back of the locker; it was hidden by stacks of cardboard boxes.

"Yeah, at least it did. Grandma used to listen to it all the time. Dad kept it going for her. He was always fiddling with it, replacing tubes and wires and . . ." Jenny paused. "Oh, my gosh, could it be?" she said, now remembering her father's cryptic message in the videotape.

"What?"

"Have you got a screwdriver in your car?"

"No, but I've got a penknife." He reached into his pants pocket, removing a key chain.

"That'll work."

Three minutes passed. "Look at this!" Jenny said when she removed the radio's back panel, exposing its innards.

The cardboard box was resting on the wood base, underneath the shelf that held the actual radio receiver. The box was stuffed full with file folders and bound reports.

"I'll be damned," Tim said, stunned at the finding. He then leaned forward, helping Jenny extract the box.

Jenny removed one of the thick manila file folders and examined the contents. "Wow," she said, "this stuff's incredible. . . . These are Dad's original notes and calculations for MERLIN."

"They should help explain how it works, shouldn't they?"

"Absolutely. . . . They're priceless."

Five minutes later Tim discovered the real mother lode. Encased in a clear plastic Ziploc baggy, it was resting inside the RCA's electronic guts, next to a vast collection of vacuum tubes, resistors, and coils.

"What's this thing?" Tim said, pointing.

Oh, dear Lord! Jenny thought.

Jenny was now holding it. It was about six inches by ten inches. Most of the hard plastic backing that held everything together was green, but one end was blackened, scorched by heat.

"That must be the part that got fried," Tim offered.

Jenny nodded. "Yep. That fits." She opened the bag, removed the contents, and then examined the damaged area. Dozens of hair-thin wirelike lines had been fused together on one end, distorting the original geometric patterns. "What a mess," she finally said.

"What?" asked Tim.

"The circuit traces." She pointed. "They're fused together in this area and some of the chips have melted. It's a horrible mishmash."

"That must be what your father was referring to—the part of the MERLIN thing that makes it so special."

Jenny glanced back at Tim. "Maybe." She hesitated for a moment. "Anyway, I now see the problem. Dad was probably trying to replicate the exact same pattern so he could reproduce the effect. He'd have to be able to do that to make it commercially marketable. But this looks so random and haphazard that I don't see how . . ." Jenny's voice trailed off.

"You don't see what?" Tim finally asked.

"I don't see how anyone could hope to replicate it."

"So this thing's just a freak of nature."

Jenny shook her head. "I don't know. Dad's video said he'd had some success in replicating it . . . but it's hard to believe that this jumble of circuit traces and silicon chips could do it. There must be more to it than just the fire damage." She gestured toward the cardboard box. "Maybe Dad's research notes will tell me what's really happening." She took a deep breath. "Anyway, all of this is still a paradox to me. There's no reason why this damn thing should work, but . . ."

"But it does work," offered Tim. "We saw that in the video."

"I know, I know. And standing here, holding this thing in

my hands, really gives me the creeps. So many people have died trying to get it." Jenny again shook her head, confused, scared. Part of her wanted to throw it onto the floor so she could crush it to pieces with her shoes. But the engineer in her wouldn't let her do that.

She slipped the circuit board back inside the baggy and then turned to face Tim. "So what do we do now?"

"I want to get you out of here and let things·settle down."

Jenny handed Tim the baggy. "Maybe we should just give this to the FBI and be done with it."

"I don't recommend that. This thing's worth a bundle to you. I think we should lie low for a while and then get hold of that lawyer your dad was working with. We can let him negotiate with the feds."

"Okay, I guess that makes sense."

"Good." Tim checked his watch. It was half past ten. "Well, let's get going. We're supposed to leave in thirty minutes."

"Do you think those gunmen will be able to trace us?"

"No. I doubt it. I didn't use my real name and we'll pay with cash from now on."

"If we just stop by the bank, I can get some more money."

"That's not necessary. We've got plenty."

Tim was, indeed, flush with cash. After spiriting Jenny out of North Bend, he'd driven straight to his Kirkland office. The bank he used for his business had a branch a block away. When it opened at nine o'clock he withdrew $8,500 in cash. He'd already liberated another $3,000 that was stashed away in his office safe. The eleven-plus grand would go a long way.

Along with the spare money in the safe, Tim also removed Dr. Richmond's legal papers and his farewell video to Jenny, Tim's own passport, a portable phone, and his compact Glock 26. The loaded 9 mm semiautomatic pistol came with two extra ten-round magazines.

"Tim," Jenny said, "when things calm down, I'll reimburse you for all of this."

"Don't worry about it—money is the least of your problems now."

"Yeah, I guess you're right."

Tim handed Jenny the plastic bag. He then leaned over to grab the bulky cardboard box.

"Let's go," he said after lifting the box. It was heavy but his six-foot-one, 180-pound frame hardly noticed the load.

Jenny followed as he headed down the long hallway.

The main conference room of the FBI's Seattle field office was packed. The agents were chatting away, waiting for their boss to arrive. The meeting had been hastily ordered just minutes earlier.

He walked into the room and moved to the head of the mahogany table. His charges continued to talk as he placed a file folder onto the tabletop. And then he took charge.

"Okay, people," he said, his deep voice resonating throughout the room, "listen up."

The decibel level plummeted as all eyes turned to face the tall, muscular, brown-skinned man who stood at the head of the table. A former varsity college baseball third baseman, SAC Ricardo Molina was an icon of masculinity.

"I've got bad news." Molina paused, gathering his thoughts. "Our Cascade unit was hit last night. We lost four agents: Thompson, Billings, Chavez, and Taylor."

The roll call of death stunned the assembled. The tight-knit group of FBI personnel had all lost friends.

Ricardo continued. "Agent Jordan was also badly wounded—gunshot to the back. She's been airlifted to Harborview. The doctors still don't know if she's going to make it. Agent Kwan should be there by now. She's going to try to get a statement from Audrey."

Molina stared down at the table, letting his words sink in. No one spoke.

Finally, one of the agents at the opposite end of the table broke the ice. "Sir, what happened?"

Ricardo looked up. "We really don't have much. The unit radioed the ops center around oh three hundred hours this morning that they were under attack. That was the last communication we had. By the time our SWAT unit heloed into the site, it was all over."

"What happened to the witness?" asked another agent.

"She's missing." Rick opened up the folder and then held up a black-and-white photograph. "Her name's Jennifer Richmond. Thirty-three years old, five-foot-six, hundred twenty pounds, red hair, brown eyes, lots of freckles.

"Apparently, Audrey was able to get her off the mountain. They ended up in an emergency room near North Bend. We think Richmond drove her there—Audrey was in pretty bad shape by then. But after dropping Audrey off, she disappeared. We eventually found Audrey's Expedition at a nearby truck stop."

"Do you think the perps got to her?" asked the same man.

"It's possible, but I don't think so. I think she took off on her own."

A female agent sitting two chairs away from Molina spoke up next: "Sir, why wouldn't Ms. Richmond wait for the police or our people to show up? Clearly, she must have been scared that these characters would come after her again."

"That's right, but think about this: We'd sequestered Ms. Richmond in our most secure facility—against her will. She was guarded around the clock by a well-trained team of agents and then the place gets hit, right out of the blue. I think that might cause her to doubt our ability to protect her."

There was a uniform sigh throughout the room. They all understood. The elite FBI had failed in its mission. And four of their brethren had died as a result.

The same woman asked another question: "But how could this have happened, sir?"

"It's obvious to me." Molina then hesitated for a long moment. "There's a leak. Someone tipped these bastards off as to the location of the Cascade unit."

The fourteen men and women sitting around the table all wanted to ask the same question: Who? But no one volunteered. Rick did it for them.

"But who could have done it?" He paused again. "Maybe it was one of you."

Molina took another moment to survey his charges, eyeing each one as he scanned around the table. And then he said:

"But I don't think so. I think it came from outside the bureau."

Most of the assembled shuffled in their seats, as if suddenly freed of an oppressive burden.

"Any ideas, sir?" asked a new voice.

Ricardo raised his hands, signaling his frustration. "Hell, I don't know. The Air Force's heavily involved, as well as a number of other DOD and DIA staff people. So's NSA, and even the CIA. It could be any of those." He paused once again. "But from here on out, everything we do regarding this case stays in-house. Here, in Seattle. This is going to be a closed investigation until we get to the bottom of it. And that's one of the reasons I've called all of you here together. No one outside this room, with the exception of Agent Kwan, is to know about what happened or what we're doing about it. That's the only way we can hope to keep a lid on things."

A man sitting next to Molina responded next: "What about the press? Do they know anything?"

Rick spoke directly to the man: "Dan, the only thing the press knows is that Audrey was wounded. They don't know why or how, and we intend to keep it that way. We're now putting together a cover story and will be sending out a press release this afternoon."

The man nodded.

Rick looked over the rest of his staff. "I know all of you have been briefed on MERLIN and why it's imperative that we get Jennifer Richmond back."

The tension in the room skyrocketed. The agents could sense the special assignment that was coming.

SAC Molina leaned forward. It was time to get down to business. "Now here's what we're going to do. . . ."

The inland sea seemed to stretch to infinity. There were hardly any clouds and absolutely no wind. It was a perfect day to fly.

They were in the backseat, behind the pilot. Jenny sat on the left, Tim on the right. The drone from the Cessna's engine was oppressive. They both wore earplugs.

The charter plane was flying along the western shore of

San Juan Island heading north. Vancouver Island and Victoria were far off to the left, across the shimmering waters of Haro Strait.

Jenny turned toward Tim, stealing a long moment to take in his form. Although a decade her senior, Carpenter didn't fit the image of the typical middle-aged male. There was no potbelly, no glasses, no sagging chin or bald spots. He kept in shape: tan, powerful arms and upper torso; trim buttocks; and long, sinuous legs. Best of all was his face: a chiseled chin, high cheekbones, teal eyes, and a perfect nose. His thick sandy blond locks, neatly combed, covered the top half of his ears.

He wasn't perfect, though. The scars were barely visible, faint traces of something gone wrong years earlier. The tan helped disguise the damage, as did the long hair, but if you looked close enough the blemishes were apparent—at the top of his forehead near the hairline, on the palms of both hands, and on the undersides of his forearms. And one of his ears looked as if it had been mauled.

Hundreds of tiny surgical stitches had been made to repair the torn flesh.

I wonder what happened to him.

Half a minute passed and then Jenny touched Tim's left shoulder.

He turned to face her.

"Are we getting close?" she asked, shouting to be heard over the engine.

Tim glanced at Jenny for a second before turning back to the window. He then tapped the Plexiglas with his right hand. "We'll be landing pretty soon," he yelled, "right near the north end of the island, just up ahead, in a sheltered bay."

Jenny nodded and then reached down and pulled on her seat belt, tightening it a notch. She relished the scenery yet remained apprehensive. She had flown in a small airplane only once before—and never one that landed on water.

Three minutes later the pilot banked right and went into a slow spiral, burning off altitude as he picked his landing site. The bay was filled with pleasure boats. A large marina was located to the east and scores of vessels were coming and going. There were also dozens of other yachts anchored in the bay.

The landing was smooth. The aluminum pontoons sliced into the calm waters with just a slight shudder. Jenny was relieved. It hadn't been so bad after all.

As the plane slowed up, turning into a boat, the pilot cocked his head toward the right. While still looking through the windshield, he called out to Tim: "Which one of these piers is your place?"

Tim unsnapped his seat belt and leaned forward. He pointed over the unoccupied copilot's seat. "It's just ahead, a little to the right. The one with the flagpole."

The pilot nodded. "Got it."

The docking was uneventful. The pilot maneuvered his craft alongside the seventy-foot-long concrete float, being careful to avoid the creosote pilings that moored it to the harbor bottom. A twenty-four-foot speedboat was tied to the shore end of the float.

After Tim and Jenny deplaned, the pilot handed over the cargo: Tim's briefcase and the box of files recovered from the storage locker.

Tim thanked the pilot and then helped him launch the craft. Two minutes later, Tim and Jenny watched the Cessna take off.

"That was sure easy," Jenny commented.

"Yeah, this isn't a bad way to go. Sure beats the ferry and all that driving."

Roche Harbor was about a hundred miles north of Seattle. To get there without flying, you would have to drive to Anacortes, catch a ferry to San Juan Island, and then drive another ten miles to reach Roche Harbor. From there, you'd have to get in a small boat at the marina and then motor a quarter of a mile to another tiny island before finally arriving at your destination. The trip could easily take four to five hours. The charter plane ride from Lake Union had taken just fifty minutes.

Jenny turned around and looked toward the shore. The two-story beach house was striking. Designed as a northwest traditional, it complemented the natural beauty of the shoreline. Tall stands of cedars and Douglas firs ringed the home, isolating it from the neighboring homes. There was even a small sandy pocket beach in the center of a 250-foot-long rocky coastline.

"When did you guys get this place?" Jenny asked.

"We just closed on it a couple of weeks ago."

"Wow," Jenny said as she walked landward, "this is great. No one will find us up here."

"Right."

5 THE RETREAT

"She got away."

"What?"

"We almost had her, but she got away."

"This is a fucking disaster, Peng."

"I know."

"How could it have happened?"

"Bad luck, Gérard. Nothing more than that. I got it straight from Wu. I picked the team up when they landed. They got chewed up pretty good." A slight pause. "The damn FBI had an emergency escape route—a tunnel under the house. *Your* MAGNUM didn't tell us anything about it. That's how they got her out."

Allen Peng was calling from a pay phone in the lobby of a downtown Seattle hotel. His name was an alias, deliberately Westernized.

The man Peng was speaking with was 150 miles to the north in Vancouver. He was also using a public phone. The emergency communication plan had been established earlier. It was simple but effective. Both men wore pagers. Whenever they needed to talk—without fear of being wiretapped— they simply dialed into the local paging network where their contact was operating and left a special return number on the digital readout. The bogus code simply informed the receiver that the caller needed to speak. They would then use preestablished telephone numbers to call each other. In this case, Peng had paged Gérard Rémy. Rémy then had half an hour to drop what he was doing and get to the designated public phone. It would begin ringing exactly thirty minutes after his pager was activated.

When Rémy's pager went off, he was in a restaurant having lunch with a new friend and maybe, just maybe, a future lover. If the call had been from anyone else, he would have ignored it.

"You know that we'll never get another chance to get her," Rémy said. "The Americans now know they've got a bad leak."

"Of course. But all is not lost. I do have encouraging news."

"What are you talking about?"

"We're certain she was at a hospital emergency room, about twenty miles from the safe house."

"She was hurt?"

"No. We don't think so. Apparently she drove one of the FBI guards to the hospital. The agent was wounded, a woman."

"How do you know this?"

Peng smiled. He had lived in the United States on and off for almost ten years now, yet it continued to amaze him. "It was on the television. A Seattle station picked up police radio traffic about a shooting involving the FBI. They sent a mobile news crew to the hospital and made a live broadcast for their early morning news program. One of my people saw it."

"What about Richmond?"

"We sent one of our operatives to the hospital. Her cover was a newspaper reporter."

"And?"

"She interviewed someone on the hospital staff. He was in the emergency room when the FBI agent was brought in. He confirmed that the wounded agent wasn't alone. She then showed him a photograph of Jennifer Richmond and he positively ID'ed her."

"Shit. Then they got her back."

"We don't think so. The man said he reported the gunshot wound to the police, but by the time they were ready to investigate, the Richmond woman had already left."

"What do you mean?"

"She took off."

"Then the FBI must have picked her up."

"We don't think so. When our agent finally arrived, the hospital lobby was filled with FBI and police. The injured woman had already been airlifted to another hospital. Apparently, they interrogated the same hospital staff person thoroughly. We got to him after they finished. He said they seemed to be pretty upset about the woman leaving."

"Then they don't have her, either?"

"That's right. It appears she gave them the slip."

"So where did she go?"

"That, my friend, is what *we* must find out. And *we* must do it before the FBI does—or we will truly have lost."

"How the hell are we going to do that?"

"I have a backup plan." Peng paused to gather his thoughts. "It's more than a plan now—it's already been implemented."

"What are you talking about?"

"During our earlier surveillance of Miss Richmond we discovered that she has a boyfriend. Actually he's her fiancé. His name's Wilcox. Chris Wilcox."

"Yes, I remember. Isn't he the one that works for Microsoft?"

"Correct. We're now in—"

"I see what you're doing," interrupted the European. "She might have called him for help. He may even be with her right now!"

"We don't think they're together—at least not yet. I've already placed Wilcox under surveillance and as of five minutes ago he's still in his office in Redmond."

"Dammit. If he's still there, then that means he probably isn't hiding her."

"Yes, I agree, but he may know where she is."

"Of course," Rémy said. "Can you get to him before the American police figure it out?"

"We're working on it."

"Good! Let me know what you find out."

"I will." Peng again paused. "But I think you should come down anyway. We might need your help."

Rémy hesitated for a long moment. "Yes, you're probably right. I'll leave immediately but it'll probably take me a couple of hours to get there. The border crossing will be a mess this time of day."

"We may have some answers by then."

"Good, that should work."

"One other thing," Peng said. "Because of what has happened, and assuming that we're able to locate her before the FBI does, I recommend that we immediately come up with a contingency plan to get her out of the country. The Americans will have everything sealed up. We just can't take a chance on the plane."

"But the others aren't going to like that . . . it's not what we agreed on. The repercussions will be severe if it fails."

"I know. But things have changed. Do you have a better plan?"

Silence and then: "All right, you're probably right. Start setting something up."

"I will."

Jenny and Tim were seated in the expansive living room. She was sipping a Coke; he had a Bud. The view of Roche Harbor and the entrance to Mosquito Pass was gorgeous.

The room was only partially furnished. About half of the new furniture Tim and his wife had purchased had not yet been delivered.

Jenny turned from the view, looking at Tim. "How'd you guys keep this a secret? Laura hasn't said a word about it at work."

Tim smiled. "Well, that's one of the reasons we're here now. You're right, no one at LorTech—or for that matter, no one else besides the attorneys—knows we bought it. Everything's listed under one of our holding companies."

Jenny frowned, not understanding.

"We wanted a retreat where we could get completely away

without having to go too far from home. And without everyone around us knowing who we are."

Jenny now understood. Laura Lorence was a local celebrity. Her Seattle-based software firm, Lorence Technologies—LorTech—was a budding Microsoft. With nearly six hundred employees and gross revenues approaching half a billion a year, LorTech was a rising star in the robotics software business.

Although nowhere near as rich or famous as the Microsoft elite, Laura Lorence was nevertheless frequently sought out by the press and all kinds of people and groups looking for everything from computer advice to charitable contributions. After a steady dose of that kind of attention, just about anyone would cherish anonymity.

Acquiring the Pearl Island property was Tim's idea. It was for Laura.

Tim was fiercely proud of his wife's achievements—both professionally and financially. Yet he was growing weary of the consequences of her success. Like many of Laura's contemporaries, male and female, she spent far too much time away from home—either at LorTech's downtown Seattle headquarters or crisscrossing the nation in jetliners. Not yet forty, the competitiveness of Laura's business was beginning to take its toll on her well-being. Tim could read the storm warnings like a barometer: utter weariness brought on by sleep deprivation; the noticeable weight gain caused by a lack of exercise and too many business lunches and dinners; and frequent bouts of dejection brought about by feelings of guilt and fear—guilt because she was often forced to ignore her four-year-old twin sons, and Tim, and fear because she worried that she might make a horrible business decision that would ruin her company.

Tim had observed it all before—firsthand; his own dark, hellish days. He'd barely survived himself. He was determined to prevent his wife from enduring a similar destiny. The Pearl Island property was the start of his campaign to restore Laura's health—both physical and mental.

Jenny took another sip of her Coke. "How long do you think we'll have to stay here?"

"I'm not sure. At least a couple of days, until I can get you out of the country."

Jenny nodded and then finished off the Coke. She placed the empty can on the coffee table. "Does Laura know that we're here?"

"No. I wasn't able to get ahold of her before we took off." Tim paused as he remembered something. "And now that you mention it, I need to do something about that right now."

He stood up and walked to the kitchen counter. His brief-case was sitting on top of it. He placed the beer can on the countertop and then opened up the case. As he searched for something inside he said, "Laura left yesterday afternoon for L.A. Some kind of software conference or exhibition down there."

Jenny stood up, shocked. "Oh, that's right. It's a technical conference on robotics software."

"Yeah, that's the one," he said, continuing to riffle through the briefcase.

Jenny shook her head, disgusted. For the past nine years, since earning her master's at Caltech, she'd worked for Tim's wife. Jenny was now one of LorTech's key employees, a senior vice president. She headed up the Deep Space Ro-botics Division.

Jenny flopped back onto the couch. "I was supposed to give a speech there—on our new artificial intelligence soft-ware for the NASA project."

Tim found what he was looking for. He looked up. "That's right. Laura said she was subbing for you. When the FBI placed you under protective custody, she knew there was no way that you were going to make it down there."

Jenny moaned. "This whole thing's such a mess. I've got both you and Laura embroiled in my problems—I'm so sorry."

"Hey, don't worry about that. Laura was going anyway so it's no big deal." Tim decided not to mention the planned postconference vacation that he and Laura had set up for their sons and Tim's mother. All three were currently visiting with his sister's family in Newport Beach. That, too, would gnaw away at Jenny's conscience.

Jenny was about to comment on the conference when she spotted the portable telephone.

"You've got a cell phone," she said, standing up.

"Yeah, we still don't have a phone here. Takes forever, so I brought this along." He held the unit up. "It's one of those new combo cellular and satellite phones. Laura bought it for my birthday."

Jenny was now standing beside Tim, eyeing the phone. Tim continued: "I haven't used the satphone much—you've got to be outside with nothing overhead before it'll work. But the cell works just fine in here."

"Please, let me call Chris first so I can let him know that I'm okay."

"I really don't want to use it much. They can be traced."

"Please! I'm dying to talk with him."

"All right," he said, handing over the phone. "But you can't say where we are."

"Okay."

Jenny struck out. Chris Wilcox wasn't at his Redmond office nor at his Kirkland condominium. And his cell phone wasn't answering. Finally, she gave up.

After placing a call to Europe, via cell mode, it took Tim five more calls and nearly two hours of waiting before he finally connected with his wife. She had just returned to her hotel suite, frazzled from her public speaking duties.

The timing of Tim's call was fortuitous. Jenny was in the shower. There was no way that she could hear.

"Look, Laura," Tim said, "I know you don't want to go, but you've got to. I just can't risk it."

"But Tim, we were supposed to take Tyler and Cody to Disneyland and then I've got a million things to do back in Seattle. We've got a board meeting coming up, and I've got to oversee the acquisition of that firm in Portland. What you're asking is impossible."

Tim was growing impatient by the second. CEO Laura Lorence was being stubborn—as usual—and he hated making confidential calls on cellular phones. You never knew who might be listening in.

"Come on, honey, give me a break. I need a little breathing room—it'll only be for a few days—a week at the most."

"I don't know, Tim. The timing is bad."

Tim decided to play hardball. Up until now he'd only told Laura that Jenny had been released, and that he had decided to move her to their new acquisition, taking care not to name the location over the open phone line. But it was now time to level with her.

"Laura, they tried to get Jenny last night. They took out four FBI agents in the process. Four of them—gone. Those bastards are deadly serious and I can't protect her if I'm worrying about you and the boys and Mom."

Laura let out a deep sigh. "They were killed?"

"Yes. Gunned down. And they almost got Jenny."

"Oh, my God."

"Can you see what I'm trying to do now?"

"Yes."

"Then you'll do it?"

"Of course." Laura hesitated for a long moment. "But, Tim, what are we going to do about passports? Won't we need them?"

"Oh, shit, I forgot about that. . . . Where's yours?"

"At home, in my desk."

"Maria's working today, isn't she?"

"Yes."

"Okay, good. The boys' passports should be in the file cabinet in the den. Call up Maria and have her get them and then—"

"But what about your mother? Do you think she has her passport with her?"

Tim sighed deeply. His carefully constructed evacuation plan was about to fall apart. "No way. I'm sure it's in her condo, locked up with all of her other records." He paused. "This is getting complicated. Do you have someone at LorTech that you can really trust?"

"Of course, many."

"Okay. Call one of them up and tell them to get over to

our house ASAP. Have Maria give them the passports and the key to Mom's condo. It's in my desk with her name on it. Maria should be able to find it."

"Okay."

"Tell your employee to go to Mom's place and . . ." Tim proceeded to give detailed instructions on how to gain access to Doris Carpenter's Meydenbauer Bay condominium and locate her passport. It was only a few minutes away from Tim and Laura's Evergreen Point home.

"That's it, you've got it," Tim said after Laura repeated his instructions. "Now don't waste any time. Get your people working on it right away. If they have to, tell 'em to charter a jet but make sure they get those passports to you by nine o'clock tonight."

"We'll do it."

"Good. As soon as you've got that set up, call Bill at his office and tell him what's going on. He'll explain it to Karen and Mom—just make sure he gets the boys and Mom to LAX on time."

"What about Karen's family—will they be in danger?"

"I don't think so—just level with Bill. He'll know what to do."

Tim's sister, Karen, was married to a real estate developer. Like Tim, Bill Cummings had been in the military, a former Navy fighter pilot.

"Okay."

"All four of you must be on that BA flight. Tony's taken care of the booking and your tickets. All you have to do is show up at the terminal and get on. He'll pick you up at Heathrow when you get in."

"Okay, got it."

"Good. And one more thing, use a pay phone to make all of your calls from now on. Don't use your cell phone or your hotel room phone. You never know who might be listening in."

"Okay."

"Honey, I know this is a pain, but it's got to be done."

"I understand." She paused. "Please be careful."

"I will."

"Love you."

"Love you."

Tim flipped the phone off. A little of the pressure had just vented. *At least I don't have to worry about that*, he thought.

The risk hadn't hit Tim until just after arriving at the Pearl Island estate. If Dr. Richmond's abductors could compromise the FBI in their attempt to get Jenny, then that meant they were capable of just about anything. He figured that, one way or the other, they'd eventually find out about him and then come looking. His immediate family would be the perfect bait to entrap him. Give us Jennifer Richmond and we'll give your wife back; or your sons; or your mother; or all four. What better leverage?

Tim hoped that he had just thwarted that tactic. With luck, before midnight this evening his loved ones would be on a nonstop jumbo bound for London. A longtime friend of Tim's would be waiting for them.

Tim had met Anthony Urban when he was stationed in Europe. At that time they were both in the service. Tim was in the U.S. Army, an officer assigned to the Intelligence and Security Command—INSCOM. Urban was with the British special forces, the elite SAS. Long retired from the military, Urban was now a partner in a London-based private security firm. He was one of the best bodyguards in the business. That gave Tim a whole lot of comfort.

6 THE PLUMBERS

At first, the agony was worse than anything he had ever imagined. They had beat him with such savagery that he expected to die right there, strapped to the chair. But then they stopped. A few minutes after the two men left, he fought to free himself. He rocked from side to side, trying desperately to loosen the layers of duct tape that bound him to the metal frame. But in that process he accidentally knocked the chair over. When his head slammed into the rock-hard floor, he nearly knocked himself out.

He was now lying on the cold concrete, blood dripping from his nose and a torn cheek. He had been groggy for several minutes. He opened his eyes, his vision blurry.

Chris Wilcox tilted his head, staring at the ceiling. A single sixty-watt bulb illuminated the tiny room. Although all of his senses were in shock, he could still smell the mildew. It reminded him of his parents' basement. He turned back, now focusing on the wood door to the ten-foot-square room. *What the hell happened?* he thought. And then he remembered.

It all started at the office, several hours earlier. He was in a meeting when the emergency call came in. The caller identified himself as an FBI agent and told him that Jennifer had been involved in a kidnapping. She was now missing and the FBI needed his help to find her.

"Of course I'll come," Chris had said, his voice filled with anger and dread. "Where do you think she is?"

"We can't say over the phone," the caller had said. "We have a command post set up in the search area and one of our agents is on the way to your office. He'll take you to where we are."

"All right, I'm ready."

Ten minutes later, Chris was in a blue Chevrolet, heading north on Interstate 405. He asked the driver, an FBI agent who had identified himself as Andy Chen, where they were going. Chen reported that the search was centered in the city of Edmonds. He spoke perfect English and Chris had no reason to suspect that his credentials were bogus.

The residence was located on a hillside overlooking Puget Sound. Chris suspected nothing. He followed Chen into the house from the garage.

He was stunned the instant he walked into the spacious living room. The water view was breathtaking, but that wasn't what overwhelmed him. The four men standing by the window wall were all Asian. They were dressed in casual attire and two gripped semiautomatic pistols in their hands.

"Hey, what's going on here?" Chris called out, now confused as he stepped into the room.

His answer came from the side. The driver, the one named Chen, launched a lightning-quick jab, striking Chris in his lower right back. The blow knocked him to the floor.

Stunned, Chris turned to look up. The five men now surrounded him. There was no escape.

And then the interrogation began.

Chris tried once again to free himself, using what little energy he had left to struggle against the bindings. It was useless.

He had just shut his eyes, hoping the nightmare would end, when the door opened. His tormentors were back.

Without saying a word, the two men gripped the chair, pulling it back upright. Once Chris was sitting up, he was hit again, this time in the stomach. The larger of the two men threw the punch. It was a sledgehammer. The blow knocked the wind out of him.

"Where is she?" demanded the other man, his accent thick. He was board-thin compared to his husky companion.

Chris shook his head, he could hardly talk. "I don't know."

He was hit again, this time on the face. More flesh ripped. Blood spurted from a new tear.

"Where is she?" repeated the voice.

The question was always the same. It was deliberate. The interrogators were now convinced that Wilcox did not know Jennifer's whereabouts. They were about to shift into the next cycle.

The big one prepared to strike out again. Chris clamped down his swollen eyelids, cringing at the expected blow. But nothing happened. Instead, right on cue, the door flew open.

"Stop," commanded a new voice, one with a different accent.

The guard relaxed, dropping his clenched fist.

"Get out!" ordered the man standing in the doorway.

The two guards exited the room. Chris watched them leave and then he focused on the visitor. He was Caucasian. Midforties. Jet black hair. Six feet tall. A skinny 165 pounds. Dressed in an expensive dark blue suit with white shirt and tie, he could have stepped out of any corporate boardroom.

Gérard Rémy kneeled down beside Chris.

"My God, what have they done to you?" he asked.

Chris let out a sigh of relief. *He's not going to beat me.*

Rémy removed a handkerchief from a jacket pocket and dabbed at the new tear in Chris's right cheek. The American was more than handsome. "I'm sorry that you had to suffer through that. Those two are pigs."

"Who are you?" Chris managed to ask.

"A friend. My name's Gérard. Call me Jerry."

Gérard Rémy was one of a half dozen cover names he used. Only a select few in Paris at the *Direction Générale de la Sécurité Extérieure* were aware of his true identity. The DGSE was responsible for the external security of France. The successor of the scandalous SDECE—which was born out of the infamous Deuxième Bureau—the DGSE spied for France, targeting both her enemies and her friends alike.

"But what do you want from me . . . Jerry?" Chris pleaded. "I don't know anything. I tried to tell them that but they just don't believe me."

"I know, they're barbarians. Just give me a few answers and then we can let you go." Rémy stepped back a pace to better view Chris's tall, slim build. *Excellent, just excellent!*

Chris Wilcox remained confused and desperate, believing everything Rémy said. "I'll tell you anything I can . . . just don't let them hit me anymore."

Rémy wanted to smile but didn't. The ancient technique had worked well. The subject's defenses were thoroughly compromised. Wilcox would now talk freely, believing that Rémy was his savior.

"I know that you don't know where Ms. Richmond is but—"

"That's right," interrupted Chris, thankful that he was finally believed. "I tried to tell them that but they refused to listen."

Rémy nodded, signaling his understanding. "I believe you, but you must tell me, what did she say when she phoned you?"

"Phoned me? What are you talking about?"

"The call she made from the hospital."

Chris shook his head. Nothing made sense. "Hospital? Was Jenny hurt?"

The French agent studied his subject. Wilcox's confusion was authentic.

"No, Jenny's fine. But she called someone from there—someone we think you might know." Rémy was bluffing. He still had no hint as to how Jenny managed to disappear.

"I don't know who that could be—maybe an FBI agent or someone like that."

Rémy shook his head as he paced in front of the chair. "No, Christopher, we're certain she didn't contact the authorities. It must have been a friend—someone she trusted. Perhaps someone from LorTech—a coworker or maybe a girlfriend."

"LorTech? Maybe, but I don't know anyone . . ." Chris's voice trailed off as a new thought developed.

"What?" asked Rémy.

"It must have been that P.I.!"

"P.I.?"

"Yeah, the private investigator Jenny hired to help find out what happened to her dad." Chris smiled. "Yes, that's it, it's got to be Tim."

"Tim who?" asked Rémy, instinctively knowing he had finally hit pay dirt.

The security system was a challenge. It was top of the line. But the man was an expert. After just ten minutes he disabled the entire network. The team could now move throughout the lakefront residence without fear of triggering an alarm.

There were three of them—Allen Peng's men. They came in from the water by boat, under the cover of darkness. They could have used the lift—a cart that ran on steel rails up and down the steep incline. Instead, they scaled the slope on foot, using the narrow-gauge rails as handholds.

After reaching the summit, they moved southward along the edge of the bluff line. The Lorence-Carpenter residence bordered the home with the new beach elevator.

The men started searching from the top floors down. As expected, all six bedrooms were empty. No one was home.

They were methodical in their examination of the 8,500-square-foot Lake Washington palace. Anything remotely fitting the request was examined and, if deemed useful, taken: framed photographs of friends and family; all of the files in a desk in Tim's office; and a dozen 3.5-inch floppies and assorted CDs sitting in plastic containers next to Laura's PC. They even stole a stack of unopened mail the house cleaner had left on a kitchen counter.

It took about ninety minutes for the burglars to finish their work. The megahouse was now a shambles, the chaos left on purpose to make it look like a home invasion. The intruders then retraced their steps to their beached runabout, each carrying a black plastic garbage bag full of trophies.

DAY 2

ADVENTURES IN PARADISE

7 A NEW LEAD

It was a quarter past six and Tim Carpenter had been up for an hour. He had watched the predawn darkness transform into a dazzling sunrise. The cloudless sky was now a beaming blue. It would be another perfect summer day in the San Juan Islands.

Tim loved the morning hours. An early riser for as long as he could remember, he cherished this time of solitude. When at home he almost always rose before Laura—and the boys. After brewing a pot of coffee, he'd walk out to the driveway and retrieve the morning paper. And then, while sitting at the garden court table that overlooked the lake, sipping from the steaming mug and scanning the newspaper, he'd light up that first cigarette. There were no interruptions, no phone calls, no TV. Just the combined rush of caffeine and nicotine.

After a twenty-minute workout on the treadmill, showering and shaving, and then a light breakfast, he would drive to his office. He could have worked out of LorTech's offices; the firm occupied half a dozen upper floors in one of Seattle's most prestigious skyscrapers. Instead, he chose a rather plain, two-story office complex near downtown Kirkland. It was just ten minutes away from home. The commute to Seattle, in contrast, was a regular nightmare.

Avoiding the traffic was Tim's excuse for not taking up Laura's offer to work out of LorTech. The real reason, however, was his desire for independence. He had to have something that was just his own.

There was no need for him to work—Laura's net worth was staggering. Yet he had his pride. But more important, he had to keep his mind occupied.

Tim's firm had grown a little since he'd first launched his one-man shop seven years earlier. He had two employees, a part-time receptionist-secretary-bookkeeper-gofer and a full-time computer technician. Not much, but all he needed.

Tim's private investigation firm, Carpenter Computer Security, specialized in the mundane but lucrative practice of investigating computer theft. It was a worldwide chess game to him, tracing stolen electronic funds or hijacked data, and then assisting the appropriate authorities in apprehending the perpetrators. It was sometimes boring, yet Tim had relished the challenge of the technology. Over the years he had become proficient in using computers to trap criminals.

Tim had learned his basic computer skills while in the military; at that time he had access to the U.S. Department of Defense's vast computer databases and used them to help track down bad guys—illicit arms dealers, drug smugglers, KGB operatives and their agents, American traitors, and terrorists.

After leaving the service, Tim continued to apply his digital skills, working for two large P.I. firms that specialized in high-tech security and then, eventually, starting his own business.

That's how he met Laura.

Tim and Laura were introduced to each other six years earlier. She'd hired him to run a security check on LorTech's computer systems. A hacker had broken in and raised hell. The FBI, assisted by Tim, tracked down the culprit—a local high school junior with too much free time on his hands. Tim then helped LorTech build a layered defense system to fend off future attacks.

Laura was more than grateful for Tim's help. The mutual attraction had been there from day one. She'd actually asked him for the first date.

They married eight months after Tim's assignment was completed. A year later they were blessed with twin sons, Tyler and Cody.

Tim Carpenter was highly skilled at his craft. He'd always had a knack for mathematics and he loved chess. It was only natural that he was attracted to computers. But there was another side to his makeup; his late father had been a police officer—a homicide detective with the LAPD, and Tim's paternal grandfather had also been a beat cop—a thirty-year veteran with the Chicago PD. The Carpenter cop gene had been passed on to Tim.

All along Tim had planned on a career in law enforcement. Some twenty-three years earlier, when he joined the U.S. Army as a future officer, he had expected to serve out his service commitment as an MP, or possibly in the CID as an Army detective. He would then resign and join the FBI.

Tim's career path was diverted prior to earning his commission. Because of his superior marks, and at the recommendation of one of his instructors, he was recruited by Army Intelligence. INSCOM was looking for the brightest officers, especially those who excelled at computing. He was offered a career that blended both of his interests: computers and hunting bad guys. He accepted.

After extensive postcommissioning training, including Ranger and Airborne schools and a six-month tour as an infantry platoon leader, Lt. Tim Carpenter was transferred to Germany.

As a U.S. Army intelligence officer stationed in Europe, Tim's specialty had been finding not so nice people who did everything they could to prevent being found. Using the latest computers, in concert with tried-and-true detective work, Tim excelled at his craft. There was no thought of leaving the Army.

For the most part, the bad guys—and gals—were elusive prey, yet Tim Carpenter managed to root them out with ever increasing efficiency. But then one wintry morning in Munich, everything changed.

It had been over fifteen years since the incident. He rarely revisited that day, at least consciously. The pain was muted, buried under the surface, never quite fading to black.

And now—just a few weeks earlier—his dormant skill had been reawakened. The missing university professor—Jenny's dad—had been a challenge he couldn't resist. When Laura asked him to help Jennifer, he had looked forward to the new assignment with enthusiasm.

But not anymore.

* * *

This morning Tim was sitting in a chair on the timber deck, located off the kitchen. There was just a touch of an offshore breeze, wind milling the anchored yachts as if they were performing in a synchronized ballet. Roche Harbor was once again packed with hundreds of boats. The marina was overflowing and those not able to tie up to the docks were anchored out. A sleek sixty-foot power boat had dropped its hook about four hundred feet offshore of Tim's residence. The yacht had come in just after midnight.

From the privacy of his bedroom, Tim had observed the crew through a set of binoculars. It took only a couple of minutes for him to decide that the visitors were not a threat. There were two adults and three small children aboard, and they all appeared to be worn out. A wealthy family out for a weekend of cruising, Tim had concluded.

Tim remembered checking on Jenny just before the yacht anchored. She was in the study, next to the living room. For hours she had been reviewing the documents recovered from her father's storage locker. The horror of the previous evening had been replaced with utter astonishment.

"Tim," she had said, "this material is absolutely amazing. Dad was so close to replicating the effect that I'm convinced that it really can be done."

She then held up a page of complex calculations—she had made them. It looked like ancient hieroglyphics to Tim.

"See, it's right here in this power transfer function. If I can figure out how to solve it, then I think that I just might have the answer." She paused, taking the time to focus on Tim's eyes. "After reviewing Dad's test results, I'm convinced more than ever that he was definitely heading in the right direction." She paused again. She had been speaking more to herself than to her companion. After picking up the MERLIN device, she continued: "It's got to be superconductivity that's making it so efficient. Somehow, when electricity flows through this thing"—she'd pointed to the scorched amalgam of silicon chips and warped circuit traces—"it magnifies the discontinuity. Now, if we can just develop a carrier medium that mimics the focusing effect, then we can . . ."

Tim took another sip of coffee and smiled to himself as he recalled how excited Jenny had been. She was like the proverbial kid in a candy shop. She could barely contain her joy.

Tim hadn't a hint as to what she was talking about. All he remembered was Jenny's conclusion: the phenomenon was real and it probably could be replicated.

Jenny had continued to recite her theories until Tim eventually convinced her that she needed sleep. She resisted at first. Her excitement was genuine, but there was also an undertone of fear. She remembered with clarity the killings at the FBI safe house. It had all started when she was asleep.

Finally, around 12:30 A.M., Jenny climbed into her bed. Within a few minutes she fell asleep. Later she would dream about her father, Chris, and a chalkboard full of complex equations.

Tim turned away from the water, looking up at the second floor of his house. Jenny's bedroom was right above the deck. He hoped that she would sleep until noon.

Tim drained his coffee cup and then stood up. He was wearing a plain gray cotton sweatshirt and blue jeans. A pair of leather sandals covered his bare feet. And tucked into the small of his back, behind the leather belt, was a ten-shot semiautomatic pistol. The Glock 26 was always there, ready for instant use.

The floor of the spacious living room was covered with documents. The two men sat cross-legged on the thick carpet, scouring through the reams of paper. They examined everything: canceled bank checks, credit card statements, phone bills, utility receipts, real estate tax billings. But it was all routine. They found nothing unusual—the content of the Carpenters' household records was similar to what would be found in most American families—except that the amounts were far above normal. Laura Lorence ran at least $10,000 a month through her Gold MasterCard account. Tim Carpenter was more restrained; he only spent a few thousand each month. And there was no mortgage payment on the $6 million waterfront estate.

Allen Peng was convinced that the burglary had been a waste of time. They still knew nothing about where Carpenter could have taken Jennifer Richmond. His agents continued to scour the Seattle area, looking for any clue that might point them in the right direction. A carefully conducted telephone inquiry to LorTech revealed that Laura Lorence was away on a business trip. Further attempts to locate her proved fruitless. The LorTech receptionist was expert at protecting the privacy of her boss.

And then there was Chris Wilcox. He remained tied up in the basement. Although Peng had yet to decide on his fate, the man sitting next to him had. Gérard Rémy still had high hopes for Chris.

Peng tossed down a telephone billing and turned to face Rémy. The French spy was examining a framed document. "What's that?" Peng asked.

Rémy turned the frame around. It was a diploma. "Our Mr. Carpenter's been in the military—graduated from West Point."

Peng nodded, mildly impressed. "Anything else about his military background?"

"No. That's it." Rémy continued to study the diploma. A moment later he asked: "How about you—find anything interesting?"

"Apparently they both use cellular phones. I've got billing statements for two accounts."

"Good. We might be able to do something with them."

"Right. I'll have Wu check into it." Peng paused, now eyeing his partner. "Besides that diploma, did you come up with anything else?"

"Maybe." The French spy set the frame on the carpet and then picked up a small booklet. The burglars had found it in a drawer under the phone stand in the master bedroom. "Address book," he said. "Has lots of names and addresses; most have phone numbers." He tossed it to Peng.

Peng thumbed through the directory. The entries were handwritten, the script neat and legible. He looked back. "Must be the woman's."

Rémy nodded in agreement. They had both studied samples of Tim Carpenter's handwriting—notes written into the margin of various bills and bank statements. Tim's script was sloppy, almost illegible.

Peng continued to examine the directory. There were several hundred entries. All they needed was one: a friend, a relative, a business associate. Someone who could lead them to Carpenter. *The answer is here*, thought Peng. *Someone will know where he is.*

Peng was trying to decide how to make the first inquiry when Rémy spoke up. There was excitement in his voice. "I think I've got something here!"

"What?"

"It was in the unopened mail. A letter from a Seattle law firm. It's about some kind of real estate purchase they made and there's a deed attached to it."

"What good is that?" Peng hadn't made the connection yet.

"It's for a house."

"Where?"

"Someplace called Pearl Island but I don't know where that is."

"Let me see it."

Peng read the letter and then examined the deed. He was vaguely familiar with American real estate transactions and understood enough to know that the find was, indeed, important. He turned to look at his companion. "This legal description . . . it says this property is located in San Juan County."

"Those are the islands north of here?" asked the French spy.

"Yes." Peng stood up. "I've got a map in the car." He headed to the garage.

Two minutes later both men were huddled over the dining room table, studying the Chevron road map. The small-scale map didn't have a lot of detail to it. Only the larger islands were called out: Orcas, San Juan, and Lopez.

"I don't see anything called Pearl Island," Rémy finally concluded. "It must be too small for this map."

Peng nodded. "We need a more detailed map—a chart of

the San Juans. Do you know where we can get one?"

Rémy had started to shake his head when he remembered. He then smiled. "Yes, I know. Come with me."

It took just seven minutes to make the drive. They parked in a stall outside the building's entrance. When they walked into the store, it was right where Rémy had remembered, tacked to a wall by the counter.

The nautical chart of the San Juans was one of several displayed in the marine chandlery. Rémy had visited the store once before, after making arrangements to sublet a slip at the nearby marina. The speedboat they had used to help kidnap Dr. Richmond was still moored at the marina.

Peng and Rémy clustered next to the NOAA chart. Peng spotted it first. The tiny island was barely noticeable. "There!" he said. He tapped the chart with the tip of his right index finger.

Rémy stared at tiny, crescent-shaped Pearl Island. It was at the very tip of giant San Juan Island. It guarded Roche Harbor from the open waters of Spieden Channel.

Rémy turned toward his partner. Both men smiled.

Ricardo Molina walked out of the hospital lobby and headed for the car. By the time he reached the Ford sedan, the skin of his forehead had begun to glisten. It was a scorching afternoon, ninety degrees.

Ricardo had just left Harborview's intensive care unit. Special Agent Audrey Jordan was still recovering from the previous day's emergency surgery; she wasn't conscious and might not be for hours yet. The catastrophic loss of blood from the gunshot wound had almost killed her.

Although there was little chance that Audrey would be awake, Ricardo made the trip anyway. The visit to Harborview had been symbolic. Audrey was his friend—he wanted to pay his respects. Besides, he needed to get out of the office. He had been running full steam for over thirty-six hours, only catching a few hours' sleep on the couch in his office.

Before leaving the hospital, Ricardo's directive to the two FBI agents guarding the entry to the ICU was crystal: the moment Audrey was coherent they were to call the office. They were further instructed not to ask her any questions about the attack. Only Agent Kwan, or Ricardo himself, would conduct that interview.

Special Agent Jordan was SAC Molina's only hope for the moment. Everything else had failed. So far, the special task force he had launched the previous morning was drawing blanks. They were no closer to locating Jennifer Richmond than to finding Seattle's notorious Green River serial killer. She'd vanished.

Ricardo turned the starter and the engine roared to life. He rolled the window down on his side. It would take about five minutes before the air conditioner kicked in.

After strapping on his seat belt, Ricardo reached into a pocket of his blue blazer and removed the phone. He punched in one of the two-digit memory numbers. It was answered on the second ring.

"Agent Kwan."

"Hi, Vicky, it's Rick."

"How's Audrey?"

"Still out, but the doctors say she's holding her own."

"She going to be okay?"

"Yeah, I think she's outta the woods now."

"Thank God."

"Vicky, anything from LorTech yet?"

"I talked with the senior vice president . . . just a sec. Ah, Bill Silverman. He said that Laura Lorence left last night from Los Angeles."

"Where'd she go?"

"He didn't know; she just left word that she was taking some time off and would call in for messages."

"How about Carpenter's mother?"

"No answer. We did get hold of the building manager. He said she was in California, too."

"And I suppose there's nothing new from Carpenter's office?"

"That right. He hasn't called in, just left the note saying he'd be gone for a few days."

Dammit to hell, Tim, Ricardo thought, *what the hell are you up to now?*

Ricardo was well aware that Tim Carpenter had been working for Jennifer Richmond, trying to find out what happened to her father. Tim had come to talk to him about it several weeks earlier. He and Tim were buddies.

Tim and Ricardo went way back—to the early days when they both were intelligence officers in the U.S. Army. They'd served in Europe at the same time.

Although Tim remained in the Army for eight years, eventually earning the rank of major, Ricardo resigned his commission as soon as his commitment was up. He then joined the FBI. Now a sixteen-year veteran and currently the top federal cop for the Pacific Northwest, Ricardo Molina was on the fast track. His next assignment would be as SAC at one of the FBI's megafield offices: New York City, Washington, D.C., or Los Angeles.

"If Carpenter's wife and mother aren't around," Kwan said, "what'll we do?"

"How about that Microsoft guy?"

"Chris Wilcox?"

"Yeah."

"No sign of him yet. He didn't come to work today nor did he show up at his place or Jennifer's condo."

"The receptionist is sure the guy said he was FBI?"

"Yep, he even showed her his badge."

"Then they must have snatched him like you suspected."

"I think so."

"Shit."

Victoria waited for a long moment. "Rick, I don't think we have a choice now. You want me to send it out?"

"Yep. We can't waste any more time. Go ahead and do it."

"Okay. I'll get right on it."

Five minutes later, a special bulletin was transmitted via the Internet from the Seattle field office to the FBI's National Crime Information Center in Washington, D.C. A nationwide alert had just been issued for Jennifer Richmond and Timothy Carpenter. They were now wanted as material witnesses in the slaying of four federal law enforcement officers. Within the hour, black-and-white photographs of the pair, along with physical descriptions and, in Tim's case, his fingerprints, would be faxed to hundreds of police stations and sheriff's departments throughout the nation.

It was a desperate measure—and not quite kosher. The FBI had no concrete evidence that Tim or Jenny had broken any laws. But it was all that Ricardo had left.

The FBI was still rolling snake eyes when it came to identifying the perpetrators. Other than hundreds of spent shell casings, all wiped clean of any fingerprints prior to firing, and the expended bullets, many embedded in the bodies of the four dead agents, the bad guys had left nothing behind at the Cascade safe house.

Then there was Dr. Richmond's abduction. He had been snatched right out of his University of Washington laboratory a month earlier, and then a couple of weeks later his corpse washed up on a Whidbey Island beach. Again, not one solid clue.

And finally, not one of the nation's other premiere intelligence organizations had anything to offer as to who was behind it all. The perps were an enigma.

Maybe, just maybe, Ricardo thought as he drove out of the hospital parking lot, *some deputy sheriff or state patrolman will spot Tim and Jennifer in time*.

He hated to think what would happen if the killers found them first. The MERLIN prize would surely be lost if that happened, and so would his friend.

8 SURVEILLANCE

"That must be the place. Here, have a look." The man handed the pair of binoculars to his companion.

"But I don't see anyone there. It looks deserted."

"You can't tell that from here."

"But there's no boat at the dock, not even a rowboat. How would they get there?"

"They've got to have a boat. They're probably out in it."

"Doing what?"

"I don't know. Maybe they're fishing."

The two men continued to parry back and forth as they stood at the end of the pier. Although there were dozens of people nearby, the observers were ignored. Wearing Bermuda shorts, T-shirts, and tennis shoes, they blended in perfectly with the other boaters and tourists who crowded the visitors pier. The fact that the two men were of Asian descent, and spoke only in their native tongue, didn't raise any eyebrows. The world-class resort attracted thousands of foreign visitors each year.

They had arrived at the Roche Harbor Resort about an hour earlier. It was now almost two in the afternoon. They took a commuter flight from Sea-Tac International to the Friday Harbor airport and then hired a cab, driving the length of San Juan Island to Roche Harbor.

It was the high season, and the resort was overflowing. All of the hotel rooms and cabins had long since been rented out. And every one of the 380 boat slips was spoken for.

The lack of accommodations wasn't a problem. The two men wouldn't be staying long. Their assignment was nearly complete.

"Do we need to rent a boat or something to get closer?" asked the shorter of the two men.

"No. We can't get too close. They might see us."

"So, I should do it from here?"

"Yes. And when the charter plane comes for us, we will have the pilot fly near it when we take off."

The short man nodded his understanding. He then pulled out a collapsible tripod and a 35 mm Nikon. An enormous telephoto lens was mounted to the body of the camera.

While the photographer set up his equipment, the other man removed a small pocketbook from a shoulder bag he carried. He then began thumbing through it.

The book was an illustrated guide to marine birds of Puget Sound. Neither man cared one iota about ornithology, but the cover was ideal: two Chinese gentlemen, outfitted in tourist garb, standing on a busy pier in the middle of one of the most popular yachting resorts in the Northwest, photographing bald eagles and diving cormorants. Who would ever suspect they were spies?

Tim had the engine cranked wide open. The Sea Ray rocketed across the emerald waters at thirty-five knots. The ride was smooth, just a slight vibration in the fiberglass hull as it planed over the rippled surface. A long trail of white marked the course as the twenty-four-foot boat headed westward down Spieden Channel. It had just passed Davison Head.

Jennifer Richmond was standing next to Tim, both hands gripping the rail mounted on the dash. Her scarlet mane trailed out from behind her head, caught by the windshield's slipstream. She was laughing, having a blast.

"Are we getting close?" she yelled, over the heavy drone of the high-performance engine.

Tim smiled and then pointed over the port bow. A few seconds later he turned the steering wheel in the same direction.

The Sea Ray raced forward for another half mile and then Tim pulled back on the throttle. When the runabout slowed, its hull settled back into the water, burning off speed at a prodigious rate.

Now traveling at just fifteen knots, Jenny released her grip on the stainless steel bar. "Wow, that was fantastic," she said.

Tim smiled again. "Yeah, that really gets your blood going."

Jenny settled back into the pedestal-mounted chair next to the helm. She pulled her knees up to her chest. She was wearing a pair of cotton shorts, an extra-large sweatshirt, and tennis shoes. All borrowed from Laura's bedroom dresser.

Just before noon, Tim had decided to take Jenny for a cruise. She needed the diversion. Earlier in the morning he had found her curled up on the rug in her bedroom, her father's papers scattered across the floor. She was weeping, the grief over her father's death still fresh.

"That engine must guzzle fuel doing that," Jenny offered,

now peering aft at the Sea Ray's motor cowling. "What's it get, three or four miles to the gallon?"

Tim shook his head in amazement. He'd expect a comment like that from another man, but a woman—no way. But then he remembered: *Damn, she's an engineer. She probably knows more about that V-8 than I'll ever hope to know.*

"I don't know, Jenny. When the tank gets low, I just fill it up." Tim then looked at the instrument panel. The fuel tank gauge was just registering slightly above the "E" mark. "And it looks like we'll need to fuel up today."

A few minutes later Tim was guiding the speedboat through the narrow gap between Pearl Island's eastern shore and San Juan Island. Several boats were heading out so he hugged the starboard side of the channel. Jenny remained by his side, sipping an ice-cold can of Diet Pepsi.

Just as the boat entered the sheltered waters of Roche Harbor, they heard the heavy roar of a racing engine. Both automatically looked toward the noise. The float plane was accelerating across the harbor, heading their way. It looked like a whirlwind of silvery metal and sea spray.

"It's coming right for us," Jenny called out, her voice strained.

Tim was more relaxed. The harbor was again jam-packed; the pilot was obviously trying to avoid the vessels. "We're okay. He knows what he's doing."

The Cessna's aluminum pontoons broke their bond with the water a thousand feet from the Sea Ray. As soon as the plane was free, it soared into the sky, banking toward the left.

"See," Tim said, watching the float plane climb higher, "what'd I tell you? No problem."

Jenny nodded. "I guess he was farther away than I thought."

"Yeah, sometimes it's hard to judge distances over the water."

Jenny grinned, relieved. "Okay, what do we do now?"

"Let's go fuel up at the marina first. We can get some

more groceries there, too. Then we'll head back to the house."

"We still going to leave tomorrow?"

"Yep. We've been lucky so far and I want to keep it that way."

They would leave early the next day. It had taken Tim all morning to arrange. It would start with a half-hour run in the Sea Ray to Friday Harbor and then a taxi ride to the local airport. The charter plane, a twin-engine Bonanza, would then fly them to Portland, avoiding Sea-Tac Airport like it was infested with the plague. Tim and Jenny would next catch an Alaska Airlines flight to LAX. After a two-hour layover, they'd board a southbound Mexicana jet.

Tim had spent considerable time in Mexico City on another case. He could hide Jenny there until things calmed down.

The float plane made three orbits around Pearl Island before heading eastward. The Asian with the Nikon shot two thirty-six-frame rolls.

9 THE *ZHONGDUI* AND THE PEASANT

"How do you stand him?"

"What do you mean?"

"He's such an arrogant bastard. He treats my men with hardly any respect. It's like we're from the backwoods."

Allen Peng grinned. "He's French—what do you expect?"

Wu shook his head. "But the way he talks down to us, it's contemptible."

Peng took a sip of tea and then glanced through one of the nearby tempered glass windows. Water everywhere. He and Wu were alone, seated in a ridiculously opulent setting; it could have been the living room of a Hollywood mogul or a Fortune 500 CEO. Instead, they were in the grand salon of a luxury motor vessel. The 144-foot *Orca* was homeported in Vancouver, B.C., but on this day, she was patrolling U.S. waters.

"I've been around others like him before," Peng finally said. "The English can be just as bad—the Japanese, too."

"Is he a racist?"

Peng laughed. "If it were only that simple." He took another sip. "Race is part of it—always has been and always will be. But what really drives someone like Rémy is the fact that he's having to play second fiddle to us."

Wu cocked his head to the side. "Second fiddle?"

"Sorry, I've lived in America too long. The French have little to say in this entire operation. Financially, they're an equal partner with us . . . as are the Germans. But tactically they both have little to contribute. Their combined North American intelligence operations are minuscule compared to our own."

"So why are we even working with them?"

"They needed us, we needed them."

Wu shook his head, confused.

"One of my people, here in the Seattle area, picked up that the U.S. Air Force was up to something unusual with Boeing. At first we thought it was the ABL program."

"ABL—what's that?"

"Airborne laser. You know, knockdown ICBM warheads with a laser beam fired from a 747. Star Wars stuff."

Wu nodded.

"Anyway. That wasn't what they were working on."

"So it must have been the jetliner project."

"Correct. We knew there was classified work being done in Everett on a new 777, but we could never penetrate the security. We really didn't have any idea as to what it was all about." Peng paused. "The German government, on the other hand, provided the first hard evidence about the MER-LIN technology."

"If the Germans were involved, how did we end up in bed with the DGSE?"

"One of our operatives in Europe made that connection—

in Berlin, actually. It came from the German government—
the particular minister was charged with looking after Airbus's interests."

"We had him under surveillance?"

"Yes." Peng drained the cup and placed it on the coffee
table. "All of the Airbus partners—the governments of Germany, France, Britain, and Spain—they've had some impressive aerospace technological breakthroughs lately so it's
in our best interests to know exactly what they're up to. We
do the same with the Americans, but they're harder to penetrate now."

"Why?"

"Much better security—after our Los Alamos operation
finally unraveled."

Major Wu knew that tale. It had gained legendary status
in the PLA. MSS deep-cover operatives—*chen di yu*—executed a near flawless looting of America's most secret secrets. The problems at the Los Alamos laboratory were a
smoke screen. The real damage took place at other Department of Energy facilities, and the consulting firms that supported DOE.

The detailed design of DOE's latest strategic nuclear warheads—H-bombs—was simply transferred onto a PC from a
top secret mainframe at the targeted weapons lab and then
emailed out. Classified design data on assorted other high-
tech weaponry and gadgetry was similarly hijacked from the
computer systems of several private consulting firms that
were under contract with the U.S. government.

The agents of the PRC—non-Asian American citizens—
were paid hefty fees by the *chen di yu* for the information.
These traitors delivered the priceless—and deadly—data on
a silicon platter to the PLA's top military scientists and engineers. With just a few clicks on the email SEND icons of
the renegades' PCs, China had gained at least ten years'
worth of technology. It was that simple.

Allen Peng continued. "To prevent more security leaks,
the NSA, FBI, and even the CIA are now all working together. They know what they're doing." Peng hesitated for
a moment as another thought developed. "Their civilian

counterparts are also getting tough to crack these days. They now take industrial espionage seriously, too."

"But they're still vulnerable."

"Of course." Peng smiled, a toothy grin. "We just have to work a little harder. You know the routine . . . kiss lots of ass and make big donations to the right people. Money still works wonders here."

Wu grinned. "I understand that, sir. But I still don't see the connection . . . why are we working with Europeans?"

"From our German minister contact we knew that he was concerned about something called MERLIN. All we knew at the time was that it was related to Boeing. At first, we thought it was just the same old rivalry between Boeing and Airbus Industrie. Both fighting for their share of the world's jetliner market. But then one of our Seattle operatives heard the rumor about the special 777 in Everett. It wasn't long before we confirmed the presence of the U.S. Air Force at the plant. That's when we speculated that there might be a connection."

Peng reached into his coat pocket to pull out a pack of cigarettes. He offered one of the Camels to Wu. After they both lit up, Peng continued. "Suspecting that the 777 project might be related to MERLIN, Beijing decided to take a chance on something that I, quite frankly, was amazed at."

"What do you mean?"

"We approached the Germans and the French about pooling our information on what the Americans were up to . . . and they accepted." Peng sucked in another lungful. Exhaling, he continued: "Eventually, we met with our German and French counterparts in Hong Kong. That's when I first met Rémy. The British we're not invited—still too close to the Americans; nor were the Spanish—they just don't have the horsepower. Anyway, it was quite a poker game." Peng smiled once again, knowing Major Wu was an avid gambler. "We anted up with what we knew about the 777 project, and they called with MAGNUM."

Major Wu again nodded, already privy to the American mole. MAGNUM had provided the location of the FBI's Cascade safe house.

The commando unconsciously massaged his right wrist with his left hand. The wound was healing but still remained stiff. "Do we know anything about this MAGNUM?" he asked.

"No, other than the Germans suspect that he might be FBI."

"Is he the one that provided the video of the airliner experiment?" Wu was referring to a 105-minute-long VHS tape of a MERLIN test. Mounted in the cockpit of a Boeing 777, the camera recorded the entire test: sunset takeoff from Everett's Paine Field, high-speed acrobatics over the Cascade Mountains, and then a flawless touchdown at the Grant County Airport near Moses Lake in eastern Washington. During the entire trip, not one human aboard the craft touched the flight controls.

"Yes," Peng answered, "MAGNUM sold us that one plus several other tapes."

"That was just an amazing video—it's still hard to believe they can do that!"

"I know. At first we thought this whole thing might be bogus—the Americans trying to throw us all off course by concocting an outrageous red herring. But unfortunately for all of us, they've really done it, or I should say, Dr. Jeff Richmond really did it."

Wu's interest spiked at the mention of the University of Washington professor. "His daughter, Jennifer—you remain convinced that she has access to the technology?"

"Absolutely. We're convinced more than ever that she knows where her father hid the prototype unit—Dr. Richmond didn't come right out and say it when we had him, but all the indications point right to her."

"Did he tell you much at all?"

"Not a lot. If we had known about his poor health, we would have taken a different approach with the interrogation." Peng glanced down at the deck for a moment. "Both Rémy and I were too rough on him during the questioning."

"Just what happened to him?"

"Heart attack. Died right here." Peng pointed at the thick

carpet a few feet away from where they were sitting. "There was nothing we could do for him."

Wu knew the rest of that story too. The *Orca*'s crew dumped the corpse overboard but it was poorly weighted. It later surfaced, eventually washing up on a beach north of Seattle.

Major Wu shook his head, now putting together all that he had just heard. "You know, sir," he said, "this whole operation is so risky—it could backfire on everyone."

"That's right. Nevertheless, we must continue. The French and Germans are scared shitless that Boeing's going to bankrupt Airbus—this MERLIN thing could be Airbus's coup de grâce. The airline companies will be switching to Boeing in droves."

"Why?"

"Because their operating costs will be so much less. You know how much those pilots make, don't you?"

Wu laughed—finally making the connection.

Peng sucked another drag from the nearly spent Camel. "Anyway, the cost savings is only part of the story. For us, it's the military applications where this MERLIN gadget really works best. If the technology is as advanced as we suspect, all the *billions* that we've spent to modernize our own air forces, and are *still* spending, will be for naught. Just about everything that we've got in the air will be vulnerable."

"So the Americans will remain the world's only superpower."

"Yes, they'll be untouchable—more arrogant and pushier than ever." Peng again paused, this time crushing out the butt in an ash tray. "But it's *our* prime directive, Major, to see that does not happen. We either get access to the technology or we make certain they cannot use it against us."

"The woman—this Jennifer Richmond—she's the key to everything."

"That's right."

Wu stood up. "Well, sir, it's time for me to check on my men. I want to go over the plan with them at least once more."

"Very well," Peng said as he, too, rose. He was six inches

taller, yet Wu's bulk more than made up for the difference. Peng eyed Wu. "Major, we can't afford another debacle like what happened at the FBI safe house."

"I know, sir."

"We either capture her or we make sure that she's useless to the Americans. It's that simple."

"Understood, sir. It will be done."

Allen Peng remained in the grand salon, alone. Another Camel drooped from his lower lip, its stink polluting the opulent compartment.

The mammoth yacht was barely under way, using just enough power from the twin turbo diesels to maintain steerage. They were ahead of schedule. Nothing to do but wait until the sun dipped behind the peaks of Vancouver Island.

He sucked in another lungful. The nicotine helped, yet he remained on edge. *It's all happening too fast. . . . Wu says his men can do it, but after that other fiasco . . . one dead, three wounded, including Wu himself . . . Shit! I just don't know!*

Despite his reservations, Peng did admire Major Wu. Or maybe it was envy. Anyway, Wu had the right stuff. Peng had made that finding several weeks earlier when he returned to Hong Kong. The briefing file had spelled it all out in black and white.

Major Wu Jin Li was on the fast-track career path in the People's Liberation Army. The son of a deputy to the general secretary of the Chinese Communist Party, he could have had any number of cushy government jobs. Proletariat perks. But to his credit he chose an honest profession.

Although originally trained as an infantry officer, Wu never served in a line unit. Instead, he had been recruited by military intelligence after receiving his commission. It was his command of the English language, coupled with his stratospheric IQ test scores, that attracted the military spy masters of the Second Department.

For the first three years of his career Wu served with a special forces naval team operating out of Shanghai. There were twenty-two men in the unit—all young army and navy officers. Approximately half of the *zhongdui* unit's time was spent in the classroom. The instruction was intense: advanced English, Western economic theory, accounting basics, computer programming, American history, and, of course, a steady diet of Communist doctrine. The remainder of the soldier's time was spent in the field: commando training.

The young officers became proficient with a multitude of small arms, expert in the use of explosives, highly competent with high-tech communication and surveillance gear, and as deadly as king cobras in hand-to-hand combat.

The blend of the MBA-level education with the art of killing was designed to create a new type of warrior—one far more deadly than any conventional soldier. The special *zhongdui* graduates would become the leaders of a new force—not an army created just for physical conflict, but, instead, an army of intellectual combatants.

Wu and his comrades had been trained for a single purpose: conduct military espionage operations in the West, with the United States as their prime target.

Peng crushed the spent Camel in an ashtray and glanced out the port window wall. Lights from the nearest shore were just flickering on. *Won't be long now,* he thought.

He stood up and then stepped aft to the bar—an elegant creation of the finest hardwoods and gleaming mirrors. Nearly every imaginable spirit was available, yet he chose a bottle of mineral water. Plain and simple, like his own demeanor.

The vessel's lavish setting had minimal impact on Allen Peng. To him it was just a tool, an elaborate disguise, something necessary for the success of the mission.

Pure b.s. Deep down, embedded under his skin, the truth reigned: *Don't get used to it. . . . Remember, now, they'll pull the rug out from under you. . . . You're not right for it. . . . You don't fit in!*

Allen Peng, indeed, did not fit in with China's ruling class. There had been no perks, no privileges, no one in his family tree to pull magical strings. Unlike Major Wu, every step up the success ladder that Peng took was earned by his own merits. And it had been a grueling climb.

It started some thirty-nine years earlier in a village on the outskirts of Shanghai. Wang Keung—Allen Peng—was the sixth child out of seven: number two son. He would have been doomed to a life of abject poverty if it hadn't been for his mother.

The Wangs were peasants, one step above coolie class. Although much of their time was spent working on the local commune farm, they also tended a tiny plot of their own. It helped feed and clothe the eleven members of the clan: seven children, both fraternal grandparents, and young Keung's mother and father.

The quarter-acre parcel had been awarded to Wang Chen, Keung's father, after China's collective farm system suffered successive crop failures. By parceling out tiny plots to individual households, and allowing them to keep a portion of the food they produced, Beijing avoided wholesale famine. This new policy was the prelude to China's current grand economic experiment: a return to capitalism, but without democracy.

Allen Peng could barely remember his father; he was just a blur now.

The Red Guards stole Wang Chen when Keung was six years old. One sweltering August afternoon, the soldiers rounded up half a dozen men from the village. Labeled dissidents by the reigning czars of the Cultural Revolution, none ever returned home. Wang Chen's crime: he attended a meeting at a neighboring village where an ex-professor of history from Shanghai University (who at that time was forced to survive as a common farm laborer) spoke on the failure of Mao Zedong's agrarian reform policies.

Exceptionally bright, Keung excelled in the village school, always outperforming his classmates. Yet he had no future. There was little hope of any education beyond grade school, and his brother, number one son, had already inherited the family farm. Keung would have to fend for himself when he reached adulthood.

Despite her own meager education, Wang Yow recognized her son's potential. If he could receive a proper education, then he just might be able to escape.

When Keung was ten, his mother launched an all-out campaign to save him. Barely able to read herself, Wang Yow begged, borrowed and swiped every book, pamphlet, and newspaper she could find. Almost everything she obtained was state-sanctioned propaganda.

A voracious reader, Wang Keung absorbed it all—like the memory core of an Intel chip. And then, by relentlessly courting the neighborhood *danwei* official—the CPC's local contact—flaunting her son's near flawless regurgitation of Communist doctrine, Wang Yow eventually succeeded.

When Keung turned fifteen, he entered the elite Commissar's Revolutionary School of Higher Learning in Shanghai. From there he graduated to the Beijing College of International Relations, the People's Republic of China's spy school. He was subsequently drafted into the PRC's equivalent of the CIA, the Guojia Anquan Bu, a.k.a. the Ministry of State Security. It was then sixteen years of foreign assignments, all in the West, most in the United States.

With the exception of just a handful of one- to two-week vacation visits, Allen Peng had lost contact with his family. Nevertheless, regardless of where he was stationed, a third of his salary was sent home each pay period. It was his one feeble link to his former life.

Allen was now standing on the *Orca*'s fantail, elbows planted on the oak guardrail. The sun had finally departed. The cross-breeze flowing down Haro Strait ruffled the fringes of his thick, ear-length sable locks. He had lit up again— now up to three packs a day. His one sin.

As he inhaled, taking another chemical hit, he thought ahead, beyond the mission. *Maybe it's time to go home . . . Mama's getting old . . . I should help her more. Yes! That's what I'm going to do. I'll put in for an extended leave when this is over. . . . It's time to take a break.*

"Damn! I've never seen anything move like that before."

"Neither have I."

"Those turns . . . and the acceleration . . . it's just amazing."

"Yeah. And what's with that funny exhaust trail? It looks like puffs of smoke to me rather than a solid stream."

Tim Carpenter shook his head. "Beats me. Must be some kind of new propulsion system . . . maybe a pulse jet or something like that." He turned to face Jennifer. "Do you think your dad was working on it, too?"

"Probably."

Darkness had engulfed Roche Harbor an hour earlier. Tim Carpenter and Jennifer Richmond were in the living room of Tim's beachfront home, watching videos.

It had been a remarkable evening. After dinner, Jenny and Tim retired to the living room. Neatly organized on the nearby coffee table were a half dozen stacks of her father's research papers. After the speedboat excursion, Jenny had spent all afternoon continuing her examination of the technical data. There were hundreds of pages of documents to review. So far, she had managed to read about a third.

And then there were the tapes. A couple of hours earlier Tim finally hooked up the new video player and television set. Both had been sitting in the corner of the room, sealed up inside their shipping crates.

First, they again viewed the video that Dr. Jeffrey Richmond had made for Jenny. The sealed tape had been locked up in a Seattle law firm's records vault, only released to Jenny upon her father's death. Jeff had recorded it the previous winter.

For over an hour Dr. Jeffrey Richmond, in person, spelled it all out for his only survivor: the experiments in his University of Washington Artificial Intelligence Laboratory; the design of his prototype AI microprocessor; the lightning-induced electrical power surge in the lab that caused an arc over in the computer's main circuitry; the accidental discovery of the phenomenon which he nicknamed MERLIN, after the mythical magician; his efforts to replicate the MERLIN effect; the Pentagon's offer he couldn't refuse; and finally, the cryptic riddle of where his research papers and the original MERLIN microprocessor were hidden.

The narrative put the pieces together, but it was the Mercedes-Benz that had the greatest impact on Carpenter. Like when he first viewed the tape, just before the FBI sequestered Jenny, Tim was awestruck by the experiment. With a large aluminum case buckled into the driver's seat and Dr. Richmond sitting in the passenger seat of the sedan, the AI pilot drove the vehicle from Jeff's Montlake residence in Seattle, across the 520 floating bridge to Bellevue, and then back again, finally parking the car inside the professor's garage. The test had been run in winter, during peak evening rush hour traffic. And it had been raining—Northwest style. Not once during the seventy-five-minute round-trip did Jeff touch or adjust the controls.

When Dr. Richmond's farewell tape finally turned to static, Jenny had briefly burst into tears. Her loss was always there, just under the surface.

The next pair of videos that Tim and Jennifer viewed had been liberated from Dr. Richmond's storage locker the day before. There was no definitive identification as to the contents of the tape, just handwritten cassette labels: "VORTEX-Run 21" and "VORTEX-Run 32." Each video ran for about twenty minutes. There was no sound. No narration. Just color images.

The object was the same in each tape. It was delta-shaped, maybe twenty feet across at its widest. There was no tail or rudder assembly. It was metallic black with no identifying markers or discernible cockpit.

In the first video the craft sped down the dry lake bed runway and hurled itself into the crystal morning sky. The ground-based camera then tracked the vehicle as it executed a series of high-altitude, high-speed turns. Even with the camera's extreme magnification, the craft was just an ant speck on the TV screen. Nevertheless, its five-mile-long contrail, shaped like doughnuts on a string, scripted a zigzag path across the cerulean stratosphere that would draw any naked eye to it.

The mystery aircraft made one low-altitude pass over the high desert base before consummating the flight with a textbook landing.

In the second VHS tape, the camera was mounted inside the cockpit of an unidentified chase plane. Tim and Jenny were still watching it.

"What is that?" Tim asked, pointing to the right corner of the Sony. The object was a silvery blur.

"It kind of looks like another airplane to me," Jenny answered, now eyeing Tim.

"Yeah, you're right." He leaned closer to the set. "It does kind of look like a Raptor."

"A what?"

"Raptor . . . F-22. A new Air Force jet. It's just coming out. Real hot bird."

"Oh," Jenny said. She was mute for a few seconds and then continued, "It looks like it's going after the little black one."

"Yeah, this must be some kind of dogfight test."

"So what are they . . ." Jenny's voice trailed off as her eyes again focused on the television set. It happened in a heartbeat. One moment the F-22 was closing in behind the tiny, black-hulled craft, lining up for an apparent missile shot. The next instant, the mystery craft darted to the right at an incredibly sharp angle and then dropped altitude by several thousand feet. Before the F-22 was a quarter of the way through its own supersonic turn, the mystery aircraft was just a few hundred yards behind the twin tail assembly of the fighter. A few seconds later the tape turned to static.

"Good Lord!" Tim said, shaking his head. "That's just incredible. I've never seen anything move that quick before. How in the world could the pilot take those kinds of G's?"

Jenny shook her head. "I don't think anyone could."

"What?"

"Now I think I finally understand what's going on." Jenny hesitated for a long moment. "That thing—the black jet . . . it's a UAV—an unmanned aerial vehicle." She paused again. "There may not be a human inside but it does have a pilot."

Tim frowned, not yet making the connection.

"It's got to be piloted by Dad's MERLIN processor, like with his Mercedes." She took a deep breath. "From what I've seen tonight in these videos, and what I've managed to read so far, I think that when Dad's MERLIN computer is coupled with the right kind of sensors, the system is quite capable of total autonomous control."

"Are you trying to tell me that MERLIN thing can replace a human pilot?"

"Yep."

"*No way!*"

The two couples were seated across from each other inside the spacious cockpit of the sailboat, sipping a Yakima Valley merlot. There was a whiff of a breeze blowing up Mosquito Passage, just enough to windmill the bow of the anchored fifty-four-foot ketch into the wind. The women had already slipped on their windbreakers. The two men, however, had not yet succumbed to the night chill that swept across the harbor—their blood remained fortified by the generous measure of wine they had already consumed.

One of the men noticed it first, a huge black hole of a shadow heading northward, toward their anchorage. "Wow," he called out, "look at the size of that sucker."

The others turned.

The approaching yacht was well over a hundred feet in length; the hull was silhouetted by its cabin and running lights.

"I wonder what they're going to do," said one of the women.

"Probably going to drop their hook," offered the owner of the ketch. "Just like we did." He then turned to the side, looking back across the waterway toward the east. The Roche Harbor Resort Marina was jam-packed with hundreds of boats. There wasn't a spare slip anywhere to be found in the marina. He again faced his guests. "I knew I should have called ahead for a slip reservation. I apologize again for having to anchor out."

"Hey, Pete, don't worry about that . . . it's fantastic out here. We love it—right, Marlies?"

The pretty blond nodded her approval.

"And so do I," offered the skipper's wife. The stunning brunette was nestled at her husband's side.

Pete grinned as he slipped his right arm around her shoulders. He then faced his friend. "Matt old boy, how about cracking open another bottle of vino?"

"Happy to!"

Tim and Jenny were now in the kitchen, sitting at the counter. Tim had just brewed a pot of coffee—decaf. They were still discussing the videos.

"Tim, that black jet has to be a direct military application of Dad's technology."

Carpenter nodded, taking another sip from his mug. "Was there anything in your dad's papers about it?"

"No. Nothing like what we saw on those tapes. So far, all of the records that I've read have dealt with peaceful applications of MERLIN, like with Dad's Mercedes."

Tim shook his head. He could never see himself turning control of his Porsche over to a computer.

Jenny continued: "Besides that application there was a description of a new space probe for NASA and something to do with a deep ocean submersible for the UW's Oceanography Department. Oh, and there was one report about a Boeing project."

"Military project?"

"No, it was for a jetliner."

"No fighter aircraft?"

"That's right. It concerned adapting MERLIN to a 777. The idea was to—"

"That stuff all sounds impressive enough," Tim said, interrupting, "but they're nothing quite like what we saw on those tapes." He made direct eye contact. "You still think that thing was flying on its own?"

"Absolutely, it makes all the sense in the world."

"How so?"

"As near as I can make out, the MERLIN processor, combined with Dad's AI software, has computing power on the same scale as the human brain."

"Oh, come on, now!"

"No. I think that's exactly what's going on."

"I thought that was impossible." Tim looked away, momentarily surveying the interior of the spacious room. He turned back. "I remember reading someplace that it would take a computer the size of this house to even come close to replicating the human mind."

"Yeah, that was the case, but not anymore." She took another sip from her coffee mug. "To begin with, Dad was always on the cutting edge of AI technology. That was one of the reasons I went into the computer science field myself." She eyed Tim. "But this MERLIN phenomenon is so advanced, so radical, that it represents a mammoth expansion of electronic brain power."

"How does it do that?"

"I'm not totally clear on it yet. But from what I've read so far, it has something to do with a molecular change in the integrated circuits. Remember the power surge that Dad talked about in the video?"

"The lightning strike."

"Yes. Somehow, that high-voltage jolt changed the composition of the chips on one of the circuit boards."

Tim pointed to the clear plastic baggy resting on the countertop. Jenny had been examining it while he made the coffee. "That thing?" he asked.

"Right." She reached forward, picking up the bag. "This board has gone through an amazing metamorphosis." She now held it at eye level. "On first glance, it doesn't look all that different from anything you'd find inside of a PC or Mac."

Tim nodded.

"But believe me, it's different. For starters, instead of using normal silicon chips with aluminum conductors, Dad's MERLIN computer had advanced chips. They used an exotic blend of copper and some other trace materials. Strontium, I think, plus a few other things. Anyway, that by itself dramatically increased computing power."

"How?"

"Simple: copper carries electricity a lot faster than aluminum."

"So the juice flows quicker."

"That's right. Everything in the CPU runs faster. The chips also had a lot more storage capacity." Jenny hesitated. "Dad needed all that extra computing power to run his artificial intelligence software. The system needs to run incredibly fast because he used parallel processing—the CPU runs thousands of problems simultaneously, each one feeding off the other. It's a way to mimic how the human mind works."

"How fast are we talking?"

"Tens of trillions of operations a second."

"Wow, that's really pushing the envelope."

"Yes, for the relatively small size of the MERLIN unit, it was one powerful little computer."

"Okay, that all sounds impressive, but what about this special effect—the power surge thing?"

"Well, when the electrical overload fried the processor, it radically changed things in one of the circuit boards—on a subatomic level. Dad's notes stated that the arc over somehow induced a new kind of superconductivity in the copper oxide conductors."

"Superconductivity?"

"Yeah, it's a phenomenon where a certain type of material, for all practical purposes, has no resistance to electricity."

"Oh, yeah, I remember now. That's what happens when they cool down a special metal with liquid hydrogen or something like that."

"Correct. Usually it's liquid nitrogen, because it's a lot cheaper. Some supercomputers use circuitry that's cooled down to near absolute zero."

"But your dad's magic circuit board has superconducting properties without having to freeze it?"

"In a nutshell, yes. The MERLIN circuitry exhibits super-conducting properties near room temperature. But there's more to it than just that." She hesitated for a moment. "Through microminiaturization, hundreds of millions of circuits can be compressed onto a single chip. Now, when a couple of those chips are interlinked and then MERLINized, they can take on the computing power equivalent to a supercomputer."

"A Cray from a handful of chips?"

"Something like that."

"That's incredible."

"That's right. Dad stumbled onto something brand new."

"Are you certain that's the right one?"

"That's what they told me."

The two men were on the fantail of the yacht, peering aft. They spoke in their native Mandarin. Dressed in black from head to toe, the *zhongdui*s were essentially invisible. The only light on the fantail came from a pair of overhead-mounted amber lights that cast just enough illumination to keep one from running into "things."

There was another boat anchored nearby—a sailboat. It had been there when they arrived. The ketch's cabin lights were still on but it wasn't the focus of the commandos' attention. They were looking toward the shore; it was just a few hundred meters away.

"When do we go?"

"Not for several more hours."

"I hate waiting."

"I know."

"Did your dad ever tell you about the MERLIN project— before he died, I mean?"

"Never. I knew about his work on the advanced AI processor. He told me about that a couple of years ago . . . but this other thing . . . the power surge. No way. His video message was the first time I heard about it."

Tim and Jenny were still in the kitchen. He stood up and began pacing back across the tile floor. He stopped half a minute later. Now facing Jenny, he said, "I think I finally see what's going on. Your dad's breakthrough will revolutionize the design of computers. Tons of computing power in a tiny package. The applications are mind-boggling."

"That's basically it . . . but there's a problem."

"What?"

"To make the phenomenon useful, it has to be replicated. And that's what Dad was having trouble with. Remember what he said in the video."

"Oh, yeah. I see what you're getting at . . . that's why he went to the feds."

"Yes, he'd had some success with the replication process but it was a long way from a perfect duplication. To make it commercially marketable would require millions in additional R and D."

"So the feds jumped in."

"Correct. His contract with the government called for a dual effort: civilian applications and—"

"And military applications," interrupted Tim.

"Yes."

Tim returned to the counter stool. "I think I'm beginning to understand. Obviously, your dad was working on the practical applications—like with the car and the other stuff—while the Air Force headed up the . . ." He stopped in midsentence, remembering. "You said your dad was working on a Boeing project. Just what was he doing?"

Jenny smiled, wondering when Tim would finally make the connection. "What Dad's always dreamed about."

Tim cocked his head to the side, puzzled.

"Dad's master's and Ph.D. were in electrical engineering. But his undergraduate degree was in aeronautical engineering. He was always fascinated by flight. But when he got his bachelor's, there was a huge recession going on, especially in aerospace. He couldn't get a job. That's why he went into electrical engineering. Anyway, to make a long story short, he had this vision of designing a computer system that would fly a plane by itself. He used to talk about it all the time when I was a kid."

"The autopilot airliner."

"Right."

"I thought they could already do that."

"They can, pretty much, but the systems are limited. They require constant human monitoring. Anyway, what Dad had in mind went way beyond that. Complete autonomous control of the aircraft—the engines, navigation and communication systems, external sensors, flight controls, everything. That was to be one of the applications of his AI work."

"So he was working with Boeing?"

"No. Not directly, at least that's what his papers indicated. It was through the Air Force. They had the contract with Boeing to test MERLIN on a 777. The 777 test was part of his deal with the government."

"Civilian applications."

"Yes."

"Well, I bet the airline pilots won't care for MERLIN one bit."

"I'm sure they'd oppose it, but they'd still be needed."

"How's that?"

"The computer would control the plane from takeoff to landing, but there'd be a human in the copilot's seat—for PR reasons."

"Public relations?"

"That's what one of Dad's reports said. The pilot wouldn't be needed, of course. But it would ease the passengers' apprehension. They'd need to do that in order to sell it to the public."

"Okay, so what's the big advantage?"

"It could operate in virtually any weather conditions: fog, high winds, snow, rain, you name it. The AI computer wouldn't need to 'see' like a human pilot. Instead, it would use infrared, radar, laser beams, and a host of other sensors to see—in every direction around the entire aircraft—with every sensor hardwired right in the MERLIN processor. Just like what I think was going on with that tiny black jet in the videos." Jenny took a deep breath. "That would certainly speed things up for the civilian air transport business by improving overall operating efficiency and safety. But that isn't all. The big deal, the thing the airlines would love, is the elimination of one of the pilots in the cockpit. The cost savings in labor alone would be gigantic."

"I see what you're getting at. Eventually, after it's been used for several years, and the public gets used to it, they'll start phasing out the humans entirely."

"Yep, that's my guess too."

Tim shook his head. "Never happen, Jenny. Not in a million years." His actual thoughts were even more direct: *No frigging way I'll ever get on a plane with just a computer at the stick!*

Tim continued: "Maybe you'll get it down to one pilot but there'll always be a human aboard to oversee."

Jenny laughed. "Yeah, you're probably right." Her instant thought was of the once exalted airline pilot relegated to bus driver status. "But even so, it would still be a huge deal."

Tim just nodded, turning away to look through the kitchen windows. Other than the marina lights across the harbor, and the cabin lights of a couple of yachts anchored offshore, the bay waters were pewter-black. After sipping from his mug he again faced Jenny. "You know, Jenny, this whole business of civilian applications of MERLIN—jetliners, robot-controlled cars—it just doesn't sound right to me. Why would the Pentagon ever allow such a fantastic secret to get out? Anyone who bought a plane or car with the system in it could take the damn thing out and reverse engineer it. It happens all the time."

"I wondered about that too." She pointed to the baggy with the circuit board; it was still resting on the countertop. "Dad's papers indicated that replicating the MERLIN effect would be virtually impossible without access to the original circuit board and to his notes. Re-creating the phenomenon requires exacting standards. Without knowing the precise composition of the original semiconductor components and just how the power surge energized the unit, trying to back engineer it could take forever."

"Why?"

"Because there are millions—billions—of possible combinations. Only one works."

"But couldn't they just analyze the thing—take it apart—figure out its components?"

"That's what's so unique about MERLIN." She held up the baggy. "The microchips in this thing are completely new. The original chips were transformed—metamorphosed, if you will, on a quantum level—into an entirely new material. There's nothing to compare with."

Tim mulled that over for a long moment. "So it's kind of like the secret formula for Coca-Cola, or maybe the Colonel's special recipe. Competitors having been trying to duplicate 'em exactly for years—all without success."

Jenny laughed. "Yeah."

Tim took another sip from his mug. "What you say may all be true, Jenny, but I still don't think that we're going to be seeing any civilian applications in the near future. The technology's just too important for now."

"You're probably right. Dad's papers said that first priority would be given to military applications." Jenny hesitated, remembering something. "In fact, there's a clause in his contract with the government that specifically addressed that very issue."

"What clause?"

Jenny shook her head. "Damn—that's got to be it—I didn't pay any attention to that before but now it makes perfect sense."

"What are you talking about?" Tim asked, confused.

"The contract—it specifically states that before MERLIN could be used for civilian purposes, a way had to be devised to regulate its sensitivity." Jenny shook her head, clearly stunned at her revelation. "That must have been what Dad was doing with the Boeing jet."

"Doing what?"

"Trying to come up with a way to lower MERLIN's sensitivity so that it could be used for nonclassified purposes. That way, the original system—the one that works one hundred percent—would remain secret."

"Hmmm," Tim muttered. "I think I see what you're getting at. It would be kind of like what the government can do with the GPS system—vary the computing precision of the satellites. Ultrahigh precision for military applications, lower precision for general civilian usage."

"Exactly."

Tim waited a long moment before responding. "So, how would you go about regulating MERLIN?"

"I don't know—maybe by calibrating the speed of the chips, filtering the system somehow—something like that."

Tim nodded. "Now it's all starting to come together for me. The 777 project was a test with the low-power version of MERLIN . . ."

Jenny finished: ". . . and the video with the little black jet must be the high-power version—unfiltered, the full effect!"

"That's got to be it—that little bastard must have been using the full-strength MERLIN."

"Right."

A couple of minutes passed. Tim refilled his mug and replanted himself on his stool, facing Jenny. "You know, that little bugger we saw in the video could have some real advantages from a military standpoint."

"Like what?"

"For starters the aircraft would have to be a hell of a lot cheaper to build. Without having to worry about the pilot, you wouldn't need a life support system, an ejection seat, or even a cockpit. That stuff takes up a lot of room and costs a bundle."

"So they'd be smaller."

"Right, just like that little sucker in the videos." Tim pushed against the countertop while tilting back on his stool, balancing it on the back legs. "That means a smaller radar cross section, making 'em tougher to see. But the big advantage would be maneuverability. Without having to worry about keeping a pilot conscious, that thing could probably turn on a dime, pulling twenty, thirty G's or more. That's gotta be a colossal advantage in any kind of air-to-air combat."

"Plus, if something goes wrong, you've just lost the plane. Not the pilot."

"Exactly." Tim leaned forward, returning the stool to all

fours. "No wonder the feds have had you under a micro-
scope. This MERLIN thing's going to be a huge, huge deal
for the Pentagon—a whole new way of conducting aerial
combat."

"I know ... and it's really starting to scare me." Jenny
reached up with her right hand and massaged the back of her
neck. "Besides the obvious military uses, Dad's breakthrough
has so many applications that it's almost ... no, it is just
plain priceless."

"It certainly is. And from what your dad said in the video
about his contract with the government, you're going to
make a mint from it."

"Yeah, I guess so. But to be honest, money's the last thing
I'm thinking about right now. When word of the discovery
gets out, everyone's going to want access to the MERLIN
technology. It will have worldwide ramifications."

"The word's already out, Jenny."

"What?"

"Those people that attacked the FBI cabin ... they know."
He then pointed to the MERLIN circuit board. "You can bet
your last dollar, they wanted you so they could get that
thing."

"Oh, you're right, I forgot." Jenny sighed and then a ka-
leidoscope of all too fresh images flashed into view. "I wonder what happened to Audrey."

"Audrey?" And then Tim remembered. "The agent that got
you out?"

"Yeah." Jennifer sighed again, deep, and then she lost
it. Tears spilled down her cheeks. "Oh, Tim, it was so horrible ... those poor guys getting killed, and Audrey lost so
much blood ... I don't even know if she made it."

Tim moved to her side, offering his shoulder. She accepted.

"It's okay, kiddo," he said, "let it all out."

It was now a quarter to midnight. Tim Carpenter was inside
the master bedroom. Cried out and worn down, Jenny had
retired to her own bedroom half an hour earlier.

Tim had just made one last check of the security system.

One of the remote monitors was built into the wall by his bed.

The previous owners of the Pearl Island retreat, an elderly couple who used to live in Chicago, took their personal security seriously. Sensors throughout the five-thousand-square-foot home were wired to the central alarm system. There was even a motion sensor on the dock.

After checking that his Glock was resting on the nightstand, Tim climbed into bed. It was time to rest after a whirlwind of a day.

Jenny's dad must have been quite a guy, he thought as he stretched out, enjoying the coolness of the sheets. Then, as he relaxed, allowing sleep to approach, he continued to marvel at what he had learned earlier in the evening. *This MERLIN thing's just incredible. The Air Force must be desperate to get that circuit board thing back. And what about those bastards that shot up the FBI safe house? You can bet your butt, Tim Carpenter, that they won't stop. Dammit, we should have left today!*

Tim's last conscious thoughts were directed to an old friend: *Lord, Jenny's a sweet, innocent kid. With her dad gone, she's all alone in this world. So please give me strength to get her through this mess.*

DAY 3

ON THE LAM

Tim had been asleep for almost three hours when the alarm went off. The piercing tone jolted him awake.

He flipped onto his side, searching for the alarm clock. But then he noticed the blinking light on the wall. *Now what?*

Tim slipped his long legs over the side and stood up. He walked to the wall-mounted burglar alarm panel and switched off the enunciator. And then, squinting at the dim light, he examined the LED readout next to the still pulsing light. That's when he finally made the connection: *It's the dock!*

He was now beside the bedroom's main window, peeking through an edge of the drawn curtains. "Son of a bitch!"

A small inflatable—a Zodiac with oars—was riding high in the water, tied off to a cleat on the concrete float, just a few feet away from his Sea Ray. And crouched down on the dock, silhouetted in the moonlight, were two men.

The intruders were garbed in black, head to toe. They cautiously crept along the float, heading toward the shore.

The light sensor on the floating pier had worked as designed. When the first man pulled himself onto the float his body intercepted the invisible beam. With the circuit broken, the dock-mounted transmitter broadcast the warning signal.

Tim didn't waste a second. He threw on a pair of jeans. Then he pulled on a sweatshirt and slipped his feet into a pair of deck shoes. With his 9 mm Glock 26 tucked in the small of his back and two extra magazines stuffed into his rear pants pockets, he quietly opened his bedroom door and stepped into the hallway. A moment later he was in Jenny's room.

"Jenny, it's Tim, wake up." He was kneeling by Jennifer's bed, his hand hovering near her mouth, ready to clamp down should she call out in fear.

Jenny's eyes snapped open.

He raised his left hand to his lips. "Shhh!" he said.

Jenny sat up. She was wearing one of Tim's sweatshirts. "What's wrong?" she asked, her voice faint.

"We've got visitors."

"Oh, God, not again."

"I don't know who they are—maybe they're just burglars but we can't take any chances. I want you to get dressed and then stay here. Keep your door locked and don't come out until I tell you. And don't turn on any lights."

"What are you going to do?"

"Find out who they are and make sure they stay out."

Tim was about to leave when he remembered. "Where did you put all of your father's things?"

"They're over there." She pointed to the canvas bag sitting in the far corner of the room. She had packed away all the MERLIN documents before retiring. She and Tim were planning to leave Pearl Island later in the morning.

"That circuit board thing in there, too?"

"Yeah, it's inside the container you gave me."

"Okay, good. Now just stay put until I get back."

By the time Tim walked downstairs, the intruders had reached the house. They were one floor below, under the huge deck that projected off the living room. The two men were huddled next to the doorway that led to the basement.

The solid-core door was giving them trouble. One of the men had picked the lock but the door refused to open. The locksmith turned to his companion and whispered in Mandarin: "Must be bolted from inside. We'll never get in this way, unless we blow it."

"All right, let's try the main floor."

Tim stood in the shadows of the living room, next to the still empty floor-to-ceiling bookcase. He could see the deck in the distance. He knew they'd eventually try this way. The sliding glass doorway that opened onto the deck offered the least resistance. All of the other doors to the house were independently locked from the inside with a separate dead bolt.

Tim never heard a thing. The intruders moved with the stealth of Ninja warriors. In the blink of an eye the black-clad figures appeared out of nowhere, slipping over the top deck railing with the grace of a pair of cats.

When they reached the doorway, Tim spotted the sub-machine guns. *No way these guys are thieves!* He pulled out the Glock and chambered a round.

One man kneeled down and began working the lock mechanism. His partner crouched beside him, holding his SMG at the ready.

The locksmith worked on the lock for just a few seconds and then Tim heard a distinctive click as it opened. The intruder pushed on the slider. It moved about a quarter of an inch before stopping. A dark metal rod placed in the track prevented the door from opening. The intruders couldn't see it from their position.

Tim smiled. *They must be getting pissed by now.*

The well-secured home was only slightly challenging. The visitors were prepared. Without commenting, the locksmith reached into the knapsack he carried and removed a suction-cup device. He secured the black rubber housing to the outer glass panel of the double-pane slider, in the center of the lower half of the doorway. He then took a steel blade embedded with industrial-grade diamonds and scribed a rectangular pattern in the glass. It was about two feet square.

After grabbing the handgrip of the suction cup with one hand, he gently tapped the perimeter of the scored glass with a tiny rubber hammer. A moment later the pane popped free. He placed the glass panel on the timber deck, released the suction grip. He then began the same process with the second pane.

Tim was pumped now. *These guys are real pros!* When the first one was halfway through the opening, crawling on his hands and knees, Tim let him have it: "Freeze, you bastard, or you're dead."

The intruder complied. The voice was somewhere to his left. Without raising his head, he rolled his eyes upward,

straining to see through the shadows. Nothing. He then
slowly raised his left foot a few inches and began rotating
his ankle, pointing to the left.

Tim couldn't see the movement. The lower half of the
intruder's body was still on the deck. The intruder's companion, however, instantly recognized the warning signal.
Something was wrong. The two men had worked together as
a team for five years. They were almost symbiotic.

The man on the deck didn't hesitate. He flipped the SMG's
selector switch to auto and, with the metal stock jammed into
his right armpit, he fired.

In just a heartbeat, the Heckler & Koch MP5 spit twelve
rounds through the glass opening, just inches above the head
of the first intruder. The suppressor worked flawlessly. The
noise of the escaping bullets and gases sounded like the closing of a jacket zipper.

Tim wasn't prepared for that response. First, the muted
SMG's muzzle flash caught his eyes. Then the subsonic 147-
grain lead slugs began tattooing the stucco wall near where
he was standing.

His reaction was instinctive. He dove for the floor; his left
knee smacked into something on the way down. He was
immune to the pain and let loose with his Glock, aiming at
the base of the sliding glass door. He pulled the trigger six
times before finally stopping.

Tim's hands remained clamped to the pistol. He was prone
on the hardwood floor, both arms extended in front. His ears
were ringing from the report of his pistol. The pungent stink
of spent gunpowder filled his nostrils. Tiny rivers of fear-
sweat cascaded down his forehead.

With the heightened reflexes of a leopard on the prowl,
Tim's eyes searched for movement, ready to pounce.

He waited almost a minute, never moving. Tim could still
see the first one. The man was slumped down, half in, half
out of the doorway. Blood seeped from holes in his upper
body, pooling on the floor under his head. There was also a
nasty glass shard embedded in his shoulder. Tim's torrent of
pistol fire had blasted the remaining sections of the sliding
glass door into a galaxy of shrapnel.

The other man—the one who had fired—was still on the deck. But Tim had no idea if he had hit him or not. He had fired blindly, the first flash from his own pistol destroying what was left of his night vision.

Maybe I got him, too!

Tim was just about to crawl forward when it happened. The object sailed through the now glassless doorway. It was about the size of a soup can. It bounced off the wall and then rebounded back toward the main part of the living room. It slid across the hardwood floor, finally coming to rest under a leather-lined couch. And then it exploded.

The grenade was not designed to kill. Its sole purpose was to immobilize. The concussion of the blast, accompanied by the blinding flash, was intended to shock the victims into submission. Developed for use in hostage rescue situations, the stun grenade had proved exceedingly useful.

The weapon would have done its job had it not come to rest under the couch. The $2,000 hunk of furniture was built to last. The welded steel frame and the thick foam cushioning under the leather absorbed most of the blast.

Nevertheless, the detonation was violent. Tim thought his eardrums would burst from the concussion.

An instant after the grenade detonated, the surviving intruder burst through the now open doorway, leaping over the body of his partner. His finger was glued to the trigger of the submachine gun. He hosed the room.

Tim's head felt like it was about to burst. And he couldn't hear. But he could still see. The man crouched in front of him was firing into the center of the living room.

Tim didn't have to think. His reaction was pure impulse. The Glock roared four more times, one round finding its mark.

The gunman collapsed.

Tim remained glued to the floor. He had just ejected the spent magazine and inserted a new one. The Glock was again ready. But it was no longer needed.

The entire attack, from the intruder's first shot to the last firefight, had taken fifty seconds. But it felt like a lifetime. Tim's heart continued to race like a freight train heading down a steep mountain grade. Sweat streamed from his brow. And his hands were now shaking. He could barely hold the pistol.

Tim's self-talk was on hyperdrive. *What if there are more out there? No, there were only two. You saw them get off that boat. . . . But where'd they come from? Shit, I don't know . . . maybe from one of the boats in . . . That's got to be it. They came from one of those yachts anchored out front. Jesus, we've gotta get out of here. Now!*

"Pete, Pete! Wake up!"
The man rolled from his back onto his left side and then grudgingly opened his eyes. The light on the headboard over the double berth blasted into his face. He blinked several times, fighting off the glare and the waves of drowsiness that continued to consume his consciousness. Finally, about a quarter of a minute later, his brain kicked into gear and he began to reenter the real world.

His wife was standing next to the bed, leaning over him. Her lovely face was wrinkled with concern. "What's wrong, Jeanne?" he asked, now alarmed.

"Didn't you hear it?"

"Hear what?"

"Gunshots, and then an explosion."

"What are you talking about?" He was still half asleep.

"I just came back into our cabin, after getting a drink of water. There was gunfire—I'm sure that's what it was—half a dozen shots or so. And then a terrific blast of some kind. It echoed across the harbor. Sounded like thunder."

"Are you sure it was—"

Peter was interrupted by a soft knocking sound on the cabin door. And then a new voice called out: "Pete, are you awake?"

Jeanne stepped across the deck, opening the cabin door.

"Oh, Matt," she said, addressing their guest, "did you hear that racket?"

"Yeah. I sure did." He then turned to face his friend. "Pete, let's get topside and take a quick look around. I think something's going on."

"Okay."

* * *

Allen Peng and Gérard Rémy had watched the assault from
the darkened pilothouse of the *Orca*. Earlier in the evening,
the superyacht had anchored in Roche Harbor offshore of
Pearl Island's southern shore, mooring near a sleek two-
masted sailboat. The Carpenter-Lorence residence was just a
few hundred meters away.

The commandos that had just assaulted the home were
among the elite of the PLA's special forces. The day before,
the two *zhongdui* had flown from Hong Kong to Vancouver,
B.C. Fresh recruits were needed for the Roche Harbor job.
With the exception of Major Wu, all who had participated
in the assault on the FBI safe house had been sent home.
With the Americans now on the rampage, it was too risky
to employ their services again.

A stray fingerprint, a shoe impression, or even a strand of
hair, left at both crimes scenes, was all it would take for the
FBI to make the connection.

Peng raised the night vision device to his eyes, focusing
on the first floor of the Carpenter residence.

"Can you see anything different?" he asked.

Rémy was standing a few feet away. Like Peng, he was
viewing the house through an NVD. The greenish tint of the
light-enhanced device helped turn night into day. "No. I
don't see any movement at all. How about you?"

Peng unconsciously shook his head. "No. How long has
it been since the firing stopped?"

"Maybe five minutes."

Peng lowered his NVD. He then scanned the surrounding
harbor, looking for activity. Other than a couple of cabin
lights on the nearby sailboat, all remained normal at Roche
Harbor. No new lights on the yachts in the marina, no police
cars racing down the road to the harbor area. *Amazing,* he
thought, *all of that racket and no one's yet stirring.*

Although the PLA commandos had used sound suppres-
sors on their weapons, the man guarding Jennifer Richmond
had not. The heavy reports of the pistol, the glass panels
shattering, and then the blast of the grenade, had resonated
across the quiet harbor.

"Do you think the woman was injured?" Rémy asked, his eyes still scanning the house through the NVD.

"She better not be. They were told not to harm her." Peng then turned, facing another man who stood in the background. "Right, Major?" Peng asked.

Major Wu Jin Li stepped forward. "Correct. They only had permission to take the man out."

Gérard Rémy shook his head. "I hope they followed your orders, or all of this has been for nothing."

The current operation had started the day before when the *Orca* was pressed into service. The 144-foot megayacht sailed south from Vancouver, heading into Washington State waters. She eventually took up station in Haro Strait, several miles offshore of San Juan Island. Throughout the long afternoon she jogged, waiting for the various parties. Major Wu and his two shooters arrived first, landing in a float plane. The recon team that photographed the Carpenter-Lorence Pearl Island residence came next. And then, an hour before dusk, Peng and Rémy boarded, flying in from Seattle on another chartered float plane.

While the yacht slowly made its way toward Roche Harbor, Major Wu and the two-man hit team now observed by Peng and Rémy, continued to refine the plan. Aided by high-quality photos of the target area, developed from the yacht's onboard photo lab, the assault had been planned to the nth degree. To a man, they all thought it would be a piece of cake.

The French intelligence officer was the first to spot the movement. It was at the base of the deck, on the basement level. "I've got something," Rémy said. "On the ground floor, under the deck."

Peng raised his NVD and scanned the house. He then spotted two figures. The timber columns and diagonal bracing that supported the balcony deck partially obscured his view. "I see them," Peng finally responded.

"They're coming out now. Looks like they're heading for

the dock." Rémy paused. "I only count two—how about you?"

Peng increased the magnification on his NVD, hoping to improve his view. The two figures moved quickly down the embankment and then onto the approach pier. One appeared to be limping. Peng was having difficulty tracking the figures because they were hiding behind the pier's wide timber railing. *What the hell are you two doing?* he said to himself.

"Your men look like they're coming out empty-handed. They must have killed them both," Rémy said. The tone of his voice clearly expressed his displeasure at what he was seeing. He handed his NVD to Major Wu.

Peng and Wu watched as the two figures slowly worked their way down the slope of the aluminum gangway ramp. They were crouched down, hiding behind the guard railing. Peng thought their movements were a little odd. But Wu was alarmed. Something was wrong.

Tim and Jenny were huddled together, at the very end of the gangway. The long concrete float stretched out before them. Tim turned to face Jenny. "It looks clear. Now, I want you to stay here until I check the boat. If it looks okay, then I'll signal you like this." Tim raised his right hand and pumped his wrist.

"Okay."

"Good. Now, you sure you can manage the bag and my briefcase?"

"No problem." Jenny reached down and patted the canvas duffel bag. It was filled with her father's research papers. Next to the bag was Tim's attaché case. She looked back at Tim. "But what about your knee—can you walk all right?"

The first surge of adrenaline from the gunfight had worn off. His left knee was on fire. "I'll be okay."

"Please be careful. There might be more of them out there."

"I'll be ready for 'em," Tim said. He then looked down at the black metallic object that he held in his hands. Tim had liberated the H & K from one of the dead intruders. The submachine gun was ready to kill: safety off, auto selector on, full mag inserted, and a round in the chamber.

Tim hadn't fired an automatic weapon in years, but his military training had done him well. He held the weapon with confidence. His hands were steady, his grip firm. He took one last look around. *Okay,* he said to himself, *let's do it.*

Peng, Wu, and Rémy watched as the figure scurried down the floating pier. And then, before they realized what was happening, the man climbed into the Sea Ray.

"Major," Peng called out, "why aren't your men using the Zodiac?"

The Chinese army officer did not reply. Instead, he cursed to himself. *Dammit! What's going on?*

Tim made a quick check of the speedboat. Everything looked normal. He then reached under the cushion of the passenger seat and removed the starter key. He inserted it into the ignition switch. After advancing the throttle he pushed the start button. The V-8 roared to life.

He looked back down the dock and then raised his right hand.

Jenny spotted the signal and started running.

"It's the woman!" Rémy shouted, now recognizing their quarry. After the yacht anchored, both he and Peng had ID'ed her. At that time, Jennifer Richmond was in the kitchen, along with a man. They were both sitting at a table, sipping from coffee mugs. Jennifer had been facing the water; her head had been clearly visible through the NVDs. This allowed a direct comparison with a photograph that the MSS had obtained for Peng. The photo of Jennifer had accompanied a professional article that she had written for a robotics software journal. It had been published a year earlier.

Although they never got a good look at the man—they had one photograph stolen from Tim's house to compare with—they'd assumed that he was the private detective Carpenter.

Rémy turned to face Peng, stunned at the observation. "What the hell is going . . ." And then he figured it out.

"That's gotta be Carpenter in the boat. He must have taken out your men."

Peng just shook his head in disgust.

Major Wu was mortified. He couldn't believe what was happening. "Impossible," he shouted, yet knowing he was wrong.

Jenny released the stern tie while Tim uncleated the bow line. Tim then shoved the gearshift into reverse and added power. The Sea Ray backed away from the pier in a wide circle. Once clear, Tim shifted into forward and shoved the throttle to maximum.

It took almost five minutes before the *Orca* was able to give chase. The anchor had to be reeled in and the engines started. But once the ship was ready, Peng wasted no time. He ordered the captain to flank speed.

The superyacht's powerful turbo diesels belched inky soot from the exhaust ports. White water churned at her stern as the forty-eight-inch-diameter wheels cavitated.

It was almost high tide, allowing the monster vessel to follow the same path as the Sea Ray—through the narrow passage that separated Pearl Island from San Juan Island. Otherwise, it would have had to detour to the other side of the island.

When the *Orca* entered the narrow channel it was already moving at sixteen knots. The three-foot wake it generated would soon raise havoc with the scores of vessels moored in Roche Harbor.

"U.S. Coast Guard, this is the sailing yacht *Nooschkum*, come in, please. Over."

"*Nooschkum*, Coast Guard Station Port Angeles. What assistance do you require? Over."

"Ah, I'm not sure but I think there may have been some kind of trouble here."

"*Nooschkum*, Port Angeles. State your location. Over."

"We're moored in Roche Harbor, anchored about three hundred yards southeast of Pearl Island. Over."

"*Nooschkum,* Port Angeles. What's the situation? Over."

"Well, we think there's been some kind of explosion and gunfire, maybe on a boat or possibly onshore. Anyway, this superyacht, maybe a hundred and fifty feet long, was moored near us and it just reeled in its anchor and then . . ."

12 EVASION

The Sea Ray blasted over the water at forty miles an hour. It was much too fast. The darkness of the early morning hours, combined with the boat's excessive speed, made it almost impossible to see anything in the water. And there was always something to hit. The logs and other driftwood that plagued the San Juans were like mines. Slamming into a three-foot-diameter Douglas fir would certainly ruin anyone's day—or night.

Tim Carpenter and Jennifer Richmond had no choice but to run full-out.

After escaping from Roche Harbor, Tim powered northward into the Spieden Channel. But now, after just a few minutes at full power, he chopped the throttle back and switched off the engine.

"Why are we stopping?" Jenny asked.

"I want to see if we're being followed."

"By another boat?"

"Yeah. Our visitors either launched from someplace onshore or came off one of those yachts in the harbor. If they came from another boat, then we'll know shortly."

Tim had his answer a few minutes later when the *Orca* powered around Pearl Island's eastern end. Her running lights were off, like the Sea Ray, but the main salon remained lit up. And the heavy drone from her screaming diesels filled the still night air.

"Shit, I knew it," Tim said.

"What do we do now?" asked Jenny.

"We run."

"Can they catch us?"

"That thing's a big sucker, but there's no way it can keep up with this baby." Tim punched the starter. The engine surged. He turned to face Jenny, a thin smile on his face. "Hang on, now. We're going to go like a bat out of hell!"

"Do you see it?" Gérard Rémy asked. He was standing in the *Orca's* pilothouse, next to the high-tech instrument panel.

Allen Peng was staring at a TV-sized screen. It was part of the radar unit. The color monitor displayed a computer-generated image of the surrounding landforms and waterways. Spieden Island was to the starboard, Henry Island was to the port. And scattered across Spieden Channel were several fluorescent targets. Most of the blips were navigation buoys, marking reefs.

Peng looked up from the screen. "I can't tell. There's no traffic. Nothing's moving."

"Then where could they have gone?"

"I don't know," Peng said as he turned back to face the screen. A moment later, one of the blips began flashing. The radar's computer had just picked up a moving object. "Wait a minute," Peng said. "I've got something now." He paused, waiting for the digital readout. And then a small window in the upper right corner of the screen blinked on. "That's got to be it. It's heading northwest into Canada—forty knots plus."

"How fast can this thing go?"

"Twenty-five knots, max."

"Shit, we'll never catch it."

"In this, yes. But one of our launches might." He turned to face Major Wu. "Let's get it in the water. We haven't got a second to waste."

"Yes, sir."

It took six minutes to launch the *Orca's* Donzi. The twenty-two-foot speedboat was shaped like a stiletto. Powered by a huge V-8, the craft could reach speeds of seventy knots or more.

The three men accompanying Major Wu in the launch were equipped with submachine guns. Wu was armed with a cellular phone. By using the *Orca*'s radar, the Donzi could be vectored to the fleeing Sea Ray—just like a jet fighter attacking an enemy bomber.

The chase lasted twenty minutes. The Donzi had closed to within a few miles of the Sea Ray when the *Orca* lost radar contact.

Without assistance from the mother ship, the Donzi was blind. Major Wu tried to follow, but it was hopeless. Like the San Juans, the Canadian Gulf archipelago consists of a vast collection of islands, ranging in size from mere rock outcrops to twenty-mile-long giants. And mixed in with the islands are a maze of coves, bays, channels, and passes, most capable of concealing a tiny vessel like the Sea Ray.

"Do you think they're still following us?" Jenny yelled over the drone of the screaming engine and the vibrating hull. She was still standing beside Tim, her hair glued to her scalp by the Sea Ray's speed.

"I don't think so. I'm pretty sure we lost 'em back there when we backtracked through Navy Channel."

Tim and Jenny had just powered into an immense inland sea. Stretching from the San Juans to halfway up Vancouver Island, 140 miles, the Strait of Georgia was like the ocean to Tim.

They could really make time now. With the throttle wide open, the Sea Ray was a water rocket. Nothing could catch it.

"Where are we going?" Jenny asked.

"We've got to hide this thing and I know just where to go."

"Where?"

"You'll see. Just hang on."

It was half past nine. The drive across the 520 bridge had been a disaster. There was a wreck on the drawspan that jammed up the morning commute. Ricardo Molina wished he had taken I-90 instead.

From the exterior, the Evergreen Point residence looked normal when he drove down the brick-lined driveway. It was just like he remembered it. But inside was something else. Throughout the huge home, the interior was a shambles. Every drawer had been riffled. All of the cabinets were opened and their contents scattered across the floor. Carpeting had been ripped up. Even the wall-mounted paintings and photographs had been removed and their backings slit open. The home invaders had been thorough. Short of leveling the multimillion-dollar structure, they had examined and probed nearly every conceivable hiding place.

Ricardo walked out of the master bedroom, disgusted at the mess he had found. Special Agent Victoria Kwan was at his side. As usual, she was immaculately dressed: pleated silk crepe skirt, cotton blouse, bolero jacket, black pumps. With her petite figure, just about everything was fashionable on her.

"The police think this happened two nights ago?" Ricardo asked. They were walking down a hallway, heading for the stairway.

"Probably. The housekeeper discovered the mess when she came in yesterday afternoon. She had the morning off. Everything was okay when she left the day before."

"How come the locals took so long to let us know about the burglary?"

"They didn't make the connection until last night. The home's ownership is listed under Laura Lorence's name, not Carpenter's. Our alert only mentioned Carpenter and Richmond. It was just luck that the night-duty sergeant figured it out. He knows both Laura and Tim."

Ricardo nodded. *Details,* he thought. *It always boils down to the details.* "No alarms went off?" he asked.

"No. These guys are real pros—state-of-the-art equipment. They disarmed the entire system without triggering a thing. The security company had no idea that the home had been penetrated until the local PD called 'em."

"It's got to be the same bastards that hit our people."

"No doubt."

Ricardo started down the stairway, Agent Kwan at his side. "Still no word from Laura Lorence?" he asked.

"No. Nothing yet. I managed to get hold of her general manager at his house this morning. He found out about the burglary last night and then alerted Laura's insurance people."

"What did he say about Laura?"

"Like when we talked to him earlier, he still doesn't know her whereabouts. He's been expecting a call, but hasn't heard anything from her yet."

"Our surveillance people confirm that?"

"Yes. She hasn't called the corporate office or the manager's home." Agent Kwan paused. "I think he's being up front with us. He really doesn't know where she is."

Ricardo stepped onto the main floor and then stopped. He slowly shook his head. "Dammit, Tim," he muttered to himself, "this is getting out of hand."

"What?" asked Kwan as she stepped next to Molina.

"Carpenter . . . he's sharp. We're never going to hear from Laura Lorence until he wants us to."

"What do you mean?"

"I know Tim well. We served in the military together—Army Intelligence. We spent a lot of our time tracking terrorists in Europe." Ricardo paused. "These people after the MERLIN technology are just as ruthless as the bastards we were tracking. And Tim knows it. There's no way he'll let Laura or any of his loved ones get involved. That would do him in for sure."

Ricardo turned to face his aide. He recognized the confused look. "I don't think I ever told you this, but Tim lost his first wife—and their daughter. They were killed by a car bomb in Munich; Tim had been the target but Eva and Emily took the car that morning."

Agent Kwan gasped, more than touched by the story.

Ricardo continued: "Needless to say, Tim took it bad, real bad. He eventually left the Army over it."

"How awful."

"It was."

Both were silent for a long moment and then Vicky said: "So Laura Lorence's really not on a business trip—he had her leave the country."

"Yep. I'm certain of it, along with their sons and his mother." Ricardo hesitated. "And I don't have the slightest idea of where to look for them, let alone Tim and the Richmond woman."

"What do we do, then?"

"We wait."

"For what?"

"When Tim's ready, he'll call me. Then we'll know."

The room had a magnificent view of the harbor. The hotel was perched high up on the shore, right in the middle of the downtown core. The twenty-story building complemented the dozens of other nearby high-rises that made up the spectacular skyline.

It was midmorning in Vancouver and there was a flurry of traffic on Burrard Inlet. The sleek Sea-Bus passenger ferry from North Vancouver had just departed from its downtown berth and was now churning its way across the blue-green waters of the harbor. A commuter helicopter from Vancouver International had just touched down at the floating heliport. Over a dozen passengers had climbed out of the aircraft and were now working their way into the terminal. And about a mile offshore, toward the center of the harbor, a nine-hundred-foot-long Japanese containership was slowly steaming westward, preparing to pass under the Lions Gate Bridge.

Closer in, just west of the heliport, was another gigantic ship—over two and a half football fields long. The white-hulled goliath was berthed at the Canada Place cruise-ship terminal. The Norwegian-based vessel had docked earlier in the morning, completing a five-day journey down the Inside Passage. Its 1,600-plus Vancouver-bound passengers had already departed and the ship was now in the process of preparing for a new contingent. It was scheduled for a 5:00 P.M. departure, retracing its course back to Alaska.

Tim Carpenter had always enjoyed his visits to Vancouver. It was one of the most exquisite cities in the world. The modern architecture of its downtown buildings, its extensive water settings, and the surrounding ring of white-capped mountains all combined to create a truly unique cityscape. It was like visiting Hong Kong and Switzerland in one trip.

But today, Tim wasn't enjoying the scenery. Instead, he wondered if he'd live to see another day.

He was stretched out on his back, lying on a leather couch in the living room of the hotel suite. A black plastic bag filled with ice was resting on his left knee. It was an old injury that, thanks to the trouble back at Roche Harbor, had come back to haunt him.

Years before, when Tim had been blasted to the rock-hard pavement of a suburban street, his left knee had absorbed much of the impact. Cartilage and ligaments had been shredded. The trauma to his knee had been the least of his problems, though. He nearly lost his life. Three operations later, he could walk.

Jennifer Richmond was in the adjacent bedroom, sound asleep. Tim wanted to sleep—needed to sleep—but he was too keyed up. It had been a whirlwind morning.

After evading the attackers, Tim and Jenny had continued running northward up the Georgia Strait. Tim's goal had been to sneak into downtown Vancouver, tying up at one of the marinas near the old Expo site. But it didn't quite work out that way.

At around 4:15 A.M. they ran into a fog bank offshore of Roberts Bank. The mirk was syrup thick. The Sea Ray wasn't equipped with radar or any other navigation aids, except for a compass. Consequently, Tim was forced to cut the throttle back to a crawl and wait for the fog to lift.

By six o'clock, Tim could finally see enough to estimate their position. They were just north of Westham Island, about a mile offshore. Tim advanced the throttle and turned the wheel toward the right.

"Are we heading to shore now?" Jenny had asked.

"Yeah," Tim had said, "but not into False Creek. Too much light out now, and a ton of people live around there. Someone might turn us in."

"To Canadian Customs?"

"Yeah, or their immigration people. My boat's only registered in the U.S. We'll stick out like a sore thumb if we tried sneaking in there now."

"So what are we going to do?"

"I think I know another place where we can dock."

"Where?"

"Just sit back, you'll see."

Several minutes later the Sea Ray sped into the mouth of the south arm of the Fraser River. After running nearly five miles inland on the rural waterway, they stopped at a marina near the George Massey Tunnel. During previous trips to Vancouver, Tim had recalled seeing the river marina from the highway.

At a quarter to seven, they tied up the Sea Ray to an empty berth along the river channel. Tim and Jenny had then loaded up their gear and walked ashore. The marina office had not yet opened and no one else was around. Tim found a pay phone and called a cab. Thirty minutes later they checked into the hotel.

Tim tossed and turned on the couch for a few more minutes before finally giving up. *Screw it,* he said to himself as he stood up. The ice bag flopped onto the carpet. His knee throbbed but he could walk.

There was no way he could sleep. Still dressed in the same clothes he wore the previous night, Tim picked up the phone. He dialed room service and ordered breakfast for himself plus a bottle of Advil.

While waiting for his meal, Tim unzipped the duffel bag that he and Jenny had taken from his Pearl Island residence.

It was filled with Dr. Richmond's research papers and the sealed container with the original MERLIN device.

Tim wasn't interested in the scientific paraphernalia. It was the SMG hidden under the paperwork that he wanted. He had commandeered the Heckler & Koch MP5 back at Roche. A favorite of the British SAS and legions of other security services, the 9 mm submachine gun was a reliable and efficient killing machine. And Tim's weapon was deadlier than most; screwed onto the stubby barrel was a salami-sized sound suppressor.

Tim removed the magazine. He then cleared the chamber, ejecting a live round. There were two more fully loaded thirty-round mags in the duffel bag, also liberated from the gunmen.

Now satisfied that the H & K was safe, Tim returned the weapon to the duffel bag. He then made a mental note to visit a sporting goods store later in the day to purchase a rifle cleaning kit. Although the weapon appeared to be in perfect working order, his military training wouldn't allow him to take any chances. Later he would break down the MP5 and then clean and lubricate all key parts. It was SOP for any combat unit.

14   A NEW WOMAN

Victoria Kwan received the news at a quarter to noon. She had just returned to her office from the Evergreen Point trip when the receptionist routed the call to her desk.

"Special Agent Kwan," Vicky said after picking up the phone.

The voice on the other end of the line paused momentarily, having expected to be connected with a male. "Ah, ma'am, this is Deputy Sheriff Jackson, San Juan County Sheriff's Department."

"Yes, Deputy. How can I help you?"

"I'm responding to a bulletin you folks issued a couple of

days ago, about a Mr. Tim Carpenter and a Ms. Jennifer Richmond. Are you working on that case?"

Victoria sat up straight in her chair. "Yes, I am," she answered. *What the hell have you got!* was what she really wanted to say. Instead, she held back her emotions, just as she had been trained.

"Well, ah, I think I've got some news for you. It turns out that this Carpenter fellow and a woman, who we believe not to be his wife, were up here yesterday. We know for sure they bought some fuel at—"

"Wait a second, Deputy," Victoria interrupted. "Just exactly where are you talking about?"

"Oh, sorry, ma'am. Roche Harbor, on San Juan Island."

"Hang on a second, please." Victoria placed the handset on her desk and opened a nearby file drawer. She removed an inch-thick booklet. It was filled with USGS maps of Washington State.

After she turned to the map of·San Juan Island she continued: "Sorry for the delay. I've got a map in front of me now. You were saying you spotted them at Roche Harbor?"

"Correct. We know for sure Carpenter tied up at the resort's marina yesterday afternoon. The dock boy remembers him. Topped off the tanks for his Sea Ray and bought some groceries."

"What about the woman?"

"Yeah, he's pretty sure she was there, too, but he didn't get a chance to talk with her."

"So where'd they go?"

"Well, it turns out that Carpenter just bought a place on Pearl and was heading over there after fueling up."

"Pearl? What are you talking about?"

"Oh, yeah, sorry. Pearl Island. It's right at the head of Roche Harbor."

Victoria located the crescent-shaped island on the map. "You say he bought a place there?" This was news to Agent Kwan. The FBI had no record of Tim Carpenter or Laura Lorence owning any·property in the San Juans.

"Right. Apparently he just bought the house—a local Realtor told us this morning—it used to belong to the Williamses but they moved out last fall, to Phoenix, I think."

Victoria's heartbeat accelerated. *So that's where you've been hiding out!* "Can you tell me exactly where this cabin is located?" Already her mind was a whirlwind: *I'll find Rick, we'll get the plane, and in a couple of hours we'll have 'em both in custody.*

"Oh, sure," replied the deputy. He then described the location.

"Do you have the suspects under surveillance now?"

The deputy laughed before replying: "Ah, no, ma'am, I'm sorry, we don't have a clue as to where they are."

"But you just said they're at a cabin on this place called Pearl Island."

"Well, we think they were, but after last night, with all that shooting, I expect they're halfway to Hawaii by now."

"What are you talking about?"

"We got a call early this morning from the Coast Guard. A boater anchored in the harbor heard gunshots and some kind of explosion. They radioed the Coasties. We dispatched a deputy to the scene but when he finally got there everything was okay." Jackson paused. "It wasn't until later in the morning, around seven o'clock, when the bodies were discovered."

"Bodies?"

"Yeah, one dead guy, another shot up pretty bad."

"At the Carpenter residence?"

"Right. One of the boats leaving the marina passed by the old Williams place. Someone onboard spotted a body lying on the float. Apparently, that guy managed to crawl down from the house. He left a hell of a blood trail. We found the other one in the house. They both were dressed up in commandolike gear. Pretty strange."

Victoria unconsciously shook her head in awe. "Do you have any idea where Carpenter and this woman might have gone to?"

"Not a clue. The fuel dock boy at the resort said Carpenter had a Sea Ray. If they took off in it—fully fueled—they could head just about anywhere from up here at thirty-plus knots."

"Do you have the boat's registration number?"

"Sorry, you'll have to check with the Coast Guard for that."

I will do just that, Kwan said to herself. "Ah, how about these men—have you been able to ID them?"

"No ma'am." He hesitated for a moment. "But there was something weird about one of them—the dead guy. The ME spotted it at the crime scene."

"What?"

"Both of the victims are Orientals."

Asians, Deputy. Asians. That's what we're called, Victoria wanted to say. Instead, she held her thought. A third-generation American, she was still proud of her Chinese heritage.

Jackson continued: "The dead guy had this weird tattoo on his back. Some kind of a dragon with flames shooting out of its mouth and stuff like that. Anyway, the ME thinks it's some kind of gang symbol. If she's right, then maybe these guys are from down your way and this was some kind of drug deal that went bad." He paused. "Is that why you're after this Carpenter guy—is he a drug dealer or something like that?"

"Deputy Jackson, I can't comment on that right now. But what I can tell you is that we're now invoking federal jurisdiction. I'm going to fly up there in the next hour. Is the crime scene still secure?"

"Yes, ma'am. Our detectives are still on-site checking the place over. The wounded guy is in surgery right now at the hospital."

"I want a guard on him immediately. You understand that?"

"Yeah, sure. But he's not going anywhere. There's a good chance he won't make it through the afternoon."

"I don't care. I want him under guard until we get there."

"Okay, you got it."

"What about the other man?"

"Well, we did remove him. It's getting warm up there and, you know, all those boats going by, in and out of the resort. It was causing a problem."

"And where is it now?"

"In the county morgue—here in Friday Harbor."

"Okay, just keep him on ice. I'll be arranging for our own forensics people to conduct the autopsy. Your coroner will be invited to participate."

"Yes, ma'am. Whatever you say."

After hanging up, Agent Kwan shook her head in amazement. The MERLIN case was becoming more convoluted by the minute.

As she headed out her door on her way to Ricardo Molina's office, one thought repeated itself: *What the hell happened to Tim Carpenter and Jennifer Richmond?*

Tim and Jennifer had just returned to the high-rise hotel suite. It was early afternoon.

The transformation was like magic. It took about two hours and just a hundred bucks. She was a new person.

Jennifer Richmond stared at her reflected image in the mirror. Her scarlet, shoulder-length hair was gone, hacked down to a bob and then dyed India ink black. Her usual prim lipstick coloring had been replaced with a hideous fluorescent pink-orange. And the pale, freckled skin of her face and neck was now tanned and glowing, the result of an off-the-shelf chemical tanning treatment.

The biggest change of all, however, was with her body. Instead of the tight-fitting blue jeans and blouses that she had been wearing, she now wore garments several sizes larger. The baggy pants and billowing sweatshirt added thirty illusionary pounds to her normal 120.

Topping off the disguise were the glasses. With perfect vision she didn't need corrective lenses. But the fake spectacles really helped. Purchased at a novelty shop, the clear-glass lenses and thick plastic frames looked as if they had been manufactured in the sixties.

Jenny abhorred her appearance. But Tim loved it.

She turned away from the mirror, looking back at Carpenter. He was sitting on the edge of the bed.

"Well," Jenny said, her hands flowing down her sides to emphasize her baggy attire, "do I pass?"

"One hundred percent. If I hadn't been with you this morning, I'd have a hell of a time recognizing you."

Tim Carpenter was serious. Jenny's metamorphosis was radical. It had to be. It was designed to save her life.

Jenny eyed Tim. He had had his full sandy blond mane cut down to a Drew Carey crew cut, and, like Jenny, he had purchased a pair of fake glasses. "You look real cute," she said, "like when guys first go into the military and get their heads shaved."

She had not asked about the scars. With his hair trimmed away, the stitches along the scalp line of his forehead and around the top of his left ear were even more apparent. The surgeon's skill had been exceptional; nevertheless, Tim remained scarred forever.

Tim reached up and brushed a hand over his thinned-out dome. "He took off more than I wanted."

"Jenny smiled. "I like it—it's the new you." She paused. "But I think you should dye it black too, along with your eyebrows. Then you'll really look different."

"Yeah, sure," Tim muttered, "just like a middle-aged skinhead freak." He grinned. "Anyway, it's your disguise that I'm counting on. If those bastards are around here, then I want 'em following me, not you. That way you can get to the airport."

"Well, I still think you should come with me."

"Not now. They'll be looking for both of us. It's just too risky to travel together anymore."

Jenny shrugged. "Okay, boss, whatever you say." She paused after turning back to look at herself. She then shook her head in awe. "Lord, I look like a pig."

"Hey, don't worry about it. It's perfect."

"When I get there, I'm going to trash this stuff."

"Yeah, that's fine, but only after Tony says it's okay."

Jenny turned back, grimacing. "You mean I'm going to have to wear this crap in England?"

"Just until you're out of danger. Once you join up with Laura, I'm sure she'll be able to fix you up."

Jenny nodded. "Good. That'll work."

* * *

Tim's plan to evacuate Jennifer was in motion. He had used a public phone in a nearby department store to set it all up. Early the following morning she would take a cab from the downtown hotel to Vancouver International Airport. She would then board a nonstop Air Canada flight to London. Once the jumbo jet landed at Heathrow, Tim's buddy Anthony Urban, the ex-SAS officer, would take charge of Jenny's safety. Within a few hours, Jenny would join Laura, Tim's sons, and his mother at a well-guarded country retreat.

The only problem had been Jenny's passport—she didn't have one. It was back in her Seattle condominium. Before being permitted to board the jet, she'd have to prove to the airline that she had a valid passport. And upon landing, British Customs would once again demand to see her travel documents before permitting her to enter the country.

At first, the passport problem had been the fatal flaw in Tim's plan—just like with his own family. But then he remembered that he had brought his own. It had been packed in with the cash and other items he had taken from his office.

It took Tim a little over an hour to find the right man. He concentrated on Vancouver's Asian district. Like other ethnic neighborhoods across the globe, Vancouver's underground economy was thriving and Tim, thanks to his years as an intelligence officer, knew how to tap into it.

The Pakistani forger had demanded $500 American up front. It was highway robbery, but Tim paid. He left his own passport with the forger along with a freshly printed photograph of the new Jenny. The photo had been easy—there were shops everywhere offering instant turnaround.

The false passport did not have to be perfect. Jenny was traveling to Great Britain as a tourist—not reentering the United States, where it would be subject to far more scrutiny.

Jenny's passport would be ready by five P.M. Her new name would be Thelma Carter.

"Now really, Tim—*Thelma?*"

Tim had just informed Jenny of her new moniker. She was still standing in front of the mirror.

"Hey, the guy said that the fewer changes he had to make

to my name, the better it would be. Changing Carpenter to Carter was a no-brainer—cut out a few letters and paste it back together. But the first name was the big problem and the only female name that I could come up with that was remotely close to Timothy was Thelma."

Jenny grinned. Tim caught her mirrored reflection. "It's fine, Tim." She then stepped away from the mirror, now walking toward the windows. It was almost one o'clock. The sun was high overhead and the harbor sparkled. "Do you think we could go out to a real restaurant—now that I'm in drag?"

"I don't think that's a good idea. We took enough risks this morning getting your hair done and the photo. I think we should continue to use room service."

"Yeah, you're probably right."

Tim's security precautions were certainly warranted. However, he had an additional motivation. Tim had managed all of the walking from earlier in the day—thanks to a heavy dose of ibuprofen—but his left knee was once again in rebellion. He desperately needed to ice it down.

Tim reached for a phone. Before dialing he asked: "What would you like to eat?"

"A cheeseburger and some fries. And a glass of milk. Nonfat."

"You got it."

15 BREAKOUT

They found the Sea Ray in midafternoon. It had been a Her-culean effort. Over a hundred men and women were in the field, canvassing every marina, harbor, and moorage facility along the southern Strait of Georgia, in both Canada and the United States. Most traveled by automobile and then on foot, but several small boats and two aircraft were also mobilized.

The core of the search group originated from greater Vancouver. With several hundred thousand citizens of Asian descent, and a substantial percentage of those immigrants from China and Hong Kong, Vancouver provided a vast pool of talent to call upon.

Most of the agents that were activated had been planted years earlier by the PRC's Ministry of State Security. Referred to by the MSS as "fish at the bottom of the ocean" (*chen di yu*), the deep-cover agents were directed to infiltrate high-technology businesses as well as federal and provincial government organizations. The sleeper agents were now permanent fixtures within their local communities. Their talents deliberately covered a broad spectrum, ranging from business owners, doctors, lawyers, and engineers to schoolteachers, construction workers, and airline pilots.

They were alerted by phone. A special code word identified the caller and then the instructions were given. No explanations were offered. The agents were expected to carry out the instructions. And they did.

Not all of the *chen di yu*s were motivated patriots. They were just frightened. The threat was always there, in the background, a notch below the surface. Their loved ones—those that remained behind in the People's Republic of China—were forever at risk.

A forty-two-year-old nurse from Tsawwassen found the Sea Ray. Alerted just before the noon hour while at work in a local clinic, she feigned a migraine headache and left early. Instead of driving to her nearby condominium, however, she proceeded southward down Fifty-sixth Street. Her primary target was located just a few minutes away, at the very tip of the Tsawwassen Peninsula.

After passing through a tiny border station, she drove into Point Roberts. The six-square-mile American enclave was surrounded by water on three sides. Its only land access was through British Columbia.

Point Roberts is American territory, part of the state of Washington, yet it is owned and used mainly by Canadians. It has miles of sandy beaches, hundreds of cabins and beach houses, a golf course, and a scattering of other tourist-related businesses. Its star attraction, however, is the marina. With over a thousand slips, the Point Roberts Marina Resort is one of the largest privately owned marinas on the West Coast.

Lien-hua Ainsworth had been certain that she'd find the renegade craft at the marina. It was the perfect place to hide: instant access to the Strait of Georgia but still in U.S. waters. And she knew the marina well. Her late husband, a Canadian liquor distributor she had met in Hong Kong, had kept a boat at the marina.

George Ainsworth never had an inkling that his union with Lien-hua had been orchestrated by the PRC's Ministry of State Security. Lien-hua's natural beauty had been the bait. George had been visiting Hong Kong on business. Almost twenty years her senior and two years a widower, he walked into the honey trap—eyes and fly wide open.

Almost four years into the marriage, George died. Heart attack.

Lien-hua's grief was genuine. She had grown to care for George. In any case, now a Canadian citizen and gainfully employed, her cover was solidly in place. She loved Canada and never wanted to return home. But the leash was always there. Her mother and three sisters still lived in Beijing. Easy pickings.

Lien-hua spent most of the afternoon walking the docks at the Point Roberts Marina, looking for the Sea Ray. But it was a waste of time. Defeated, she drove back to Tsawwassen. Before returning to her condominium, however, another idea suddenly developed. "Of course," she had said to herself, "it could be there, too."

She discovered Tim Carpenter's runabout a few minutes after three P.M. It was tied up to a floating pier at a river marina near Ladner. The markings were unmistakable: U.S. Coast Guard numbers and Washington State license decals. The Yankee boat stood out like a bone-rotted leper in the crowd of Canuck vessels.

Located along the banks of the Fraser River, near the George Massey Tunnel, the marina contained berths for several hundred boats. Lien-hua hadn't visited the marina in years but that didn't matter. Before relocating to Point Roberts, she and George had moored their thirty-six-foot cabin cruiser at the river marina.

* * *

"So we know they're here," Gérard Rémy said.

"Yes, at least sometime today they were," replied Alle
Peng.

Both men sat in the *Orca*'s main salon. The yacht wa
now moored to the visitors' berth at the Royal Vancouve
Yacht Club on English Bay.

"You think they might have gone back to the States?"

"Maybe, but if I were them, I'd hole up somewhere i
Vancouver. This is a big place. Besides, if those report
we're getting about the FBI search are right, then it make
even more sense for them to stay in Canada."

"That does make sense," agreed the French agent. "Th
FBI will have more difficulty working in Canada, despite th
close ties between both countries."

"But that will only last for a short time, Gérard. You ca
be certain that the Americans will eventually get complet
cooperation from the Canadian authorities. They want th
woman back—just as bad as we want her."

"So what do we do now?"

"Our people are working the problem," Peng said. "W
think they must have come in early in the morning. Ther
are no reports of any missing or stolen boats in the marin
and no stolen car reports, so we're pretty sure they got a rid
out."

"From whom?"

"We're checking with the cab companies right now. Sho
of hitchhiking, that appears to be the only way they coul
have left."

"So we still have a chance?"

Peng pointed to the cellular phone sitting on a nearby co
fee table. "We should know within the next half hour."

The call came twenty-two minutes later. A local cab com
pany reported picking up a fare at a river marina just befor
seven A.M. About half an hour later, the passengers, a ma
and a woman, were dropped off in downtown Vancouver a
the corner of Burrard and West Pender.

"What are you going to do now?" Rémy asked after Pen
briefed him on the call.

"We accelerate the hunt. I'll bet my last dollar that they're still here."

"Good, let's get on with it."

"This guy's Asian all right," Ricardo Molina said as he stared at the body. He then turned to face his companion. "Can you tell what he is?"

Victoria Kwan surveyed the corpse. They were in the tiny morgue at the San Juan County facility in Friday Harbor. The male had been in his late twenties. Although slightly built, his upper torso, arms, and legs were well muscled, indicating that he had been fit. His hair had been cut close to his scalp, military style. The puncture wound in the chest was hardly noticeable. The exit wound in the lower back, however, told the real horror of his death.

"You know, Rick, it's not so easy for us either. He looks Chinese, but he could be Korean, maybe even Japanese."

"Yeah, I know what you mean. I have the same problem with my own people." He then pointed to part of the tattoo that originated on the dead man's back and flowed over his right shoulder. "How about that thing—could he be one of the Japanese thugs?"

"You mean a *yakuza?*"

"Yeah."

Victoria hesitated before responding. "Maybe, but we don't have any intel that suggests the Japanese mob is mixed up in this mess. Besides, that kind of tattoo is not unique to the Japanese. Certain Korean gangs use them, as well as Chinese triads."

Molina shook his head. "We still don't know anything. This guy's no help at all, and from what that doc said, the other one's probably not going to survive the night. Shit! We're no closer to solving this mess than I am to flying to the moon."

Victoria Kwan felt the same frustration. Once again, their investigation had hit a brick wall. *What do we do now?* she wondered.

The FBI agents were just about to walk out of the examination room when a middle-aged woman dressed in a white lab coat walked in. Scarecrow thin, she had shoulder-length blond hair and stood nearly six feet tall.

"Hi there," she said. "You two must be with the FBI."

The introductions were made and then the chief pathologist for San Juan County continued: "You able to ID this guy?"

"No, not yet," replied Molina.

"You still sending in your own forensic people?"

"Yes. They should be arriving tomorrow."

"Well, make sure that you tell them to check out this guy's dental work."

"What do you mean?" Victoria asked.

"It looks a little unusual for this neck of the woods." She paused, moving closer to the body. "I don't know a lot about dentistry, but the hardware in this fellow's mouth sure wasn't done in the States. Very crude work." She paused again as she inserted her gloved fingers into the man's mouth. She pulled the jaws apart and looked into the opening. "I spent some time with the UN a few years ago. Worked in the former East Germany and then the Balkans. I saw a lot of similar work there."

"This guy is from Eastern Europe?" Ricardo asked.

"I doubt that. But the dentist that worked on him might have been trained there—probably in Russia."

"A Russian dentist?" Ricardo said, confused.

"No. The dentist was probably Chinese. You know, from the People's Republic." She hesitated. "Lots of Chinese medical professionals received their training in Russia—the Soviet Union—back when the Soviets and Red Chinese were on good terms with each other."

Ricardo Molina waited a few seconds for her words to register. "So this guy could have received his dental work on mainland China?"

"Yeah, I think there's a good chance of that. Anybody around here that did a job like that would lose their license." She paused again, removing her hand from the body. "And another thing, from the amount of the hardware in his mouth, I'd say he probably didn't have the work done until he was in his late teens. That would be typical for some of the poorer places in China."

"How could you know that?" asked Victoria.

"I don't know for sure, but, if I had to guess, I'd say this guy was in the military at one time. He probably didn't get any decent medical attention until he went into the army or whatever. Once he joined up, they'd take care of him—one of the perks of being a soldier. Too bad, though, some old fart must have worked on him, because their new docs wouldn't do work like this."

Chinese military? Soldier? thought Ricardo. *What the hell is going on here?* And then it hit—like a mountain avalanche. The two Asian gunmen at Roche Harbor—the intruders that attacked the FBI safe house—the abduction of Dr. Richmond. *My God! The Chinese Communists. Could they be the ones trying to steal the MERLIN technology?*

Chris Wilcox had been working on the bindings for hours. He had made the most progress with his left wrist. It was slightly loose, enough to encourage him to keep trying.

He was lashed to a metal chair. The guards used a whole roll of duct tape to bind his body to the steel frame. Layer after layer of the gray tape was wrapped around his legs, arms, and waist. They even sealed his mouth with the sticky tape. As an extra measure, they had bolted the back of the chair to an adjacent wall. It prevented him from generating momentum with his body to tip it over. And finally, as a last-ditch effort to confine him, they had used a pair of handcuffs. One cuff was locked on his right wrist. The other cuff was locked onto the steel armrest of the chair.

The room that he was locked inside seemed no larger than a closet. But then, he really couldn't tell. There was no light to speak of. Just a little diffraction under the bottom of the door.

Chris had been imprisoned for just a few days, but it seemed like a lifetime. After the savage beating and then the miraculous rescue by the man with the French accent, they had locked him up in the basement cell. He had been abandoned until late the first evening. That's when the Frenchman returned.

"How are you feeling?" Gérard Rémy had asked that night, his voice soft, affectionate—too affectionate.

"I'm okay," Chris had answered, on guard.

"Good, good. I'm glad to hear that." Rémy then stepped closer and leaned over, further examining Chris's battered face. "Those pigs really hurt you. I'm so sorry."

Chris stiffened in his chair, now alarmed. *Something's wrong here. Watch out!*

Rémy reached forward and gently brushed an errant blond lock from Chris's forehead. It was almost a caress.

Chris jerked his head back.

"Don't be alarmed, Christopher. I can be a very good friend to you." He paused for a moment, casting a more than friendly smile. "All I ask from you is a little cooperation and then we can work things out." The DGSE operative again reached forward and . . .

"No damn way I'll do that!" Chris said aloud, remembering what his captor had hinted he could do to gain his freedom. Chris again twisted both arms, testing the bindings. The left arm moved a little more.

After vehemently rebuffing Rémy's advances, Chris was left alone. He had now lost all sense of time. And right now there was a jackhammer working overtime inside his skull. His mouth had the texture of sandpaper. No one had brought him any food or drink, let alone attended to his wounds. But worse—he had not been allowed to use a bathroom.

At first, the indignity of having to urinate in one's own trousers had been too much for Chris. He held it back until his bladder was about to burst. Unable to stand it any longer, he relieved himself. From then on, it was not a problem.

Convinced that his captors had deliberately abandoned him, expecting him to starve to death, Chris fought the bindings. Nearly every conscious minute was spent twisting, turning, probing, hunting for a weakness. He was now exhausted and his body was brutally sore, the result of the earlier beatings and his constant struggle to free himself.

He might have given up hope if the left wrist binding hadn't given a little. He could feel more movement. The guards, impatient to complete their work, had wrapped fewer layers of tape on the left wrist. It made all the difference.

Chris rested for half a minute and then, after sucking in a great breath, he put everything he had into his left arm. The tape tore and his left hand and lower arm broke free.

"Thank God!" he exclaimed ardently.

He rested again, gaining new strength. Now, with part of his arm free, he shoved it forward. The tape bit into his biceps. Just before the skin would have ruptured, the duct tape tore. It was the sound of victory.

Ten minutes later Chris had removed all of the tape. But he wasn't free yet. His right wrist remained handcuffed to the chair and the chair was bolted to the wall.

Still in the dark, Chris kneeled in front of the chair and grabbed one of the front legs. And then, with all of his might, he yanked upward and outward. The cantilever force tore the bolts out of the wall. He was finally free.

He used the chair as a battering ram to break open the door. He no longer cared about noise. And then, with the chair firmly gripped in his right hand, he headed upstairs. He found a phone a few minutes later.

He dialed the only numbers he could think of.

"Nine one one. Is this an emergency?" asked the operator.

Chris waited a second. The female voice was the first human contact he had had in a long time.

"Ah, I've been kidnapped and I . . . I just escaped."

"Are you hurt, sir?"

"A little, but I'm still kind of tied up."

"What do you mean, sir?"

"There's this handcuff—it's still locked to the chair and it's hard for me to get . . ." Chris stopped as a new horror rocked him. "Operator, I don't even know where I am."

"That's okay, I have the address you're calling from—its automatic with the system. Now, what's your name, sir?"

"Wilcox, Chris Wilcox. Can you send someone?"

"Yes, the police are on the way. They'll be there in a couple of minutes." The operator paused. "Now, why don't you relax and tell me what happened."

"Yeah, okay."

DAY 4

THE *EMERALD SEA*

16 THE WAITING GAME

Under normal circumstances the FBI's Seattle field office would have been staffed by just a few personnel at quarter past midnight. But nothing was normal about this evening. The office was packed. Dozens of special agents had been called in, most rousted from their homes.

The hunt for Tim Carpenter and Jennifer Richmond had been kicked into overdrive. Ricardo Molina made the decision. He really didn't have a choice.

The acceleration started several hours earlier, when the Edmonds Police Department called the FBI. Chris Wilcox was now in their custody. Within minutes, a squad of special agents was dispatched to Edmonds. The four men and two women began a thorough search of the home that had been used to imprison Chris. Every conceivable surface would be fingerprinted, hundreds of photos taken, and dozens of hair and fiber samples collected. Nothing that could possibly be used to identify the abductors would be overlooked. It would take the forensics team all night to conduct the investigation.

Another team of agents escorted Chris back to downtown Seattle. Special Agent in Charge Ricardo Molina, assisted by Victoria Kwan, was now interviewing him.

"These people that beat you, they were all Asians?" SAC Molina asked. He looked as if he had slept in his clothes, which he had.

Chris nodded. He was now dressed in a pair of orange prison coveralls, compliments of the Edmonds Police Department. He had refused to touch his own soiled clothing after showering.

Ricardo continued: "But this other guy, the one that talked the most, he wasn't an Asian?"

"Right. He was white—European, I think. He had an accent."

"What kind?" asked Agent Kwan.

Chris turned to face the woman. Despite the late hour, Victoria's appearance was immaculate. Even her makeup was perfect. "I'd say French, maybe Swiss, something like that. Anyway, he sounded just like that karate movie actor guy . . . Claude something."

"Jean-Claude Van Damme?" offered Victoria.

"Yeah, that's the one."

Ricardo frowned. This was a new complication. The Chinese connection was only part of the equation. "This European guy," Ricardo said, "he's the one that asked the most questions about MERLIN?"

"Yes."

"What did he tell you about it?"

"Not much, only that Jenny's dad, Dr. Richmond, was behind it. Some kind of secret military thing. I really don't know what he was talking about, though." Chris paused as a new thought developed. "But he kept implying that Jenny was helping him with it, like she knew all about it."

"But you think Jenny was in the dark, like you?" Ricardo asked.

"Yeah. I would have known something about it if Jenny were involved. We've been going out for a year and she's never kept anything hidden from me. I'm certain she wasn't working with her father on some kind of super-secret government project."

"Do you think you could recognize these people if we showed you some photographs?"

"Maybe. But you gotta remember, they beat the hell out of me. Everything's still foggy." *But I'll never forget him!* was what Chris wanted to add, but didn't. He was too embarrassed to tell that part of the tale.

Gérard Rémy's face was fused into Chris Wilcox's memory core. He wanted to hate the man, yet, strangely, he did not. Rémy had been decent, almost kind to him, even after Chris had rejected his advances. There was a soft side to this Frenchman; it was all a contradiction to Chris.

"Okay, Chris," Ricardo Molina said, "but whatever assistance you can give us with the photos will be greatly appreciated."

"Sure, I'll try."

"Good, I'll get someone to bring you the photos." Ricardo then started to push his chair away from the table, signaling the interview was over.

Chris leaned forward. He wasn't done. "Just a second," he said. "Before I do anything else, I'd like a few answers."

Ricardo settled back in the chair, stealing a glance at Agent Kwan. Her face was neutral, but he could tell she had the same thought: *Here it comes!*

"What do you want to know?" Ricardo asked.

"Well, for starters, where the heck is Jenny? You have her in protective custody someplace and I'd like to see her."

"I'm sorry, but we can't do that."

Chris shook his head, now disgusted. "Come on, you guys, at least let me talk to her on the phone. She's my fiancée, for crying out loud."

"Please believe me, Chris," Ricardo said, "I'd like nothing more than to be able to pick up a phone and get her on the line. But I can't."

"What do you mean?"

"We're not sure where she is." Molina hesitated for an instant as a new thought developed. "In fact, Chris, maybe you can help us. Do you have any idea where Jenny might go to hide out—you know, a special place to get away?"

"What the hell are you talking about?"

Agent Molina had no obligation to say anything more, but he did. It was the only decent thing to do.

It took Ricardo ten minutes to tell the story: the attack on the Cascade Mountain safe house, the dead and wounded FBI agents, Jenny's escape with Tim Carpenter, the burglary of Tim and Laura's Evergreen Point residence, and finally, the attack at Roche Harbor.

Chris was stunned. "Do you think these pricks got Jenny and Carpenter?" he finally asked.

"No. There's no evidence of that," answered Ricardo.

"But where could they be then?" Chris had nothing to offer on the possible whereabouts of his lover.

"We're working on a couple of leads. We think they might be holed up somewhere else in the San Juans, possibly even the Canadian Gulf Islands. Tim might be waiting for things to cool down before bringing Jenny back."

Ricardo was guessing. He didn't have a clue as to the location of Tim Carpenter and Jennifer Richmond. He just hoped that they were still alive.

One of the Seattle FBI computer technicians hit the jackpot a few minutes after one A.M. He had been working with his counterparts at AT&T and several other telephone service providers for over an hour. They were jointly reviewing every call that had been made to and from the Edmonds residence. Surprisingly, not one long-distance call had been placed from the home. However, by employing a special screening program developed by the FBI, the technicians discovered that dozens of foreign telephone calls had been placed to the Puget Sound residence. Most of the calls originated from two principal locations: Hong Kong and Paris. And just recently, there had been a barrage of activity from Vancouver. All of the incoming calls from B.C. originated from cellular phones or public phones. The pattern was clear to the FBI technician. He had observed it before. A foreign intelligence operation had been conducted from the Edmonds residence.

The call for assistance came in at 0528 hours EDT. The CIA watch officer logged in the electronic request and then routed it to the Office of Counter-Intelligence. Because the request from the FBI's Seattle office used the code word MERLIN, a copy of the report was automatically filed electronically with the CIA's Office of Technology Transfer. The message, decoded, printed, and sealed in an Eyes Only envelope, would be delivered to MAGNUM's office later in the morning.

The *Orca* remained moored at the Royal Van. Although it was three in the morning, the main salon of the megayacht was lit up like the Academy Awards. Allen Peng and Gérard

Rémy had been up all night, coordinating the search. So far, though, they had nothing to show for their efforts.

"They must be hiding out somewhere in the downtown core," Rémy suggested. "That's where the cab dropped them off."

"Maybe," Peng responded, "but remember, Carpenter's a professional. He'd know that the cab route from the marina could be traced. He could easily have taken another cab back to the airport or someplace else after the first one dropped them off. We might not be able to trace that second route."

Rémy nodded. "Yes, but we know they haven't used the airport since the morning. Your people would have spotted them."

"True, but they could have just as easily boarded a bus or rented a car to get back to the States."

"Yes, but I don't believe they want to go back to America, at least not yet. It's still too hot down there for them. Remember the nationwide bulletin the FBI sent out."

"Well, I hope you're right because that gives us a chance. If they're still here, we'll eventually spot them, given enough time."

"Yes. But our window of opportunity is narrowing by the hour. It won't be long before the American authorities start pressuring the Canadians. Once that happens we'll have to shut down the operation."

"I know but . . ." Peng stopped in midsentence as one of his aides walked into the salon. The young Asian frowned. Something was wrong.

The man walked up to Peng's side, bowed slightly, and then began speaking. The conversation was short, all in Mandarin.

Rémy watched the neutral expression on Peng's face melt. "What's wrong?" asked the French spy.

"It's not good. One of our people in Seattle just phoned in. He was returning to our operations center to check on Wilcox." Peng paused, drawing in a deep breath. "Apparently the police have discovered the house."

"Dammit. Did they get any of your people?"

"No. The house was deserted at the time. Luckily, our man

followed standard protocol when he went to check it. He drove by it, on the street just below. There were lights on everywhere—there should have just been one in the upper bedroom. He used his cellular phone to call the house. A male voice answered when no one was supposed to answer."

"It's got to be the FBI."

"Probably."

"Then that means they've got Wilcox."

"Yes, but he's no threat to us."

Rémy stared at Peng. "For you, probably. But remember, he saw me. I questioned him after your goons softened him up."

"You should have taken Major Wu's advice."

The *zhongdui* had wanted to eliminate the American, but Rémy insisted on keeping him alive. Insurance, he had called it. But it was a deep-seated longing that really drove him. And utter loneliness was near the core of that need.

"I suppose you're right," Rémy said. But it's too late for that now, isn't it."

Peng nodded. "So you think he might be able to identify you?"

Rémy stood up. He was visibly shaken by the turn of events. *Identify me?* thought Rémy. *He probably hates my guts.* "The Americans have data processing skills far beyond anything either you or I have. I'm sure they have a dossier on me, maybe even fingerprints. But surely photographs."

"Why would they have that? You're supposed to be an ally."

"We've been dueling with the Americans for years, mostly friendly encounters. Usually, we just test each other's intelligence services, that kind of thing. But with the end of the Cold War, and all of the emphasis on economic espionage, things have really changed. We now spy on them, and they spy on us, regularly."

Peng nodded. None of this revelation was news to him. Long ago, China's intelligence services adopted a similar strategy. The MSS and its companion military branches had been spying on everyone for decades.

Gérard Rémy continued: "The principal reason I was assigned to this case was my background with Boeing. We've been covering all of their European operations for years. When our people got wind of Boeing's involvement with MERLIN, I was a natural to get involved."

"So what's the problem?"

"They know me."

"Who?"

"The CIA, the FBI."

Peng stood up, stretching his arms. "Okay, so they know you. That doesn't prove anything. Besides, you're not in the States anyway. This is Canada. They can't touch you up here."

"You don't get it," Rémy said. "The French government was never supposed to be implicated. That's why we went to such extremes to use your people—they're untraceable. All the Americans were supposed to know was that an Asian consortium was responsible for stealing the MERLIN secret. If they discover our involvement . . . I don't know what will happen."

Peng wanted to laugh, but managed to hold it in.

The two spies talked for a few minutes and then headed to their cabins. There was little else they could do for now.

Two hours later, just before falling asleep, Peng recalled Gérard Rémy's earlier words. He chuckled at the French spy's fear that the Americans might discover the real truth. *What fools!* Peng thought. *How could the French have ever thought that the Americans wouldn't figure it out?*

To Allen Peng, Rémy's confessional had cemented his belief that all Caucasians were really alike. On the exterior they professed equality with everyone else. But on the inside, where the real feelings lie, the tone of superiority always dominated. The white Anglo-Saxon . . . and *Franco* . . . creed was universal: *We are better than you and we will always be your superior.*

From the very beginning, when the European intelligence operatives joint-ventured with their counterparts in Beijing, Peng and his MSS comrades were aware of the French and

Germans' true intention: China was destined to be the fall guy.

It was an ideal setup. Communist China would be blamed for stealing the MERLIN secret. But there was little America could do in direct retaliation. With over a billion citizens and dozens of ICBMs—each armed with a copycat U.S. nuclear warhead and guided by state-of-the-art electronics supplied by the former Clinton Administration—Red China was immune from any possible military action. And when the Americans finally broke the economic ties that linked the two nations together, as they most surely would have to do to save political face, the Europeans, led by France and Germany, would gladly step in to fill the void. And then through a prearranged deception designed to hide the real truth from the Americans, the Europeans would agree to a joint venture with China in the development of the MERLIN technology. It was a perfect plan to prohibit the Americans from dominating the twenty-first century with the MERLIN secret. Except for one flaw.

If America discovered that she had been tricked by two of her closest allies, there'd be hell to pay. It was bad enough to be assaulted by a mugger. That was to be expected. But to be gang-raped by trusted blood-relatives was unthinkable. The harm would be permanent. America would never forgive such treachery.

The motel room was nothing like the palatial suite he had rented earlier in the day. It was a dwarf in comparison. There was no view and it had only a shower stall instead of a full bath. The single bed was decent and Jenny had offered to share it, but there certainly wasn't much room for two. That didn't matter, though. Even if the bed had been king-size, Tim would have avoided it like it was infested with lice. He was married, and no matter how dire the circumstances were, he wasn't about to get in the same bed with another woman.

Tim Carpenter liked to think it was his loyalty to Laura that was responsible for his noble caution. What really drove him, however, was his fear that he might give in. Tim had

always found Jenny attractive and tonight he had been un-
duly tempted.

Privacy in the tiny room was at a premium and when
Jenny walked out of the bathroom after showering, she wore
a skimpy T-shirt and not much else. Her exposed flesh was
beyond desirable.

And then came the offer to share the bed. Another mixed
signal.

Under the circumstances, it was far safer to take the chair.

The economy motel was situated in the heart of Vancouver's Chinatown. It was an ideal place to hide: nondescript
and the manager didn't ask any questions.

Tim had planned to remain in the high-rise hotel, but late
in the afternoon he elected to move. It was too risky to stay
in the same place for very long. *The bastards are out there,
no doubt looking under every rock,* he had concluded. *Sooner
or later they'll come looking.*

The minuscule room was unlit, but there was just enough
outside light penetrating through the curtains to see. Tim
checked on Jenny. She had her back to him, a sheet wrapped
around her slim shoulders. Her newly clipped and colored
jet black mane shimmered. Her breathing was slow, steady,
almost sensuous . . . *Stop thinking about that, you idiot!*

Tim turned away and slumped further into the chair, trying
to get comfortable. His knee still hurt, but not like the previous day. He hoped the worst was behind him.

The Glock was on the dresser top, just a few feet away.
The MP5 was on the carpet, within easy reach. He glanced
down at his wristwatch: 3:14 A.M. He next checked the
Seiko's alarm setting. It was set for five o'clock. He doubted
that he would need it but decided not to take any chances.
Jenny's flight to London didn't depart until 8:50 A.M., but
he wanted to make sure they had plenty of time to get to the
airport.

He closed his eyes. *I'll just doze for a few minutes,* he
told himself, not really tired. A minute later he was unconscious. He would dream up a storm until the alarm finally
brought him back to reality.

17 MAGNUM

She arrived at her office at five past seven. She really didn't like getting up early, but the traffic was so horrible later in the morning that she put up with the lesser of the two evils.

Her secretary had preceded her by fifteen minutes and a full pot of coffee was now simmering on the stand next to her credenza. She poured herself a cup, mixing in two spoonfuls of sugar.

She took a sip and turned to look out her windows. The view of the Virginia countryside was superb. Her office had one of the better views on her floor. It wasn't one of the huge power corner offices—she'd never get one of those—nevertheless, it was quite pleasant.

She was nearing middle age and could see the changes. Once quite slender, she now weighed about thirty pounds too much for her five-foot-five frame. Her face remained pleasing—almost attractive. There were just a few wrinkles and she really didn't need much makeup. Her hair was short, a couple of inches off her shoulders. The curl from her last permanent was wearing off and her dark roots seemed to appear sooner and sooner after each coloring. She needed to call the salon.

She sat down behind the desk and opened her appointment calendar. There were no meetings until 9:30. *Good,* she thought, *that'll give me time to catch up on some paperwork.*

She pivoted her chair until she was facing the credenza. She slid the oak panel aside, uncovering a small stainless steel safe. She dialed the combination and opened it. Inside were a stack of files, half a foot high. She removed the top two folders and then closed the safe, resetting the combination.

She had just started to open the first folder when her secretary walked in through the open doorway.

He was twenty-five. Tall. Barrel-chested. Brunet. Clark

Gable mustache. A real hunk. "Morning, ma'am," he said with a friendly smile.

Marsha Lewis, assistant director, Office of Technology Transfer, Department of Science and Technology, Central Intelligence Agency, smiled back. "Good morning, Paul."

"Ah, this was just delivered from Communications. It came in last night." He held up a sealed nine-by-twelve envelope. The code name MERLIN was machine-printed in black letters on the outside.

She reached forward as he handed her the document. "Thanks."

"Anything I can get for you?" he asked.

"No, Paul, I'm fine."

The man turned around and headed for the door.

Marsha's eyes followed him. She liked looking at him, especially his trim rear.

Paul automatically closed the door on the way out.

Marsha checked the seals on the envelope. They were intact. She then ripped it open. Inside was a status report from the FBI. *Well! well!* she thought as she read through the opening paragraph. *So the Chinese are involved, too.*

All along Marsha suspected an Asian connection but could never verify it. The Germans and French were supposed to be allies of the United States so it was almost a certainty that they would insulate themselves from the real dirty work. Besides, there was too much happening for the Europeans to manage it all by themselves. They would need all the help they could get.

Marsha would have picked the Japanese or South Koreans. They were far more predictable to work with than Chinese Communists. But then again, China had a huge intelligence organization with hundreds of agents located along America's West Coast. The mammoth size of the Chinese operation dwarfed anything that the other Asians could offer. And that provided unique opportunities, especially for the Germans, who had a very modest American espionage operation.

The French probably didn't like it, thought Marsha. *But they'd put up with the Chicoms if the Germans insisted.*

Marsha swiveled her chair, now facing the distant tree line. *I wonder how much they'll pay for this.*

Marsha Lewis was already a millionaire. But you would never know it. She lived in a modest rental apartment, purchased off-the-rack clothing, and rarely vacationed. She had just over $24,000 in a federal credit union CD as well as a modest pension set aside. Her only visible luxury was the two-year-old Acura sedan she leased.

Almost all of Marsha's real wealth, however, was discreetly tucked away in Switzerland. She never touched that money—now totaling $2 million plus change. It wasn't time quite yet.

So far, Marsha had been careful, very careful, indeed. Aldridge Ames had been her case study of what not to do.

She'd remain in her position for four more months, until she had her twenty years in. Then she'd retire. No one would notice.

She thought the south of France would be nice, maybe even northern Italy, on the Med, of course. She'd go on a diet, get her figure back, take on a lover, and then live the good life. MAGNUM could hardly wait.

Marsha Lewis dealt only with the Germans but she never once met her German contact. There was no need for such a risky encounter. Everything had been done remotely, through the mail and with electronic communications.

Five months earlier she made the initial solicitation to a midlevel intelligence officer in the German government. The forty-four-year-old man was an expert in aviation matters. Marsha had his complete file in her office, one of the benefits of working in the CIA's Department of Science and Technology.

Included in the man's file was his home address and the Internet email address for his Bonn office.

Marsha's first untraceable electronic message was to the point:

HAVE INFORMATION. WILL SELL. SAMPLE IN MAIL.
                                        SIGNED: MAGNUM.

A week later, Marsha sent the videotape to the man's home address. Prior to mailing, she completely sanitized the cassette, the mailing envelope, and the stamps. There would be no fingerprints to trace, no stray hair samples to analyze, no saliva DNA to check. Marsha took her trade craft seriously.

At first, Marsha planned to mail the package from New York City, purposely concealing her real location. But then she changed her mind. She wanted the Germans to know where it came from—they would likely backtrack the package's initial mailing point.

Marsha drove across the Potomac, entering the District of Columbia. She dropped off the package at a post office near the Washington Monument. When the Germans checked, they would discover that the FBI building was just a few blocks away.

It was a nearly flawless setup. The Germans took the bait without hesitation. The MERLIN project was like nothing they had ever come across. And the possibility that another senior FBI official was willing to sell the secret was just that much more enticing.

Marsha could have revealed her real government connection. The lure of a CIA mole would have been far more attractive to the Germans. But that was too close to home. If something went wrong, or if the Germans refused the bait and reported the solicitation to Washington, she would be protected. Security experts would spend years trying to ferret out the make-believe traitor in the Justice Department.

Marsha's video of one of Dr. Richmond's early MERLIN experiments sent shock waves through the German intelligence community. If the Americans had, in fact, developed an autonomous flight control system, then the entire European military and civilian aviation industry might be in jeopardy. America, led by the Boeing Company, would continue to dominate far into the next century.

The German government could not let that happen, especially after having spent billions to prop up the European aircraft industry. Finally, after decades of struggling, Airbus Industrie was now almost on a par with Boeing, the giant

American aircraft manufacturer. But with this leap in technology, Airbus might again be left in the dust.

At first, MAGNUM did it for revenge. Pure and simple. And then greed took over.

Marsha Lewis had spent almost her entire professional career with the Agency. For over fifteen years she was posted overseas, first in Europe and then South America. She had worked like the proverbial coolie, never complaining, always completing her assignments, whatever they might entail. And because of the nature of her work, there was never any serious thought of marriage.

As a category B intelligence officer in the CIA's Directorate of Operations, it had been Marsha Lewis's duty to recruit agents. And she was good at it, using both her brains and her sex to win over new spies. Almost all of her contacts were men.

She had relished the challenge, especially the macho Latin males, and she won continual praise from her superiors, all men. Marsha steadily advanced in the DO. But then she hit the wall. The promotions and titles plateaued. The plum assignments went to others. She was off the fast track.

Marsha was never able to determine who had derailed her career, only that the decision had been made back in Langley, almost certainly by a male. But she wasn't alone. Similar roadblocks had been raised for other aggressive DO females. The underlying cause of action had been the unwritten decree: Women just can't hack it as spies in culturally chauvinistic foreign countries.

Many of her contemporaries revolted. Several hundred female DO case officers filed a class action suit against the CIA. They eventually won, each receiving a modest monetary award and the promise that the sexual discrimination would cease.

Marsha Lewis remained on the sidelines, not participating. She knew it was a lost cause. They'd win the battle, but still lose the war.

It was a smart move. Marsha's male superiors rewarded her silence. First, she was transferred to the Department of

Science and Technology. Her undergraduate degree in biology had opened that door. And then, late last year, just after her annual polygraph, she was promoted to assistant director level and assigned to the newly created Office of Technology Transfer.

The new position was a godsend for Marsha. She could seek retribution and get rich in the process.

Marsha finished reading the memorandum and tossed it onto her desk. It would be simple to just ignore the news and go about her daily business. But she couldn't. The news probably wouldn't be of great use. By now the Chinese must also suspect that the Richmond woman and her companion were hiding out in Vancouver. Nevertheless, they would probably appreciate knowing that the FBI was closing in.

Then how much should I charge? she asked herself.

With the last payment she had promised herself that she would stop. She didn't need more money. The nest egg she had salted away overseas was plenty to retire on.

The Germans had paid half a million U.S. dollars for the location of the FBI safe house. But the new info wasn't even in the same league.

Maybe it's worth ten or twenty grand—but that's just chicken feed. Besides, it's such a hassle to get the money— they have to wire it to my account first and then I . . .

In the end her decision was based on a perverse sense of loyalty to her illicit benefactors. *What the heck. I'll give 'em this last one for free. Then I'll be done for good.*

Marsha checked her wristwatch. It was 7:25 A.M. She'd take care of it after work tonight.

18 A FISH AT THE BOTTOM OF THE OCEAN

"Just black, right?" asked Tim Carpenter as he poured the coffee.

"Yeah, that'll be fine."

Tim handed Jenny the plastic mug.

"Thanks," she said as she began to sip the steaming brew.

Tim drained the rest of the tiny pot. It was from the complimentary coffee machine on the counter next to the bed. It was about the only amenity that the cheap motel room offered.

Tim dumped a packet of whitener and a bag of sugar into his mug, stirring the concoction with a plastic stick. "Not bad," he said, after sampling the contents.

"Yeah, it sure hits the spot," agreed Jenny.

Tim walked to the nearby window and peeked through the still closed curtains. The sun was rising—it was half past five. It would be a warm, clear day. He scanned the parking lot and the other motel rooms. Everything was quiet.

Tim turned back to face Jennifer. "You all set now? Everything packed?"

"I think so. She stood up for inspection. She wore the same outfit from the previous day: fake spectacles, baggy sweatshirt, and a bulky pair of cotton pants. "Do I pass?" she asked, pirouetting in place.

"Fine. You look totally different—the hair and the clothes, they did wonders."

"Okay, good. So what's next?"

Tim checked his watch. "Well, I guess it's show time." He walked over to the edge of the bed and picked up the phone.

From the exterior, the Ford van was nondescript. It was a utility-type vehicle, designed for hauling and delivering small loads. The rear half of the body had solid side panels instead of windows. It was painted a dull gray. There were no identifying marks, other than the provincial license plates.

The Ford's only distinguishing feature was a pair of tiny black wires that penetrated the roof. At first glance, they looked like cellular phone antennas. But closer examination would reveal that they served another purpose.

Behind the driver's seat, in the cargo bay, sat two technicians. They had been parked along the street all night, monitoring intercepted radio transmissions. The equipment mounted inside the van was far more sophisticated than was really needed. There was no electronic code to break; no frequency-skipping transmissions to worry about; no cellular nets to penetrate; no cryptic discussions. It was simple stuff.

The man sitting toward the rear picked up a new transmission in his earphones. He leaned forward, ready to record the message.

"Three-Two, Three-Two, Base," announced the caller.

"Base, Three-Two," came the reply.

"You've got a pickup for the airport." The caller then read off the address.

"Right. On my way," replied the cabby.

The technician's interest spiked. *Finally*, he thought, *maybe this is something.* It had been a boring morning; there had been only a few calls after two A.M., mostly drunks and partygoers wanting a ride home. And this was his first call to the airport. His partner, sitting just a few feet away, had already intercepted three airport-bound calls.

The two men in the van were part of a team of electronic eavesdroppers. Their assignment was to monitor the radio transmissions from a local cab company. There were several other similarly equipped vans scattered throughout the city, all parked near the various headquarters for the cab companies. Each van-team's job was to monitor all transmissions and report any that fit the target profile: rides to the bus station, train station, and especially the airport.

The technician reached for the portable Motorola cellular phone on his console. He punched a single memory button on the keypad and then hit SEND. The call was answered almost instantly.

"Command here," replied the voice, using his native tongue.

The caller made his report, also in Mandarin: "This is Unit Three. I've got a pickup for the airport." He read off the address.

"Got it, Three. We'll take it from here."

His formal name was Chou Haixing but all of his Western friends just called him Harry. It was easier that way. Harry was asleep when the portable cell phone announced its presence. It was on the passenger seat. The piercing tone jolted him awake.

Harry Chou sat up, blinking his eyes. He tried to focus but instantly turned away. He was facing directly into the rising sun. It had been dark when he drifted off, ninety minutes earlier. His twenty-year-old Toyota Corolla was the only vehicle parked in the tiny lot just off of Keefer Avenue.

Chou picked up the receiver. "Yes," he said.

"There's a pickup for the airport," replied the caller, speaking in English this time. The caller read off the address. He then finished with: "Check it out and report."

"Right," replied the University of British Columbia graduate student. He reached down and turned the key. The engine turned over five times before finally catching. He let it warm up for half a minute before pulling onto the street.

The cab arrived right on time. Tim and Jennifer climbed into the backseat, carrying their own luggage. Jenny's duffel bag, purchased the day before, contained her new wardrobe. But the garments occupied only a third of the space. The remainder was taken up with her father's research papers. She also carried a small handbag. It was full of cosmetics and other female things.

Tim had his attaché case and the other duffel bag. It was sitting on his lap. The MP5 was inside. The weapon was now thoroughly cleaned and it was loaded with a full magazine. Also inside were several garments Tim had purchased, along with four white towels from the motel room. The towels gave the bag a little more bulk, helping to disguise the telltale outline of the submachine gun.

And stashed away at the very end of the bag, still enclosed within a plastic cylinder, was the MERLIN control device. Tim decided it was too risky for Jenny to try to bring it aboard the airplane. Instead, he would take charge of it.

After settling in, Tim looked forward. The Sikh cabby wore a plain white turban. He had a full beard and wore a pair of thick glasses. "Driver," Tim said, "how long will it take to get to the airport?"

"About twenty minutes, sir."

"Good, let's go."

Harry Chou was late. His Toyota stalled out when he pulled up to a stoplight. It wasn't the first time it had happened. But it was getting worse. The carburetor choke wasn't working right. He tried to restart the stubborn engine. It refused to light.

Harry climbed out and opened the hood. He knew what to do. After fiddling with the hardware for half a minute he climbed back in and turned the key. The engine caught on the first crank. *I better let it warm up a little more,* he thought.

His ancient vehicle needed a new choke along with a major tune-up. But Harry was broke. Like many of his fellow grad students, he lived on a shoestring budget. The university granted him a stipend, but it was barely enough to live on. Harry had never dreamed how expensive it would be to live in the West. Back in Nanjing, where he had graduated from Hohai University, he could have lived like a king on the $700 a month he received in Vancouver.

Well, he thought, as he cycled the accelerator pedal, helping to warm up the engine, *at least after today I'll have enough to get this thing fixed.*

The call from the resident MSS agent came in the day before when he was in the laboratory, running a test. He had no choice but to cooperate. If he didn't, they would certainly arrange for his instant return. And then the real trouble would start.

Harry abandoned the experiment, immediately following the orders to report to a downtown office building. Like many of his fellow countrymen and -women fortunate enough to receive a Western education, he was absolutely obligated to cooperate with the local MSS spymaster.

In a way, Harry didn't mind this assignment. The lure was the money. He would receive $500 cash for his efforts. By now, the MSS had learned that national loyalty wasn't always enough to motivate its cadre of student *chen di yu*.

Harry was almost finished with his master's degree. His course work was complete and all he needed was to finish his thesis. But he wasn't about to stop at that point. They might make him return to China. Instead, he had already applied to a dozen other universities, most in the United States. If he was lucky, he could string out a Ph.D. program for another three, maybe four years. He'd worry about his repatriation commitment at that time.

Harry was studying civil engineering at UBC. His specialty was coastal engineering. After receiving his graduate education, he was programmed to return home where he would be assigned to China's equivalent of the U.S. Army Corps of Engineers.

The Toyota was now warmed sufficiently so that it wouldn't stall. Harry glanced at his watch. It had been six minutes since receiving the call. *Damn, I better get going.*

He pounced on the accelerator.

Tim was just settling in when he spotted it. The Toyota sped around a corner about half a block ahead, turning north onto Main Street. Its squealing tires, protesting the excessive speed, gave it away. Tim watched as the car approached. It was about half a block away.

There it is, thought Harry Chou. He arrived just in time. Another minute and the Chevy cab would have been gone.

Tim watched as the Toyota drove by. He would have ignored it if the driver hadn't been so obvious. The car deliberately slowed up as it approached the cab and then the man behind the wheel turned his head, looking directly into the passenger compartment.

Two passengers, male and female, Chou thought after passing the cab. He pulled over to the curb and reached for a file folder sitting on the seat. There were two color photographs. The woman he had just observed was not a match to the female photo. But there was something about the man. He stared at the photo—it was a poor copy. *Maybe,* he thought. *I better check them again.* Harry looked up, scanning the rearview mirror. The yellow cab was now heading south down Main Street. It was two blocks away.

Harry checked for other traffic and then swung left, making a wide U-turn. Now on the same side of the street as the cab, he floored the throttle.

Tim stared through the rear window. *Trouble,* he thought as the Toyota turned around and began its tail. He reached down and unzipped the duffel bag.

Harry followed the cab as it turned onto Broadway and then onto Oak Street. He had already phoned in his observations. The airport surveillance teams had just been put on alert.

When the Toyota turned onto Oak, now about half a block behind the cab, Tim finally made up his mind. Without saying anything to Jenny, he leaned forward. "Driver," he said, "I need to make a quick phone call. Please find me a pay phone."

The bearded man nodded. About a minute later, the cab was parked in the parking lot of a shopping center located just off Oak. The phone booth was a few feet away from Tim's side of the car. Before exiting the cab, Tim whispered into Jenny's ear: "Just sit tight. I need to check something out."

Tim stood inside the booth, handset glued to his right ear. He appeared to be making a call. But it was a ruse. He ignored the dial tone. Instead, he focused on the target.

The Toyota was parked on a side street about a block away. There was one occupant.

All doubts were now gone. *Okay, now I know for sure,* Tim thought. He hung up the phone. A moment later he was leaning in the cab doorway, speaking to Jenny: "I'll be right back. I want to pick up some cigarettes." He then gestured to the twenty-four-hour convenience store located behind the cab. "You need anything?"

Jenny wanted to ask Tim what he was up to but refrained. Instead, she just said, "No, thanks, I'm fine."

"Good." Tim looked toward the driver. "This'll just take a couple of minutes. We've still got plenty of time to get to the airport, don't we?"

"Yes, sir. No problem." The cabby didn't mind the delay at all. The meter was still running.

Harry Chou watched the man as he disappeared inside the store. *What the heck is he doing?* he wondered.

Tim was now standing outside the rear entrance to the store. The door opened onto a service alley. There were dozens of cardboard boxes stacked next to an already overflowing Dumpster. He looked toward the left, where the alley connected with a side street. *Good,* he thought. He started running, his left knee protesting.

Tim had simply walked right through the store. There were just a few patrons inside so the cashier noticed him the moment he walked in. When he ignored the displays and walked into the back room at the far end of the store, she reacted.

By the time the woman reached the storage area, however, Tim had already exited through the rear doorway. When she opened the door and looked down the alley, she spotted him just as he sprinted onto the side street. *What a jerk,* she thought. She slammed the door shut and locked it.

Harry Chou inhaled deeply, drawing in another lungful of smoke. Like hundreds of millions of his fellow countrymen, he was hooked. Smoking was sanctioned in China. Despite his own intellect and the mountains of scientific evidence about the harmful effects of smoking, he was powerless to stop.

Harry exhaled, expelling a thick cloud through the open side window. He continued to watch the rear end of the cab, wondering what was going on. A minute earlier he had phoned in a status report, informing the controller of the temporary delay. He had been ordered to call back the instant the cab started up again.

Harry never saw it coming. It happened in an eye blink. There was a blinding flash of light and then darkness.

Tim pulled the butt end of the Glock through the open window. The blow was right on target. One moment the subject was alert and conscious, the next he was out cold.

Tim took a quick look around. The side street was still deserted. He opened the door and leaned in. He picked up the smoldering butt from the passenger seat and crushed it out in the dashboard ashtray. He then grabbed the unconscious man by the arms and began shoving him to the side.

Although Chou was slightly built, weighing only 145 pounds, Tim struggled to remove him from the bucket seat. It was like trying to push a sack full of Jell-O into a keyhole. Tim finally managed to relocate the unconscious man, dumping him into the adjacent passenger's seat. He then climbed in and started up the engine.

Two minutes later the Toyota was parked in the alleyway behind the convenience store. Tim emptied part of the Dumpster, making room for a new deposit. Just before shutting the lid, Tim leaned into the trash bin and checked his victim. He was still comatose. Tim hoped the man wasn't hurt too badly.

The controller was concerned. Chou hadn't reported in for over fifteen minutes. He dialed the man's cell phone number. It rang and rang. *Come on, Chou*, thought the man, *answer the damn thing!*

Jenny stared at the portable cell phone sitting on the Toy-ota's dashboard. The annoying electronic pulse continued to announce its presence, demanding to be answered. Jenny turned toward Tim. "What do you want to do with it?" she asked.

Tim didn't bother to face Jenny. Instead, he stared through the windshield. They were now in downtown Vancouver, just entering the financial district. The early morning traffic was picking up and he had to concentrate on driving. "Let it ring. When it stops, flip it open and then switch the damn thing off."

Half a minute later the cellular phone was silent. Jenny deactivated the device. She then turned toward Tim. "Maybe we should keep this thing. It might come in handy."

"No. I don't trust it. When that guy turns up missing they might try to trace it. Besides, I've still got my own phone." He gestured toward the backseat. "It's in my briefcase. We can use it if we get in a real jam but I'd just as soon not. You never know who might be listening in."

"Okay."

"What's in that notebook?" Tim asked.

"Oh, yeah, just a second." Jenny reopened the three-ring binder resting on her lap. She had discovered it in the backseat. She paged through the document for nearly a minute and then turned to face Tim. "These are some kind of research records, something to do with ocean wave forces . . . on a breakwater."

"A breakwater?"

"Yeah, looks like that guy might have been a grad student."

Good Lord, Tim thought, *could I have made a mistake?* "You think he really was a student?"

"Who knows? After all that's happened, I'm not surprised at anything anymore." She held up the binder. "This thing could also be part of an elaborate cover." She shook her head, annoyed. "Anyway, that guy was following us and now he isn't. That's all I know."

Tim just nodded.

Jenny slipped the binder onto the floor. After a long moment she again faced Tim. "What about that cabby? Think he'll do it?"

"Well, I hope so. I sure gave him enough of an incentive."

Tim had paid the cabdriver $500 U.S. to drive around north Richmond for twenty minutes as if he were continuing on to the airport. He was then supposed to report that he had dropped off his fare and was going off duty.

"He seemed honest," Jenny offered, hope in her voice.

"Yeah, I think he'll do us right—it should buy us some time."

Jenny again turned toward Tim. "So what are we going to do now?"

Tim shook his head. "I don't know. If I hadn't spotted the turkey driving this thing, we'd be up a creek by now."

"So going to the airport on our own is out?"

"Definitely. Too damn risky. The bastards are everywhere—they must be monitoring the cab dispatchers, so you can believe they'll be all over the airport." Tim faced Jenny—just a quick glance before turning back. "Even with your disguise, they might spot you, especially if the guy in this thing called in a report."

"Do you think he did?"

"Probably. Ten to one, he recognized me. And he may have seen enough of you to blow your new cover."

Jenny shook her head. The bad dream continued. "Are we going to drive out of here, then?"

"No way. It won't be long before they figure out their man is missing. You can be sure they know what this thing looks like, as well as its license number."

"Then we better hide it. That way maybe they'll think we drove out of the city."

"Exactly. As long as we stay one step ahead, we've still got a chance."

Jenny scanned the roadway. They were now surrounded by high-rise office buildings. "Maybe we can drive into one of the parking garages for these buildings," she suggested.

"Yeah, that's not a bad idea, but I've got a better place."

"Where?"

"Down by the harbor—Canada Place. It's close, just a few blocks away. There's a huge public parking area under it. Lots of tourists use it. I don't think they'll expect that."

"So what are we going to do when we dump the car off?"

"I'm not sure yet. I'll figure out something then."

"Okay."

19 THE BRIEFING

There were a dozen men and women sitting around the conference table. The meeting had been hastily arranged. The telephone call from the Vancouver director of Canada Customs to the U.S. border station at Blaine had set off a chain reaction south of the forty-ninth parallel. It all started when the general manager of the river marina called the local Customs officer to report an unauthorized Yankee boat moored in his facility.

The visitors had arrived with hardly any warning. Just twenty minutes earlier their helicopter landed at the Burrard Inlet heliport. There were three of them: two men and a woman. The female was in charge.

"I'm really sorry to barge in on you like this, but we really didn't have any choice." FBI Special Agent Victoria Kwan paused, scanning the assembly of Canadian police officials sitting on the opposite side of the table. There were five senior officers from the Vancouver Police Department, the assistant director of Canada Customs, and three members of the Royal Canadian Mounted Police.

Victoria continued: "We believe there's a good chance that Ms. Richmond and Mr. Carpenter are still in your city. It is vital that we find them. We think—"

"Agent Kwan," interrupted the only other woman in the group. She was one of the highest ranking officials in the Vancouver Police Department. She was also of Asian ancestry, but ten years senior to Kwan. "What makes you believe they're still here?"

"Well, thanks to your efficient Customs officer who found Carpenter's boat"—Victoria paused, turning momentarily to smile at the Canada Customs official—"we don't think they've left yet. They'll need new IDs for any foreign travel from here and that can take some time to arrange."

The female police officer nodded. "These two people that

you're after," she said, pausing to check her notes, "Richmond and Carpenter, besides being material witnesses in the slaying of your people, they're also in possession of classified documents. Are they wanted for espionage, too?"

Victoria shifted position in her chair. She had expected the question. It would be a very sensitive subject. "At this time, no. They have not been charged with espionage."

"Then on what legal authority are you pursuing them?"

"We only want them brought back for questioning about the shootings."

"Questioning?" The frown on the Vancouver policewoman's face telegraphed her confusion.

Victoria leaned forward, focusing on the policewoman. "Legally, we can't charge them with anything regarding the documents. What they probably have are privately owned but they're of such a sensitive nature that if they fall into the wrong hands, there will be severe consequences."

"What kind of consequences?" asked one of the Mounties.

Victoria turned toward the man. It was time to close the sale. "The information that Richmond and Carpenter possess has direct military application. All I can say at this point is that the technology concerns high-performance aircraft and if this material is transferred to nonfriendly parties, it will result in an enormous problem for our military forces." She paused for effect. "And your own military forces will be severely impacted as well."

Frowns and questioning looks broke out in the Canadian ranks. A few seconds later the Vancouver policewoman continued her questioning. "You indicated that this man and woman are being pursued by others. Just who is after them?"

"Just a sec," Victoria said. She turned to the agent sitting on her right side. "Sid, let me have the photos now."

The man reached into a nearby briefcase, removed a manila folder, and handed it to Agent Kwan. Victoria opened the folder and removed the first photo. It was an eight-by-ten color print of a corpse. She handed it to the policewoman.

"This is one of the men that attacked Richmond and Carpenter in Roche Harbor. As you can see, he is of Asian ancestry."

She removed another photo. It was a close-up of the man's upper torso, emphasizing the shoulders and upper back. The multicolored tattoos were striking. "We have identified the tattoos as of Chinese origin."

Victoria removed the next photo. It was a blowup of the dead man's exposed teeth. "Our forensic lab has identified the man's dental work as most likely originating from mainland China. We think he's probably from—"

"So this man is Chinese," the policewoman said, breaking off Victoria's narrative. "I'm sure that's obvious to all of us." She quickly surveyed the rest of her companions. They all nodded in agreement. She then turned back to face the FBI agent. "So what's the big deal?" The woman's tone was not friendly.

Victoria kept her cool. She could not afford to alienate any of the assembled. "Ma'am, we're convinced that this man"—she glanced down at the photos—"is an agent from the PRC's Ministry of State Security or possibly from one of its military intelligence units. And we have reason to believe he was operating from a cell located right here in Vancouver."

"Impossible," stated one of the Mounties. "We'd know about that."

Victoria expected the resistance. It was time to bring out the heavy artillery. She turned to the other FBI agent sitting on her left side. "Go ahead and show 'em, David."

The forty-five-year-old man reached into another briefcase and pulled out a half-inch-thick bound report. The words *Top Secret, Authorized Personnel Only* were stamped in bright red ink on the cover. The warning filled the entire front cover sheet of the document.

He placed the report on the tabletop, turning it around so the others could clearly read the warning. "Ah, folks, this document was prepared by the CIA and your Canadian Security Intelligence Service." He flipped the cover page over. The report title stunned the Canadians: "PRC Covert Operations in Western Canada."

The agent began his narrative: "For the past couple of years, the CIA and the CSIS have been jointly monitoring the spying activity of the Chinese in western Canada, particularly the Vancouver region. We have confirmed that there are over a hundred operatives currently . . ."

The briefing took half an hour to complete. The Canadian police officials were in denial. Most were generally aware that Chinese agents occasionally operated out of Vancouver. But not one of them had an idea of the extent of the activity. It was almost endemic. MSS operatives were everywhere.

The senior Mountie now took charge. "Agent Kwan, the contents of this document are damning, to say the least. Do you really expect us to take the word of *your* CIA after what happened at *your* Los Alamos lab?"

Although the RCMP was Canada's national police force, the Vancouver regional office had been left out of the loop regarding the joint CIA/CSIS study. The senior Mountie was more than perturbed, suspecting that the CIA had bullied its Canadian equivalent into keeping the local RCMP ranks in the dark. This was particularly annoying because until 1984—when the CSIS had been created—national intelligence for Canada had been the RCMP's turf. The Mounties were stripped of their spy-busting activities after it was revealed that the RCMP had been involved in numerous black bag jobs—mail tampering, illegal wiretaps, and break-ins.

Victoria anticipated the Mountie's resistance. "No, sir, of course not. But we don't have time to go through normal channels. That's why I was given authorization to show you this document rather than having to wait for the CSIS to formally distribute it." She paused, glancing at her wristwatch. It was half past noon. "In fact, right about now our ambassador should be meeting with your prime minister in Ottawa. We're also making a formal request for your help and we're hoping that you'll receive official sanction early this afternoon."

"They're meeting now?" the man said, clearly astonished.

"Yes, we haven't got a moment to waste. Now, if you'll allow me, I'd like to explain our plan. That way, when we get final approval, we'll be able jump right on it."

The RCMP officer looked toward the senior Vancouver

police officer. She nodded. He turned back to Agent Kwan. "Well, okay, go ahead."

"Good, now, we think you should . . ."

The parking garage was enormous. It extended over a thou-sand feet into the bay. The stolen Toyota was parked on the lowest level, almost at the very end of the structure. Tim Carpenter sat in the front seat. A nearly spent cigarette hung from the edge of his lower lip.

Tim had done his best to disguise the car. Earlier he exchanged license plates with another car parked dozens of spaces away. The Buick was covered with a thick coating of dust, like it had been parked in the garage for some time. Tim was counting on the owner not showing up for the next few hours.

The Toyota was parked so that it faced the driveway, providing Tim with a commanding view down the long aisle. Any vehicle or person heading toward the end of the pier would be easy to track. So far, the passing traffic had been light.

Tim took one last drag from the butt and then dropped it out the open window. It landed on the concrete deck, adding to the other half-dozen remnants he had already discarded. He glanced at his watch. It was half past one. Tim next looked down the long row of cars. They seemed to stretch into infinity. *Where the hell is she?* he thought.

"I'm sorry, ma'am, but I think it's all booked up. Those spaces usually go months in advance." The middle-aged man looked away from his computer terminal, scanning the client. He liked what he saw.

"Well, could you check anyway?" the young woman said. "Maybe someone's canceled."

"Of course. But I'll have to call the company headquarters direct. There's no way I can tell from the computer this late."

"Fine."

Jennifer Richmond settled back into the chair. This was the fourth travel agency she had visited so far. She was beginning to think it was nothing but a waste of time. *At leas this place is willing to check,* she thought. The other firms would only consult their computer terminals; they all said it was hopeless.

Jenny listened to the man as he made his telephone inquiries. He wore a headset and used a computer keypad to dial the call. She didn't need to hear the other half of the conversation to learn the answer.

The agent looked up from his keyboard. "I'm sorry, miss, but they don't show anything. If you could just wait a few more days, I'm sure something will turn up. We have several other lines operating from here."

Jenny shook her head as she started to stand up. "Well, I appreciate your help anyway. I only had enough time to make the trip if something was available today. I'll just try next season."

The agent was about to kiss off his commission when a new thought suddenly occurred to him. "I have another idea. If you can wait just a few more minutes, I'd like to check it out."

Jenny glanced at the wall clock. She had been gone longer than she expected. *Tim's probably climbing the walls by now.*

"Okay, sure I'll wait."

Tim Carpenter was puffing away on his last Marlboro. He was more than worried now. *Something must have happened. Dammit! I shouldn't have let her go alone.*

He had just about convinced himself to leave his cover and start looking when he spotted her. Jenny was about fifty yards away, walking down the center of the aisle. She reached the Toyota a minute later.

Tim's greeting was a mixture of aggravation and joy: "Geez, I was getting a little concerned—you were gone for so long."

Jenny smiled as she slipped into the front passenger seat. She automatically looked back down the length of the garage. No one was following. She then turned to face Tim. "Sorry, but it took forever. I had to try four places."

"And?"

"We lucked out. There was one spot left—they normally

don't use it anymore because of the complaints, but I took it anyway."

"Complaints?"

"Yeah, it can get pretty noisy there."

"Why's that?"

"The agent said something about vibrations making it hard to sleep."

"But you got it?"

"Yep. It's tiny—has bunk beds instead of regular ones. But it does have a window."

"Perfect. When's it leave?"

"At five P.M., but boarding starts at three."

Tim nodded his head in approval.

Allen Peng and Gérard Rémy were in the grand salon of the *Orca.* Neither man was in a good mood. The search for the Americans was floundering.

"So where is this jackass?" asked Rémy. He was sitting in a chair facing one of Peng's MSS agents. The thirty-four-year-old man was in charge of the Vancouver search teams.

"We don't know. He called in early this morning to report that he was following a cab to the airport, as he had been ordered. He said he was too far away to positively identify the passengers, but he did indicate that the man could possibly be Carpenter. After that we never heard back from him."

"What about the cab?" asked Peng. He was sitting next to the agent. "What happened when it reached the airport?"

"It never arrived, sir. At least we never saw it."

"Dammit," Rémy said as he stood up. *What idiots!* he thought. *How could they let them slip away?* His heart rate accelerated as he began pacing across the carpet. A moment later he looked back at the Chinese agent. "What did the cab driver have to say? Did he ID them?"

"We're still working on that, Mr. Rémy. When he returned to the dispatch center, he went off duty, complaining about a stomachache. We've got people staking out his apartment, but he hasn't shown up yet."

Rémy shook his head, now turning his attention to Peng.

"Until we can get positive confirmation to the contrary, we must assume that it was Carpenter and the Richmond woman and that they somehow compromised your man. Do you agree?"

"Yes. Everything seems to point to that." Peng paused as he lit up a cigarette. Unlike the French secret service officer, Peng was quite calm and collected. After inhaling a lungful, he continued. "This Carpenter character is extremely cunning. If it was him in the cab and he discovered our tail, then he could have easily arranged to take the man out. The observer was just a college student."

"You should have used someone trained for the mission. A student! That's fucking crazy!"

Peng was tiring of Rémy's intolerance. He'd never cared for the Frenchman. There was something about him, deep down, hidden, that went against Peng's grain. Nevertheless, he kept his emotions in check. His response was controlled: "Come on, Gérard, you know there wasn't time. We had to mobilize everyone we've got. If it turns out that it was Carpenter, then it was just bad luck. We couldn't have done anything different."

Rémy continued pacing. He wasn't interested in excuses. "Okay, whatever. Now, we must further assume that Carpenter spotted your man and took him out—how he did that is no longer a concern." Rémy paused, thinking out his next statement. "Now, since your man's vehicle hasn't been spotted that probably means one of two things: Either Carpenter and the woman took off in it and are heading south or east, trying to get away as fast as they can. Or they've dumped the car and are still hiding out in Vancouver."

Peng responded: "I don't think they'd risk using the car for very long. Carpenter's got to know the driver would be missed and that we'd start looking for him and his vehicle." He hesitated for a moment. "Besides, we're monitoring every border crossing along the B.C.-Washington boundary. He'd figure that out, too."

Rémy nodded. "Yes, you're probably right." He paused to sit down. His blood pressure was returning to normal. He turned to face the other MSS agent, the man in charge of the search. "So I guess that leaves my second scenario. There's an excellent chance that they're still someplace in the Vancouver area."

"Yes, sir. We're inclined to agree. Our search efforts have continued. In addition to the Americans, our people have been instructed to look for Chou and his Toyota."

"Good. If you find him or the car, that should help us track down Carpenter and the woman."

"We have every operative looking right now. It should be just a matter of time and then something will turn up."

"Well, keep the pressure on. We don't have much time left."

"I know."

20 NORTHBOUND

"Where are you, Tim?"

"I don't want to say. It's too risky. I don't trust these phones."

"Well, what's been going on? Is Jenny all right?"

"Yeah, she's fine. I just wanted to check up on you. Tony treating you okay?"

"Oh, yes. He's a perfect gentleman, and so are the men that work for him." Laura Lorence paused. She was about to begin her own interrogation when Tim cut her off.

"Mom and the boys okay?" he asked.

"They're fine. Would you like to speak with them? They're asleep but I can go—"

"No. That's all right. I don't have the time and it's too late to wake them. I just wanted to make sure that you're all okay."

"We're all perfectly safe here." Laura hesitated for a moment. "But what about you, Tim? Are those people still after you and Jenny?"

"We've given them the slip and plan to lie low for a few more days. I need time to let things simmer down."

"What about Ricky? Can't he help you?"

Tim Carpenter laughed. "Eventually, maybe. But not now. The feds have got a giant security leak. Until it gets plugged I don't dare deal with any of them."

"But what are you going to do? You can't keep running forever."

"I know. This whole thing's turned into a bad dream. Maybe in a week or so we can—"

BLAHHHHHHHH!

Tim's words were drowned out by the deafening roar. It filled the hallway where he was standing. It was as loud as a cannon blast.

"What the heck was that?" Laura asked.

Geez, I've got to get going, thought Tim as he turned, looking through the wall-to-ceiling windows. His ears were ringing. "I'm sorry, honey, but I've got to go right now. I'll call you in a few days. Give everyone a hug for me."

"But Tim . . ."

"Don't worry—everything's going to be fine. We're just going to hide out for a few days and then we'll figure out a way to join you."

"Now wait a minute. I want to know when—"

"Love you, sweetie. Gotta go." He hung up the phone. And then, with the carrying strap of the duffel bag draped over his right shoulder and his attaché case in his left hand, Tim began fast-walking down the hallway, his injured knee preventing him from running. The hall appeared endless.

"Good afternoon, sir. Are you traveling with us today?"

"Yeah," Tim Carpenter said as he approached the young woman. He was no longer winded but his knee hurt like the devil. He hadn't needed to hurry. About two dozen other latecomers were still lined up behind him.

The metal detector he had just passed through was not top of the line, and there were no security guards—just a couple of boarding agents. He'd verified the poor security measures earlier. It made his task much simpler.

The twenty-something agent standing nearest to the gate wore a uniform-type dress—blue blazer with a white knee-length skirt. A silver logo in the shape of a water wave was pinned to the lapel of her jacket.

"May I see your boarding pass?"

"Sure, just a sec." Tim reached into his pants rear pocket and removed a folded-up slip of paper. "I think this is it," he said as he handed it over.

She nodded and then began to examine the document, checking it against a computer printout attached to the clipboard that she carried.

"Oh, I see that your wife has already boarded."

"Yeah, that's right."

"Well, welcome, Mr. Carter. Just head down the hall and then onto the gangplank. We'll be getting under way in about fifteen minutes."

"Thanks."

Tim had limped about a dozen paces when another young uniformed woman approached him. She flashed a toothy grin and then handed him a plastic-wrapped basket full of fruits and assorted confections. Dozens more were stacked on a folding table behind her. "Compliments of the Emerald Line, sir," she explained.

Tim had barely managed to express his thanks when a cockney-accented voice belted out: "Smile there, mate!" And then a brilliant flash exploded in his face.

Tim automatically turned away, furiously blinking his eyes. When he looked back, he spotted the photographer. Already the man was lining up on the couple that had followed Tim.

The woman with fruit baskets read Carpenter's confusion. "We give everyone a complimentary boarding photo, too. They'll be ready tomorrow afternoon."

"Oh, okay," Tim said, still slightly stunned. He then moved forward, stepping onto the steel gangway. He hardly noticed the towering white hull that stretched for what appeared to be miles along the face of the wharf.

The *Emerald Sea* was 712 feet long. About average size for a cruise ship.

* * *

"I was wondering when you'd finally show up," Jenny said as Tim walked into the cabin.

"Yeah. I was talking to Laura."

"Everything okay?"

"Yep. They're all fine."

"Good."

Tim dropped his duffel bag on the deck and then began to survey the compartment. It was tiny, but nicely appointed. The oak-lined bunk beds were anchored to the far wall against the ship's steel hull. A small vanity with a full mirror was located at the aft end of the bunk beds next to the porthole. There was one chair near the lower berth with a reading light. An oak-lined closet divided the living space from the bathroom. And near the aft end of the closet was a built-in television set.

"Hey," Tim said, "this isn't so bad."

"Yeah, I kind of like it. It's small but quite functional."

Tim turned and took a step into the bathroom. There was the standard sink, mirror, and toilet. There was even a bathtub, but it was only about two-thirds the length of a normal one. It would be a tight fit for him.

Tim next walked to the vanity and looked out the porthole. The ship was slowly moving northward as it backed out of its berth. He could see Coal Harbour in the distance. There was a slight vibration in the deck. He turned back to face Jenny. She was now sitting on the lower berth.

"It's moving," he said.

Jenny glanced at her watch. It read 5:04 P.M. "Not bad. Almost on schedule."

Tim nodded. "Beds any good?" he asked.

"Okay, but the pillows are a little hard for me."

Tim started to check out the upper berth when he heard a knocking from the cabin door. He froze in place. He whispered to Jenny. "You expecting anyone?"

She shook her head.

Tim turned. "Who's there?" he asked, raising his voice.

"Ah, sir, I'm your host. May I come in, please?" The female voice had a heavy Eastern European accent.

Tim raised his eyebrows. "Host?" he whispered.

Jenny raised her hands, signaling her own confusion.

"Just a minute."

Tim removed the Glock from the small of his back, slipping it into his coat pocket. With his hidden right hand still gripping the pistol, he flipped the lock on the door with his other hand. He backed up and then said, "Come in."

She was in her midthirties. Short brownish-blond hair. Five-foot-six and a little on the thin side. She had an attractive face, but her front teeth were horribly crooked. Her uniform was white and blue—the cruise line's official colors—and there was a name tag above her right breast: Zena. She was holding a medium-sized box decorated with colorful wrapping paper and ribbons.

"I'm sorry to intrude on you, sir, but I wanted to introduce myself. I'm Zena. I will be your host for the cruise." She hesitated and then looked down at the package. "And this is for you."

"What is it?" Tim asked, playing dumb. By now he had removed his hand from the pistol.

"It was delivered to the purser's office this afternoon—from a well-wisher, I believe."

Tim accepted the box, opening the card taped to the outside. He then turned to face Jenny. "It's from Bob and Judy Marshall—a bon voyage gift."

"How thoughtful of them."

"Right." Tim turned back to face Zena. "Thanks for bringing this."

"Happy to, and if there's anything I can do for you, please don't hesitate to contact me."

Tim smiled. Already he liked her. "Okay, but I think we're doing fine for now." Tim turned to face Jenny. "Honey, you need anything?" he asked.

Jenny moved a few steps, coming into view. "Well, now that you mention it, I could use another pillow." She moved toward the lower berth, removing the single pillow. "This one's hard as a rock. Do you have anything softer?"

"Oh, yes, ma'am. I'll arrange for a replacement one. Anything else?"

Jenny shook her head.

Zena faced Tim. "And you, sir?"

"Well, you could just answer one question for me."

"Certainly."

"Your accent, is it German?"

Zena smiled. "I'm Polish, sir. I'm from Warsaw."

"Ah, well, I wasn't too far off. I used to live in Germany."

Zena smiled again but didn't reply.

Jenny spoke next: "Do you live on this ship full-time?"

"Most of the time. But I will be taking a month off at the end of the year to return home."

"To visit with your family?"

"Yes, my son and daughter live with my parents. I always spend Christmas with them."

Jenny was aghast. "It must be hard, being away from your kids like that."

Zena shrugged. "We're a poor family and things are still hard in Poland. This job helps a lot."

Jenny beamed, now understanding the woman's sacrifice. "Well, thank you for stopping by."

"Yeah, thanks," Tim echoed.

"You are welcome. Enjoy the cruise."

After Zena left, Tim turned to Jenny. "Nice gal."

"Yeah. We should tip her well when we leave."

"Right."

Tim returned to the porthole. The ship was now turned around and was slowly heading toward the center of Burrard Inlet. "Why don't we go up on deck? We can see the sights."

"Sure, but in a minute." Jenny stood up and walked into the bathroom, locking the door.

Tim sat down at the tiny table and started thumbing through the cruise ship directory, not looking for anything in particular. A moment later, when he finally looked up, he spotted the duffel bag—and the gift box. *Oh, shit, what am I going to do with those?*

The sausage-shaped canvas bag that he had carried aboard was packed with Dr. Richmond's research documents, including the thermoslike cylinder containing the MERLIN circuit board. Either Jenny or he would have to keep the bag in sight at all times, no matter where they were.

But that wasn't the only problem. It was the gift box. Tim had packed it; Jenny wrapped it. The top half contained what you might expect: a bottle of wine, a brick of cheese, boxes of crackers, several cans of smoked salmon, and some fine chocolates. Underneath the foam divider, however, were the real goodies. The MP5 was broken down into its principal components—suppressor, pistol grip housing with the stock folded over, and three thirty-round mags. Also included were two spare magazines for Tim's Glock.

He'd carried the Glock aboard—unloaded—in the small of his back. He'd known its plastic housing would not trigger the metal detector alarm. Nor would the half-loaded magazine buried deep inside the duffel bag. He'd learned how to defeat metal detectors and X-ray machines while in the Army.

Smuggling the MP5 aboard was even simpler. Tim had slipped the deckhand he'd recruited on the wharf $50 U.S. to deliver the gift box to the purser's office. "A special bon voyage treat for a passenger," he had explained. It was that easy.

The gift box was now open and the MP5 reassembled.

What the hell should I do with this? he thought. Tim scanned the cabin, looking for a hiding spot. He finally shook his head. He didn't dare leave this thing here. He had to find someplace else where he could safely stash it. But someplace easy to get to. But where?

Ten minutes later, Tim and Jenny were on the main deck, leaning against a polished oak guardrail. Like most of the other nine hundred passengers, they were taking in the sights of picturesque Vancouver Harbor as the ship headed toward the Lions Gate Bridge. No one paid the slightest attention to the couple.

The carrying straps from the nylon duffel bag were draped over Tim's right shoulder as he stood next to Jenny. He rested his arm on the top of the bag. Despite the internal padding, he could feel the barrel of the SMG. He was still trying to figure out where he could hide it.

* * *

Raul knocked on the door three times before using his key. He walked into the cabin, carrying a down-filled pillow. After placing it on the lower berth he started to head for the door. He stopped when he noticed the half-open closet door. He could see the expensive leather-lined attaché case.

The nineteen-year-old removed the case and placed it on the lower bunk. He then stole a quick glance at the door. *Plenty of time!* Back in Caracas, he had learned his trade well. Despite the combination lock on each latch, he opened the briefcase in seconds. He was after cash, credit cards, traveler's checks. But he drew a blank. Tim Carpenter carried those items with him at all times.

It wasn't a complete bust, though. Hidden at the bottom of the case, under a stack of cruise-related documents and a thick airline schedule booklet, he found treasure.

Raul pushed the power key. The display screen lit up. *Good, it works. I'll just borrow this for a while,* he thought as he slipped Tim Carpenter's new portable phone into his coat pocket.

The lines seemed to stretch for miles, but Tim and Jenny didn't mind. There was no rush. They would wait. It had been a long time since either felt secure enough to relax. And the bar was just the right place to wait.

It was dinnertime aboard the *Emerald Sea*. Most of the passengers were already queued up at the ship's stern, waiting like cattle to pass through the dual buffet lines. It was the ship's first night at sea and, by custom, the meal arrangements were informal. On the following night, however, the twin four-star dining rooms, each with its full complement of maitre d's, tuxedoed waiters, and uniformed busboys, would be ready to pamper its guests. Reservations required. But tonight it was first come, first served.

Tim took another sip of his whiskey. The Crown Royal was silky smooth—it helped dull the fire in his knee. "How's your wine?" he asked.

Jenny nodded. "Good. It sure hits the spot."

Tim and Jenny were sitting in a corner by themselves. There were a few other patrons inside the Cascade Lounge.

Within an hour or so, however, that would all change.

Tim looked out one of the nearby windows—the kind made for viewing, not a tiny porthole. The sun was sinking behind the mountaintops of nearby Vancouver Island. "Sure is beautiful."

"Yes, it is," Jenny said as she stared at the distant view. "Dad and I made a few trips up north in our sailboat. We always liked it up here."

At the mention of her father, Jenny was flooded with memories. Dr. Jeff Richmond's death was always there, an undertone of grief. And then there was the attack on the FBI safe house. *All of those men killed. And poor Audrey, so badly shot up.* More blood and gore at Roche Harbor. The escape in the speedboat. Hiding out in Vancouver. And finally, there was Chris. *Whatever happened to sweet Chris?* she wondered. Jenny desperately missed her fiancé.

Tim took another sip while glancing at Jenny's pretty face. She was on another planet. *Poor kid,* he thought, *she's been through hell.*

"It's definitely being used, sir. We've picked up two transmissions already."

"You're positive?" asked Major Wu.

"Absolutely. We've been monitoring Carpenter's cell phone ID code by computer since yesterday and it started up about fifteen minutes ago. It's somewhere in the local net."

Major Wu and the PLA electronic surveillance technician were in the penthouse suite of one of Vancouver's tallest skyscrapers. An assortment of high-tech antennae had been installed on the roof of the spire the previous day. The monitoring equipment inside the office was state of the art. Much of it was based upon American military technology.

After a PRC jet fighter collided with a U.S. Navy electronic surveillance aircraft in international air space over the South China Sea, the spy plane made an emergency landing onto China's Hainan Island. The EP-3E's crew managed to destroy most of the data and disable the key hardware before the plane was boarded by the Chinese military. Nevertheless, PLA engineers and technicians had unrestricted access to

America's most secret electronic communications eavesdropping gear for weeks. Skilled at reverse engineering, the top secret equipment proved to be a treasure trove for China's SIGINT experts.

"Can you trace it?" asked Wu.

"We're working on it. If it stays on long enough, we might be able to triangulate the position."

"Excellent, keep on it."

"Yes, sir."

   The deck was located at the very stern of the ship, just aft and one deck below the swimming pool level. It was reserved for the crew. And about twenty off-duty personnel were lined up.

Raul was positioned at the head of the line, right next to the ship's railing. He charged five bucks U.S. for ten minutes of air time. It was a bargain. Nearly every one of the assembled crew lived half a world away. Already calls had been placed to Cairo, Istanbul, and Nairobi.

Raul had never used a phone like the one he had "borrowed" from the Americans' cabin. It was both a cellular phone and a satellite phone, all in one unit. He had set it to automatic mode and extended both antennas. The thick tubular sat antenna, angling off the side of the plastic case, dwarfed the wire-thin cellular antenna.

The global telephone worked just fine, each international call going through without a hitch. Currently, the phone was working on its digital cellular mode. The Vancouver region had broad cell coverage that extended far up the Strait of Georgia.

The battery readout indicated that the unit was fully charged. Raul figured he probably had a couple of hours' worth of air time before it petered out. He'd make at least fifty bucks.

And later that evening, when the guests were out of their cabin, he'd replace the phone. When the Americans eventually checked it, they'd wonder about the low battery light. But they wouldn't discover Raul's thievery until they returned home and received next month's billing in the mail.

The alarm on Raul's wristwatch began beeping. He looked at the thirty-two-year-old woman standing next to him. She was one of the hundred-plus maids aboard the ship. She was from the former East Germany.

"One minute to go," Raul said, raising a finger.

She nodded while continuing to jabber away in her native tongue.

"This is really weird, sir," the PLA electronic intelligence technician said, addressing Major Wu.

"What?"

The calls, sir. We've identified five so far. They're all over the place: Europe, Africa, even one to Bombay, India."

"India?"

"Yes, sir." The tech hesitated. "Why would he be making calls like that?"

"I have no idea." Major Wu moved closer to the technician, now standing next to the seated man. "What about the location? Has the computer got a fix yet?"

"Just about, sir. It's running another confirming plot. We should have some rough coordinates in a minute or so."

"Why's it taking so long? Is there a problem with your equipment?"

"No, not at all. These cellular systems are quite simple to penetrate with our monitoring equipment, especially when we know the transmitter's ID code. However, the transmission point appears to be constantly moving. That's what makes it difficult to pinpoint."

"Moving?"

"Yes, it's probably in a car."

Major Wu nodded.

It took another three minutes before the computer screen finally displayed a set of earth coordinates. Wu scanned the longitude and latitude readings. It meant nothing to him. "Where is this?" he asked.

"Just a moment, sir." The technician pushed away from the computer terminal. Half a minute later he had unfolded a large map of British Columbia onto a nearby table. He was now leaning over the map, using a plastic scale to plot the coordinates.

He used a pencil to make an *X* on the paper surface. He then looked up at his superior. "It graphs out right about here, sir."

Major Wu scanned the map. "But that's in the middle of the Georgia Strait," he commented.

"Yes, sir. And I expect that when we take another fix, we'll find that it's moved."

"So they're on a boat."

"It would certainly appear that way, sir."

Wu smiled. Finally, they had something. "Excellent. Keep monitoring the position."

"Yes, sir."

21 JUST DESERTS

MAGNUM was careful with her phone calls. Never the same place twice. And never near Langley. This evening was no exception.

After work, Marsha Lewis crossed over the Potomac and drove into the District of Columbia. She found the shopping mall near the west end of the capital. She had never visited this area of the city before, but that didn't matter. The row of public telephones mounted outside the main store was her target.

It was a few minutes after eight o'clock when she pulled into the half-empty parking lot. She managed to find a stall only a few rows away from the phones.

She walked up to one of the phone stations near the middle of the group. She picked up the receiver. No dial tone. She tried the next one. No handset. Finally, the fifth phone, the one nearest to the doorway, worked.

Marsha reached under her coat, removed a rubber-cupped device, and slipped it over the handset. The acoustic coupler was wired to an Apple. The laptop was in a leather bag, suspended by a carrying strap draped over her right shoulder. Marsha's knee-length coat concealed the portable computer.

She dialed. It was a local call.

Marsha waited for the high-pitched tone to signal that the receiving computer was ready. It took a couple of seconds for the two computers to exchange handshakes and then MAGNUM was logged on. A moment later, Marsha pulled up the keypad and hit the "command enter" key. The 235-character message, already addressed and stored in the Apple's memory, was automatically transmitted into the public telephone system. A fraction of a second later it was parked in an anonymous account in an Alexandria, Virginia, Internet service provider.

Within the next few minutes, when space on its European line opened up, the local server would deliver the email message to a certain address in Bonn.

The whole process took about a minute. That was it. No personal contact whatsoever. No need for drop-offs and pick-ups, signal markers, and all of the other espionage trade craft. Just a quick phone call and then a push of a button or two.

Marsha was so good at the process that, unless you were standing right next to her, you'd never know what she was doing. It looked like she was making a normal phone call—nothing more.

MAGNUM disconnected the computer hardware and started back toward her car. It was only then that she noticed the two men. They were behind her, about a dozen paces away.

They really weren't men quite yet—teenagers was more accurate, both around sixteen. But they both looked awfully big to her.

Marsha didn't hesitate. She reached the Acura and within seconds slipped inside, instantly locking her door and automatically buckling her seat belt. She had just started the engine when one of the boys climbed onto the rear fender. He then began jumping up and down, violently rocking the car.

Marsha turned toward her right, looking back over her shoulder, trying to figure out what was happening. The distraction always worked. The other one stood just behind the driver's door. The window shattered into hundreds of tiny fragments when his lead-filled pipe smashed into it.

The exploding glass was like a rifle shot. It so startled Marsha that her heart skipped a beat. A moment later the door was wide open and one of them was yanking on her arm, trying to pull her out of the car. But she couldn't move. Her seat belt locked her in place. And then the second one joined in, also trying to yank her from the car. The strain on her arm was unbearable as the tug-of-war continued.

"Get outta the fuckin' car, bitch!" ordered one of the attackers.

Marsha screamed. But no one came to her rescue. About a dozen other mall patrons, either entering or leaving the main store, watched the assault from the entryway. They all stood like granite statues, fixed in place as the real-time horror continued.

Marsha fought with all her strength, which was considerable. She actually managed to push one of the assailants to the ground and was now trying to throw the transmission into gear. She would run them over if necessary, anything to escape.

"Do her, man, do her now," shouted the one on the asphalt.

Another second or two and she would have made it.

Marsha never saw the gun. The one who had jumped on the fender had it. He shoved the Saturday night special against her left side and pulled the trigger. The .32-caliber slug ripped through a lung before shattering her heart.

The instant she stopped struggling, the gunman reached inside and released the lap belt. MAGNUM flowed out of the doorway and spilled onto the asphalt.

The thugs never bothered to take her handbag. Nor did they discover the $2,500 computer under her coat. All they wanted was her car.

"How's it going up there?"

"Slow. They're having a hard time with the CIA report. I think it really shocked 'em."

"Well, I'm not surprised," replied Ricardo Molina. He was

in his Seattle office, leaning back in his chair with his shoes
resting on the desktop. He held a fat cigar in one hand, occasionally raising it for a puff, while holding the phone handset in his other hand. "Hell, I'm having a tough time with
what the Chinese are doing down here—it's hard for me to
believe, too. We were supposed to have a handle on all of
this—after the Los Alamos fiasco."

"I know. Anyway, I think they'll come around," Victoria
Kwan said, "but it's going to take some time." She was in
her hotel room, high up in a downtown Vancouver tower.
She had just taken a shower and sat on the edge of the bed,
her delicate body encased by a towel. "Rick," she continued,
"anything new from that house in Edmonds?"

"Not yet. We lifted a ton of prints and our people will be
running them through NCIC computers tonight. We might
know something in the morning."

"How about LorTech? Were they any help?"

"No. Nothing. Silverman still claims he doesn't know
where Laura Lorence is and he hasn't heard a word from
Carpenter or Richmond."

Victoria let out an audible sigh. "Well, I'm beginning to
think we're on a wild-goose chase."

"What do you mean?"

"What if they never made it to Vancouver—or if they did,
what if they've already left? Took off for Europe or Asia.
You can fly just about anywhere from here. How are we
going to know?"

"We won't know for sure—until they turn up. But what
alternative do we have? If we don't keep the pressure on,
then the People's Republic is going to get the MERLIN device and/or Jennifer Richmond and Tim Carpenter are going
to end up dead. I don't see it any other way—unless we
continue to intervene, and unless we get some help from the
Canadians."

Victoria hesitated before replying. *He's right. The Chinese
will not stop—we've got to keep going.*

Despite her Asian heritage, she felt nothing for the Chinese
Communist cause, not one iota. She was as American as
apple pie. "You know, Rick," she finally offered, "I think

that if I could just talk with Jennifer for a few minutes I could convince her to come in. We seemed to get along pretty well in the past."

"Well, I don't know about that anymore. We really blew it bad on the Cascade compound. She was supposed to be safe up there and somehow the bastards tracked her down. I'll be amazed if she'll ever voluntarily talk with us again."

Mention of the attack on the FBI's Cascade Mountains safe house jogged Victoria's memory. "Oh, geez, Rick," she blurted out, "I completely forgot. How's Audrey doing?"

"Okay. I called her late this afternoon. She's still drugged up pretty good, but sounded a lot better than when I last visited her." He paused to take another puff from his cigar. "She still doesn't remember much about that night."

"Well, that's not surprising."

Ricardo sat up, planting his shoes back on the rug. It was time to get back to business. "So what are our friends from the north doing, anyway?"

"Despite their skepticism regarding the CIA/CSIS report, the RCMP did acknowledge that they suspected the MSS might be operating in Vancouver. The local police also acknowledged problems with Asian gangs and reluctantly agreed that some of that could be subversive activity related to ongoing Chinese intelligence operations."

"Yeah, okay. That all makes sense, but what are they doing about helping us find Carpenter and Richmond?"

"So far they've agreed to circulate their photos and ID data to all local police jurisdictions as well as all international border crossings. They won't issue arrest warrants. Instead, they're listing Carpenter and Richmond as wanted for questioning only."

"Well, that's a start."

"Yes, and they also agreed to post observers at Vancouver International, the train station, and the bus terminal."

"Good. What about the local MSS operatives? If they could just haul in a few of those cell leaders, we might get some help."

"Ah, that's the problem area. They're not going to touch that without specific instructions from Ottawa. And as of seven-thirty this evening, when I finally left, the local RCMP official still hadn't heard anything from the prime minister's office." She paused to catch her breath. "It's just too political for the locals to act without federal intervention."

"Son of a bitch," Molina said, his blood pressure building, "those Mounties know the bastards are spies. They should be thrown in the clink instantly."

"It's not that simple, Rick. First, Vancouver has a huge Chinese population. Second, the people in question—the key ones identified in the report—are for the most part well integrated into the local scene. Almost all of them have been here for ten years or more. Most are Canadian citizens by now. And they have their families here." Victoria paused, collecting her thoughts. "Just think what a political mess it would be if the RCMP suddenly rounded up a dozen prominent Asians—businessmen, doctors, lawyers, engineers— and accused them of spying for the People's Republic of China. There would be an avalanche of protests—everything from racism to envy would be brought out. And then, wait and see what would happen when the press finally figured out it was the U.S. that prompted Canada to prosecute the spies because our own CIA was covertly operating in British Columbia."

Ricardo Molina rolled his eyes back. He had heard enough. "I see what you're getting at—it'd turn into a shitstorm for sure."

Victoria wouldn't have used such a descriptive term. Nevertheless, she agreed.

Ricardo stood up, the phone still glued to his right ear. "Well, I guess I should be thankful for what they're doing now. Thanks for the report."

"Of course. Anything else?"

"No. Not now. Try to get some rest and we'll talk in the morning."

"Okay."

"That's got to be it!" the man announced in his native Mandarin.

"Yes, there's nothing else around for miles."

"Can you make out its name?"

"No, not yet."

"Okay, I'll take us down for a closer look."

The pilot banked right and dove the twin-engine plane. Within a minute it was racing just a hundred feet over the water surface. The stern of the huge vessel loomed in the distance.

"Got it," called out the passenger as he lowered his binoculars. "It's the *Emerald Sea*, out of Nassau."

"Good," the pilot said as he pulled back on the wheel, easing the propeller-driven craft into a climb.

The Bonanza was now approaching Vancouver. The passenger was speaking: "What do you think is so important about that ship, anyway?"

The pilot shook his head. "I have no idea. All I do know is that Peng and that French prick are pissed about something."

"Something to do with that ship?"

"Maybe, but I don't think Wu has told them about it—that's why we were sent out there first—to find what it is."

The passenger remained silent for a while, lost in thought. And then he put it all together. "You know, it must be about those two Americans."

"Americans? What do you mean?"

"They must have somehow managed to get on that ship!"

The pilot turned to face the passenger. His face broadcast the astonishment he felt. "You're right. Wu must think they're on the ship . . . otherwise why would he send us out here?"

The passenger smiled. "No wonder we couldn't find them—no one ever thought of that."

"They were right under our noses all along. Very clever."

"I'll say. Damn clever."

The Golden Grotto was packed. At least three hundred were in attendance, a third of the *Emerald Sea*'s fare-paying passengers. It was a few minutes before eleven P.M. and the second show of the evening was well under way.

The lounge reeked of cigarette smoke, perfume, and liquor. But no one seemed to mind. The steady stream of performers worked the crowd with the kind of expertise that only comes from repetition. None were of real star quality but, nevertheless, they were entertaining.

Tim Carpenter and Jennifer Richmond sat in one of the far corners, taking in the spectacle. The duffel bag with the MERLIN documents rested by Tim's feet. The bag was considerably lighter. About an hour earlier he had found a suitable place to hide the submachine gun.

Tim was working his second bourbon on the rocks while Jenny nursed a Coke. The emcee had just called for a ten-minute intermission—enough time to refill drinks, hit the head, and give his performers a breather.

"You want another Coke?" Tim asked.

"No, thanks. I'm fine." Jenny paused for a moment. "How's your knee?"

Tim raised his drink. "Good medicine."

Jenny smiled.

Half a minute went by and then Tim lit up another Marlboro. He inhaled deeply and after holding it in for a few seconds slowly exhaled, directing the plume away from the table.

"You know," Jenny said, "they put on a pretty good show. I'm really having a great time."

Tim smiled. "Yeah, they're not bad." He took another drag. "I'm glad you suggested that we go. Beats sitting in the cabin."

Jenny swiveled her head, scanning the vast room. "This really is a neat old ship. I like all of the antique furnishing they have here. Makes me feel like I'm aboard the *Queen Mary.*"

Tim nodded. "Yeah, she's not a sleek racehorse like those newer cruise ships you see everywhere, but she's still got a lot of character." He then surveyed the compartment. A moment later his eyes caught something of interest. He pointed to the left, toward a bulkhead thirty feet away. "Isn't that a console radio like the one in the storage locker?"

Jenny squinted, peering through the maze of guests and

the pallor of smoke that covered everything. "Yeah, it sure looks like Grandma's RCA." She paused, turning back to face Tim. "I wonder if it still works."

"Maybe." He shook his head. "That was a clever hiding place. Only you would have been able to figure out the solution to your dad's riddle."

The mention of her late father's good-bye video jarred Jenny's sense of well-being. She leaned across the tiny table. There were dozens of others nearby and Tim had warned her to be careful. She whispered: "Do you think they have any idea where we are?"

Tim moved closer, feigning an intimate conversation with his lover. "Probably not tonight, but sooner or later someone will figure it out."

"So what will we do?"

"We maintain a low profile for the next two days—until we get to Ketchikan. Then we'll get off and fly out from there."

Jenny nodded. "Yeah, that's a good plan. But I'm so tired of running that the thought of hiding out on this ship for a week sounds wonderful." She sighed heavily. "But you're right. It's too risky to stay here for very long."

Tim smiled again. "It'll be okay, kiddo. Once you get to London, my buddy will take good care of you."

Jenny smiled. "That does sound nice." She paused to take another sip and then looked up again. "Are your sons and mother still with Laura?"

"Yep. They're all together. Tony and his boys are watching the whole clan for me."

"Where do you know him from—this Tony guy?"

"We were both stationed in West Germany in the mid-eighties."

"What were you doing?"

Tim smiled but did not respond.

"Tim?" she said, cocking her head to one side.

He turned away, breaking eye contact.

"Well?" Jenny persisted.

"I really can't say much other than we made a few excursions into the East."

"You were a spy?"

"We did a little recon work on the other side. That's all."

I bet! thought Jenny. She sensed there was a lot more to that story, but now was not the time to press the issue. "Hmmm, recon work," she said. "Well, that was probably interesting."

Tim just nodded and then took another slug of bourbon.

Jenny finished her own Coke. "I'm looking forward to meeting this Tony. Sounds like Mr. James Bond to me." She paused, once again eyeing Tim for some sign of a reaction—nothing. She continued: "Anyway, it'll be good to visit with Laura. Maybe we can get some work done."

Work! Jenny instantly thought. It had been days since she had thought about LorTech and the projects she was supposed to be managing. *It'll be so nice just to get back to my dull old routine.*

DAY 5

OLD WOUNDS

22 BAD NEWS

The pulsing tone would not go away. He rolled over and peered at the digital clock's readout. It was sitting on the nightstand next to his head. "Dammit," he muttered, "three frigging o'clock." He was still not quite conscious yet. The telephone continued to announce its unwelcome presence.

"Larry," called a female voice, "are you going to get that darn thing or not?"

The DCI ignored his wife as he reached for the handset. "General Carson here," he answered, automatically using his rank as a greeting rather than the conventional hello, yes, or who the hell is this? After four decades in the Army, it just came naturally.

"Sir, this is Condor One. We have a situation here that needs your immediate attention." The caller had just identified himself as the night watch commander at Langley.

The retired four-star general sat up, slipping his legs over the side of the bed. "What's going on?" he asked.

"Sir, we need you here now. We have a possible PRIME-TIME situation developing." There was a slight pause. "Your driver has been alerted and should be pulling up to your main gate within twenty minutes."

"Okay. I understand."

Even though the dedicated telephone line from CIA headquarters to the director's Chevy Chase estate was secure, the code word that had just been used by the watch commander indicated that the situation required the DCI's immediate presence before they could speak. PRIMETIME indicated a possible internal security breach.

The DCI glanced at the clock again. "I'll be there by four."

"Very good, sir. We've alerted your deputies and all division heads. They'll be waiting for you."

"All right, thank you."

The director of Central Intelligence replaced the handset and then switched on a nearby lamp. He turned to look at the tiny lump curled up on the opposite side of the king-size bed. His wife was buried under a pile of blankets, topped off by a down comforter. She had just pulled a pillow over her head, trying to block out the offensive light. "Sorry, honey," he said, "but I've got to go to the office now."

"Larry," called out her muffled voice, "it's Saturday morning, for crying out loud. Can't those people ever leave you alone?" She never got used to the middle-of-the-night emergency calls. There had been dozens since her husband took the nation's top intelligence job. "What's going on this time—another Desert Storm or something like that?"

"No, nothing like that. Just a little internal brushfire. Hopefully I'll be able to douse it and then I'll be back before lunch."

"You promise? Barb's been planning the party for months."

"I know. I'll be there."

The DCI was looking forward to his youngest grandson's first birthday party. It was almost a family reunion. All five of his children would be there, along with his nine grandchildren.

Unfortunately, he'd never make it. The brushfire was about to explode into a conflagration.

Tim Carpenter took one long last drag and then flipped the butt overboard. It disappeared into the churning wake. He was standing at the stern, beside the fluttering ensign. He had the fantail deck to himself. The giant ship was still in its slumber mode. Most of the crew and all but a handful of passengers remained below, snug in their cabins.

Tim turned to his left, still looking aft. A distant blanket of fog shrouded the British Columbia coast, ten miles away. Only the snowcapped peaks of the jagged mountain range managed to penetrate the veil. The northern end of Vancouver Island, fifteen miles to his right, was fog free.

The sun had been up for about half an hour and the *Emerald Sea* was now crossing Queen Charlotte Strait. The sea was as flat as a billiards table and there was no wind, only the ship-generated breeze as it sped northward.

Tim took in a deep breath. Despite the lingering remnants of the tobacco, the pungent aroma of the sea air managed to penetrate. It was a good smell, clean and pure. He liked the idea of living near the ocean.

Tim yawned. He was still tired. At first he'd had a tough time falling asleep. Jenny's pointed questions about his Cold War "activities" had stirred up old memories—wounds that had never quite healed. After finally flushing those thoughts he managed to get about four hours' sleep, but that was it.

As soon as the *Emerald Sea* had passed the confined waters of Broughton Strait, its speed increased from a leisurely twelve knots to the normal cruising rate of eighteen knots. Most of the slumbering passengers never noticed. But Tim sure did. *Now I know why no one wanted that cabin!*

Tim and Jenny's cabin was located directly over the starboard propeller. When the turn rates doubled, boosting the ship's speed, the mild vibration that had been tolerable transformed into a seagoing torture chamber. Tim, laid out in the top berth, awoke instantly. The bed frame rattled as if it were connected to a dozen washing machines, all running on the wash cycle. Somehow, Jenny slept through the racket.

He hadn't paid much attention to the vibration the day before. On the run up the Strait of Georgia at eighteen knots, they'd been out of the cabin, first for dinner and then the show. When they finally returned—around midnight—the ship had passed Campbell River and was well into Discovery Inlet. It had already reduced its speed to twelve knots. The inland passages for the next one hundred miles were narrow and shallow and crowded with traffic.

Tim knew further sleep was a lost cause so he'd climbed out of the berth.

After dressing, he left a note, telling Jenny he'd be back later.

In spite of the noisy cabin, Tim was impressed with the ship. The *Emerald Sea* wasn't nearly as modern as most of the other vessels that cruised the Alaska circuit. But then again she wasn't quite ready for the breakers yard. Built in the early sixties and upgraded in the late eighties, she had a few good years left.

He especially admired the woodwork. It was everywhere. From the oak guardrails on the main salon stairway to the teak decking on the promenade deck—it was all of top-notch quality. Even her lines were impressive. The massive white hull was not nearly as sleek as her current competition, but it had a mature elegance that the others could never equal.

Tim glanced at his wristwatch. It was almost half past six o'clock. *Good,* he thought. *Now maybe I can get some coffee.* He turned around and began heading forward. The sign on the door of the dining room indicated that the breakfast buffet would open at 6:30 A.M.

Tim desperately needed that first caffeine hit to get him going. At the moment, he felt like a slug. Lack of sleep and the ever lingering pain in his left knee had dulled his senses, like a once-sharp blade that had lost its edge. And that was just not acceptable. If he was going to prevent Jenny and himself from falling into the cauldron that constantly threatened them, he had to remain razor sharp.

Even though they were safe at the moment, that could all change in a heartbeat. The danger was always there, lingering just under the surface, ready to erupt into a torrent of violence and death.

"You're certain they were booked on the *Emerald Sea?*"

"Yes, ma'am. We know they boarded yesterday, in Vancouver."

"Well, I'm sorry, sir, but we just don't have any record of a Mr. Tim Carpenter or a Jennifer Richmond."

"Would you please look again? It's vital that I locate them."

"Okay."

The MSS operative stared at the thirty-something Caucasian as she once again scrolled through the passenger list of the cruise ship. The customer service representative was sitting across the desk from the Chinese operative. They were inside the Emerald Line's San Francisco corporate headquarters.

A massive computer monitor occupied nearly half of the woman's desktop. The screen was filled with what appeared to be an endless column of names. There were 892 fare-paying passengers aboard the *Emerald Sea*.

She looked up, locking onto the visitor's eyes. "I'm sorry, sir, but they don't show up on the manifest."

He frowned and ran his hand through his jet black hair. He then let out a deep sigh while tilting his head down. With his chin resting on his chest he spoke, just loud enough for her to hear: "Dear Lord, what am I going to do now?"

The clerk fell for his act. "Is this some kind of an emergency?"

The spy wanted to smile but refrained. Instead, he looked up. His eyes continued to broadcast depression. "Kind of. Miss Richmond is a close friend of our family. My sister passed away yesterday." He paused for effect. "She was killed in an automobile accident. The funeral's on Monday—in San Jose—and I know Jennifer would want to be there."

"Oh, I'm so sorry, Mr. Lee." She hesitated. "I'd like to help, but I can't do anything if they're not on the manifest."

The man nodded, pretending to accept defeat. He stood up, offering his hand in thanks. He had just started to turn when he stopped. He looked back. "You know, it's possible that they didn't register under their real names."

The clerk flashed him a puzzled look. "Why would they do that?"

The MSS operative shook his head, as if troubled. "It's her jealous ex-boyfriend. He's been stalking her for months."

"Oh! Now I see," she said, looking concerned.

He shrugged, as if signaling "what can I say?"

"Any idea on what alias they might be using?" she asked.

"No. The only thing I can think of is that they might have booked passage at the last minute. We know Jenny and Tim weren't planning the trip until just a few days ago. They were in the Seattle area, visiting friends, and then they decided to head up to Vancouver to see if they could book passage. We think they boarded, but we don't know for sure. They could have done something else."

The clerk nodded. "Ah-ha. Now that helps."

She turned back to the monitor and began attacking her keyboard. She hit pay dirt thirty seconds later. "This looks interesting," she said. She then waved him to her side of the desk.

"Now this particular cruise has been booked solid for months, but yesterday morning the manifest was updated." She pointed to the screen. "See, right here. Cabin 345. It's normally not used because it's right over the propeller—the passengers hate the noise and vibration." She paused. "But yesterday it was taken."

That's got to be them, thought the operative. "Can you check the names for me?"

"Sure, just a sec."

She again attacked her board. A moment later two names were displayed: Mr. and Mrs. Thomas Carter.

"There you go," she said.

He pulled out a ballpoint pen and notepad and jotted down the name and cabin number.

"Do you think it's them?" asked the customer service rep.

"Maybe, I don't know. At least it gives me a start."

"If you want to get a message to the ship, we can do it from here. Send a fax or radiotelephone?"

"Oh, that might be very helpful. I think that . . ." He stopped in midsentence, as if he had just thought of something. But like everything else, it was a counterfeit gesture. "Where's the ship docking first?" he asked.

She again glanced at the computer screen. "It arrives in Ketchikan on Sunday, nine A.M."

"No stops in between?"

"Nope. Just cruises up the Inside Passage." She then handed him a four-color company brochure that contained a small map with the ship's course plotted out. It also contained color-coded layouts of the ship's various decks with each cabin number called out.

He studied the map for a few seconds and then looked up. "So, if Jennifer's really aboard, then Ketchikan is the only place where she could get off—tomorrow morning—to catch a plane back to San Francisco?"

"Right."

He held up the brochure. "May I keep this?" he asked.
"Of course."

As he folded up the advertisement, he began the last phase of his carefully executed interrogation: "Thanks to your assistance, I think I know what to do now." He paused to smile. It was friendly, almost a kindly gesture. "I would like to take up your offer to radiotelephone the Carters to see if it's really Jennifer or not. But before I can do that I need to check a few things out with my family regarding the various arrangements." He looked down, checking his wristwatch. "It'll take me an hour or so before I can return. Could we do it then?"

"Oh, sure, I'll be here until four."

"Excellent." He stood up. "Thanks; thanks very much. I really appreciate your help."

"No problem. See you later this afternoon."

The PRC agent exited the office. He would never return. There was no need. He had obtained everything he needed. Peng would be pleased.

Ricardo Molina was sitting behind his desk, leafing through a pile of reports and assorted interdepartmental mail. He tried to concentrate. But it was a struggle. He was bone tired and frazzled.

Agent Molina had been up since five o'clock. It was now half past two in the afternoon and about the only thing that kept him going was caffeine. He held a half-empty mug of tepid coffee in his right hand. It was his seventh of the day so far.

Where the hell could Tim be hiding out? he thought as he scanned over an RCMP report on its Vancouver surveillance operation. Victoria Kwan had faxed it to the Seattle office twenty minutes earlier. It was not encouraging. The Canadian authorities had yet to uncover one solid lead. Other than Carpenter's boat, they didn't have a hint as to where Tim and Jenny were hiding out or, for that matter, if they were even in the Vancouver area at all.

Ricardo tossed the report on the table and then took another sip of the brew. It had transformed into battery acid.

He abandoned the mug and swiveled around in his chair, facing the window wall.

He had a partial water view from his office. A huge containership had just sailed past West Point, entering Elliott Bay. As Ricardo focused on the vessel, a new idea began to gel. *Hmmm, I wonder if Tim could have—*

His train of thought was brutally interrupted by the ringing phone. He turned around and picked up the handset. "Molina speaking," he answered.

"Rick, this is Bob Logan."

Ricardo leaned forward, flabbergasted. Robert Logan was the director of the Federal Bureau of Investigation—the FBI's top dog. And he was calling Ricardo on a Saturday afternoon. Something was very wrong.

"Hello, sir," Ricardo replied.

"Rick, it looks like we've finally got a lead on what happened with your Cascade unit."

They found the mole! Ricardo thought. "Was there a leak, sir?"

"Yes. But not from us." Logan waited a moment. "It was the CIA. I was just briefed by the DCI himself."

"The CIA?"

"Yes, it turns out that one of their analysts—a woman named Marsha Lewis—had turned rogue. She sold us out on MERLIN, pure and simple. Apparently, it all started . . ."

As Director Logan started to explain what the CIA had uncovered, Ricardo's reaction was instantaneous: *Dammit, this is going to be a frigging disaster!*

23 PICKING UP THE CHASE

The spacious pilothouse could easily accommodate a dozen or more, but this evening there were only three occupants. The vessel's master sat in the leather captain's chair; it was mounted directly behind the wheel. The other two were off to the starboard side, huddled around the Furuno monitor.

The yacht was on autopilot so the captain wasn't burdened with the monotonous chore of manually steering the 144-foot-long vessel. Instead, he held a pair of binoculars to his eyes. He scanned the distant horizon, probing the darkening sea-air interface, searching for the telltale speck that would confirm the radar sighting. *Where the hell are you?* he thought. Nothing but green and gray.

He lowered the binoculars and, out of habit, glanced down at the instrument panel. There were dozens of digital gauges and readouts clustered in an oak-lined housing that extended halfway across the windscreen. With the finesse of a jumbo jet pilot, he scanned the instruments, seeking out any hint of trouble. All systems were normal. Everything was just fine aboard the *Orca*.

The captain turned to his right, studying the guests. They had arrived about two hours earlier. "That contact still showing up?" he asked.

Allen Peng looked up from the radar screen. "Yes. It's now about forty kilometers . . . twenty nautical miles away and maintaining the same heading." He paused. "Can you see it yet?"

"No. It's too far away for a visual. Besides, it's getting too dark to see much of anything."

A new voice joined in: "Then how will we know for sure if that's it or not?" It was Gérard Rémy. He was standing next to Peng.

The captain glanced at his wristwatch and then back toward the two men. "Right now we're overtaking it at just about seven knots." He made a quick mental calculation. "So in a little over three hours, say around midnight, we should be able to get a good visual."

Peng nodded. "Midnight—that should work. That'll give us plenty of time to get ready."

Rémy wasn't convinced. "What about other ships? Could we be following the wrong one?"

"It's possible," replied the captain. "But that radar contact plots out almost exactly where the schedule says it should be." He paused. "Now, if you really want to know, we can send the helicopter ahead and get a positive ID. But I don't know how much spare fuel there is to try that."

"That's a good point," Peng said as he stepped away from the Furuno unit. "We burned a lot getting here."

Peng took a few steps aft and stopped. He was now looking through a porthole toward the stern. The ex–U.S. Army McDonnell Douglas 500 Defender squatted on the elevated deck, fifty feet behind the pilothouse. Its hull was solid black; there were no ID markings on it. The cockpit's bulbous windscreen, the dropping rotor blades, and the short stubby tail assembly all combined to gave the aircraft a sinister appearance. It looked like a gigantic bug.

Peng and Rémy had arrived in the 500MD, landing just before seven P.M. They had remained in Vancouver most of the day, coordinating the overall operation. The long flight from Vancouver had been exhilarating. First, they traversed the length of the Strait of Georgia, flying just a couple hundred feet above the emerald inland sea. They then followed Vancouver Island to its northern limits, landing at Port Hardy. They stayed just long enough to refuel.

Once again airborne, the Defender headed across Queen Charlotte Sound, skirting the coast. It finally caught up with the *Orca* about eighty miles north of Bella Bella.

The superyacht had been running at flank since late the previous evening. Peng had ordered the yacht to give chase after the patrol plane confirmed that the calls from the missing cellular phone originated from the cruise ship. Before departing from Vancouver, however, the *Orca* was delayed for a couple of hours as Major Wu waited for fresh troops. Earlier in the same day, the PLA's Military Intelligence Department dispatched twelve new shooters from Hong Kong. The Air China flight didn't touch down at Vancouver International until nine P.M. that evening.

Peng turned back to face Rémy. "I think we'll be okay if we wait. I don't like the idea of cutting into our fuel reserve unless it's absolutely necessary."

Rémy nodded, capitulating. "All right. You're probably right." He paused to pull out a cigarette. As he lit up he raised a new concern: "Do you really think six men will be enough?"

Peng shrugged. "I'd certainly like more, but there won't be time for more than one helo run. We're fortunate to have the lead team. They've been trained for this already."

"Well, I hope you're right." Rémy took a deep drag and then looked down at the hardwood deck. The French spy wasn't convinced. He would have much preferred having his own people conduct the mission. But then, Rémy wasn't in any position to protest. He was just an observer.

Rémy exhaled. He looked back up, now seeking Peng's eyes. "Since we've got several hours, I suggest that we head below and go over the plan with your men again. Practice makes perfect."

"Fine, let's go," Peng said, using as polite a voice as he could manage. But it was a facade. He now abhorred the Frenchman. Rémy was much too transparent. His contempt for the MSS was always there, lying just under the surface. *Damn Frogs! What egos!* Peng thought as he headed down a ladder well. *They think they're better than anyone else.*

Rémy, a few steps behind Peng, had similar thoughts: *Goddamn Chink bastards, they'll probably fuck this one up, too!*

Gérard Rémy's distrust of Peng and the MSS was born more out of frustration than actual performance. Rémy was used to being in charge. It was harsh being relegated to the bleachers.

The entire operation was now under Beijing's direct control. During the past forty-eight hours, the Ministry of State Security's Foreign Operations Department, assisted by senior officers from the PLA's Second Department, developed a dozen contingency plans for Peng's mission. The PRC was committing enormous monetary and military resources to recover the MERLIN technology, yet neither its French or its German coconspirators had been consulted.

The stakes were now too high for Beijing to worry about its Western partners. They were redundant, their usefulness expended. Peng understood that. He had read the briefing report prior to starting the mission. China's economic—and political—future might very well depend on what happened in the next few hours.

"Capitalism without democracy." That had been the keystone concept stressed in the briefing report. Some twenty years earlier, Deng Xiaoping and his cohorts had hatched the notion. It was now close to maturity.

"Money equals power." That was another mantra that China's ruling class had preached among themselves, knowing it was the key to their individual survival. They had all witnessed the disintegration of the Soviet Union, spent into oblivion by Ronald Reagan and the U.S. Congress.

"Grow the economy—it will lift the masses from the mire of poverty to the glory of personal wealth." That had been the politburo's official public theme. The "masses" swallowed it, and so did the West. The United States and its allies all believed—hoped—that with rapid economic growth and wanton consumerism, China's billions would demand personal freedoms that would eventually evolve into a democratic society.

But it was all a deception.

The real plan—the hidden agenda—was simple yet diabolical: Grow the economy to raise the standard of living of the masses severalfold. The people will be overjoyed with their newfound wealth and will produce even more. As the economic engine gathers further steam, carefully siphon off most of the surplus for the state's needs, but always remember to kick a little back as an incentive, like dangling the proverbial carrot before the donkey.

The West couldn't wait to fuel China's economic engine. They lined up at her doorstep, eager to invest their dollars, yen, deutsche marks, francs, and now euros, attracted by the PRC's bargain-basement labor market and China's legions of future consumers, all ripe for Western exports.

It was all based on numbers. With well over a billion potential earners, increasing the average hourly wage from ten cents to fifty cents—petty by Western standards—would yield an enormous increase in China's gross national product. Much of the extra wealth would be used to improve China's visible infrastructure—roads, airports, harbors, medical facilities, universities, public buildings—but the lion's share would be diverted to just one entity: the PLA.

Paramount to China's modernization revolution was the creation of a formidable military. A standing army of millions, equipped and trained with the latest weapons, would intimidate any potential external foe, but more importantly it would deter internal opposition. Aided and abetted by state intelligence organizations like the domestic arm of the MSS, the People's Liberation Army would be ready to quash any rebellion.

China's leaders had demonstrated their resolve in 1989, ordering the PLA to terminate the new China's first flirtation with freedom. The Western powers were swift to condemn the "Butchers of Beijing," but almost as quickly turned a blind eye to that first warning sign, all eager to continue lining their pockets with gold.

China's leaders' grand plan to maintain control was for the most part solidly in place. Yet there was a storm brewing on the horizon that threatened to undermine everything.

China remained a technological misfit. Despite her past history of innovation, and the individual intellect of her people, she rarely invented anything new. Instead, China played catch-up, buying, trading, and—when that didn't work—stealing high-tech marvels.

America was the ultimate typhoon—an enormous vortex of innovation, sparked by the personal freedoms upon which it was founded. China's Communist leaders knew they never could duplicate the United States' success. At best, they hoped to limp along in its wake.

But now they were about to be left high and dry on the rocks.

MERLIN was the immediate fear. It would result in a quantum leap in high technology. Military application—revolutionary robotic aircraft that would rule the skies, rendering China's newly modernized air force to second-rate status—was the initial threat. But it was the other applications of Dr. Richmond's discovery—software, supercomputers, manufacturing, telecommunications—that was the greatest threat.

America and her true close friends would share the new high-tech bounty, enriching themselves. China would be left behind, forever relegated to second world status.

Without an expanding economy and saddled with a mediocre military, China would be ripe for internal dissent. And that would eventually mean the end for China's elite.

"No money, no power." It was that simple.

China's ruling class was determined to not let that happen.

24 LOST LOVE

There was a festive mood aboard the *Emerald Sea*. The companionways and assembly areas were filled with hundreds of passengers. Most were decked out in formal attire: crisp black tuxedos and elegant glittering evening gowns. Those that had it, or wanted others to think they had it, flaunted their wealth—the males with Rolexes and gold pinkie rings; the women with diamond earrings and pearl strands.

About half of the passengers were now waiting for the second sitting in the multiple dining rooms. The others, literally stuffed full from their first formal dinner, were ready to start the evening's entertainment. They were heading to the ship's various bars and lounges, the Golden Grotto nightclub, the Caravel ballroom, the casino, and the two movie theaters. The less adventurous could find solace in the library, work out in the gymnasium, or take a long leisurely soak in the spa. Even the children aboard had their own entertainment center. There were video arcade games, Ping-Pong tables, a small basketball court, and dozens of other games to keep them occupied while their parents played. The ship's owner spared no expense when attending to passenger entertainment. There was something for almost everyone.

It all started at seven P.M. when the first sitting for dinner was announced over the ship's intercom. The announcement was first broadcast in English and then followed up in French. Almost all of the passengers were American, with a smattering of Germans, Swedes, and a small contingent from Mexico City. There was no one from France or Quebec aboard. That call was for form only. It was a tradition aboard the *Emerald Sea;* the French announcement provided that little extra ring to an otherwise routine broadcast.

While most of the ship's passengers prepared for the evening's events, Tim and Jenny declined. Tim wanted to keep a low profile. They had eaten dinner an hour earlier. The buffet was always open to serve those passengers who avoided the formal dining rooms. They were now back inside cabin 345. It was half past eight o'clock.

Jenny was sitting cross-legged on the lower berth, poring over her father's research papers. Tim rested above. The bulkhead at his feet vibrated, excited by the enormous propeller that churned away just twenty feet below their cabin. The ship's speed had been nearly doubled a few minutes earlier. Tim had been dozing. He woke instantly.

"Good God," Tim groaned.

Jenny cocked her head upward, reacting to Tim's remark. "What's the matter?" she asked.

"I hate this."

"What?"

"The noise and propeller vibration—don't they bug you?"

"It's a little loud, but it's not so bad." She paused, still looking up. "I kind of like it in here—it's warm and cozy."

Tim shook his head. "Well, this racket's driving me nuts."

"You should go take a walk—get some fresh air."

"Maybe later."

"You want something to read? I've got a bunch of my dad's research reports here—they're real thrillers!"

"No, thanks. I'll just try to get some sleep."

But that was going to be impossible for Tim. A light sleeper all of his life, there was no way he would get any rest this night.

He hated the tiny compartment. The cabin's appointments were adequate, but the drone from the propeller was overwhelming. He stuffed Kleenex in his ears. It didn't help.

And on top of all that Tim's left knee still ached.

Tim lay back, now studying the overhead, just an arm

length away. It was painted white like the rest of the cabin. The odor of the fresh paint still permeated the air. He watched for the resonance to reappear. It came every ten seconds or so. For just an instant, the thick steel plate shuddered as if connected to a gigantic kitchen blender. The cavitating propeller continued to assault the tiny compartment. *Dammit,* he thought, *this just sucks. No wonder they don't try to rent it out.*

The short, squat man scowled as he adjusted his tie, jamming the knot hard against his Adam's apple. *Too damn tight,* he thought as he stared at his reverse image in the mirror. He loosened the knot, just a little. *Better.* He then ran a comb through his brownish-blond hair. There wasn't much to work with on top, just a thin facade covering his tanned dome.

He leaned a little closer to the mirror, now exposing his front teeth. And then, with a dab of toothpaste on his brush, he polished them. He was proud of his teeth. Even after half a century, they remained nearly perfect: ivory white, straight as a flagpole, and nicely proportioned.

He picked up a cologne bottle and shook a few drops onto his hand. He patted his cheeks. The musky fragrance flooded his nostrils. A moment later he stepped back from the sink for a final inspection. His physique was not impressive, just five-six and 170 pounds, but his uniform made up for those shortcomings. There were four gold stripes on the sleeves of his sparkling white jacket.

Captain Markos Demetriou, master of the *Emerald Sea,* smiled at his mirror image. He liked what he saw. *You're still a looker!*

He glanced at his wristwatch. He was due in the main dining parlor in a few minutes. The second sitting was about to commence and it was his turn to sit at the head table. His second in command had already completed the honors for the seven o'clock event.

Before Captain Demetriou could take his ceremonial seat he had a quick stop to make. He walked out of his cabin and headed forward. Twenty seconds later he stepped onto the bridge. The compartment had just been rigged for night running—subdued red lighting replaced the normal fluorescent fixtures. The sun was still dropping, not yet extinguished. The thick overcast that blanketed the western horizon soaked up what light remained. The sea surface was flat, broken only by the occasional whitecap from the fifteen-knot breeze.

"Good evening, sir," called out the officer of the deck. The thirty-two-year-old third officer was standing next to the windscreen, just forward of the helmsman. There was a pair of German-made binoculars draped around his neck.

Captain Demetriou nodded. "Evening, Nicki." He then walked next to the helmsman, glancing down at the compass's digital readout. The ship was on a magnetic heading of 325 degrees. He next checked the log. The ship continued to plow ahead at a steady eighteen knots. The boat had been running at full for about half an hour. For most of the day, however, the *Emerald Sea* had been cruising at a leisurely ten knots. Late in the morning the ship entered Milbanke Sound and began heading north up the Laredo Channel. Later in the afternoon it passed into the Principe Channel. The scenery of the placid British Columbia passages was awe inspiring—a hint of what was to come in Alaskan waters.

The ship had just cleared McCauley Island and was now in the Hecate Strait, away from the protected channels of the B.C. coast. The weather was beginning to be a problem.

The captain stepped forward, standing next to the OOD. "What's the latest forecast?" he asked. "That storm front still moving in?"

"Yes, sir. We can expect some nasty water offshore of Prince Rupert. It continues to blow force nine in the Dixon Entrance."

Demetriou glanced at a nearby bulkhead wall. The ship's clock read 2055 hours. He had a quick decision to make. If they continued at the ship's present speed, it would arrive in the thick of the agitated waters around midnight. Normally, that wouldn't be a problem. Most of the passengers would already be in their berths and might not even notice the increased rolling and pitching that would inevitably occur. But tonight was different. The ship's hotel manager had a special midnight buffet planned. It was one of the cruise's highlights. Elegant ice sculptures had already been ordered; hundreds of pounds of caviar, shrimp, and salmon were being prepared at this moment; and dozens of pastries, cakes, and other fine desserts were in the ovens.

If the seas were as sloppy as predicted, the special event could turn into a nightmare. The spectacle of nine hundred passengers puking their guts out flashed through his head. He turned to the OOD. "I want to get through that damned midnight ice party thing before we hit the Dixon Entrance so reduce your speed to eight knots, hold this course."

"Reduce to eight knots. Maintain same course. Aye, sir."

The OOD repeated the order to the helmsman. He, in turn, relayed the instructions to the engine room via the bridge telegraph. Within seconds the giant diesel-electric drives, deep below in the bowels of the vessel, were throttled back and the thirty-thousand-ton vessel began slowing.

Satisfied with the state of his vessel, Demetriou walked off the bridge and headed aft. It was now time to switch roles: from master mariner to shipboard celebrity. He wondered who would be sitting at his table this evening. He hoped that at least one of the women would be young and attractive.

"That damn bitch must have set 'em up! No wonder they all got butchered!" FBI Special Agent Victoria Kwan's voice was seething with wrath. If her blood could have boiled, she would have exploded by now.

"Yep," Ricardo Molina replied. He was on the other end of the telephone line back in his Seattle office. Victoria was still in Vancouver. "Our Cascade unit didn't have a chance," he said. "That assault team had plenty of hard intel on the safe house. It could only have come from her."

"Good Lord," Victoria said, shaking her head, "then it's just a fluke that Audrey got that Richmond woman out of there at all. By all rights, those bastards should have had her back then."

"Yes, and then they would have the MERLIN secret, too." There was an awkward silence for a few moments and then Agent Kwan responded: "How could this have happened? She was a senior officer, for God's sake. If we can't trust those people what the hell are we to do?"

"I don't know."

Ricardo empathized with his assistant. He had had a similar reaction hours earlier when Director Logan had told him the bad news. Although MAGNUM never brought her personal laptop to her CIA office, she'd been careless with its security. She had used her late mother's birth date in reverse order, as the password to her encrypted files. She had kept a copy of everything. SAC Molina's head was still spinning from all of the damage that the CIA turncoat had caused.

Victoria sat back down on the edge of the sofa and looked out the hotel room window. Vancouver was lit up with a carnival of lights. It was just as beautiful at night as during the day. But she could care less. Right now all of her thoughts were centered on Marsha Lewis. *Shot to death in a carjacking—at least she got what she deserved!*

"Vicky," Ricardo said, "I know this is all a shock to you but what's done is done. Right now we've got to concentrate on finding Jennifer Richmond before those people do. They're absolutely ruthless and will not stop."

Victoria stood up, instantly switching mental gears. She was ready to continue the hunt. She'd been running full out all day. "You're right."

"Okay. Now what have you got to report?"

She sighed. "Unfortunately, not much. Our State Department boys finally got through to the crowd in Ottawa, and the RCMP's now cooperating fully but . . ." She hesitated.

"What?" Ricardo asked.

"But we can't find 'em. The Mounties have got people everywhere: airports, bus and train terminals, the ferry at Tsawwassen, and every one of the border stations from here to Minnesota are operating under emergency conditions." She paused again. "Rick, I even sent two of our people down to Point Roberts to check that place. Nothing. Not a hint as to where they are."

"Yeah, well, that's not much of a surprise. Knowing Tim,

if he doesn't want to be found, he's quite capable of disappearing indefinitely."

"But what are we going to do, then? I'm sure those MSS teams are still scouring the countryside for them."

"We keep looking, that's all I can say. Washington's not able to roll over on this."

"All right. I'll keep the pressure on. But I'm not optimistic, not at all."

"Yeah, I know."

"What's wrong, Jenny?" Tim said. He was standing by the bathroom doorway, having just returned from a smoke break. Jenny's deep sobs stopped him cold in his tracks. It was half past midnight. Several hours earlier, the annoying drone of the ship's propeller had magically faded away, restoring the cabin to a normal sound level.

Jenny cracked open the door. Her eyes were puffy red. Tears streaked down her face. "I'm okay now," she said, reaching up with a Kleenex to dab her cheeks.

"What happened?"

"Oh, nothing. Don't worry about it."

Tim smiled. "Come on now, Jenny," he said, his inflection sympathetic. "What happened?"

Jenny shook her head. "Oh, I don't know. I was just reading some of Dad's research papers . . ." She gestured toward the lower berth. It was littered with MERLIN secrets. "And then I had this flashback. Me and Dad were camping out at this lake near Mount Adams. I was just a kid back then, but we had so much fun. Fishing, hiking, picking huckleberries." She hesitated. "But now I'll never be able to do that with him again. It's just not fair!"

Fresh rivulets cascaded down her cheeks.

Tim reached forward and slipped his right arm over her shoulders. He pulled her close, cradling her head against his chest. "It's okay, Jen. Let it all come out."

Jennifer did. For ten minutes she vented, the murder of her father foremost in her torment.

And then it was Tim's turn.

"The pain will eventually fade," he said, his voice tender,

consoling. They were now both sitting on the edge of the lower berth, side by side. "It'll probably never go away completely, but you'll learn to adapt to it. Please believe me."

"But how? I seem to be getting worse."

"I know. Right now you're under maximum stress. It's only natural that it brings back the bad memories." Tim paused, now looking down at the deck. "I know about what this kind of stuff can do. I've been there, too."

Jenny turned to face Tim. His forehead was contorted, the faint scars highlighted. She sensed the pain. "What happened?" she asked.

He sighed, crushed. "I lost my first wife . . . and my daughter. Fifteen years ago . . . when I was in the Army."

"Oh, I'm so sorry."

"They were killed—by a car bomb that was meant for me."

Jenny gasped. She was aware that Tim was a widower. All along she had assumed that his first wife had died of natural causes. And she knew nothing about a daughter.

A solitary tear streamed down Tim's right cheek, splashing onto the mattress. "They were both torn to shreds . . ." His voice choked up. "Somehow I survived, but I shouldn't have—why I was spared . . . I don't know."

More tears.

Jenny extended her arm around his waist, hugging him. "I didn't know, Tim. I'm so sorry for you. It must have been horrible."

Tim brushed the wetness away. He tried to smile. "Afterwards, I just about went nuts. The FBI and CIA have spent years trying to find the bastards." He shook his head. "Nothing but dead ends. They'll probably never be found." He hesitated. "Jen, you just can't imagine what that's like. If you let it get to you, it'll just eat your guts out."

Jenny remained mute, stunned.

Tim continued: "The grief almost killed me. I was blind to its impact—all I could think about was revenge."

Twenty minutes had passed. While still seated on Jenny's bed, Tim had made his confessional: the years of psychiatric counseling, the battery of antidepressants, the horrible flash-backs that had plagued him for so long, and then, finally, his recovery.

When Tim finished, Jennifer's distress abated, replaced with a deep-seated fervor that for days had been suppressed, but was now about to erupt. *You poor wonderful man! Your life's been ripped apart at the seams, but here you are putting yourself on the line for me.*

Without one thought of the consequences, Jenny reached up with her right hand and stroked the back of Tim's neck, her fingertips electric. And then, ever so delicately, she leaned forward, her lips slightly parted, the tip of her tongue just tracing the lower lip, her breathing condensed, fiery . . .

DAY 6

DEATH DAY

25 LOVERS' LAMENT

There was a solid knock on the pilothouse door.

"Come," called out Allen Peng, using his native tongue.

The door opened and a man walked in. Like Peng, he was tall for an Asian, nearly six feet. And his medium build was brick solid. He wore black from head to toe. A web harness crossed his chest. It was filled with spare SMG magazines.

"Sir, Major Wu asked me to tell you that the launch just returned. They made positive identification."

"You're certain? There are many others like it operating in these waters."

"No question about it, sir." He then handed a Polaroid snapshot to Peng. It had been taken just forty minutes earlier—at 12:36 A.M.—when the *Orca*'s launch powered up to the stern of the huge cruise liner. There had been just enough hull-generated light to take the photo.

Peng smiled as he read the name plate: *Emerald Sea, Nassau.*

He had been watching it for twenty minutes. When he first noticed the luminescence, it was too diffuse to give any indication of its source. There was no distinct outline, just a glowing orb on the distant night horizon, like a midnight mirage. But now, as it passed abeam of the *Emerald Sea,* the aberration had metamorphosed into a crystal spectacle.

The white-hulled behemoth was over eight hundred feet long. She was graced with modern slick lines, marking her as one of the newer cruise ships. And every light aboard appeared to be on. The Vancouver-bound vessel was nearing the end of its week-long excursion in Alaskan waters.

Tim Carpenter watched the floating palace sail by. It plowed through the choppy waters at uncommon speed, as if running away from something evil that lurked in its wake.

The *Emerald Sea* was also running hard. But in the opposite direction, toward the troubled waters. Tim could feel the straining engines in his feet, the steel deck plates rattling. He was baffled as to the ship's erratic speed. Early on in the evening it had been "full speed ahead!" and then, for several hours, the ship crawled across the ocean like a sea slug. And now, once again, it was "damn the torpedoes!"

"Dammit," Tim muttered, leaning against the railing, "why are we moving fast? What the hell's going on?"

Tim's self-talk was a diversion. What really occupied his mind—cluttered his objectivity and gnawed at his conscience—continued to hammer away with the repetition of a metronome: *Carpenter, you damn fool . . . what the hell were you thinking?*

It had started a couple of hours earlier. Jenny's first kiss ignited the firestorm.

Never once had he strayed, not when he was married to Eva all those years, nor now that he was with Laura. And there were temptations everywhere. His rugged Harrison Ford looks were like a night candle to a flight of moths. But tonight his ice will had flashed to steam—torched by raw lust.

They were both animals—100 percent instinct. He ripped the buttons from his shirt; she slipped out of her T-shirt. He tasted her breasts; she caressed his manhood.

They were near the point of no return when it happened. It was the propeller.

When the midnight buffet ended at one A.M. and the ship's speed was increased, the vibration and noise level of cabin 345 quadrupled. It was like the inside of an alarm clock.

Thank God! Tim thought, once again remembering.

The unexpected racket broke the spell. Tim had rolled away. "I can't . . . it's wrong . . . I'm sorry."

"It's okay," Jenny had whispered, equally relieved.

The wind ruffled Tim's hair as he watched the lightship trail away. Within minutes it would be a tiny speck on the coal black sea-sky interface.

He turned back toward the bow. The light radiating from the *Emerald Sea* illuminated the sea surface around the hull for nearly fifty feet. Relentless trains of six-foot rollers, each crowned with a windswept crest, smashed into the ship.

The 712-foot vessel was now beginning to feel the storm that had been brewing all night in the Dixon Entrance. It wasn't a big disturbance, just a nasty summer tempest that had its origin in the Gulf of Alaska. The worst of it would be over by sunrise. But until then, the *Emerald Sea* would be at its mercy.

Tim turned away from the rail, cupping his hands as he lit up the Marlboro. He inhaled and then turned back to face the sea. He peered into the blackness. *I wonder where we are?*

The *Emerald Sea*'s watch officer stared at the radar screen. It was set to the maximum range, 120 nautical miles. The surrounding terrain was displayed by thin luminous green lines. Rose Point, at the northeastern tip of Graham Island, was off the port beam. The seaport of Prince Rupert, tucked away on the British Columbia mainland, was to the starboard. And dead ahead, across the Dixon Entrance, was the start of a vast archipelago. Southeast Alaska extended northward for over five hundred miles.

The watch officer looked up, now peering through the bridge windows. Raindrops the size of dimes suddenly began blasting the tempered glass. The racket sounded like machine-gun fire. A few seconds later the ship began a slow roll to starboard, responding to the swells that had now transformed into mountains of green. They relentlessly bore down on the ship. He grabbed one of the stainless steel handholds next to the radar unit, steadying himself. And then a brilliant flash erupted across the pewter sky, filling the pilothouse with light many times brighter than the noonday sun. Within a heartbeat, a thunderclap rattled everything.

"Getting pretty rough, sir," called out a voice, using his native language.

The officer turned to his left, looking back at the helmsman. The Greek crewman stood stoically behind the wheel, watching the gyrocompass as the autopilot magically steered the vessel.

"Are we having any trouble holding the course?"

"No, sir. But it must be getting pretty bad down below."

The officer nodded. "Yes, but we're all right for now. We'll be out of this crap in a couple of hours."

"Yes, sir."

The helmsman's comment had hit home with the watch officer. It did make sense to slow up, but that would mean waking up the captain. And he really didn't want to do that. His orders had been explicit.

After the midnight buffet, and after disembarking the Canadian pilots at the Triple Island Pilot Station, Captain Demetriou had ordered the ship's speed increased to eighteen knots. By running at full, they could still arrive on schedule, making up for the lost time earlier in the evening.

The *Emerald Sea* was due to dock in Ketchikan at nine A.M. And it was absolutely against company policy to be late for a docking.

Another flash of lightning burned the night sky. The instantaneous boom rattled the windows. And then a huge wave broke against the bow, sending a seismiclike shudder through the entire hull. *Sweet Jesus,* he thought, *maybe I better slow up.*

He looked at the bridge clock. It was 2:32 A.M. Thirty minutes earlier all of the ship's clocks had been rolled back one hour to conform with local time. The watch officer next made a quick mental calculation. *No way we can slow up,* he concluded. *We've got to keep going.*

Like the *Emerald Sea*'s officer of the deck, the *Orca*'s captain was glued to the Furuno radar display. The giant cruise ship created a huge reflection on his screen. It was a dozen miles ahead, just inside the Dixon Entrance. And the static fluff erupting around the bright blip told the skipper it was rough ahead. The radar pulses were reflecting off the towering seas that engulfed the waters that lay ahead.

The superyacht had not yet encountered the bulk of the storm. The waves and wind around the vessel were still tolerable. But that would all change within the next hour. It was now or never, he finally concluded.

The captain turned away from the screen, looking at the man who stood next to him. "I don't think you should delay. If we wait much longer, it may be too rough."

Allen Peng nodded. He then picked up a microphone and gave the order. A moment later he turned around and peered aft through a porthole.

The 500MD had been idling for five minutes, its engine now fully warmed up. The beat of the rotors increased as the pilot spooled up the power level. And then it lifted off in a fury of turbulence, the turbine screaming a high-pitched whine.

Peng watched as the airship sheared off to the starboard. It then raced ahead, passing the bow a few seconds later. The helicopter remained visible for twenty more seconds, its hull outlined by the flashing anticollision strobe lights. But then it disappeared, swallowed up by the night sky. The pilot had switched off the running lights. They were no longer needed.

26 DREAMS

It was a quarter to three in the morning. The target was gleaming like the Atlantic City boardwalk. The pilot had spotted it eight kilometers out and made a beeline toward it. But now, after closing and dropping elevation, he was having trouble with his night vision gear. The helmet-mounted NVD did not provide depth perception. The luminous green image in his visor looked like something on a television screen— just a two-dimensional picture. Consequently, he took exceptional care as he raced over the water surface. If he clipped the crest of one of the monster waves that roared under the 500MD's belly, it would be all over. The forty-knot gusts and the driving rain didn't help matters either.

The helicopter was now on final approach. The *Emerald Sea* was about a kilometer out. The pilot keyed his intercom switch. "Delivery in one minute," he said, speaking in Mandarin.

"Affirmative," replied Major Wu. The assault team leader wore a flight helmet with a built-in intercom. He was in the left-side cockpit seat. Normal conversation was impossible without the intercom. All the doors except the pilot's had been removed. The rotor's deep-toned beat and the screaming jet turbine assaulted the cabin with the fury of a category 5 hurricane.

Major Wu turned to face the five other men packed like sardines behind him. They were all dressed and equipped alike: black woolen head caps, nylon gloves, and black Nomex coveralls with ankle-high leather boots. Each was armed with a suppressor-equipped 9 mm submachine gun, ten thirty-round magazines, grenades and assorted plastic explosives, a combat knife, and a semiautomatic pistol.

Wu raised his right index finger and mouthed the words: "One minute!"

His men made one last equipment check and then they were ready.

The Defender 500MD followed the ship's churning wake right to the stern. When it was about two hundred feet out, the buffeting from the wind lessened, easing the final approach.

The helo slowed up, now pacing the ship's eighteen-knot speed. The stern's huge rounded superstructure loomed in the near distance.

The pilot took a deep breath and then advanced the throttle while simultaneously pulling up on the collective. The 500MD jumped over the stern. As soon as it broke free from the hull's shelter, the full force of the wind hit it. The pilot had timed the maneuver perfectly. The helicopter was now hovering over the fantail, windmilling toward the northwest, right into the wind.

The pilot keyed his mike: "Execute, execute!"

It took only a few seconds for the six men to fast-rappel from the Defender. They deployed from both sides, dropping through the ten meters of darkness like sacks of grain.

A moment after the last man hit the steel deck, the rappel

lines were jettisoned and the helicopter flared off to the starboard. It was instantly swallowed by blackness. Like the bird of prey that had just dropped them, the commandos scurried off the fantail deck, dissolving into the shadows.

The entire deployment had taken twenty-three seconds. Two seconds less than had been planned.

Although the landing was picture-perfect, it had been fraught with risk. Even in the middle of the night, the fantail was always bathed in light. If someone had been near that area, a crewman on a smoke break or an insomniac out for a walk, they would have seen the commandos. And that would have been a disaster.

As it was, the stern was deserted. Not one of 1,433 crew and passengers aboard the *Emerald Sea* had any idea that the ship had just been invaded.

The young watch officer leaned back in the leather-lined pedestal chair, yawning. It was now 3:05 A.M., local time. He was bone weary and fought to stay awake. He hated the midwatch. Until relieved at four A.M., he remained master of the *Emerald Sea.*

He stared through the windscreen. The bow floodlights illuminated the huge plumes of spray as they blasted upward from the heaving hull. The ship was still bucking into the storm.

As expected, the Dixon Entrance had turned into a maelstrom. Eight-foot swells relentlessly attacked the hull while vicious rain gusts whistled through the superstructure's rigging.

Outside, on the open windswept decks, it was a chilly forty degrees. But inside the wheelhouse, it was short-sleeve warm. And the rich, delicious fragrance of coffee permeated the compartment. A fresh pot had just been brewed.

The watch officer reached for his coffee mug; it was resting in a gimbaled mount on the chair. He took a sip. The thick brew, a special blend from his home island of Sparta, was heavily laced with sugar. Yet it still packed a wicked bite.

He took another sip from the steaming porcelain mug and

then turned to the side, eyeing the only other person on the bridge deck. "How's it look, Vassos?" he asked in their native Greek.

The third mate was leaning over the radar monitor. "We're on course and maintaining speed. We should be in the lee of the storm in another hour or so."

The watch officer nodded. "Good, then we'll make it to Ketchikan on time. That'll make the captain happy."

"Right, shouldn't be a problem."

They were both wrong.

He was in maximum REM. It had been months since his last viewing. The images were in Technicolor, as vivid and real as if he were living them all over again.

It had snowed that December morning. Not much, just a few inches, yet it had transformed the cityscape from its drab, dark complexion into one of sparkling purity. Captain Tim Carpenter had flown into Munich the night before, catching a MAC flight out of Berlin. Christmas was three days away.

Eva had waited up for him. He had been gone for sixteen long days—another clandestine mission into the East. Their lovemaking that night was frantic—both starved.

Tim had three weeks' leave saved up. Tomorrow they would all fly back to Boston. Eva's parents were anxious to see their first grandchild.

Captain Timothy Carpenter was twenty-eight at the time. He was assigned to the U.S. Army's Intelligence and Security Command. Officially, he reported to INSCOM's 66th Military Intelligence Brigade, Munich Field Station. But he really worked for another INSCOM group: Foreign Intelligence Activity, Detachment E, European Command.

Tim would have slept till noon if it hadn't been for the phone call. Eva answered for him. He was wanted at brigade headquarters for a ten A.M. staff meeting. More Army b.s.

Tim showered, shaved, and dressed in his uniform. He was almost out the door when Eva called out: "Honey, can you take us into town before your meeting?"

"What?"

"It snowed and I don't want to drive my car—I need to

ick up a few more gifts for Mom and Dad."

Tim smiled. "Sure—where do you want me to drop you ff?"

She told him about a great little antique shop she had ound.

Tim's vehicle had been parked in the street near the front f their apartment building—a U.S. Army motor pool Chevy uburban. It was pea green, of course. But this morning it vas camouflaged by a covering of snow. He helped Eva strap Emily and her car seat into the right rear seat and then pened the front passenger door for Eva.

After Eva had climbed in and he shut the door, Tim was bout to head around to the driver's side when he remembered. *I forgot my briefcase.* He stepped back and opened he passenger door. "Honey, I forgot my briefcase." He then anded her the keys to the Suburban. "Why don't you start t up and turn on the heater?"

"Yeah, that sounds good—it's sure cold." As Tim shut the loor, she began to slide across the bench seat, heading for he driver's side.

Tim had managed to take a couple of steps when he spotted the footprints in the snow—they led from the sidewalk straight to the front end of the Suburban. He hadn't noticed hem earlier. *What the hell?*

He turned for a closer inspection just as Eva rotated the gnition key.

"NO!" he screamed.

Tim Carpenter woke with a jolt. He was trembling; his heart vas thundering like a racing locomotive; his body was slick vith sweat.

"Oh, Christ!" he moaned.

The haunting was not unexpected. Tim's confessional of a few hours earlier had stirred everything up. Sometimes he vomited afterward.

The forensics analysis team—FBI agents from Quantico, U.S. Army CID explosive experts from Falls Church, and specialists from the BND, West Germany's Federal Intelligence

Service—reconstructed the bomb. A kilogram of Semtex had been wedged into the engine compartment, near the driver's side. The brick of plastic explosive was bound with multiple layers of detonation cord, each layer knotted. Intertwined with the coils of det cord, and wired to the starting motor, were three blasting caps. The instant that Eva switched on the ignition, the caps exploded, triggering the prima cord. The knots in the ribbon of high explosive concentrated the force. The resulting shock wave denoted the Semtex.

Eva and tiny Emily didn't have a chance—the passenger compartment was eviscerated.

Tim was about six feet away from the hood when the bomb went off. The Chevy's V-8 saved his life. The massive engine block deflected much of the blast from his direction. Nevertheless, it was a narrow escape.

Instinctively, he had raised his hands to protect his face—shrapnel from the disintegrating windshield and other car parts peppered his arms, hands, and upper torso. The missiles found other marks, ripping into his forehead, peeling away part of his scalp, and mangling an ear.

The blast's concussion hammered Tim's entire body—a Goliath-sized right hook—propelling him to the pavement. His left knee took the brunt of the impact but he also broke an arm and wrenched his back.

Tim spent five weeks in the hospital before he was finally released. He didn't make Eva and Emily's funeral, back in Boston.

The top secret joint CIA/BND follow-up investigation was inconclusive. The bomb could have been placed by several likely sources: remnants from West Germany's Red Army Faction—the former Baader-Meinhof Gang, PLO terrorists operating out of East Germany, or Libyans. Tim Carpenter and his INSCOM group had been targeting all three.

What was known for certain was that the car bombing was not a random act. Tim had been set up. There was no brigade staff meeting that morning. The telephone call had been a ruse, designed to lure Tim into the Suburban. That suggested a sophistication beyond the norm of the usual suspects. As a consequence, two additional culprits were considered as possibilities: East Germany's Ministry of State Security—the Stasi—its Department XXII, in particular; and the KGB. The Cold War was winding down at the time and the losers were getting desperate.

Tim was lying on his back, catching up with his heart—and his emotions—when he felt the vibration.

A huge growler had smashed into the hull, sending a massive shudder through the ship's hull plates. The ship groaned in pain.

Tim shook his head while waiting for his weary eyes to focus. "Wow," he said to himself, "what was that?"

He was in the ship's reading room. The compartment was located in the forward end of the main superstructure, on the port side. Tim had been lying on one of the room's sofas.

Over an hour earlier he had started working on a dog-eared mystery. Hundreds of paperbacks filled the bookshelves lining the room. He should have returned to the cabin at that time but he wasn't ready. His feelings about what had happened earlier with Jennifer remained unsettling.

Tim had managed to digest a dozen pages before nodding off. And then the familiar nightmare jolted him back to life.

He stood up and stretched out his arms, yawning. His thoughts remained focused on Jenny. *You've got to do it, buddy. She's your responsibility. It's your job. She's relying on you.* A moment later he walked out of the doorway and headed aft.

Tim Carpenter dreaded the prospect of returning to the cabin. The pounding propeller would drive him nuts . . . he could live with that. It was Jenny's reception he feared. *She probably hates my guts!*

27 VIOLATION

Major Wu swore under his breath as he stared at the sheet of paper. "Shit, this is turning into a bloody mess!"

The six-man team was deep inside the *Emerald Sea*. They were now huddled together at the end of a long hallway. There were dozens of mahogany cabin doors on one side, a solid steel wall on the other. The corridor was hot, much warmer than other parts of the ship, and the air had an oily odor to it. And then there was the noise. The deep-toned rumble of racing machinery resonated through the wall almost as if the insulated steel plates were not there. The racket from the ship's engine room sounded like a dozen locomotives, all running at one hundred miles an hour.

Major Wu again squinted at the paper. It was a fax copy and its quality was poor. But that wasn't the problem. The original document had been color-coded. After it was scanned and transmitted, everything reverted to black and white.

"According to this thing," Wu said, pointing to the sheet, "we should be near it." He then looked at the steel wall that blocked their access. The watertight bulkhead completely sealed off the passageway. There was no way through it.

If the commando team leader had had the original colored brochure, he would have instantly recognized the problem. Although most of the Bolero Deck was shaded blue, a small section near the stern was marked in yellow. And a tiny note on the brochure's legend would have indicated that yellow stood for special cabin access. Another note on the brochure, typed in even smaller print but now blurred from the fax process, stated that access to cabins 340 to 345 could only be obtained by using a secondary stairway located on the deck above. The commandos, however, had used the primary access stairway.

Major Wu continued to study the deck plan. *There's some-*

thing wrong here, he finally concluded. He then glanced at his watch. *Shit, we're running out of time!* He looked back at his men. "We've got to back up and try another way."

The assistant cook had just come up from his quarters, heading for the galley, when he ran into the black-clad intruders. Before he knew it, they had him pinned to the deck, a knife held to his throat.

"Tell us how to get to cabin three forty-five or I'll cut your head off," Major Wu said, speaking in perfect English.

The cook shook his head. *"No hablo inglés,"* he replied. His normally brown face had turned to ash. He wanted to urinate.

Wu turned to one of his charges. "Tell him," he ordered in Chinese. The man repeated the order, this time in Spanish.

The cook got the message. "I don't know, exactly," he said. "We're not allowed in the passenger compartments."

The pressure from Wu's knife increased when the translation was completed, spurring the cook on. "But I think maybe I can show you how to get there."

Thirty seconds later, the commando team was on the move, led by the twenty-two-year-old Colombian. They had just turned into a new companionway when the Chinese equivalent of Murphy's Law struck again.

The passenger, an elderly woman, and her equally ancient husband were walking forward. She was herding him along, like a cowhand driving a reluctant steer. "Come on, George," she said, "the doctor's waiting."

The seventy-eight-year-old man held his right wrist with his good hand as he shuffled along the corridor. He was about as miserable as one could get. Up half the night retching his guts out, he had slipped by the toilet and fallen. In the process of catching himself, he managed to break something in his wrist. The pain completely overwhelmed the motion-induced nausea that had plagued him.

Normally, the ship's physician would have come to the cabin to treat the injury. But because of the inclement weather, she was busy attending to a dozen other seasick patients in the tiny infirmary.

When the woman spotted the gunmen, she screamed. She had the lungs of a teenager. And then, just a moment later, one of the nearby cabin doors opened. Another elderly man peered out. "What's going . . ." he started to ask but then stopped when he eyed the intruders. He instantly slammed the door.

"Stop him," Major Wu commanded.

Two commandos ran toward the door. It was locked. One blasted the lock with a burst of submachine-gun fire. The suppressor muffled the report from the nine-millimeter.

When the door sprang open, the man in the cabin had the phone glued to his ear. His face was wrinkled with terror as he started to speak. "Yes, this is Bill Wilkerson in cabin—"

He never finished. They cut him down with another burst. He belly-flopped to the floor, almost DOA.

The woman in the hallway had now been silenced. Duct tape sealed her mouth and her hands were tied behind her back. Her husband was similarly bound. The gunmen ignored his yelp of pain when they snugged up the plastic cable tie on his broken wrist.

The commandos guided the couple into the cabin, making them lie in the bed. The cabin's single occupant littered the deck space, blood now pooling around it. One of the men yanked out the phone while Major Wu leaned over and whispered into the woman's ear.

"You lie real still and keep your mouth shut for the next half hour," he said. "We'll be gone by then, but if we hear any more from you, or if you try to get out of here, I'll come back and slice your heart out. You understand?"

The woman nodded, her eyes as wide as saucers.

The PLA commandos continued heading aft, led by the assistant cook. After having witnessed firsthand the ruthlessness of his captors, he was now so terrified that he walked right by the one doorway that would have taken them to cabin 345. Instead, he blindly walked aft. All he could think of was his mother.

Tim Carpenter smelled it the instant he came down the long stairway. The air was thick with it. He stopped and took another sniff. *What the hell?* he thought as the acrid odor of cordite continued to tease his nostrils. And then he spotted the door.

The invaders had pulled the cabin door shut, using a strip of duct tape to hold it in place. But the shattered lock gave it away.

He cautiously approached the door. He moved next to it, his head cocked, listening for any telltale noise. Nothing. He gripped the handle and pushed. The tape sheared away and the door swung open.

"Good God!" he said as he stared at the corpse. Fresh blood now covered almost all of the tile deck. And then he spotted the couple lying on the bed. The woman struggled to talk, but the duct tape muffled her voice.

Tim walked forward, trying to avoid the mess. He kneeled on the bed and then removed the tape from her mouth. Before he could say anything, she started to gush out her story.

"The bastards! They just shot him down—for nothing. Cold-blooded murder. That's what it was. They didn't—"

"Who did this?" Tim interrupted.

"There were six of them—dressed in black—they all had guns. Chinamen, I think."

Tim's pulse raced. "What are they after?" he demanded.

"They didn't say."

"Where'd they go?"

"I don't know. They dumped us in here a few minutes ago. They said they'd kill us if we tried to get away." She turned to check her husband. He was fine. But by the time she turned back the visitor was halfway through the doorway. "Hey!" she shouted, "don't leave us here."

Tim ignored the woman's plea. Instead, he raced down the hall and then pushed opened a doorway. He dropped down the carpeted stairway, taking two steps at a time. When he reached the Bolero Deck he stopped, forcing himself to think ahead. Once he pushed opened the fire-door, there was no stopping. Their cabin was six doors down. If the intruders were anywhere nearby, they'd see him. *Shit,* Tim thought, *I don't have a damn thing to use.*

His Glock remained in the cabin and the Heckler & Koch

was hidden inside one of the lifeboats. There was no time to retrieve the submachine gun. But then he saw it. The emergency fire station was built into the bulkhead next to the stairway landing. Inside was one hundred feet of nylon fire hose, a chemical fire extinguisher, and a red-handled fire ax.

Tim yanked open the cabinet and removed the ax. He then pushed open the doorway, the ax ready for battle. But the corridor was vacant. He peered aft, counting doors. *One, two, three . . . six.* None of the cabin doors appeared to have been damaged.

He moved aft, the ax held at port arms, still ready for action.

He was now standing opposite the cabin door. He could hear nothing other than the constant drone of the propeller. He tested the lock. It wouldn't budge. *Good,* he thought. He inserted the key.

When the door swung open, his spirits dropped like a lead balloon. Jenny wasn't in her bed. *Oh, shit, they got her.*

A moment later the bathroom door opened and Jenny stepped out, wearing one of Tim's extra-large sweatshirts. Her complexion was waxy and pained. Something was amiss.

"Jenny," Tim said, "you're all right!"

"No, I'm not," she retorted and then flopped down onto her bed. "I'm seasick."

Tim rushed inside, dropping the ax onto the deck beside the bed. He then leaned forward and pulled her up by the arms, roughly. "We've got to go!" he ordered.

"Hey," she protested, "what are you doing?"

Tim released his grip once she was standing. He next turned to the side and grabbed a pair of her jeans that hung over the back of a chair. "Here," he said, "get dressed. We've got to get out of here."

"What's going on?"

"No time, I'll explain later." He then reached into the tiny closet and retrieved the Glock from his carry-on bag.

While Jenny yanked up her jeans, she watched Tim eject the magazine, checking to make sure it was fully loaded. He then shoved the mag in and pulled the slide back, injecting a live round into the firing chamber.

Oh, no, she thought, *not again!*

Three minutes later Tim and Jenny vacated the cabin. For both, any lingering thoughts of what had happened there just a few hours earlier had vanished, replaced with gut-twisting horror.

28 HIJACKED

"Did you see them?" Jenny asked, still slightly out of breath. They had been running for several minutes. Her nausea had miraculously faded, replaced with an adrenaline rush.

"No, but I saw their handiwork—one dead, two others tied up. The woman I talked with told me there were at least six of them, all armed." Tim hesitated. "And she said they looked Chinese."

"Oh, damn! Then it's got to be them." She could hardly forget the Asians that had attacked them back in Roche Harbor.

"Yep, they somehow managed to figure out we're aboard this thing." Tim paused. He really wanted a cigarette, but he didn't dare light up. The smoke might reveal their hiding place.

Tim and Jenny were in the forward third of the hull, tucked away in a laundry supply room next to the gymnasium. Located one deck level below their own cabin, they had taken a serpentine route through the galley to reach it. Only a handful of the crew were about and none of them challenged the "guests" when they fast-walked through the compartment.

Tim took a deep breath. "I've got to find out what those characters are up to."

"How are you going to do that?"

"I've got to head topside and check things out. There could

be an army of those bastards aboard. Until then, we'll just be guessing."

"All right, let's go, then."

Tim turned, eyeing Jenny. "No, not yet. It's much safer if you stay behind, here." He pointed to one of the canvas duffel bags resting near her feet. "You've got to watch over your dad's stuff."

"We can hide it someplace down here," she protested.

"No, I can't risk taking you with me right now. They just may settle for you, instead of the documents. Remember they've been trying to get to you all along. I gotta believe they think you collaborated with your dad."

"But we don't even know if they're after us—they could be doing something else."

"Yeah, but that's one hell of a coincidence, don't you think?"

Jenny hesitated before replying. "Okay, so it's probably them. But maybe you fooled them."

"What?"

"With the beds and our stuff."

Before exiting cabin 345, Tim had pulled up the blankets and bedcovers on both bunks, tucking them in to look as if they hadn't been used—the way the Army had taught him as a first-year cadet at West Point. And if there had been time, he would have removed all of their personal effects from the cabin. Instead, he settled for what they could cram into the duffel bag with the MERLIN documents and his attaché case.

"It might slow 'em for a while, but they'll eventually figure it out. Anyway, I want you to stay here until I get back."

"But—" Jenny said as she started to protest.

Tim shook his head, interrupting. "No. And that's final. You stay put until I figure a way out of this." He then reached into his coat pocket and removed the Glock. He handed it to her. "It's ready to fire—like I showed you earlier."

"You keep that thing—I don't want it."

He thrust the pistol forward. "Look, Jenny. I can't leave

you without some kind of protection. These damn people are ruthless."

"But what about you?"

"I'll be all right. Once I get topside, I'll get the weapon I hid in the lifeboat."

Jenny acquiesced. "All right, but don't leave me down here too long. I might get bored and decide to come look for you."

"Don't worry. I'll be back in about half an hour."

Jenny nodded. Tim handed her the pistol.

Tim was now heading up another flight of stairs. His heart was pounding like a steam engine. There was new fire in his knee. *Oh shit!* he thought, *how the hell are we going to get out of this mess?*

The PLA commandos finally found cabin 345. Remembering the debacle on Pearl Island, Major Wu took no chances with the assault. After stealthily picking the lock, a flash-bang was tossed inside. Two and a half seconds later the stun grenade exploded with a blinding light and deafening roar. Two *zhongduis* rushed in, ready to capture the occupants.

But it was all for nothing. The cabin was empty. Someone had been there, that much they were certain of. There were a half dozen garments in the closet as well as assorted female underwear in one dresser drawer. But no luggage, other than one empty duffel bag. And more troubling were the bunk beds. They would have passed a drill sergeant's inspection.

Major Wu was now standing in the hallway outside of the cabin. Smoke from the blast continued to diffuse outward, as if there had been a fire. The two men who had first entered the cabin were now frantically tearing it apart, looking for any clue that might point them in the right direction. Other than the clothing and various toilet articles in the bathroom, there was nothing to work with. Finally, the two commandos came out, shaking their heads. Their prey had again vanished without a trace.

"Dammit!" Wu shouted, cursing in his native tongue. He was now almost beside himself. The entire mission was turning into an utter failure.

"What should we do?" asked one of his men.

Major Wu was about to respond when the door of the next cabin squeaked open. All six men turned in unison.

The brunet, brown-eyed seven-year-old, wearing nothing more than a large T-shirt with a pink teddy bear clutched to her chest, stared wide-eyed at the gunmen.

Dressed in black and armed to the teeth, the *zhongdui*s were a sinister sight.

One of the commandos started to raise his weapon but Major Wu gave him a sharp look. The man lowered the SMG.

Wu smiled at the girl. "Go back inside, honey," he said, "and get back in your bed. Everything's okay out here."

The girl pushed the door shut. The lock clicked a second later.

Wu again faced his men. "All right," he said, "they're obviously not here so let's get topside. We need to inform Peng about the situation."

He was awake after the first rap on the cabin door. Like the majority of master mariners, he had learned to sleep with a mother's ear.

Captain Markos Demetriou reached up and switched on the light next to his bunk. "Come," he called out.

The watch officer opened the door. He was silhouetted by a light from the overhead just outside the cabin. "Sir, we need you on the bridge right now."

Demetriou swung his short legs over the rail. "The storm getting worse?" he asked.

"No, sir. It's abating, but we've got a situation below."

"What do you mean situation?" The captain of the *Emerald Sea* was now standing, throwing on a bathrobe over his nearly naked body. He wore only a pair of boxer shorts.

"We're not sure. But the chief steward's office just reported that several passengers are complaining about an explosion."

"What?" Demetriou said, not yet fully awake.

"An explosion, sir. Somewhere aft, on Bolero Deck."

"Have we got a fire back there?" asked the captain.

"Maybe. No heat sensors are showing, but we have one sensor showing smoke."

The watch officer now had Demetriou's full attention. A fire at sea was one of the worst horrors for any ship, especially a passenger-carrying vessel. Located throughout the ship were thousands of remote smoke and heat sensors—each linked to the main fire control computer located on the bridge. But there were no automatic cabin alarms like those found in a typical hotel room. Instead, the *Emerald Sea,* as well as most other cruise ships, manually activated all cabin alarms from the bridge. The system was designed to control passenger panic.

"Just where on Bolero is this smoke coming from?"

"Cabin three forty-five."

"You dispatch a fire response team?"

"They're on the way, sir."

"Good," Captain Demetriou replied as he stepped into a pair of slippers. He then headed for the open doorway. "Alert all senior officers and mates. I want them on the bridge in five minutes."

"Yes, sir."

"What the hell else can I say?" the voice said in Chinese. "No one was in the cabin when we got there. Over." Major Wu was now standing on the sundeck, opposite the main swimming pool. It was still raining, but the wind had dropped down to tolerable levels. A portable VHF radio was glued to the side of his head. The radio would not work belowdecks.

Allen Peng was on the other end of the wireless communication line, standing in the *Orca*'s bridgehouse. Both radios were equipped with encryption chips. Their voices sounded flat, lackluster—washed out by the crypto processors. "Then they've still got to be aboard. There's no way they could get off until the ship docks in Ketchikan. Over."

"Yes, if they were really here to begin with. Over."

"They're aboard, Major, I'm certain of it. Over."

"All right. But this is a huge vessel. It could take hours, days to search it. What do you want us to do? Over."

Peng turned to face Rémy. He translated, summarizing what the PLA commando had just repeated.

The French agent shook his head, disgusted with the new situation. He then turned away, breaking eye contact. *Idiots!* he thought, *they've screwed it up again.*

Peng ignored the man's rebuke. He'd deal with the arrogant bastard later.

"Control, you there? Over," asked Major Wu.

"Stand by, Dragons," replied Peng. He was still considering his options. It would have been so simple to just abandon the mission. Recall the team and leave was what logic dictated. But he rejected that plan. Withdrawal was not an option. Beijing had made that clear from the beginning. The prime goal of the operation was to obtain the MERLIN technology. He had to continue.

Peng keyed his mike. "Dragons, Control. You are directed to execute plan Rising Moon. I say again, execute plan Rising Moon. Over."

"Control, Dragons. Execute Rising Moon. Over and out."

Major Wu flipped off the radio and slipped it back into a pocket on the pants of his fatigues. He signaled for the other members of the team to join him as he headed toward a covered area. It was time for new instructions.

Tim Carpenter watched the collection of black-clad men as they kneeled together, forming a semicircle around the one that had just been talking on a radio.

Tim was about one hundred feet forward, standing behind a lifeboat davit. He had just retrieved the Heckler & Koch from its secret hiding place when he spotted one of the intruders. The guard was pacing along a walkway near the guardrail.

What are you turkeys up to? Tim asked himself. He then looked down at the submachine gun. The German-made nine-millimeter was heavy in his hands. He rotated the selector switch from safety to the two-round burst mode. *If I get a little closer, maybe I can nail 'em all.*

Tim again looked up, now ready to work his way aft toward the enemy. But he could hardly believe his eyes. The six men had vanished. Not one was in sight. *Shit! Where the hell did they go?*

29 TREACHERY

The sun had just risen, revealing the thick, low ceiling of dripping-wet clouds. The vapor mass enveloped the ocean for as far as the eye could see. Everything was gray, from the rolling sea to the veiled base slopes of the distant coastal mountains.

The gale had finally died out just before dawn, leaving a windless morning. The residual waves, no longer fueled by the wind, had dissipated to low, slow swells. The air had a pungent salty fragrance, as if scrubbed clean by the overnight squall.

All in all, it was a typical summer morning for the local waters. And if the sun ever managed to burn through the two-mile-deep overcast, the scenery would be truly magnificent: steep wooded mountains thrusting upward from the long, narrow, deep fjords; icy glaciers creeping down the slopes to melt into the sea; and wildlife everywhere—whales, sea lions, eagles, orcas, salmon, and bears. This was the attraction of southeast Alaska. Every summer, hundreds of thousands flocked to see its wonders, transported through the magical waters on floating palaces.

For cruise ships heading north, Ketchikan was often their first port of call. The next day they would land in Juneau, followed by Skagway, Sitka, and then finally across the Gulf of Alaska to Prince William Sound with a final docking at Whittier or Seward.

The landings and departures of the monster vessels along the Alaska ports were planned months in advance. Arriving vessels were assigned dockage space or anchorages, depending upon when they were scheduled to arrive. The wharfage, of course, was most desirable because the passengers could depart directly from the ship without having to use the shuttle launches.

On this morning, the *Emerald Sea* was scheduled to dock at Ketchikan's main berth. Located right in the heart of downtown, it was the perfect departure point for exploring the historic town and its surrounding territory. By nine A.M., dozens of buses would be queued up beside the wharf, ready to carry hundreds of passengers on their prescheduled local tours. In the waters near the ship would be a flotilla of sightseeing vessels, fishing boats, and float planes, all ready to transport more passengers to distant events. But this morning it would all be for naught. The *Emerald Sea* would never arrive in Ketchikan.

At the moment, the ship was charging westward at flank speed. It was near the westerly limit of the Dixon Entrance, about twenty miles north of Graham Island's Cape Fox. The North Pacific Ocean lay dead ahead.

The bridge deck was crowded. All of the ship's officers had been rounded up half an hour earlier. Even the ship's hotel manager and concierge had been ordered to the pilot-house. The commandos had been very thorough in commandeering the vessel.

Only one shot was fired during the transfer of power. Three of the *zhongdui* had simply walked onto the bridge and brandished their submachine guns. Captain Demetriou, at that time on watch, was too stunned to react. But the third mate wasn't. The man reached for the console and almost had removed the switch guard when he was killed. The PLA commando fired one round into the officer's chest.

The specter of a hijacking was always present and the *Emerald Sea*, like many other modern passenger vessels, was equipped with an emergency alert system. Patterned after the silent alarms that bank tellers use, the ship's alarm was located on a console next to the helm. Once the plastic guard was pushed aside and the toggle switch flipped, the system would activate. The radio transmitter was mounted on top of the radar mast. It would beam a coded digital signal to the nearest communication satellite. The signal would announce the hijacking, identify the vessel, and then provide the ship's current earth coordinates. The message would be repeated every thirty seconds.

But it would never be used. After the killing, one of the commandos deactivated the system, severing the control wires inside the console. The *zhongdui* was an electronics expert and knew what to look for.

At the same time that the bridge was being commandeered, Major Wu and two other gunmen took control of the ship's radio room. As on the bridge deck, there had been no time for the young communications officer to send out an SOS. One moment he was listening to an updated weather forecast, the next he was being herded forward at gunpoint.

Knowing that many of the passengers were affluent and expecting that some of them might have brought along their portable satellite phones just for the fun of it, Major Wu took appropriate precautions. The same *zhongdui* who had disabled the ship's hijack beacon rigged up a portable PLA jamming device and mounted its antenna to the top of the pilothouse. Grandpa and Grandma would no longer be able to phone home—or call 911.

While the other members of the assault team remained inside the wheelhouse guarding the assembled crew, the assault team leader was now standing alone on the port bridge wing. Major Wu had his back to the twenty-knot ship-generated wind. He was looking aft. The *Orca* was about a mile behind, charging forward at nearly twenty-five knots. He raised the portable radio to his lips and keyed the transmitter. "Command, Dragons. Over," he said, speaking in Chinese.

"Dragons, go," came the instant reply.

Wu recognized Peng's voice. "Sir, the operation has been completed. We have control. Over."

"Any problems?"

"Negative."

"Still no sign of the targets?"

"Affirmative."

There was a short pause. "Stand by. I'll be coming aboard."

"Very good, sir."

Major Wu slipped the transceiver back into a pocket on his chest harness. He then cupped his hands, sheltering his lighter from the breeze as he lit up. It was his first cigarette since starting the mission. The nicotine helped.

After running on adrenaline all night long, the short respite was welcome. The mission was souring. It had been geared for a quick turnaround: land on the ship, find the target, and then fly back to the *Orca*. The assault would have gone off like clockwork except for one critical element—they couldn't find the target. Jennifer Richmond was not in cabin 345, nor was her companion, the private detective named Carpenter.

They could be just about anywhere, thought the commando leader as he sucked in another lungful. The *Emerald Sea* was huge. Well over two football fields in length and with ten decks from the keel to the bridge, there were hundreds of hiding places. The interior of the ship's hull was the ultimate maze—a floating labyrinth. *How am I supposed to find them?*

Major Wu took one last drag before flipping the spent butt overboard. He then glanced at the *Orca*. The yacht was still closing. *Good, Peng'll be here soon. And then he can take over this mess.*

"Peng," shouted the voice, **"I think you're crazy to continue** with this madness!"

Allen Peng turned to face Gérard Rémy. The French intelligence operative was standing a few feet behind him. They were on the open deck directly behind the *Orca*'s pilothouse. The helicopter was about forty feet away, nesting on the cantilevered helideck. Its turbine was screaming and the rotors spinning, filling the air with an oppressive racket.

Peng yelled back: "You know we've come too far to stop now."

Rémy moved closer. "Stop it, right now! You've got time. Recall your people and we'll get the hell out of here."

Peng shook his head. "I can't do that."

"Look, we don't even know for sure if they're aboard that thing. The only solid lead we have is the cellular telephone calls but they could have been made by anyone." Rémy hesitated. "Hell, Carpenter could have lost it or given the damn thing away."

"They're aboard—it makes all the sense in the world. We just have to find them."

"Peng, we're in this thing as equal partners. We all agreed that we had to have unanimous approval. I've just made a decision for our interest—we want out. That means you must stop."

Peng didn't reply. Instead, he fired back an icy stare.

The DGSE spy continued: "If you continue with this, it'll be an unmitigated disaster for all of us." He shook his head. "My God, man, think about what you're doing—hijacking a fucking ship with nine hundred passengers—most of them American. We'll be crucified if they figure out who we are!"

"They'll never know."

"Yes they will. You can count on it."

Peng stiffened. "My orders are explicit: capture the Richmond woman; short of that I'm to make certain that she's dead." He paused, now looking the Frenchman squarely in the eyes. "I intend to carry out my orders."

Rémy remained just as steadfast. *I've got to stop this bastard or he'll ruin us all.* He stepped a little closer. His voice was raw from yelling. The din from the helicopter continued to envelop everything on the open deck.

Rémy was now just an arm's length away. He had made up his mind. *I've got to distract him first.* "All right, Allen," he said, now smiling, "if you insist on continuing, then at least let me . . ."

Peng listened as Rémy suggested a modification to the plan. His guard, however, remained on full alert. After such vehement opposition, the Frenchman's sudden capitulation was disturbing. *He's up to something.*

As Rémy continued to outline his modifications, he slowly lowered his right hand, inserting it into his parka jacket.

From the corner of his eye, Peng saw movement. *What's he doing?*

And then it happened.

Like a lightning bolt, the knife blade flashed as Rémy thrust it forward. Peng's lower abdomen was the target.

Peng would have been gutted had it not been for the cold, and his quick reflexes. He wore a heavy wool peacoat, provided by the *Orca*'s master. The blade penetrated three-quarters of the way through the dense fabric before Peng deflected Rémy's knife hand away with a downward chop from his right arm.

Rémy, instantly assessing the tactical situation, prepared for another attack, this time a slash to the neck.

Peng was ready. Instinctively, he again lashed out with his arm, blocking Rémy's second thrust. And then, with one enormous lunge, Peng slammed his full body weight against the lighter man.

Rémy reeled backward, stunned by the powerful body blow. Before he could stop himself, however, he collided with the guardrail. And then, knife still in hand, he toppled over the top oak rail and plummeted into the sea.

Peng moved forward. When he reached the railing he looked aft. Already Rémy was just a tiny dot in the *Orca*'s wake. For a fleeting moment Peng considered turning the ship around and then running the bastard down, using the propellers to slice him up like sashimi. But he dismissed that thought. There was no time for revenge. Besides, Rémy would soon be fish bait on his own. The forty-five-degree waters would suck the life-heat from the French spy within an hour.

"I need to speak with one of the ship's officers. Are there any around here?"

The deckhand scraping rust from a guardrail stanchion shook his head. His slight body was encased in a yellow slicker. "Sorry, sir," he answered in perfect British-accented English, "but I haven't seen any yet this morning. They're probably still in their quarters or on the bridge."

Tim Carpenter nodded. "Okay, thanks."

Tim continued moving aft along the main promenade deck. The young African was the only crew member that he had encountered on the exterior deck. Other than a few other early risers, out for their morning constitutionals, the outside walkways of the ship were deserted.

Tim was now near the stern, the SMG once again concealed in a duffel bag. Even with the hood of his jacket extended, he was rain-soaked. He was just heading back inside when he spotted it.

The drizzle had thickened to the consistency of fog, concealing nearly everything around the cruise ship. The boat was now about a quarter of a mile away, following in the *Emerald Sea*'s wake. It was barely visible to the naked eye, just a white aberration in a seascape of gray.

Tim moved to the seaward side of the deck. Now leaning on a guardrail, he studied the visitor as it plowed ahead into the swells, white water blasting from its bow. *It's coming up fast,* he said to himself. His heart beat a little faster in anticipation. *Maybe it's help?* He smiled. *That's it. It's gotta be the Coast Guard. Now we'll get out of this mess.*

Tim's elation eroded a few minutes later when the new arrival pulled even with the cruise ship's stern, taking up station about a hundred yards to starboard. It was not a patrol craft, but a modern yacht. A big one. Its form and shape were vaguely familiar, but that wasn't what alarmed Tim. It was the helicopter. The black-hulled craft lifted off from the yacht's helideck and within seconds landed on one of the *Emerald Sea*'s upper decks. And five men jumped out. All Asians. The first to deplane wore a heavy peacoat and appeared to be unarmed. The four that followed, however, were outfitted in combat fatigues and each carried a high-powered assault rifle.

Shit, oh, dear! Tim thought as he turned away. *Five more of those bastards aboard. Now what the hell am I going to do?*

"Morning, Rick. It's Vicky. Did I wake you?"
While holding the handset with his left hand, Ricardo Molina reached up with his other hand and rubbed his eyes. He

had been sound asleep, lying prone on the couch in his office when the telephone started ringing.

"It's okay. I was just taking a catnap." He paused a moment to check his wristwatch. It was almost seven o'clock. "What's going on?" he asked.

"We've finally got something. We think they're on a cruise ship heading to Alaska."

"What?" Ricardo asked, clearly taken aback by Kwan's statement.

"The chief RCMP investigator just showed me a surveillance video from the port. The Mounties have been reviewing tapes all night. There are a bunch of closed-circuit TV cameras around Canada Place. That's the cruise ship terminal downtown. You know the place?"

"Yeah," Ricardo replied as an image of Vancouver's monster over-the-water building snapped into focus. The twin rows of white canvas sail-like icons that jutted upward from the structure's top floor were hard to forget.

"Well, it turns out that one of the cameras happened to pick up a shot of what we believe to be Tim Carpenter. It's not all that clear of an image so we're not completely sure. That's why we're faxing you a copy—maybe you can verify it for me."

"You send it yet?" he asked, now slipping his thick legs over the side of the sofa.

"Yeah, it should be there by now."

"Hang on," Ricardo said. He pushed the hold button and then walked out of his office, heading into the communications room.

A minute later he was standing by the main fax machine. He picked up a single sheet from the output tray. It was a blowup of a video still. The original photograph had been grainy and additional quality had been lost during the fax transmission. But none of that mattered. Ricardo picked up a nearby phone and punched the flashing hold button.

"It's Tim—must have cut his hair—but there's no question about it."

"Good. Then we've got 'em now."

"Tell me more," Ricardo ordered.

"The video was taken Friday afternoon. He was in the boarding area for the *Emerald Sea*. It's one of those Alaska tour ships."

"Where in Alaska is it going?"

"Its first port of call is Ketchikan—later this morning."

"What time?"

"Nine o'clock, local time. That's one hour behind us."

Ricardo made a quick mental calculation. *Good, I just might make it,* he told himself. He then spoke into the handset. "Great job, Vicky. Keep monitoring things up there. See if you can get a better handle on the Chinese connection. We've got to find out just how much these people know about MERLIN."

"Sure, but what are we going to do about Carpenter and the Richmond woman?"

Ricardo smiled. "I'll be there right at the dock, waiting for old Tim to show up. There's no way he'll be able to give me the slip this time."

30 CLOSING IN

"Where are you hiding them? We know they're aboard."

"On my mother's grave, I don't know."

"Liar!" screamed Major Wu. And then he hit the hostage.

The butt end of the rifle stock slammed into Captain Demetriou's gut with the force of a pile driver. The master of the *Emerald Sea* doubled over, searing pain ripping through his insides. And then he dropped to his knees.

Wu raised the assault rifle, preparing to strike again.

"Enough, Major!" called out a voice in Mandarin.

Wu turned, facing Allen Peng.

"He doesn't know anything," Peng said, continuing to use his native tongue. "You're wasting our time."

"I just need a few more minutes, then he'll talk."

"No. We have to take another approach."

"What then?"

Peng turned to one of the other commandos now manning the pilothouse. "Take this one back to the others," he ordered. He then paused, scanning the clipboard in his hands. "And bring back the one named L. Weathersby."

"Who's that?" Wu asked.

"This manifest says he's the hotel manager. If anyone will know, he will."

Wu nodded as he pulled out a cigarette.

The *L* in *L. Weathersby* stood for Lindsay.

Lindsay was now planted in the captain's chair on the bridge. She was surrounded by Asians.

Peng was conducting the interrogation. He couldn't resist. The Australian was very much to his liking: blond, tan, leggy. And, of course, full-breasted.

Peng glanced down at the clipboard. He then focused on her baby blues. "Tell me, Miss Weathersby, how did someone as young as you get to be hotel manager?" He then gestured to the clipboard. "This says you're in charge of the ship's entire Accommodations Department—food service, housekeeping, concierge, entertainment. Very impressive."

"I work hard. I've been at it for ten years now."

"Where?"

"In the Caribbean, the Med, and here, of course."

Peng smiled. "That's very good; then you're just the person we need to talk with."

Lindsay remained mute, not taking the bait.

Peng reached into a coat pocket and removed a pair of photographs. He handed the snapshots to Lindsay.

"I know these two individuals mean nothing to you right now, but in about ten minutes they're going to be the most important people in your life."

Lindsay scanned the photos and then looked back up. "What do you want from me?"

"We want those two—they're registered as Mr. and Mrs. Thomas Carter—cabin three forty-five."

She shook her head. "You want me to go get them out of their cabin?"

Peng laughed. "If only it were that simple, then we would

have been long gone by now." He smiled again. "Miss Weathersby, they're not in cabin three forty-five, but we know they're aboard."

Lindsay shrugged. "What can I do if they're not in the cabin?"

"That's why you're here. We expect you to solve our little problem. We don't have a lot of time so let's get on with it."

She shook her head, confused. "I don't know what you want."

Peng's grin dissolved into an icy stare. It was time for closure. "It's this simple: use your experience to come up with a plan to find these two. Otherwise, you're going for a very cold swim."

Lindsay's body stiffened as dread swept down her spine. *My God, these people are bloody nuts!*

"Sir, I don't think this is such a good plan."

"Why not?"

"Because it may not flush them out. I'd much rather go with the other scenario."

Peng looked away from Major Wu, scanning the ocean surface through the windscreen. It was raining and everything outside appeared drab. He turned back to face his second in command. Besides the MSS agent manning the helm, just he and Wu were in the pilothouse.

"Major, if you are wrong, then we will have missed a golden opportunity."

"But they must have known we were coming, otherwise why weren't they in the cabin during the initial assault? And what about the beds—they were all made up, like they hadn't been slept in." Wu glanced at his wristwatch. "It's been a couple of hours now and there's still no sign of them."

"How would they know when we were coming?" Peng asked. He then answered his own question: "They couldn't know—it would be impossible. You and I didn't even know for certain when we'd be able to make the assault—that storm screwed up everything." He hesitated as a new thought developed. "Besides, everything we've observed about this

Carpenter character leads me to believe that he is extremely cunning. I wouldn't put it past him to mimic what Arafat does."

"What?"

"Yassir Arafat—he never sleeps in the same bed on two consecutive nights. He always moves about—the threat of assassination is always there."

Major Wu nodded. "I hadn't thought of it that way. I see your point. They may have found someplace else to hide out last night, anticipating that we just might try something in the middle of the night."

"Correct. For all we know, they're holed up in another cabin or some other nook on this tub."

Wu nodded once again but he wasn't yet ready to capitulate. "All right, that does make some sense, but let's just assume for a moment that they know we're here. What then?"

"Major, if we try your way, I'm afraid we'll have nothing but chaos. We'll never be able to control the situation."

"But we'll have the passengers motivated. That should help flush them out."

"Maybe. But you still don't understand these Americans. You've only been over here for a short time. I've lived around them for many years—they're different than at home. They always rally for the underdog. I'm convinced that it will happen here and that will be a disaster for us."

"What could they do?"

"Many things—hide them, try to overpower us, sabotage the ship, jump overboard. They're unpredictable when their backs are against the wall. It's far better for us to keep them in the dark for as long as possible."

Major Wu shook his head. "Well, sir, I can't believe that Carpenter and the Richmond woman will be so naive as to fall for this plan. The hotel manager knows this ship all right, but I can't see this working out like she thinks it will."

"It might not. But if it does, then it will be easy, no?"

"Yes," Wu reluctantly agreed. "But what happens when they don't show up?"

"Then we search. Eventually, we'll find them."

Major Wu finally surrendered. "Very well, when do we start?"

Peng checked his watch. "In fifteen minutes."

It started with the klaxons. Hundreds of the electronic de-vices were located throughout the ship. At a quarter past seven, the master alarm was activated. The obnoxious racket penetrated every cabin and compartment onboard the *Emerald Sea*. The tone was designed to wake the deepest sleeper.

"What's that noise?" Jenny asked, startled by the piercing din.

Tim stood up. After a quick topside look-see he had just rejoined Jenny in their hideout, deep inside the hull near the gym. He searched the overhead, homing in on the noise source. He pointed to a red light at the opposite end of the compartment. "It's some kind of shipboard alarm. I think it might be—"

Tim was interrupted when a voice suddenly boomed from another speaker hidden away in the overhead: "Attention, all passengers! Attention, all passengers! Please proceed immediately to your muster stations with your flotation jacket. I say again, please proceed immediately to your muster stations with your flotation jacket." The message was repeated in French, then German, and finally Spanish.

Jenny was now standing by Tim, her face wrinkled with worry. "What's going on, Tim—is this another fire drill?"

A day earlier the ship had completed its perfunctory safety drill. After breakfast, the same alarm was sounded and all of the passengers were huddled to their preassigned emergency deck stations. Attendance was mandatory. The cabin stewards had the responsibility of taking roll. And there were no exceptions. Every passenger had to be accounted for.

Tim shook his head. "Clever bastards. They're trying to get us on deck."

"You mean they want us to go to our safety stations, like yesterday?"

"Yes, it would appear so."

"But there's no way we're going to do that."

"Right. This is bizarre—it doesn't make any ..." Tim's voice trailed off as the reverse logic hit home. "Damn—they must think that we still don't know they're aboard."

"What?"

"Right now, if I hadn't spotted their handiwork, we'd have no way of knowing that anything had happened."

"But surely they'd know we weren't in our cabin."

"Maybe, maybe not. For all we know, they may not even know what cabin we were assigned to."

"But what about that woman who was tied up—didn't she say they were looking for us?"

"No, as a matter of fact, she didn't. All she said was that the gunmen were heading aft when she ran into them."

Jenny smiled. "I think I see what you're getting at—they know we're aboard, but they don't know what cabin we were in."

"Yep. And now, instead of conducting a cabin-by-cabin search, they're getting everyone on deck, just like the drill yesterday."

"And no doubt they'll be up there, looking for us."

"That's right. And with a captive audience, we'd be easy pickings—despite our disguises."

"Then what do we do?"

"We just sit tight. They won't be able to find us down here."

The starboard and port-side promenade decks were packed with passengers. They were dressed in everything from pajamas to leisure suits. But they all had one common garment: Every person, from an eighty-year-old great-grandmother to a three-year-old preschooler, wore a fluorescent orange personal flotation device. The bulky PFDs were complete with a whistle and a water-activated light.

Most of the assembled accepted the second drill as a simple annoyance. But not everyone. Complaints could be heard throughout the hordes of passengers. The protests were directed to the cabin stewards and the lifeboat crews: "We went through this crap yesterday—what are we doing out here again?" "I didn't pay good money to freeze my ass off like this!" "When do we eat?" "Is there something wrong with the ship?"

The ship's crew calmed the passengers as best they could, answering their inquires with a uniform response: "This is just a drill and you should be able to return to your cabin soon."

But it was a lie. The cabin stewards and lifeboat attendants had no idea what was going on. Not one of them had ever had a second fire drill during a cruise. Something was wrong. Nevertheless, they remained cool and professional. They had all been trained not to panic the passengers.

"Their assigned station should be just ahead," Lindsay Weathersby said as she walked aft along the open deck. Like everyone else aboard the *Emerald Sea*, she now wore a life jacket. Despite the PFD's bulk she looked stunning as her golden locks billowed up around her face, buoyed by the ship-generated wind.

"All right," Peng said. "Just act natural as we approach. I don't want to call attention to them yet."

"Okay, whatever you say."

Peng too was outfitted with a PFD. But underneath he had traded his peacoat for an officer's tunic. He had liberated the dark blue jacket with the set of twin gold strips on each sleeve from the ship's second officer. Despite his Asian features, Peng fit right in with the international crew. No one had a hint that the officer accompanying the ship's hotel manager was an impostor.

Lindsay stopped at lifeboat station 18. The lifeboat, a forty-foot-long motor launch, was cantilevered over the seaward edge of the deck, suspended from twin davits. The two crewmen assigned to the lifeboat stood stoically at each davit.

Lindsay nodded to the nearest attendant and then turned toward station 18's assembly area. It was packed with several dozen passengers, all standing and lined up like a platoon of soldiers. A woman crew member, another blond, was busy counting heads.

"Oh, Zena," Lindsay called out, trying to attract the woman's attention.

Zena turned around.

Lindsay smiled and raised her right hand, signaling. "Could I talk with you a moment, please?"

Zena approached. "Yes, ma'am, what can I do?" she answered with her thick Polish accent.

"I'm just making random checks. Everything okay here?"

For just an instant Zena looked beyond Lindsay, eyeing the officer standing behind her. She didn't recognize him and he seemed to be preoccupied with her passengers.

Zena looked back at her supervisor. "Well, ma'am, I am having some difficulty here."

"Oh?"

"Yes, I'm two passengers short. I even sent one of my orderlies back to their room. They are not there."

Peng stepped forward, taking over. "What are their names?" he demanded.

Zena glanced down at the clipboard she carried. "Mr. and Mrs. Carter, sir."

"Cabin three forty-five?" asked Peng.

"Yes, sir," she answered, surprised.

Peng silently cursed to himself. *Dammit, they didn't fall for it!* "Have you personally met these two?"

"Of course. On the first day of the trip I introduced myself."

Peng reached into a jacket pocket and produced two color photographs. He handed them to Zena. "Are these the Carters?"

Zena studied the snapshots. "I don't know. These must be old photos because they don't look too current."

"What do you mean?"

"The man—his hair is much shorter than in this photo—kind of looks like Mr. Carter."

"And the woman?"

"The Mrs. Carter I met was definitely not a redhead, I remember that for sure. Her hair was very black and cut real short. And she was a lot heavier than this woman."

"But you still think she's the same one in this photo?" Peng asked, now concerned.

"Maybe, but I can't really tell."

Peng stiffened, the bile beginning to surge. "Ah, this is real important, miss. I've got to know . . ." He paused to point to the photograph of Jennifer Richmond. "Is this the same woman you met?"

Once again Zena scanned both photos. And then, shaking her head, she replied: "If I had to guess, I'd say the woman in the photo is not the person I met, but the man might be."

Sonofabitch! Peng thought. *What the hell is going on? How could Carpenter have fooled us like this—using a substitute?* And then he remembered one of Rémy's last pronouncements: "Look, we don't even know for sure if they're aboard that thing. The only solid lead we have is the cellular telephone calls."

Dammit, Peng thought, *could Rémy have been right?*

The two women watched in silence as the color faded from Peng's face. It was like watching water drain from a sink. The man was obviously stressed.

Another chill swept down Lindsay's spine. *Oh, my God, what are they going to do now?*

So far the hotel manager had gone along with the hijacker's demands, but now that her carefully thought out scheme had failed, dread once again engulfed her. Lindsay feared not only for herself, but for Zena and her other charges.

Peng had just started to remove the transceiver from a jacket pocket, intending to call Wu, when Lindsay broke the silence.

"Zena, do you think you could positively identify these people if we produced current photographs?"

"Sure," she answered, puzzled.

"What are you talking about?" Peng interjected.

Lindsay turned to face the MSS operative. "There's a chance we might have a photograph of the woman . . . and maybe the man, too."

"Of course," agreed Zena, now making the connection.

"What do you mean?" Peng asked.

Lindsay smiled. "We need to go back to the reception area. I'll show you there."

It took only a few minutes for Zena to find them. She spot-ted Jennifer first.

The glass-enclosed display cases lining both sides of the entryway to the ship's main reception lounge were filled with hundreds of snapshots. Back in Vancouver, the ship's photographer had stood near the gangplank as the passengers boarded. The souvenir pictures, now on display, would be given to the passengers at the end of the voyage.

"That's the woman in cabin three forty-five," Zena called out, pointing to the color print near the center of the portside case.

Peng moved closer, examining the snapshot and then the photo he held. A few seconds later, he sighed. *Thank the gods!*

In spite of the clever disguise, the facial features in the two photographs matched. Jennifer Richmond had, in fact, boarded the cruise ship. *Now I know she's here for certain!*

He turned toward Zena. "How about her companion?"

"I'm still looking."

Five minutes later she found the photo of Tim Carpenter.

After removing both photographs from the display cases, Peng turned back to face Zena and Lindsay. "All right, I want both of you to follow me."

Peng and the two women returned to the bridge. Zena and Lindsay were locked up in Captain Demetriou's cabin, joining the rest of the ship's key staff. Peng then issued new orders.

While the passengers and most of the crew remained top-side, huddled about their exposed muster stations and trying to stay warm in the frigid mist, the invaders began their search. There were now a total of sixteen aboard. Twenty minutes earlier another load had just been airlifted from the *Orca*.

The assembly of MSS agents and PLA commandos started in the bow and worked aft. Everything was checked: cabins, storage lockers, mechanical spaces, electrical enclosures. Nothing was left to chance.

It was like earlier times aboard the huge sailing vessels that once plied the world oceans. When a ship's crew had finally suffered enough from the droves of rats that infested their vessel, they acted. They would start at the bow, smashing, crushing, and impaling every rodent they encountered. The terrified animals would retreat aft, only to find themselves eventually trapped at the stern by the approaching marauders. Those not slaughtered outright leaped overboard, preferring a watery grave.

The procedure worked, ridding the vessel of most of the pests. But it usually wasn't a complete success. There were always stragglers. The survivors would hole up in some obscure space. And then, when the ship returned to its normal routine, they would multiply and start the whole process over.

Unlike the sailors of old, the Chinese marauders would leave no stragglers. Their orders were explicit: They could not leave the ship until the two Americans had been found—dead or alive.

"What's wrong?" asked Jennifer.

"I don't know . . . I can't seem to get anything with it."

Tim and Jenny were still hiding out near the gymnasium, deep inside the vessel. At the moment they were huddled around Tim's open briefcase. He had just retrieved his portable phone.

"Well, I'm sure you have to be outside to pick up the satellite. It's not like a cell phone."

"Yeah, I know . . . that's what the instructions said." Tim paused as he continued to push buttons on the handheld device. "But I should at least get the display to stay on. I can't even do that now."

"Maybe the battery's dead."

"Can't be. It's brand new—I charged it up back at our place on Pearl."

"Could be a bad battery; did you bring the charger?"

"Yeah, it's someplace in here." Tim began rummaging

through the attaché case. "Here it is," he finally announced.

"Good, let's plug it in and see what happens."

The battery was indeed dead, depleted by Raul's digital thievery. It would take at least half an hour of charging before it could be used, and then only for a few minutes of air time.

As Tim and Jenny stared down at the phone, a tiny light on the charging unit pulsing away, she turned toward Tim: "Once you get it charged up, just whom are you planning to call for help?"

He met her eyes. "The cavalry—who else!"

The sixty-foot vessel had been on station for nearly twenty minutes. It was raining—southeast Alaska style. Visibility had been reduced to a few hundred yards as the gully-washer let loose.

The deluge hammered the fiberglass pilothouse, drowning out the low rumble of the idling diesels. The single wiper cycled across the windshield like the wagging tail of a retriever on the hunt.

The bridgehouse was toasty warm, but the stink of cigarette smoke polluted the compartment. There were three men inside. The first mate stood behind the helm, a smoldering Camel hanging from his lip. The skipper was huddled over the radar screen. And standing next to him was the passenger.

"You spot her yet?" asked the passenger.

The master looked up. "No, Bill, there's nothing big out there, just a few small blips, probably fishing boats."

"Well, where the hell is the damn thing, then?"

The captain shook his head. He then reached up and retrieved a handheld microphone from a VHF radio. It was mounted to the overhead. He depressed the transmit key and said: "*Argo* to *Emerald Sea,* come in, please." He waited a few seconds before repeating the message. He then turned to face the passenger. "This is weird. I've never had this happen before."

"What do you think happened to it?"

"I don't know. It should have been here by now. I better check back with the local agent."

The captain reached for another radio microphone that sat on top of the instrument panel. He keyed the transmit switch. "Dock Boss, *Argo.* Come in, please."

"*Argo,* Dock Boss; go."

"Ah, Susan, this is McGivney. We've got a little problem out here. I'm not sure but . . ."

While the captain explained his predicament, the passenger checked his watch. It was 7:58 A.M. *I should have been aboard by now,* he thought. He shook his head in annoyance and once again looked through the windshield. He could see nothing but gray sky and gray water. *What the hell happened to the ship?*

The work boat was south of Duke Island, near the north end of the Dixon Entrance. The international boundary between Canada and the United States was a dozen miles due south.

The *Argo* had been dispatched from Ketchikan an hour earlier. Her mission was to rendezvous with the *Emerald Sea.* The single passenger that the *Argo* carried was a ship's pilot. It was his job to guide the giant ship as she cruised through Alaskan waters.

The *Argo*'s skipper completed his call and then looked back at the Alaska pilot. "The dock boss doesn't know what's going on. She's going to call San Francisco and try to find out if the ship's been delayed."

"Jesus, Joe, how can they not know where that damn thing is?"

"Beats me."

The pilot turned away, shaking his head. *What a screw-up!*

31 IN OVER HIS HEAD

"Sir, I've got a call for you." The steward plugged the tele-phone handset in to a nearby jack and then handed it to the passenger.

"Thanks," Ricardo Molina said, accepting the telephone. He pulled it up to his right ear. "Molina here."

"Rick, it's Vicky. We've got a problem."

SAC Molina sat up straight in his seat. Except for the flight crew and one attendant, he was the only passenger aboard the executive jet. After the attack on the Cascade safe house, the director himself had ordered the FBI-owned Gulfstream to one-hour standby status, ready for the exclusive use of the Seattle field office. The G-IV had been sitting in a hangar at Seattle's Boeing Field.

Ricardo had been airborne for nearly an hour. The jet was five miles above British Columbia, racing north at 510 knots.

"What's wrong?" Ricardo asked.

"It's the ship—something's happened to it."

"What do you mean?"

"We just got a call from the Coast Guard base at Ketchikan. The *Emerald Sea* is late." She paused. "It was scheduled to rendezvous with the pilot boat about twenty minutes ago, but it never showed up. And they can't find it on radar."

"Well, where is the damn thing? It can't just disappear."

"No one knows yet. The Coast Guard's just getting ready to start searching."

"Can't they raise it on the radio?"

"There have been no responses. None." She hesitated. "And I just got off the phone with company headquarters in San Francisco. They're in the dark, too. They last communicated with the ship yesterday evening during a routine SATCOM call from the ship's hotel manager. Everything was just fine at that time."

"What about the Canadians—they know anything?"

"Nothing. They haven't heard from the ship since it dropped off the B.C. pilots last night."

Ricardo remained silent for a moment, staring out the porthole next to his seat. Although the jet was following the rugged B.C. coastline, he could see nothing but thick clouds. "Vicky, this doesn't sound good. I think you better get hold of General Mathews's office and apprise them of the situation. I think we're going to need some help—and quick."

"Right, I'll get right on it. I'll call you back as soon as I have something."

Ricardo switched the phone off. He again peered through the window. He imagined the blue-green ocean waters that lay under the blanket of clouds. *What the hell happened to that ship?*

The passengers were restless, like a herd of cattle pinned up in a tiny corral. They had been waiting at their muster stations for over an hour now. Most remained comfortable, warmed by the built-in heat lamps and sheltered from the dripping mirk by overhead decks and canvas canopies. The cabin stewards and deckhands kept busy by distributing steaming mugs of coffee, tea, and hot chocolate along with donuts and cookies. But the standing was beginning to take its toll. Several of the older passengers had settled onto the hardwood deck surfaces, no longer able to stand.

The crew offered no new explanations about why the drill was taking so long, only saying that it would be over soon. As the minutes passed, the complaints multiplied. Most wanted to return to their cabins, use the rest rooms, or file into the dining areas for breakfast. But they were all universally denied access to the ship's interior.

Finally, a few passengers began to suspect that something other than a drill was occurring. A rumor swept through the crowds that the ship was having generator problems. Another rumor suggested that there really had been a fire. And there was even speculation that the ship was lost. None of the nearly nine hundred passengers, except for two, had any inkling that the ship had been hijacked.

* * *

Tim and Jenny were now two decks below the Allegro Deck, heading aft through the engine spaces. Forty minutes earlier, they had been forced to flee from their original hideout by the approaching invaders. And now they just had a second close call. One of the commando teams almost nailed them three compartments forward. Tim latched the steel hatch in time. He used a section of pipe he found on a nearby work-bench to jam the hatchway shut.

"What'll we do now?" Jenny said, shaky from fatigue and fear.

"Gotta keep going aft for now," Tim replied as he searched the machinery-filled compartment.

"But what happens when we get to the stern? They'll find us for sure then."

Tim shook his head. "Somehow we've got to get behind the bastards before then—so we can head back to the bow."

"But how are we going to do that? They're everywhere."

Tim shook his head again. "I don't know right now. But I'll figure out something." He then began moving aft, holding the nine-millimeter MP5 across his chest, his right index fin-ger on the trigger guard. He was limping again—his bad knee. Jenny followed in his steps, the duffel bag with her father's research papers suspended over her left shoulder and Tim's attaché case in her left hand.

Tim's combo cell/sat phone was inside the briefcase, par-tially charged. He'd not yet had an opportunity to use it. The *Emerald Sea* was far beyond any local cellular net and the unit's satellite antenna would only work in the open, not buried deep inside of a steel hull.

"Unit Four to Command," the voice announced in Mandarin.

"Command, Four; go ahead," replied Allen Peng.

Peng had returned to the *Emerald Sea*'s bridge; he was surrounded by his own men. The ship's real officers and key hotel personnel remained crammed inside the master's quar-ters, located just aft of the bridge deck. A commando guarded the open doorway.

"Sir, we think they're heading for the engine room. They

blocked one of the hatches just forward of it, but we should be able to get around it."

"Excellent. Keep the pressure on them." Peng paused. "Now, remember, do not harm the woman. She's who we want."

"The other one . . . we're still free to take him out?"

"Absolutely, get rid of him."

"Yes, sir. We should have them within the next thirty minutes."

"Good, proceed."

Peng replaced the handset on a nearby console. The soldiers conducting the search were using the *Emerald Sea*'s internal intercom system to communicate with the bridge. There were hundreds of similar handsets located throughout the ship. Their own handheld radios were not effective when operating deep inside the vessel. The massive steel hull blocked the RF signals.

Peng walked forward and leaned against an oak rail located just below the windscreen. Beyond the foredeck, he could see nothing but gray. It was raining again, hard. The cruise ship continued to charge westward into the calm sea, running at twenty knots. It was now well out into the Pacific Ocean. *Thank God for this shitty rain,* he thought.

The inclement weather was, indeed, a lucky break. One of the few they had had during the mission. None of the passengers yet suspected that the ship would never reach Ketchikan. The distant shore remained shrouded in rain-rich clouds. But better yet, the thick overcast would hinder search efforts that would undoubtedly be launched within the near future.

I've got to keep the Americans off guard for as long as possible, Peng acknowledged. His Beijing masters had made that directive unambiguous in an encrypted SATCOM message received minutes earlier. *But how? And what if we don't find Richmond in time?*

Allen Peng was in over his head and he now knew it. *I'm not a warrior! They should have given command to Major Wu, not me!*

Peng turned about and walked aft a few steps to the chart

table. One of Wu's men was keeping a running fix on the ship's position, using the ship's primary GPS monitor to plot out the course.

"How far?" Peng asked.

The commando placed a plastic scale on the table, setting one end by the *Emerald Sea*'s current position and then running its length past an *X* mark that had been penciled onto the NOAA chart. "We've got about 420 kilometers to go, sir."

Twelve more hours! Peng calculated.

32 RAT PATROL

The United States military installation was on full alert. An hour earlier, just a handful of officers and technicians had occupied the spacious command center. But it was now packed with some sixty-five men and women. Most wore headsets with companion boom mikes, and they all seemed to be talking at the same time. Their collective voices created a machinelike clamor that resonated with the flood of information that poured into the top secret facility.

The National Military Command Center (NMCC) occupies two floors within the Pentagon. Although it was originally designed to fight a land war in Europe with the Soviet Union, it now serves as the nation's focal point for monitoring worldwide hot spots. And on this day, a brand-new cauldron had just ignited, this time in America's own backyard.

The first indication of trouble originated from another office within the Pentagon. Normal protocol would have called for the Defense Intelligence Agency duty officer to report the FBI's call for help directly to her commanding officer, General Mathews. Mathews, a one-star, would then report to his superior, a two-star. The two-star, in turn, would report to his superior . . . and so on up the chain of command until the buck finally stopped.

But this morning, there hadn't been time for all that. General Mathews was in Nevada so the aide called the Office of the Chairman of the Joint Chiefs of Staff directly. By employing the code word MERLIN, she gained instant access to the four-star admiral. Within a few minutes of the conversation, the National Military Command Center was notified of the impending crisis.

The chairman himself was now monitoring the command center from his own console, located just behind his subordinates. He was currently listening to the cross-talk between the NMCC's senior watch commander, an Air Force brigadier general, and a civilian operative at the National Reconnaissance Office. The NRO, located near Dulles International Airport, functioned as the Pentagon's eyes. Its fleet of reconnaissance satellites spanned most of the globe, allowing near instant imagery of the earth's surface.

"Has that bird been retasked yet?" asked the NMCC watch commander.

"Affirmative," replied the unseen NRO technician. "You should be receiving images momentarily."

The one-star waited, staring at a projection screen that covered the wall in front of his console. It was blank—just a blue tone. An instant later, it blinked with a flash of white and then a nondescript dark gray image materialized.

At first glance, the screen appeared to be blank, just a change in background color. But upon closer examination, two tiny white objects could be seen near the center, one much larger than the other. Although they looked like the kind of flaws or imperfections that sometimes occur when developing photographic film, the objects were very real.

The satellite that created the electronic image was currently scanning the North Pacific Ocean from its 350-mile-high orbit. Because a two-mile-thick band of clouds obscured the ocean surface, it was using its radar transmitter, rather than its cameras, to track the objects.

The NMCC watch officer keyed his mike. "Got something now."

"Right, we've got it here, too," replied the NRO technician.

"I see two targets," the NMCC commander said, "one's

obviously much larger." He paused. "Can you improve the resolution?"

"Roger. Magnifying by one hundred now."

The screen blinked again. This time the same two objects were transformed into remarkable detail. The reflection from the synthetic aperture radar unit was not quite as sharp as a real photo. Nevertheless, it was more than enough.

"That's got to be it. But what's that little one?"

"Looks about the size of a yacht to me, maybe a tugboat."

The general stared at the screen. "Yeah," he replied, "and ten will get you one, the bad guys came off it." He hesitated for a moment. "Have you got a speed estimate yet?"

"Yeah, just a sec. Ah, sir, they're both moving at about twenty knots on a westerly heading."

"Okay, keep the feed open. We'll be getting back to you soon."

"Yes, sir."

The Military Command Center watch commander turned to his right, looking back at his boss. "Sir," he said, "that's got to be the *Emerald Sea*. How do you wish to proceed?"

"What assets have we got in the immediate area?" asked the chairman.

The one-star turned to scan a monitor on his console. A few seconds later he looked back at the four-star. "Sir, the Coast Guard has got two helos, a C-130, several patrol boats, and one cutter—a 378—stationed in Ketchikan."

"Good, get that cutter going."

"Ah, there's a problem, sir. She's currently down with a turbine problem. Won't be ready for at least ten to twelve hours."

"You've got nothing else that floats?"

"Just the patrol boats, an eighty-two-footer is the largest. It's armed with M-60s."

"That's next to useless for this mission."

"I agree."

"Have the aircraft manned and placed on standby status. We're going to need 'em."

"Yes, sir." The watch commander turned to one of his aides and nodded. He then turned back to the chairman. He had a new idea. "Sir, I'd like permission to check with the Canadians. They might have something in the area that could help."

"Yes, good idea. Do it."

Once again the order was delegated and then the NMCC commander turned back to face the chairman. "Sir, in addition to the Coast Guard aircraft at Ketchikan, our nearest military air asset would be NAS Whidbey. When we first got wind of this situation, we contacted the base CO. They now have an Orion ready to launch. It can be on scene in about two hours." He paused. "The bird's equipped with a TV camera and satellite transmission system so we'll be able to get real-time images."

"Excellent, get her going."

While the watch commander executed the order, the CJC fidgeted in his chair, trying to get comfortable. The mounting pressure of the developing crisis was beginning to take its toll on his delicate lower spine.

Thirty seconds later the one-star made his report: "Sir, Whidbey reports the P3 will be rolling in five minutes."

The admiral nodded and then responded, "What's the status of our assault units?"

"We've got a SEAL platoon at Coronado on alert right now. They can be airborne within an hour."

"Okay, good. Get them on the way to Ketchikan. We'll base them from there. Hopefully, we won't need 'em. But if we do, I want them close by."

"Yes, sir." He paused. "Anything else?"

"I guess not. But I sure as hell wish we had some real sea power in the area. Aircraft only go so far."

The one-star glanced down at his computer monitor and then back at the chairman. "Well, sir," he said, "we do have one capital asset in the general area."

The chairman's eyes widened. "Good Lord, man, why didn't you say so before?"

"Well, sir, it's not so straightforward. You see, it's . . ."

The G-IV had hardly touched down at Ketchikan International when Ricardo Molina was once again airborne. This time he was in a U.S. Coast Guard Aerospatiale HH-65 Dolphin. The French-built helicopter had just lifted off and was heading southwest over Gravina Island.

Ricardo was the only passenger aboard the search and rescue craft. He sat in the rear compartment with the crew chief. The pilot and copilot were forward in the cockpit.

Like the rest of the crew, Ricardo wore a fluorescent orange survival suit; it covered him from head to toe. He looked like a blowup of the Pillsbury Doughboy in the bulky garment.

The chopper would soon be flying over the ocean and if it had to ditch, the buoyant and well-insulated survival suits would be the crew's only protection from the freezing water.

Ricardo was also outfitted with a white fiberglass flight helmet. It was equipped with a set of built-in headphones and a lip mike. Although the Dolphin was quieter than most helicopters, it was still noisy inside the cabin.

Ricardo was using the helmet's com system to communicate with the pilot. "How far out is it now?" he asked.

"The last report we received from the Pentagon said it was about eighty nautical miles offshore."

"Still heading west?"

"Yes."

"Do they have any idea where it's going?"

"No, sir. At least they haven't told us."

"What about our friends, are they still on schedule?"

"Affirmative, sir. We should make the rendezvous right around ten hundred hours."

Ricardo reached down and pushed the watertight seal away from his wrist, exposing his watch. It was 9:12 A.M. local time. "Can you land this thing, or will I have to be reeled down?"

"It's got plenty of deck space so we should be able to set down real easy. But if there's a problem, we'll use the basket."

Ricardo glanced down at the aluminum gurney. It was resting on the deck at his feet. Ricardo eyed it with suspicion. When compared to his own bulk, it didn't look all that impressive. And he certainly didn't like the idea of being low-ered from the helo in it.

Agent Molina next looked out the cabin window. The Dol-phin was now over water, crossing Clarence Strait. He could see a thick band of clouds to the south. He spoke again: "Lieutenant, are we going to have to fly through that stuff?"

"Yes, sir."

"How will you find it, then?"

"Our nav computer will get us close, and if it's still crummy out there, they'll bring us in with their radar. Its got everything on it."

Ricardo unconsciously nodded and then said: "Has anyone told 'em that I'll be their contact?"

"Don't know, sir. We're all kind of in the dark about this. And I have a feeling they're wondering about it, too."

Ricardo didn't reply. His gut rumbled. It wasn't hunger. *Shit, what the hell did I get myself into?*

The *Emerald Sea*'s engine compartment was hell on water. The noise was deafening; the air stank of burnt oil; and it was hot enough to fry an egg.

The two motor diesels, each rated at 15,000 hp, raced at a furious rate. Not since the first sea trials had the engines been pushed so hard and for so long. Despite the abuse they did their job, powering the twin banks of electric generators, which, in turn, drove the two propellers. The result was speed. The *Emerald Sea* was now charging westward at 20.7 knots—23.5 miles an hour. The ship had never moved faster.

Tim and Jenny were standing next to the base of the port diesel, using a huge engine mount for cover. They had just stuffed Kleenex in their ears, trying to muffle the oppressive racket. For the moment, they were alone. Earlier, all of the maintenance personnel had been ordered out of the engine compartment. There were now just two crewmen in the power plant's sound-insulated control room two decks up. They were guarded by one of the hijackers. It was the com-mando's job to insure that the crewmen maintained flank speed.

Although the oilers and motormen had vacated the compartment, Tim and Jenny took special care to avoid the main walkways and service bays. They were potential death traps.

When they had first entered the engine room, Tim spotted a closed-circuit TV camera mounted on a nearby bulkhead. It was wired to a bank of monitors in the control room. Fortunately, the camera's field of vision was directed away from Tim and Jenny's position. To avoid the electronic eyes, they dropped down a ladder to the bilge level. They were forced to stand in a slurry of calf-deep water, oil, and other chemicals that, over the years, had drained into the sump. It was not a pleasant experience.

But merely hiding wasn't enough. Tim and Jenny were running out of ship. The only place left to retreat to was the alleyway that housed the propeller shafts. It offered little protection and there was absolutely no way out once they entered that compartment. It was a dead end.

Tim decided to make a stand where they were. His submachine gun was locked and loaded. The selector switch was set to burst. He was standing, peering down the weapon's barrel through a six-inch gap in a metal grill next to the engine mount. He was eye level with the top of the steel catwalk that led to a hatchway from which they had just come. It was the only access point to the engine room from the forward compartment.

When the intruders opened the hatchway and stepped onto the steel catwalk, Tim would hose them down using controlled bursts. The targets would never know what had hit them. And neither would anyone else. The background racket from the diesels was so overpowering that the SMG's suppressor would be superfluous.

The thought of what he was prepared to do didn't phase Tim in the least. His dormant combat skills had kicked back in—Ranger school, Airborne training, special ops with the Delta Force. He was also operating on sheer survival instinct. *It's either them or us,* he repeatedly told himself.

Tim never told Jennifer what he was planning. The screaming diesels made conversation impossible. But she knew. And it bothered her—a lot. *He's going to shoot them in cold blood,* she thought. *There's got to be another way!*

Jenny moved forward, sliding next to Tim's side. He continued to survey the field of fire, unaware of her presence. The pounding diesel completely obliterated any noise that she might have made. She touched his shoulder to get his attention. He turned in a flash, startled. Sweat poured from his forehead, fueled by the oppressive heat, fear, and an abundance of adrenaline now surging through his bloodstream.

Jenny cupped her hands and yelled: "Can't we go somewhere else?"

Unable to hear, he gave her a questioning look.

Jenny reached into the duffel bag suspended from her shoulder and removed a ballpoint pen and a piece of paper. She then squatted down, using the back of Tim's attaché case to write on.

Tim bent down, watching.

She had just started to write the message when she happened to catch the movement out of the corner of her eye. By reflex, she jerked her head to the right.

Tim followed her eyes. And then he saw them.

Two *zhongdui* were already halfway down the catwalk, automatic weapons at port arms. *Jesus!* Carpenter thought.

They had come through the watertight hatchway just as he had expected. But Tim was no longer in the ambush position. If he stood up and returned to his firing port, they might spot the movement. If he tried to shoot from where he was, he would be lucky to hit their boots. He would have to shoot upward at an angle through the catwalk's open steel grill. And if he tried that, there was a high probability that some of the rounds might ricochet back and hit himself or Jenny.

Damn! What do I do now?

A moment later, Jenny made the decision for him. First, she slipped the straps of the duffel bag onto an edge of an engine mount. And then, holding up the briefcase with both hands, she sank down, immersing her body lengthwise into the black, stinking, slimy bilgewater.

Tim mimicked her move. He lay back, using the muck as a body cover. To his astonishment, it was refreshingly cool. He kept the submachine gun pointed upward, slowly tracking the two commandos as they cautiously walked down the catwalk. If just one of them decided to look down, Tim had already made up his mind to pull the trigger.

His heart pounded faster than the diesels. All thoughts were focused on the enemy. They were now almost directly overhead. They stopped. Through the one-by-two-inch openings of the catwalk grill, Tim could see the soles and heels of their boots. *What the hell are they doing?*

He waited. The gunmen stood still. Tim couldn't see their heads. He was beginning to panic. *Are they looking down? Do they suspect something? What should I do?*

And then he decided.

He was ready. He took aim and started to squeeze the trigger. But an instant later he stopped. The commandos were moving on.

Tim watched as the two men continued aft down the catwalk, always ready to blast them.

Finally, after they passed out of sight, he cautiously sat up. He signaled for Jenny to stay where she was. He then climbed partway up a ladder and carefully looked down the catwalk. It was clear. He turned back toward Jenny, waving his free hand.

A minute later they had retraced their original escape path through the engine hatchway. They were now heading forward, away from their pursuers.

Tim and Jenny looked like a pair of Dumpster-divers in their drenched, oil-laden garments. But they didn't mind one bit.

33 HMCS *REGINA*

The U.S. Coast Guard helicopter cautiously descended through the foglike drizzle. The moist air was so thick that it was like flying inside a Turkish bath. There was no sense of up or down. Or of sky or sea. Everything was wet and colorless.

As the pilot concentrated on the flight controls, the copilot called out their altitude: "Four hundred feet . . . three ninety . . . three eighty . . ."

Ricardo Molina listened to the call-outs while staring out the side window of the Dolphin. *Oh, man!* he thought, *I can't see squat out there. How can they know where they're going?*

"Coming up on one hundred fifty feet . . . should see something pretty soon."

"Roger," replied the pilot. He continued to focus on the instrument panel, not bothering to look away.

A moment later the colorless surface of the ocean materialized. "I've got water," the copilot announced. "Level her out."

The pilot adjusted the controls and the helicopter's descent was halted. And then, for a brief instant, he glanced through the windscreen, eyeing the ocean surface. "Where is it?" he asked.

"Just a sec. I'll get a new bearing." The copilot selected a new com frequency and after a brief radio conversation reported back to the aircraft commander. "She bears at zero three five degrees. Range five hundred and twenty yards."

"Roger."

The pilot swung the helicopter to the right and slowly applied power. As the Dolphin inched forward, he continued to rely on his instruments rather than peer through the windscreen. The precipitation-induced fog, combined with the lack of a defined horizon, made for extremely hazardous flying conditions.

About a minute later the copilot made visual contact. "There it is!" he shouted, his voice conveying relief.

Ricardo Molina strained to look over the pilot's helmet. And then he too saw it. *I'll be damned!*

The warship was an aberration, an island of green within a sea of green. It was heading into the oncoming sea, barely under way.

The copilot again switched radio frequencies. "*Regina, Regina,* this is U.S Coast Guard helo Bravo Nine Five. We have you in sight. Over."

The response was immediate: "Bravo Nine Five, *Regina,*

you are cleared for landing. Wind is from the west at four knots. Follow deck controller's wands. Over."

"Roger."

Within just eight minutes of touching down, Ricardo Molina was standing on the bridge of Her Majesty's Canadian Ship *Regina.* The 442-foot fast frigate was now churning through the swells, having just passed into the Pacific Ocean. Her gas turbines were running full out, propelling the sleek vessel at flank speed: thirty knots. The ride was smooth, like in a well-built automobile.

To Ricardo, the state-of-the-art combat vessel seemed to radiate raw power. The deck plates transmitted the engines' pulse through his shoes. The Bofos cannon mounted to the foredeck commanded respect. And the myriad sensors, radar displays, communication gear, and other electronic equipment that filled out the bridgehouse were mesmerizing.

The FBI agent could hardly believe it was all happening. Just a few hours earlier he had been in his Seattle office and now here he was, out in the middle of the ocean on a foreign warship.

"Mr. Molina, care for a cup of fresh brew?" asked a friendly voice.

Ricardo turned to his right. The *Regina*'s CO held out a mug of steaming coffee.

"I'd love some, Captain."

Ricardo sipped as the Canadian naval officer stood silently by his side. Both men stared through the windscreen, watching the ship's dagger bow slice through the oncoming swells.

As Ricardo cupped the mug, his cold fingers relishing its heat, he turned to face the Canadian. Barely forty, Captain Mark MacKenzie was young for a full captain. Medium height and slim with chestnut hair that was maybe just a bit long, he fit the image of a seasoned naval officer.

Ricardo smiled as MacKenzie caught his gaze. "Nothing like a good cup of coffee to settle you down," Ricardo said.

"Pretty wild ride out here?" the captain asked.

"I'll say. Those Coast Guard guys got a lot of balls, doing what they do." Ricardo shook his head.

"Yes, I know what you mean. I sure wouldn't want to fly in that crap either."

Ricardo turned to again look over the bow. No change. Nothing but lousy weather. "How far away is it?" he asked.

"She's about ninety nautical miles ahead, almost due west of here."

"So it'll be a while before we catch up?"

"Quite a while. That ship is running at around twenty knots. Our closure rate is only ten knots."

"I get the picture."

The Canadian nodded and took another sip from his mug.

"Where were you guys, anyway?" Ricardo asked. "I mean when you got your orders."

"We pulled into Prince Rupert yesterday evening to take on fuel. We departed early this morning and were headed back to Esquimalt when the alert came in."

"Hmmm," Ricardo said, "so I guess you're kind of in the dark about all this."

MacKenzie laughed. "You can say that again. All I know is that we were ordered to rendezvous with an American helicopter in the Dixon Entrance. We're then to proceed at flank speed on an intercept course with a Bahamian-registered cruise ship that recently departed Canadian waters." He paused. "I can only surmise that the vessel in question has been hijacked."

Ricardo nodded again, "Well, that's right." He took another sip. "Let me try to explain what's going on."

"It still isn't working?" asked Jenny.

"No. All I'm getting is static."

"Let me look at it."

Tim handed the portable phone to Jennifer. She had already opened up the operating manual.

A few minutes earlier, Tim and Jenny had finally managed to escape from the ship's interior. They were on the sundeck, temporarily hidden away inside a tiny alcove near the aft end of the main swimming pool. There were no overhead obstructions, allowing use of the phone's satellite mode for the first time. Unfortunately, the satphone was not cooperating.

Jenny finished her examination of the device. It didn't take long for her electrical engineering skills to troubleshoot the problem. "Tim, it's working fine . . . there's plenty of battery power and the transceiver diagnostics check out."

"Yeah, so what's wrong with the damn thing?"

"I'm pretty sure the signal's being jammed."

"Jammed?"

"Yes, there's some kind of radio signal on this ship that's overwhelming the frequencies that your phone operates on."

Tim Carpenter remained silent for a long moment before finally commenting. "Those bastards—they think of everything, don't they."

"It sure looks that way."

The Orion found the *Emerald Sea* a few minutes before noon. It hadn't been all that hard to locate. The cruise ship had maintained a constant speed and heading since the patrol aircraft took off from NAS Whidbey two and a half hours earlier. By flying an intercept course and periodically checking the hijacked vessel's position with satellite radar data, the four-engine propeller-driven aircraft closed to within twenty miles of the ship and its tiny companion. It then used its own onboard radar to electronically slice through the two-mile-deep overcast, pinpointing the exact location of each vessel.

The U.S Navy Orion dropped through the mirk for a visual sighting. It then began tracking the targets, establishing a two-mile-diameter orbit over the primary. From an altitude of just 1,200 feet, the P-3C skimmed the underside of the gray-black clouds. The vapor-rich mass engulfed the sky for hundreds of miles in all directions.

The Orion P-3C had been monitoring the hijacked ship and the elegant yacht for over half an hour now, watching and listening with an array of electronic sensors. After repeated radio calls to both vessels, without response, the Orion's radio officer gave up trying to make verbal contact. He did discover, however, that the cruise ship was emitting an array of unusually strong high-frequency signals. The purpose had yet to be determined.

Other than the strange RF emissions, the mission profile for the ten-man, two-woman flight crew had been strictly routine. They were all accustomed to the seemingly endless hours of ocean flying that went with the Orion's primary mission: submarine hunting. But that monotonous routine had just changed.

The Orion had de-orbited and was now passing along the *Emerald Sea*'s port side. It raced over the ocean at an altitude of just two hundred feet.

"What the hell are they doing?" asked the right-hand-seat copilot as he turned away from the windscreen, looking toward the two other flight deck officers.

"I don't know," replied the center-seat copilot-observer. He had a pair of binoculars in his hands. "But it does kind of look like they're trying to launch a lifeboat."

"But that's nuts. That ship's still tearing through the water. No one could ever survive a launch like that."

"Yeah, this is weird," joined in the aircraft commander. Lieutenant Commander Megan Andersen occupied the left-hand seat. "I'll set her up for another pass." She then paused to key her intercom mike, signaling one of the enlisted personnel inside the main cabin. "Jensen," she said, "you better get our cameras rolling again. The Pentagon brass will want to see this for sure."

"Yes, ma'am."

Four minutes later the Orion made a second pass. This time the engines were throttled back and the flaps extended, slowing the plane to just 175 knots.

The photographer's mate trained his video camera onto the *Emerald Sea*. The images it recorded were fed into one of the P-3C's computers, which instantly digitized and encrypted the signal. It then transmitted the data to an overhead satellite. The U.S. Navy bird, parked in a geosynchronous orbit 22,300 miles above the North Pacific, relayed the data back to the Pentagon.

After reformatting and decrypting, the video signal was displayed onto the main screen in the National Military Command Center.

* * *

When the chairman of the Joint Chiefs viewed the real-time video feed, he had the same reaction as the P-3C's crew: "What the hell are they doing?"

The admiral turned to face the civilian standing to his right. The retired merchant marine officer had just been summoned from his Alexandria, Virginia, residence. He had captained cruise ships for nearly thirty years.

"Captain," the CJC said, "what do you make of this?"

The tall, beefy, bearded man shook his head. "Something's very wrong here. The ship is moving much too fast for this type of operation. I've never seen anything like this."

The chairman nodded and turned back to face the watch commander. "Pete, tell 'em to make another pass." He paused. "And while they're setting up, let's replay that video, but slow it up some."

"Yes, sir."

Thirty seconds later the recording was replayed at half speed.

Everyone in the room watched in astonishment as one key section of tape appeared. "There. Freeze it there!" shouted the chairman.

The screen stopped. It flickered until the automatic tracking adjusted the frame's image. The result was startling. One of the *Emerald Sea*'s lifeboats had been lowered halfway down the hull, suspended from its launching davits by steel cables. A figure dressed in black could be seen leaning over the ship's railing. He held something in his hands.

"Enlarge that area around the lifeboat," ordered the chairman.

The screen blinked to a solid blue background. Two seconds later a new image appeared.

"Son of a bitch!" shouted the CJC. "That bastard's got a weapon, all right." He turned to face the watch officer. "We've got a hijacking on our hands. No question about it now."

The one-star nodded and then said: "Sir, the Orion's about to make another pass."

"Okay, put it on the screen."

This time the images were even more revealing. The lifeboat they had viewed earlier had now been dumped into the sea. It was already sinking. Even more ominous were the new images: two more lifeboats were in the process of being jettisoned.

"My God!" called out the chairman, "I think they're trying to scuttle all of the lifeboats!"

The two men were facing each other as they stood on the *Emerald Sea*'s bridge deck. With the exception of just one other man, who monitored the helm, they were alone. All of the ship's officers and key staff remained locked up in the captain's cabin.

"Sir, we've made a complete sweep through the ship. We couldn't find them. They must have somehow doubled back on us." He paused. "Should we start over again?"

Allen Peng stared at Major Wu. Peng was beyond anger. His carefully orchestrated plan continued to disintegrate. "Why couldn't you find them? All of the passengers are still on deck."

"Sir, my men are thorough, but there are hundreds of potential hiding places. We'd need a company to check everything. With the few we do have it could take us all day to check everything."

Peng turned away, now glancing over the bow. The ship continued to race west. The ocean surface remained calm, marked only by the slow rollers that tracked east. The near sky, however, was in turmoil. The low ceiling of gray clouds was darkening by the second. Torrential rain was just a few minutes away.

But Peng hardly noticed. He was lost in thought.

After the clandestine attempt to spirit Jennifer Richmond off the ship had failed, Peng had hoped that the hastily arranged shipwide search would pay off. But it was now a lost cause. The two Americans remained hidden. And then the U.S. Navy patrol plane showed up. It was not unexpected, but it was still a nuisance.

Peng shook his head. He had no choice but to continue with the backup plan. He finally turned back to face his subordinate, reluctantly accepting reality. "All right, Major,"

Peng said, "take your men and help with the lifeboats. They must all be jettisoned. And finish off the rest of those life rafts, too."

"Yes, sir."

As the PLA officer turned and walked aft, Peng moved to one of the two closed-circuit TV monitors that were located on the bridge. The nearest screen displayed the live feed from a camera mounted along the ship's starboard side. He could see the droves of passengers huddled on the deck. Those sitting on the steel plating used their PFDs for cushions. For the most part, they remained docile and cooperative. But that hadn't been the case just minutes earlier.

After having been forced to remain at their emergency stations for hours, a few of the nearly nine hundred passengers began to rebel. Most were cold. Many were hungry. And all of them were tired of standing, packed like sardines next to the bulkheads on the partially open-air decks.

The ship's crew that were assigned to monitor the passengers, mostly cabin stewards and lifeboat attendants, were unaware that their captain was no longer in command. None of the commandos had yet ventured onto the assembly areas. However, as the unplanned drill dragged on, the crew, too, began to wonder what was happening.

Later, when the first handful of passengers began to defect, heading back into the ship's interior, Peng was finally forced to act. Those men not searching the vessel were dispersed to both sides of the vessel. And within minutes they had every passenger's undivided attention.

They could have started by gunning down selected passengers. That would have probably worked. But Peng's plan was more sophisticated, more terrifying.

The two teams started from the forward end of the main lifeboat deck, moving aft on each side of the ship. They said nothing as they marched past the crowds. Their military apparel and Type 56-2 Chinese assault rifles said everything. When the respective teams reached their first lifeboat station, they raised their weapons and aimed at the hull. Each lifeboat was suspended above the deck by davits. The AK-47 replicas roared with hellfire.

The 7.62 mm armor-piercing rounds peppered the thin steel hulls, ripping through the interior of every vessel and then exiting through the cabin top. Those slugs marked with a dab of phosphorus could be seen arcing high into the sky.

As the PRC commandos repeated their sabotage at each lifeboat station, the assembled passengers all got the message: The ship had been hijacked and there was no escape.

At the conclusion of the live-fire demonstration, no one—not one person aboard the *Emerald Sea*—challenged their captors. Cooperation was complete.

Although the passengers were under control for the time being, Peng had another problem.

He turned away from the TV monitor, moving forward until he was standing next to a massive windshield. It stretched across the entire bridge deck. He looked toward the south. *There it is,* he thought. He raised the binoculars that were draped around his neck. The Orion snapped into focus. Earlier, one of his men had identified the aircraft as a U.S. Navy patrol craft. Peng would have preferred a little more time to get ready, but nevertheless, it was now time to deal with its presence.

The easiest approach would have been to use the *Emerald Sea*'s sophisticated communication gear to radio the P-3C with his demands. However, as with passengers, a live demonstration of his resolve would have far more impact than mere words.

By lowering the lifeboats partway down the hull, blasting them again with machine-gun fire, and then finally jettisoning each one, the message conveyed to the Orion's crew would be unambiguous: "We have the ship and there's nothing you can do about it."

Peng walked out onto the starboard bridge wing. The stiff ship-generated breeze ruffled his hair. Its frigid, moist bite was refreshing after the sizzling, stuffy pilothouse. He looked aft. Rows of oil barrel–sized white fiberglass canisters, each one containing a deflated ten- or twenty-person life raft, lined a nearby bulkhead. They had all been rendered useless, peppered with machine-gun fire. Further aft, all but one of the lifeboats had been released. In just a few minutes, it too would be gone. *Good,* he thought, *that'll shake 'em up for sure.*

"What do you think they're doing?" Jenny asked.
"I don't know, but it sure doesn't look good," Tim said. He pressed his cheek onto the porthole's chilled glass, trying to look aft.

"Can you see it?"

Tim backed away, turning to face Jenny. "They just dumped it overboard. I could see it bobbing in the wake, upside down."

"Oh, my God, you don't think there was anyone in it, do you?"

Tim shrugged. "I don't know what's going on. No one in their right mind would try to launch a lifeboat at this speed. It would be suicide."

Tim and Jenny were temporarily hiding out in a vacant cabin on a midlevel deck. After giving up on the satphone, they headed back inside the ship, moving forward and descending two levels. During their journey, they encountered no one—not one passenger, member of the crew, or, most important, any of the bad guys. They eventually took refuge in one of the scores of unoccupied cabins. Tim picked the door lock, easily gaining entry.

Had Tim and Jennifer chosen a cabin with the curtains drawn across the porthole, they would never have noticed the lifeboat as it was lowered down the hull.

"Where do you suppose everyone is?" Jenny asked, now examining the cabin's interior. It was considerably larger and more elegantly appointed than the one they had occupied.

"They must still be on deck, at their emergency stations."

"Why would they keep them there?"

"It's simple—they can keep track of everyone up there a lot more efficiently than from inside the ship." He paused. "Besides, that way they can concentrate on finding us."

Jenny frowned, now making the connection. "So if they run into anyone below, it's shoot first, ask questions later."

"You got it."

34 DESPERATE MEASURES

Allen Peng was on the bridge, looking forward. The *Orca*
was about half a mile away. He raised his right hand and
spoke into the portable radio: "All right, that's far enough.
Stop and then set the unit."

"Roger, set the unit," came the instant reply.

The brief conversation had been in English. Peng spoke
without the slightest trace of accent and the recipient aboard
the *Orca* was equally trained. It was unlikely that electronic
analysis of their voices would reveal each man's Chinese
origin.

Besides avoiding his native tongue, Peng's radio conversation had been broadcast over a public VHF ship-to-ship
marine band. He used one of the ship's handheld bridge radios. There was no need to use the assault team's special
encrypted radio transceivers for that particular message. Peng
wanted the Americans to hear his orders loud and clear.

Tim Carpenter was leaning forward, his head in the wall
depression that formed the cabin's porthole. Jenny was at his
side.

"What's going on?" she asked.

Tim turned to face Jenny. "We're definitely slowing up
now and that yacht looks like it's stopping, too."

He turned back to the view port, straining to look aft. The
Orca was now almost dead in the water.

"Maybe they're getting ready to leave," Jenny offered.

He shook his head. "Not a chance. They're not finished
with us."

The chairman of the Joint Chiefs had just left the command
center, summoned to a meeting in the secretary of defense's
office. The NMCC watch commander was now in complete
charge of the operation.

"What the hell are they doing, Commander?" asked the watch officer. He was speaking with the pilot of the P-3C as it transmitted real-time video images to the Pentagon. The Orion continued to orbit the *Emerald Sea,* standing off about half a mile and flying just under the low ceiling.

"Sir, they're definitely up to something," the female pilot replied. "The ship has slowed up and that yacht's moved off to the southwest. It's slowing up, too."

"All those lifeboats gone now?"

"Yes, sir. They've all been jettisoned."

The NMCC commander was about to ask another question when an aide walked up. He held a sheet of paper in his hand.

"General," he said, "this just came in from NSA."

The CO scanned the document. It had originated from the National Security Agency. Earlier, one of its legions of eavesdropping satellites had been tasked to monitor the air space offshore of the Dixon Entrance. One of the transponders aboard the billion-dollar bird had just picked up Peng's open microphone conversation.

The general looked back at his aide. "What do they mean, set the unit?"

The major shook his head.

"That yacht moving yet?" Jenny asked.

"No," Tim said. "It's still sitting there."

"What about the helicopter?"

"I don't see it anymore. I think it landed."

"Maybe they're picking up the rest of those pirates." There was a little hope in her voice.

Tim said nothing. He didn't know what to think. He was baffled at the latest turn of events. *Maybe she's right,* he thought. *Maybe they are bagging this whole thing.*

For the past several minutes, Tim had remained glued to the tiny porthole, watching the stationary yacht. His pulse had accelerated when he first spotted the black-hulled helicopter. It took off from its perch on the cruise ship, heading toward the yacht. It landed on the *Orca*'s helideck, but within seconds lifted off again. It then retraced its flight path back to the *Emerald Sea.*

There are at least a dozen or so of those bastards aboard, Tim thought. *That bird can take maybe six or seven passengers at a crack. What are they . . .* He then smiled as he made the connection. *That's it. They're ferrying the buggers out. They're giving up!*

Allen Peng handed the microphone to Captain Demetriou. They were standing in the ship's bridge next to the windscreen.

"Just read the script and nothing more," Peng ordered.

For just an instant, the captain turned to the right. *The bastard's still there!*

Major Wu stood at Demetriou's side. His arm was stretched out. The pistol was just inches from the captain's temple.

Demetriou cleared his voice and then depressed the transmit switch. "American aircraft! American aircraft!" he said, his gravelly voice thickly accented with his native Greek inflection. "This is the *Emerald Sea*. Come in, please."

Both Peng and Demetriou looked toward the north. The Orion was banking left as it continued to orbit the stationary ship.

Peng faced the ship's master. "Do it again," he commanded.

Demetriou repeated the message.

No response.

Demetriou looked toward Peng. "Maybe we're not using the right radio frequency. This is just a ship-to-ship channel."

Peng said nothing. He wasn't concerned. Right now, he estimated that there had to be dozens of electronic ears listening to every RF signal emanating from the ship. Other than the jamming of the portable satphone frequencies, all other radio signals from the ship were broadcast loud and clear. It would be just a matter of time before the connection would be made.

"Send it again," Peng ordered.

The link was established after Captain Demetriou's fifth call.

"*Emerald Sea, Emerald Sea*, this is U.S. Navy aircraft orbiting your vessel. State your situation."

Peng frowned. There was a woman in command. He gestured for Demetriou to proceed.

The fifty-one-year-old Greek cleared his voice and then pressed the transmit key on the microphone. "This vessel has been commandeered by the People's Army for the Liberation of Algeria. Explosive charges have been placed throughout the vessel and all lifeboats have been jettisoned. If any attempts are made to . . ."

Captain Demetriou continued reciting the script, word by word. There was a demand for the release of two dozen political prisoners held in an Algiers jail, an order that $20 million in cash be air-dropped to some remote outpost in southern Algeria, and a command that France publicly apologize for interfering with the internal affairs of Algeria.

The list of demands was punctuated with a final threat: "If our demands are not carried out within the next twenty-four hours, we will blow up the *Emerald Sea.*"

Captain Demetriou next started listing the exact instructions on how the U.S. government was to comply with the terrorists' demands. The instructions were overly detailed, deliberately conflicting, and, of course, completely bogus.

Peng had particularly enjoyed crafting the script. The implication of the French government was deliberate. It was partly payback for Gérard Rémy's treachery, but was principally designed to add confusion to the overall situation. Peng didn't expect the Americans to buy the threats of the phony Algerian terrorist group. However, the possible repercussions would keep them occupied for a while, trying to make sense of what really was going on. Ultimately, the U.S. government would discover that no such group existed. Then, once again, they would concentrate on finding Jennifer Richmond. But by that time, Peng and his men would be long gone. He would either have the Richmond woman and the MERLIN secret, or the threat that she represented would be discharged.

Captain Demetriou was now on the last sentence of Peng's script: "To demonstrate our commitment to our cause, we have prepared a demonstration."

Peng reached forward, removing the microphone from Demetriou's hand. "Very good, Captain," he said, "return to your cabin now."

As Demetriou walked away, escorted by a guard, Peng reached inside his coat pocket and removed a black case. It was about the size of a pack of cigarettes. A four-inch-long wire antenna projected from the top.

The Pentagon watch officer listened to the radio transmission from the *Emerald Sea*. The actual broadcast was delayed about half a second as it was first relayed from the Orion to an overhead satellite. That satellite relayed the message to another mini-moon, which, in turn, sent it down to NMCC.

All eyes in the command center were now focused on the main screen. The P-3C's camera operator continued to broadcast live television images of the cruise ship.

The watch commander turned to his aide, who stood by his side. "Major," he said, "what the hell's this nutcase talking about . . . a demonstration?"

The Orion was heading in from the north, closing in on the secondary target. The fire had started about five minutes earlier. The soot-black plumes billowed into the air, obscuring the aft third of the *Orca*'s once gleaming white fiberglass hull.

"Wow! That baby's really starting to fry," commented the copilot as he spotted the flames.

"That sucker's toast," added the center-seat observer.

Pilot Andersen keyed her intercom while simultaneously banking to the left. "Jensen," she said, "get ready now. I want a good shot of this thing."

"All set, skipper."

"What happened to it?" asked Jenny. She was huddled next to Tim. They were both looking through the cabin porthole.

"I don't know but it's burning like crazy now."

"Do you think they had some kind of accident?"

"Maybe."

A moment later they both spotted the Orion. It was coming in low, just five hundred feet off the ocean.

"Here comes that Navy plane again," Jenny commented.

"Yeah," Tim replied.

The P-3C was now almost over the burning boat. Lieutenant Commander Megan Andersen had dipped the left wing down for a better view. She was eyeing the yacht when it happened.

The brilliant light flooded the cockpit. It was as if a million flashbulbs had gone off in an instant. And then something slammed into the aircraft, rattling teeth and rupturing eardrums.

The one hundred kilos—220 pounds—of Semtex had been positioned over the fuel tanks. Consequently, when Peng remotely detonated the plastic explosive, the *Orca* was obliterated. The explosion, supercharged by three thousand gallons of diesel fuel, thundered upward and outward with the fury of a miniature nuclear bomb.

The shock wave hammered into the patrol craft's belly with a vengeance. Only a few hundred feet above the detonation point, the overpressure took its toll. The Orion shook as if caught in the fangs of a gigantic dragon. Almost instantly, dozens of cockpit alarm lights and enunciators went off.

"Mother of Christ," called out the copilot, "what the hell happened?"

The pilot struggled with the wheel, trying to pull the ship's nose up. "Something's wrong!" she yelled. "Give me a hand here. I can't control this thing."

The copilot grabbed his dual wheel and tried to pull it back. It wouldn't budge. *Oh, shit!* he thought, *we're screwed!*

Tim Carpenter picked himself up from the floor, shaking his head. He had been staring out the porthole, watching the yacht when it exploded. There had been no warning. Just a couple of seconds later, the concussion from the blast hammered the *Emerald Sea*. It slammed into the hull broadside with hurricane force. Tim, out of instinct, dove for the floor, once again banging his tender knee. He had pulled Jenny downward with him.

Jenny, still on all fours, shook her head. "What happened?"

Tim returned to the porthole. "Oh, my God, look at that!"

The mushroom-shaped cloud from the detonation continued to rise. But that wasn't what caught his eye. It was the Orion. The aircraft was on fire and it was going down.

"What happened?" Jenny asked again, still in the dark.

"Crew, prepare to ditch, prepare to ditch!" yelled Megan.
The P-3C was dying. Only the two starboard engines were functional; the other two were on fire. Shrapnel from the explosion had peppered the aircraft.

The two pilots struggled with their dual steering wheels, still trying to pull the Orion's nose up for an emergency sea landing. But it wasn't enough. The aircraft's horizontal stabilizer had been torn apart by the shock wave and other control surfaces were jammed. The plane's glide path was much too steep.

Tim's heart jolted when the Orion plowed into the ocean.
The plume was enormous. *Dear God,* he thought, *those poor guys didn't have a chance.*

35 UPPING THE ANTE

"What the hell happened?" asked the chairman of the Joint Chiefs. He had just returned to the command center, summoned by an emergency call. He was standing beside the watch officer.

"We're not certain, sir," replied the Air Force brigadier general. "All we know for sure is that *Regina* lost radar contact with it about twelve minutes ago and we can't raise her on any of our com links." He hesitated. "We think it might have been knocked down."

"What?"

"One of NORAD's birds spotted some type of detonation at the same time we lost radio contact. They classified it as a significant thermal burst."

"Thermal burst? What's going on here, general?"

"Something blew up out there, sir. Created one hell of an infrared spike on the satellite's Nucflash sensors."

"The P-3?"

"Possibly, but we think the big bang may have been the yacht that was pacing the ship. *Regina* can't pick it up on radar." He again paused. "But it could also be running so close to the larger ship that it's not showing up."

"What about satellite imagery—can't we see it that way?"

"The whole gulf's still socked in. The overcast is much too thick to see through and the sat-radar's resolution has the same problem as *Regina*. If the yacht's next to the ship, it won't pick it up."

"Well, how the hell are we going to know what happened?"

"We're going to get a video replay from the NORAD bird in a few minutes. NRO's processing the info right now. We might learn something from it."

"What about the Orion's camera? Wasn't it transmitting?"

"Yes, sir. And we've got it on tape. I'll replay it now."

Both officers turned toward the wall-mounted screen located in front of the watch officer's console. There were no images on it at the moment, just a background blue. The one-star flipped a switch on the console and the screen came alive.

"As you can see, sir," the watch commander narrated, "the cameraman is training the camera on the yacht."

"The damn thing's on fire!"

"Correct, sir. That's why we ordered the P-3 to check it out." He pressed a remote control, slowing the video to quarter speed. "In just a second or so you'll see it."

The four-star admiral watched as the telephoto view of the

smoldering *Orca* jolted, as if the camera had been violently struck. And then the color image of the yacht dissolved into a sea of static.

"That's it?"

"Yes, sir. That's the last transmission from the Orion."

"So what happened?"

The watch commander hesitated, glancing up at the now blank screen. He then turned to face his boss. "Sir, we're not one hundred percent certain yet, but we're beginning to think it might have been knocked down by a handheld SAM."

"From the yacht?"

"Possibly, but more likely from the cruise ship. It would have been an easy kill. It was only about a quarter of a mile away."

"Goddamn those bastards! They set our people up—murdered 'em!"

"Yes, sir, it looks that way."

Both men had similar thoughts: *The poor crew—all of them gone in a heartbeat!*

The one-star paused, clearing his throat. "Sir, if the Orion exploded from the missile impact that might explain the thermal bloom." He paused. "But it still doesn't explain why we can't find the yacht on radar."

The chairman nodded, accepting the dilemma. "What's going on with that cruise ship?" he asked.

"It's under way again, running west at twenty-plus knots. There haven't been any transmissions since the demand broadcast. *Regina* continues to track it. She's running at flank, but it'll be hours before she catches up."

The CJC collapsed into a chair next to the watch officer's console. "Have you heard anything from that Orion?" he asked.

"Nothing, sir. No radio contact. No emergency beacons. Ketchikan Coast Guard has dispatched a C-130 SAR unit to check the scene." The brigadier general glanced down at his console. "The Herc should be there in about forty minutes or so."

"How many aboard the Orion?"

"It had a full complement of twelve, sir. And there were two women aboard."

The chairman shook his head in despair. "This is all turning to crap, Sam. None of this should be happening."

The NMCC watch commander nodded.

The chairman looked up at the watch officer. "What's this bullshit about the People's Army for the Liberation of Algeria?" he asked. "Anything to it?"

"The CIA's still working on it. Apparently, there's some group like that, but the spooks don't think they're involved with the *Emerald Sea* hijacking. It's probably a cover story."

"So we're still up against these MERLIN pirates?"

"It looks that way, sir. The FBI's convinced the Chinese are still involved, but we don't have any hard intel on just who's aboard the ship. It could be anybody."

Although the watch commander remained skeptical, the CJC was convinced that the Chinese government was behind the downing of the Orion.

There had been a previous incident between the People's Republic of China and a U.S. Navy surveillance aircraft. In that event, an EP-3E Aries II spy plane—based on the same airframe as the Orion P-3C—had been accidentally rammed by a Chinese jet fighter. The Aries's crew—also based out of NAS Whidbey, like that of the Orion—survived, thanks to the superb skill of its pilots and a bit of luck. The PLA pilot, however, perished.

That incident was a diplomatic hot potato for a few weeks but eventually faded away after the PRC finally released the detained crew. This time, however, a firestorm of vengeance was brewing. The horror of what had just happened to the P-3C and her crew would not languish.

The chairman turned away from the one star, facing the civilian sitting at his side. The retired cruise ship captain had remained in the NMCC throughout the crisis, providing his expertise wherever possible. "Captain, if those pirates blow a couple holes in the bottom of that ship, how long would we have to get the passengers off before it sinks?"

"If they know what they're doing—like shutting down the power systems, opening a few critical watertight doors, and disabling the emergency bilge pumps—she'd could go under quick. Maybe an hour. Ninety minutes at most."

"And if we couldn't get any help to them right away, the passengers and crew, how long could they survive?"

The master mariner shook his head. "Admiral, without lifeboats or rafts, you'd lose most of them in the first hour. Those ships are loaded with the elderly. The cold water would kill 'em off in droves. The younger folks might last a little longer, but not by much."

"Damn those bastards to hell," the CJC muttered. He then stood up, stretching out his sore back in the process. The stress was building by the minute and he was going to have to make some very tough decisions in the next few minutes. Life-and-death decisions. He eyed the NMCC commander. "Okay, Sam, we can't screw around with these turkeys any longer. What do your people recommend?"

"Well, sir, we've got a team airborne right now and if we divert . . ."

Allen Peng paced back and forth across the bridge deck, a Camel drooping from his lower lip. He ignored the MSS agent that manned the helm.

A minute earlier he had lit up. His hands shook when he held the lighter. For the first time since boarding the *Emerald Sea* he was scared. Nothing had gone right. The entire operation was unwinding and he was powerless to stop the process. Disaster was just around the corner.

Downing the American aircraft had been an accident. Peng had timed the explosion for show only. The yacht was no longer needed and its obliteration would further insulate the PRC from direct involvement in the hijacking. Never did Peng imagine, however, the magnitude of the detonation, nor its impact on the Orion.

He was now desperate. Hijacking the ship was a despicable act, but murdering the flight crew was the ultimate sin. There would be hell to pay. And the bill collector would soon be on the way.

They'll probably attack after sunset, Peng thought, sucking in a deep drag. *That's how I'd do it.*

He expected an aerial assault, most likely from helicopters. The assault force would be overwhelming, composed of U.S. Navy SEALs or the elite Delta Force or maybe both.

Dammit, I've got to end this soon or we're going to be screwed for sure.

Peng had a dozen handheld SAMs at his disposal. They would help when the attack came. But they were of limited range and could be thrown off course with flares. Besides, he had to keep at least half in reserve for the final transfer.

Peng stopped pacing. He was now facing the windscreen. The bow of the cruise ship plunged through the oncoming swells. It was getting rougher and it had just started raining again. He checked his watch. It was 2:55 P.M. *About six more hours of daylight,* he thought.

He next moved over to the main radar display. The fluorescent green screen was clear except for one flashing blip. *So, you continue to close,* he thought as he stared at the return echo. HMCS *Regina* was now about fifty miles to the east.

Peng knew nothing about the phantom vessel. Nevertheless, he assumed that it was hostile. He wasn't particularly concerned about its presence at this point. Only if the last phase of the mission were delayed would it become a problem.

When it was time to terminate the mission, all he would have to do is stop the ship, give the backup signal, and then climb into the helicopter.

But he couldn't do it. There was one piece of the puzzle missing—a critical piece, indeed.

Where the hell are those two? Peng thought, once again pacing in front of the windscreen. He puffed away, considering his options. *What the hell should I do?*

Finally, five minutes later, he made up his mind.

Tim Carpenter remained in the vacant cabin, half a dozen levels below the bridge deck. He was sitting on the edge of one of the beds, using both hands to massage his left knee. The H & K submachine gun was sitting on the bed beside him.

Tim was still in shock. Witnessing the destruction of the Orion had numbed his senses. *No one could survive that crash,* he repeatedly had told himself. *The poor crew—their lives snuffed out in a heartbeat! Damn, I just can't believe it!*

Jennifer Richmond was standing next to the porthole, looking seaward.

Tim looked up. "You see anything?" he asked.

She turned. Her face was neutral. She too remained stunned. "No, nothing. We're all alone out here." She moved to the bed and sat next to Tim. "Do you think they'll send another plane?"

"Probably. Might take a while, though." He paused to stand. "But we can't wait anymore. We've got to get off this thing ASAP."

"How?"

"I've got an idea. It's risky as hell, but I think it just might work."

"What?" Jenny said, her voice hopeful.

Tim laid it all out.

"But won't they see us?" Jenny asked.

"We'll just have to risk it. Besides, what other alternatives do we have?"

"I see your point. Let's do it."

"First, I've got to check it to make sure it's still there. Those bastards may have dumped it, too."

"I'll come with you."

"No. You wait here. I'll be back as soon as I check it out."

"Okay."

Jenny had been alone for nearly ten minutes when it hap- pened—the voice broadcast from the emergency intercom speaker in the cabin's overhead. It jolted Jenny to her core.

"Attention, Tim Carpenter and Jennifer Richmond!"

The call was repeated two more times before continuing. "If you do not surrender within the next ten minutes, we will be forced to take drastic measures." The voice paused. "If you think we're bluffing, find a television set and turn it to channel three." The intercom switched off with a metallic click.

Jenny searched the cabin. She found the TV a moment later. Like in their own cabin, the Sony was built into a walnut-lined cabinet enclosure.

While at sea, the ship's television system offered a variety of closed-circuit broadcasts, ranging from a calendar of daily ship events to videotaped movies. And when in port, the system was sat-linked to CNN and a variety of other channels.

She switched on the set and tuned it to channel three.

"Oh, my God," Jenny mumbled as she stared at the color image.

Allen Peng stood just outside the camera's field of vision. He was on the ship's fantail, near the stern. The Greek crewman manning the minicam couldn't believe what was about to happen.

Peng keyed the camera's remote microphone. It was now linked directly to the ship's closed-circuit TV system. "All right, Mr. Carpenter and Miss Richmond, if you're watching you can see that we're not playing around here. You have five minutes to give yourselves up. Just pick up a phone anywhere on the ship and this will all end."

Jenny started to reach for the phone but stopped when she spotted the duffel bag. It was sitting on the floor next to one of the beds. It was chock-full of MERLIN secrets.

"No," she said to herself, "you can't do that. They must not get hold of Dad's papers. Besides, they're bluffing. They won't do it. No one's that cold-blooded!"

The deadline passed.
Peng nodded. The PLA commandos moved forward.

The cameraman continued to train the minicam on the victims. They were a family of four. Californians. San Jose. The mother and father were in their midthirties. The two boys were eight and ten. All four stood next to the opening in the guardrail. A churning mass of white and green wake dominated the background. The ship-generated wind blasted their bodies.

Tim Carpenter was one deck level directly below the Jack-son family. But he was oblivious to their fate or to Peng's ultimatum to Jenny. Although the platform he knelt on was open to the sea, the overhead fantail concealed him from those above. And the swirling sea noises drowned out the ship's intercom system.

Tim was busy studying the instructions. The fiberglass container was about the size of a beer keg. *Okay,* he thought, *all I have to do is pull this sucker and it's armed.*

He stood up. It was time to get Jenny. He had just taken a step when he spotted something fly by, out of the corner of an eye. He snapped his head to the right. *What was that?*

Brad Jackson was the first to go. Naturally, he resisted. But when the gunmen threatened to shred the children his resolve wilted. He kissed his wife and hugged the boys. And then, without further ceremony, he pinched his nose, shut his eyes, and leaped overboard.

After he disappeared, the mother clutched her children even tighter, fear and rage tormenting her. The boys wailed and she prayed as the commandos approached. And then they too were gone.

The cameraman zoomed in on the receding wake. The Jacksons were all afloat, buoyed by their PFDs. But they wouldn't last long. The chilled ocean waters would steal their body heat with the efficiency of a Vegas pickpocket.

The camera refocused onto Allen Peng. "Miss Richmond," he said, "give up. Right now! Or we're going to repeat this again and again and again. . . ."

Jenny turned away from the TV, vomiting.

Tim Carpenter was enraged. "Son of a bitch! They're throw-ing the passengers overboard!" A few seconds later he reacted.

Tim struggled to lift the bulky fiberglass container, momentarily balancing it on the steel combing. And then he tossed it overboard.

36 OPERATION DELIVERANCE

The pilot of the Boeing C-17 Globemaster III had received the revised orders nearly an hour earlier. Instead of heading for Ketchikan International, the giant cargo jet was diverted westward. It was now crossing the North Pacific Ocean, four miles high. But it was impossible to tell that from the cockpit. For hundreds of miles ahead the thick cloud cover completely obscured the water surface. The special operations cargo jet could have been flying over Kansas for all the flight crew knew.

A simple adjustment to the autopilot was all that had been required to comply with the new orders. But back in the cavernous cargo hold, the sudden change in plans had created a firestorm of activity. The fourteen passengers had to scramble to get ready.

They were now all set, each man outfitted with sixty-plus pounds of gear. They sat in two equal columns on either side of the cargo bay, their backs to the fuselage, resting in canvas frame seats. The cargo compartment had already been depressurized, requiring the passengers to hook up to the aircraft's oxygen system. In spite of the clumsy face masks strapped to their heads, the men chatted among themselves.

The leader of the group, a Navy lieutenant, stood near the forward end of the compartment. He was conferring with the Air Force loadmaster. Two cylindrical fiberglass containers, each about two and a half feet in diameter and seven feet long, were lined up in the center of the aluminum deck near the aft end of the hold.

On the flight deck, the C-17s copilot continued to scan the aircraft's three separate GPS navigation systems. They were all in sync, each one displaying identical earth coordinates as they independently interrogated the constellation of overhead satellites. There was no room for error. Being off by just a few seconds of latitude or longitude could result in calamity.

The copilot turned to face the aircraft commander. "Five-minute warning, skipper," he called out.

"Roger, five minutes." The pilot paused for a moment. "Better let Hamilton know."

"Right." The copilot then keyed his intercom mike and alerted the loadmaster.

It was almost time now. The C-17's aft cargo doors were open and the rear ramp partially lowered. The fourteen men were queued up, standing in parallel columns next to the gaping hole in the rear of the aircraft. Despite a reduction in air speed to two hundred knots, the noise inside the open compartment was deafening.

Although the air temperature was twenty degrees below zero, the passengers hardly noticed. Their garments insulated them from the cold.

The Air Force sergeant was in charge. He stood next to the doorway on the starboard side of the fuselage. His helmet communication system was plugged into the aircraft's intercom. He could hear the copilot calling off the countdown. "Thirty seconds . . . twenty seconds . . ."

As the ten-second mark approached, the loadmaster looked at the nearby senior officer. The Navy lieutenant's plastic face shield was partially fogged from his breath, but the two men achieved eye lock. When the copilot said "Ten," the sergeant raised both gloved hands, spreading his fingers apart. The noise from the turbulence made normal conversation impossible.

The lieutenant nodded and turned to face the opening.

The copilot continued the countdown: "Five, four, three, two, one . . . Execute! Execute! Execute!"

A green light above the ramp door snapped on while the loadmaster simultaneously gave the final thumbs-up signal. Within twenty seconds, it was all over. The U.S. Navy direct-action SEAL platoon, twelve enlisted men and two officers, along with two equipment containers, were now airborne.

"Sir," called out the Pentagon officer, "the C-17 just reported that the team has deployed."

The NMCC watch commander nodded. He then turned and looked at the wall-mounted screen. A video map of the North Pacific Ocean and the southeastern coast of Alaska was displayed. There was a blinking red light on the map about one hundred miles offshore of the Queen Charlotte Islands. It marked the current location of the C-17. *Good luck, boys,* he thought.

The ocean surface was choppy. The wind had come up an hour earlier; it was blowing about fifteen knots. And it was raining—hard.

The three men crammed into the elevated platform ignored the crummy weather. They were too busy to notice. Their collective eyes were all elevated, scanning the gray-black, moisture-dripping clouds.

The senior officer, a full Navy commander, checked his watch again. *Where the hell are they?* he wondered.

About a minute later, the starboard observer made visual contact. "I've got one," he called out, "zero three zero degrees."

The other men rotated into position, all raising their binoculars in unison. The target had just penetrated the low ceiling. "Here comes another," called out the same lookout.

The SEALs landed precisely on target, each one flying his parasail with the grace of an eagle. After free-falling for two miles, they deployed their chutes and then used GPS receivers strapped to their wrists to home in on the landing coordinates.

Within ten minutes of plunging into the cold ocean water, each man had been plucked from the sea and hustled below. It took another half hour to recover the two cargo containers, which had been blown downwind. Although they had landed over ten miles away, they had been easy to locate. The radio transmitter attached to each pod announced its location with a digital broadcast that translated into: "Here I am!"

At 4:09 P.M., a full six minutes ahead of schedule, the USS *Bellingham* flooded her ballast tanks and sank below the ocean surface. Operation Deliverance was now officially under way.

One hundred sixty-five miles to the north, Jennifer Richmond and Tim Carpenter were in the midst of a heated debate.

"Tim, I don't care anymore. I've got to stop this madness. I'm going to give them what they want." Jenny pointed to the duffel bag full of her father's research papers.

"That won't satisfy them—please believe me. They want you!"

"But I don't know any more than what's in those documents."

"They don't know that." Tim shook his head. "Think about it. They've been after you from day one. Somehow, they're convinced that you worked with your father on that MERLIN thing. They will not stop until they have you."

"Then I'll give myself up."

"No way—I'm not going to let that happen. I'll figure a way out of this mess. I just need some more time."

"But I can't let them kill any more passengers." Jenny turned toward the cabin TV. "Look, they're going to do it again."

Tim faced the Sony. Armed guards were herding a middle-aged couple toward the gap in the guardrail. *Oh, shit,* he thought.

Tim had returned to the cabin hideout twenty minutes earlier, just in time to witness another live demonstration. Two more passengers were tossed overboard. As with the Jacksons, the ship's closed-circuit television system broadcast the forced leap of the newlyweds from Denver. And now it was about to be repeated once again.

Tim picked up the MP5 and pointed it at the TV. He squeezed the trigger, blasting a single round through the screen.

37 THE WATER BULLET

Ricardo Molina was standing inside the *Regina*'s Combat Information Center. The spacious compartment, located aft of the bridge, was the nerve center of the Canadian warship. It was shirt-sleeve cool. The lighting was subdued, almost cavelike. The faint odor of hot electrical equipment tainted the compartment's atmosphere.

Besides Molina, a dozen other officers and enlisted personnel were inside the CIC. They sat at high-tech consoles, staring at color monitors. Most wore headsets and spoke into lip mikes. The CIC staff was responsible for monitoring the ship's surveillance and communication equipment: three separate radars, the latest passive and active sonar systems, and a variety of satellite-linked radio systems. They also controlled the frigate's weapon systems: an automatic cannon near the bow; an aft-mounted Gatling gun designed to shoot down cruise missiles and jet aircraft; and an antiship, antiair missile battery located near amidships.

"Did they find anyone?" Ricardo asked, addressing *Regina*'s CO.

Captain Mark MacKenzie turned to face the American visitor. He had just hung up a telephone handset. His face was strained, pained.

"I'm sorry," MacKenzie said, "but my crew didn't spot any survivors. Just an oil slick and debris, like what your Coast Guard plane reported. Apparently, it disintegrated on impact."

MacKenzie was referring to a report that he had just obtained from the *Regina*'s helicopter crew. Besides the shipboard monitoring systems, the CIC was also electronically linked with a suite of remote sensors located on its own helicopter. Nearly an hour earlier, the Sea King, call sign Air One, had rolled out of its fantail hangar, was fueled, and then launched. At this moment it was hovering fifty feet over the ocean surface, about twelve miles west of the *Regina*. The aircraft commander had just reported back to the mother ship using an encrypted radio frequency.

Ricardo peered downward and while staring at the deck shook his head. "Dammit, Captain, those poor guys on that Orion didn't have a chance."

"No, I'm afraid not."

Ricardo looked up. "Well, what are we supposed to do now?"

"I've just ordered Air One back. Your Pentagon didn't want us pursuing the *Emerald Sea* at this time, even though it's well within its flight range."

"That doesn't make any sense. If the helicopter's so close, why wouldn't they want the ship checked out?"

"I suppose they're worried about SAMs."

"Oh, yeah." Ricardo paused, thinking. "But you could have it stand off—beyond the range of any handheld missiles. That way we could at least get a look at the thing. Maybe we'd learn something."

"Right, we could do that. And our bird's equipped with flares so we could even get closer, but I don't think they want us monkeying around just yet."

"Why?"

"Apparently, your people have something else going on."

"What do you mean?"

MacKenzie frowned. "I don't know. Esquimalt didn't give me any details, only that your navy is preparing some type of operation." He paused. "That's a little bizarre to me because, technically speaking, the hijacking occurred in the Dixon Entrance—our waters. And right now the ship is offshore of our coast, not yours." He paused again. "If anyone were to launch a rescue operation, it should be us."

Ricardo shrugged. "Yeah, but remember that ship's registered in the Bahamas—neither one of us has official jurisdiction over it." He took a breath. "Anyway, those bastards still have control of the ship, and most of the passengers are American. I'd say that means we have a big stake in the whole thing."

Captain MacKenzie smiled. "Good point, Rick. Sorry about the turf hassle."

"So what do we do, then?"

"We've been directed not to close with the *Emerald Sea.* Instead, we're just supposed to shadow it, maintaining a forty-kilometer separation."

"Forty klicks—twenty-five miles! Good Lord, what good is that going to do?"

"I don't know. I just follow my orders."

Ricardo nodded. "Yeah, so do I. I guess we'll just wait and see what develops."

"Right. So, if you'll excuse me, I'm needed on the bridge."

"Sure, see you later."

After MacKenzie walked away, Ricardo turned to his side, scanning one of the nearby radar displays. He could see the flashing yellow icon near the top part of the screen. It marked the position of the *Emerald Sea.* Another flashing icon, close to the center of the screen, marked the location of the Sea King helicopter. Other than those two blips, the display was clear. There was nothing else around, not even a fishing boat. *What the hell could those Pentagon jockeys be up to?*

The USS *Bellingham* was running at flank—almost fifty miles per hour. It sliced through the abyss like a water bullet.

The source of the submarine's great velocity was its nuclear power plant. The uranium-fired reactor, located near the center of the 360-foot-long hull, was running at 104 percent of its rated capacity.

The *Bellingham*'s reactor was red-lined because it was in a race. Several hours earlier, SUBCOMPAC, acting on orders from NMCC, had directed the warship to close with the *Emerald Sea.* And at the moment, the cruise ship was still over 150 miles to the north while continuing to charge westward at twenty-one knots.

Prior to her new mission, SSN 775 had been exercising a hundred miles west of Vancouver Island. The sonar techs were running a series of diagnostic tests on the boat's passive arrays when the radio room picked up an ELF bell ringer message. The *Bellingham* was directed to ascend to VLF

dio reception depth. The VLF Emergency Action Message
rdered the warship to head north for possible action in con-
ection with a hijacking of a cruise ship. There were no other
etails.

A few hours later, as it proceeded north at flank speed,
another message was received. This time the EAM directed
the *Bellingham* to a specific set of earth coordinates. Within
ist minutes the SEALs magically dropped out of the cloud-
ceiled sky.

Once the special warfare contingent had boarded, the *Bellingham* resubmerged and continued its northerly speed run.
The extra personnel were now a major burden for the already
crowded submarine. And to further complicate matters, the
SEALs needed to rehearse as a unit as well as conduct complete weapons and equipment checks. Consequently, the only
space large enough to accommodate the visitors was the
ship's mess.

Meal service was suspended while the SEALs planned
their hastily conceived mission. The SEALs' XO conducted
the briefing.

Simultaneously with the team meeting, a second briefing
was taking place in the officers' wardroom. Only two persons
were present: the *Bellingham*'s skipper and the SEAL team
leader. Only at this time was the *Bellingham*'s real mission
being revealed. The lieutenant was explaining:

"Sir, all you'll need to do is get us a couple klicks ahead
of that bugger and then we'll take it from there."

"But what if it's still running full out?" the *Bellingham*'s
captain said. He paused, shaking his head. "SUBCOMPAC
reports that sucker's steaming at twenty-plus knots. How will
you get everyone aboard it?"

The SEAL grinned. He had planned for such a mission
for years. He could hardly wait to launch. "Not a problem,
kipper. We just swim out of your escape trunks and deploy
the boats. And then, when we get close enough, we'll hop
 right up that hull in nothing flat."

The sub commander let out a heavy sigh. "Okay, Lieutenant, but I've gotta tell you, that all sounds a bit scary to me.
A million things could go wrong." He hesitated for an in-

stant. "Anyway, once you get on that sucker, what then?"

"Oh, we'll play that by ear. We've got several contingency plans worked out."

"What about the explosive charges? Do you think they'll really try to blow it up?"

"It's possible, sir. They destroyed the yacht."

"What yacht?"

"Oh, I guess you haven't heard about that little event."

"No, please enlighten me."

The two officers talked for another ten minutes and then the SEAL leader left, returning to the galley. Commander John "Blackjack" Black, thirty-eight, fifth in his class at Annapolis, father of four, remained behind, pouring himself a fresh cup of coffee. As he sipped from the mug, his thoughts focused on his passengers: *It's all happening too damn fast. Those guys could be walking into a meat grinder and they don't even know it.*

"Come on, honey, you can make it."

"But it's so cold," she whimpered. "I can barely move my legs."

Brad Jackson reached for his wife, pulling her closer. Her face was ash white and her eyes were glazed over, almost trancelike. He reached up and pinched her right cheek. His chilled fingers could feel nothing.

Stacy eventually reacted. "Oh, stop!" she finally wailed. "That hurts."

"That a girl, stay awake now. I need your help with the boys."

Despite being numb from his armpits down, Brad managed to kick with his legs, pivoting in place.

Jeremy and Mica were just a few yards away, lashed to each other with Brad's belt. Their bulky PFDs kept their heads out of the sea but it wasn't enough. They had just lapsed into unconsciousness, their body heat stolen by the ocean.

The wind-swept crest of another endless swell rolled by catching Brad in the middle of a desperate breath. He gagged, spitting out the brine. *Oh, dear Jesus,* he prayed ke me if you must, but let the boys and Stacy live!*

Five minutes later, when Brad was about to pass out, he
aw it—a tiny speck of yellow on a sea of green. Miracu-
ously, the wind was blowing it toward them.

"Thank you, Lord," he muttered. And then a final surge
f adrenaline brought him back to life.

Allen Peng marched back and forth across the bridge deck.
is patience was nearly exhausted. So far, his carefully or-
nestrated campaign of terror was an utter failure.

It had been well over an hour since Major Wu's men be-
an tossing passengers overboard. And just twelve minutes
arlier, the latest victims had been dumped into the sea. But
ill there was no sign of the Richmond woman or of her
ompanion. *Why haven't they called in? How could they not
e impacted?*

Peng walked to a nearby intercom telephone and picked
p the handset. He punched in the number for the ship's
entral telephone exchange. It was answered on the first ring.

"Have you heard anything?" Peng asked, interrogating one
f the MSS agents, who now manned the exchange. He
aited a moment as the man answered. "Nothing?" Peng
xclaimed, his voice broadcasting his disappointment. He
oncluded with, "Very well. Keep monitoring. If you hear
nything from them, call me instantly."

Peng hung up the phone and once again took up pacing.
e ignored the helmsman, the only other person on the
ridge. His mind was running at warp speed: *We must make
ontact in no more than three hours—they will not wait long
' we don't. But somehow I've got to flush her out before
en. But how? Nothing's worked so far. And the Ameri-
ans—they will certainly act sometime this evening, probably
oming in by air or maybe by that ship that continues to
ollow us. Our radar will give us a little warning, but not
uch. But that doesn't matter. I've got to conclude this mess
efore they ever come or we're going be totally screwed!*

**"*Regina, Regina,* this is United States Coast Guard One Four
ive One."**

"One Four Five One, *Regina*. This is the commanding of
ficer."

"*Regina,* One Four Five One. Roger, sir, we just spotte
a life raft and are now orbiting over it. There appear to b
survivors aboard. Over."

"Is it from the target? Over."

"Unknown, sir. But if I had to guess, I'd say there's
strong probability. There's nothing else around out here an
it's definitely not from the Orion. We're miles from the im
pact point. Over."

"One Four Five One, do you still have a visual on th
target?"

"Affirmative, *Regina*. We can see it all right. Our rada
plots it out as twenty-three nautical miles away, still headin
west. Over."

"Can you assist the life raft? Over."

"Ah, sir, we can't do much from up here. We can tr
dropping them some survival gear and maybe a radio, bu
that's about it."

"Okay, One Four Five One, stand by."

"Roger."

Captain MacKenzie turned to his left, searching for th
American. Ricardo Molina was next to the windscreen. The
were both standing on the warship's bridge.

"Mr. Molina," MacKenzie said, "how do you want to han
dle this?"

"How far away is the raft?" Ricardo asked.

MacKenzie looked toward one of his nearby officers an
nodded. The lieutenant wore a headset with a boom mike
He was in direct contact with the senior radar technicia
located inside the Combat Information Center. He spoke
few words into the mike and waited. After receiving the re
sponse he turned toward Ricardo. "Sir, the raft does not shov
up on our radar. But the C-130 orbiting over it is approxi
mately twenty kilometers to the west."

Ricardo nodded and then addressed MacKenzie. "Give m
a moment, Captain."

"Certainly."

Ricardo turned away, now looking at the chart table. Bu

the map of the North Pacific didn't register. Instead he was lost in thought. *What's that damn raft doing out there? What does it mean?*

He then answered himself: *Maybe they tossed it overboard—just to confuse us, throw us off, like all those lifeboats.*

He paused. *That's got to be it; they're up to something! But what?*

And then a new cascade of thoughts developed: *But what if someone wanted to escape? How would they do it? Tossing a life raft overboard—from a ship running at twenty knots— and then jumping into the freezing ocean and trying to climb in? Damn, it might work, but the risks . . . who would have the balls to try something like that?*

And then it hit, like a pail of cold water in the face, a real eye opener. *Could it really be?*

Ricardo shook his head in astonishment as the idea coalesced. *By God,* he thought, *that might just explain it. But what should I do?*

Special Agent in Charge Molina now had a tough decision to make. And there was no one else to consult with. It was his call.

About an hour earlier, while still inside the *Regina*'s CIC, Ricardo had finally been made privy to the details of Deliverance. The chairman of the Joint Chiefs personally briefed him during a twenty-minute secure radio call. No one else aboard the Canadian warship, not even Captain MacKenzie, heard the conversation.

Ottawa, through enormous political pressure from Washington, had agreed to turn over temporary tactical control of the *Regina* to the U.S. military. And the CJC had, in turn, designated Molina as the on-scene commander. Consequently, for all practical purposes, Ricardo now controlled the Canadian warship.

But none of that really mattered to the FBI agent. Ricardo knew nothing about ships. His only interest was in successfully completing the mission. Everything depended upon finding Jennifer Richmond—everything!

On paper, Deliverance made sense. But a new quirk had

just popped up. The raft. It could be just a coincidence, a
fishing boat or yacht that went down earlier, with the survivors drifting into the target area. Or it could be the key to
everything.

Ricardo finally made his decision. There was only one way
to solve the mystery. He turned back to face the *Regina*'s
commander. "Captain," Ricardo said, "let's head out there
and recover that raft. I want to see just who's on it."

"Right!"

While the bridge crew began executing MacKenzie's new
orders, Ricardo stepped up to the windscreen. He could see
his reflected face in the glare of the glass. He grinned, convinced that he had the answer. *Tim,* he thought, *you clever
son of a bitch, jumping overboard with Jenny and then
climbing into the raft was brilliant. I bet those pricks on the
ship don't even know you're gone!*

He couldn't have been more wrong.

38 CAPITULATION

Jennifer Richmond was alone. Tim had taken off twenty
minutes earlier. He was on another scouting mission, looking
for a way out. Before leaving, however, he had moved Jenny
to another cabin.

The TV set he had blasted in his fit of rage caught fire.
He'd managed to douse the flames before it got out o
hand—and before the remote smoke sensor was triggered in
the bridgehouse. Nevertheless, the cabin stunk to high
heaven.

Jenny's new hideout was one deck below their last refuge.
Tim left her with the Glock. It was sitting on top of the
vanity. She hadn't touched it.

She was sitting on the edge of the bed, staring at the tele
vision set. The Sony was switched off.

Don't turn it on! she thought. *That's just what they want*

Tim had asked Jenny to stay away from the TV—no mat

ter what happened. She had agreed, knowing that the hijackers' terror campaign was aimed straight at her. Nevertheless, her willpower was beginning to mutate into mush. It started five minutes earlier when, once again, the cabin intercom system came alive with the unseen voice: "Jennifer Richmond, give yourself up. You have ten minutes or you will have more blood on your hands."

I've got to stay ahead of them. I can't give in. Tim's counting on me!

Jenny's resolve was short-lived.

Those poor people, and the children too, tossed overboard—all because of me! Oh, God. It's just not right.

The awful images were in living color, forever fused into her memory, but there remained a ray of hope.

Maybe that raft will help!

Before leaving, Tim had told Jenny what he had done. The life raft had been covered with a paint tarp on the fantail. The hijackers missed it on their earlier sabotage raid. As Ricardo Molina had guessed, Tim planned to use it for their getaway. But after the Jacksons walked the plank, he tossed it overboard.

Oh, please, Lord, let them find it!

"Last call, Jennifer," blared the intercom voice.

I can't stand this! Jenny thought, finally capitulating.

The Sony blinked on. The screen was filled with a camera's-eye view of the ship's fantail. There was no sound, just a dull electronic hum.

Dammit! Those bastards are going to do it again.

Jenny watched as the woman was herded to the opening in the guardrail. She looked to be in her seventies. She was maybe five feet tall, but weighed close to two hundred pounds. Encased by an oversized life jacket, she looked like a walking version of a Big Mac. A few seconds later, the camera focused on the male victim, another geriatric. He was planted in a wheelchair. One of the guards had rolled it up to the opening and parked the man next to the woman. The polio victim wore a light blue parka and tan slacks. No PFD for him.

The man turned and looked up. He then grasped his wife's

outstretched hand. The camera zoomed in for a closeup. Their faces told it all—absolute horror.

And then they were gone. It happened in an eye blink. From off camera, weapons had been fired. The momentum of the heavy slugs ripped into the hapless victims' flesh and bones, propelling them overboard.

Jenny's rock-solid objectivity had just been fractured by a magnitude 9 earthquake of guilt. Tears streamed down her cheeks. "Dear God," she cried out, "it's all my fault. I've got to stop this madness!"

It was almost invisible. The swells steepened, further concealing its meager profile. And radar was useless. There wasn't any metal to reflect the incident radiation. Nevertheless, one of the lookouts, an eighteen-year-old with 20/10 vision, finally spotted it. "Target, bearing zero two five!" he shouted into his headset microphone.

Five minutes later, HMCS *Regina* was dead in the water, upwind of the tiny craft. It took another twenty minutes to extract the four drenched Americans from the inflatable.

The Jacksons were now in the dispensary. The ship's medical corpsman was administering emergency care. They were all hypothermic, especially the youngsters, but they would live.

FBI agent Molina was currently waiting in the officers' wardroom, sipping his ninth cup of coffee for the day. He was alone at the moment. Captain MacKenzie had been called to the bridge.

Ricardo stared blankly at the adjacent bulkhead. He was thankful that the Californians had survived their horrendous ordeal, yet he wasn't at ease with the latest turn of events. When he had stood on the open deck, looking down at the bobbing life raft, he had been certain that his old friend, Tim Carpenter, accompanied by Jennifer Richmond, were inside. His spirits plummeted, however, when the young family from San Jose was finally hauled aboard the frigate.

Ricardo took another sip and then shook his head in disappointment. *Tim, old buddy, where the hell are you?*

* * *

Tim Carpenter was on the sundeck, near amidships. He was crouched down behind an emergency fire hose locker, using it for cover. The Heckler & Koch submachine gun was cradled in his arms. He ignored the drizzle that washed down his face. His sweater and jeans were soaked and he was shivering. But he didn't notice. What Tim really wanted, what he craved, was a smoke. But that comfort was impossible. It would give his position away. The bad guy was only a dozen feet away.

Tim cautiously extended his head around the corner of the steel box, trying to get a better look. He pulled back a few seconds later, like a turtle retreating into its shell. *He's still there!*

Tim had been on the prowl for forty minutes. So far, he had counted eighteen hijackers. Most were now busy containing the restless crowds that continued to mill around the enclosed lifeboat decks. But a few were patrolling, looking for him.

The passengers were a docile group. If they now complained at all, it was only to themselves. They had all gotten the point. Those that were not near one of the exterior TV monitors heard the rumors after the "demonstrations." They swept through the crowds like the flowing spectator "wave" at a football stadium.

During the initial live broadcasts, when the victims were forced to jump overboard, the passenger reaction had been one of open rebellion: "We should throw all of those bastards into the sea."

The brutal execution during act two squashed the bravado: "They're going to sink the ship and kill us all."

Tim had missed the machine-gunning of the Blumenfelds. Had he known that the terror campaign had been accelerated, he would have called off his reconnaissance mission. He would have decided it was too risky to leave Jenny alone. She was already on the ragged edge.

While remaining concealed, Tim checked his watch. He was late. *Jenny's probably having a fit.* But he wasn't yet ready to retrace his steps. He had one last lead to check.

It had taken him twelve minutes to get into position,

slowly working his way along the long corridor that paralleled the open deck. His knee was killing him, but he did his best to ignore it. The howling ship-generated wind helped mask his movements. Although the sun was retreating and the sky remained thick with ever darkening clouds, a modicum of filtered sunlight managed to illuminate the spacious sundeck. As a result, Tim moved at a snail's pace.

He took another quick look around the locker box. The guard remained in the same position, his back to the wind. The man had pulled up a hood on his jacket to shield his head from the rain.

It's show time, Tim said to himself. He took a deep breath and then leaped from his hiding place.

The PLA commando never heard a thing. When Tim slammed the butt of the MP5 onto the back of the soldier's head, he collapsed to the steel deck with the impact of a wet bag of cement. Glistening blood dribbled from the deep gash in the man's scalp.

Tim dragged the unconscious guard behind the fire hose locker. He took a moment to look him over. The Asian was young, clean-shaven, and appeared to be in excellent physical shape. *Military* was Tim's immediate conclusion.

He removed the man's weaponry—another submachine gun, a 9 mm pistol, an ammo pack, combat knife, and a canvas satchel filled with half a dozen hand grenades and a two-kilogram brick of Semtex.

While kneeling next to the soldier, Tim toyed with the knife. A quick thrust under the man's rib cage and he would no longer be a threat. But that draconian measure wasn't necessary. Instead, he picked up the soldier and tossed him over the guardrail.

Tim next focused on what the Asian had been guarding. The raven hull of the 500MD Defender glistened in the mist.

Jenny was almost ready. She had managed to make her way to the Golden Grotto without detection. The huge nightclub compartment was deserted. She soon found what she was looking for, off to the port side, next to a bulkhead. She knelt on the hardwood flooring and then reached into her pants

pocket, removing a red-handled object. She had liberated it
from a toilet kit in the last cabin that she and Tim had commandeered.

This'll work just fine! she thought as she pulled open one
of the half-dozen blades on the Swiss Army knife.

Tim Carpenter was about to exit the Defender, the object
of his search firmly grasped under his right arm, when he
happened to peer forward into the cockpit. It had been there
all the time, built into the center console. *I'll be damned!
Could it be that easy?*

"You have her?" Peng asked, the telephone handset glued
to his right ear. He was still on the bridge, speaking to one
of his men on a lower deck.

"Yes, sir. She called from a telephone station near one of
the lounges. She was waiting for us when we got there."

"That's excellent, just excellent." Peng paused. "Now,
what about the man—Carpenter? Where is he?"

"We don't know, sir. She said she hasn't seen him for
hours."

"All right, bring her up here. But keep your men looking
for him."

"Yes, sir."

Peng hung up the phone and turned to face his second in
command. Major Wu was standing by the radar display,
smoking.

Peng beamed. "Well, Major," he said, "you were right.
That last demonstration of yours worked. She gave up.
They're bringing her up now."

The commando nodded and then simply said, "That's
good news, sir." Although he was polite, his self-talk was
anything but: *You damn fool! If you had listened to me earlier, then we would have been long gone by now. As it is,
we'll be lucky to complete the mission without getting killed.*

Gunning down the elderly Americans had been Wu's idea.
And he had hand-picked the couple. The fact that the man
had been confined to a wheelchair had been pivotal in their
selection.

Merely pushing the senior citizens overboard, like the first group of victims, would not have had the shock value that was needed to do the job. After the first failed attempt, Wu had argued hard with Peng over that very point: "Sir, you've got to terrorize her," he had said. "Make her want to puke her guts out. That's the only way she's going to come around. And you've got to be ready to do it again and again, until she can't stand it anymore. Only then will you be assured that she'll give up!"

Major Wu had been careful not to criticize Peng directly. His comments had been directed toward resolving their current dilemma: they were running out of time, and they still had not found the Richmond woman.

Finally, after three consecutive failures, Peng had given in to the logic of his subordinate's reasoning. There would be no more attempts to appease his conscience—just death, violent and bloody and ugly.

Peng turned away from Wu and looked toward the rear of the pilothouse. Another commando was hunched over a chart table. "Fung," he called out, "what's our ETA now?"

The soldier looked up. He was young, almost a boy. "Ah, sir, we'll be arriving at the coordinates in approximately forty-five minutes."

"Very well, let me know ten minutes before and then we'll cut power and glide in the rest of the way."

"Yes, sir."

Peng faced Wu. "Major, have your men got the equipment ready?"

"Yes, sir. They'll be ready to deploy it as soon as we're stopped."

"Good." Peng checked his watch. He then looked back at Wu. "I don't want the passengers on deck when we make the transfer so order them back into their cabins."

"Yes, sir." Wu reached for his handheld radio. Just before issuing the new orders he hesitated, glancing back at Peng. "Sir," he said, "what about Carpenter?"

"What about him?"

"With the passengers flooding the ship's interior, it'll be near impossible for my men to find him."

"Major, don't worry about that son of a bitch. We've got what we want. He can't hurt us now."

I hope you're right, thought Wu, remembering an earlier briefing by Peng that had revealed the West Point diploma at Carpenter's home.

39 MAYDAY! MAYDAY! MAYDAY!

Allen Peng could hardly believe it. Finally, after weeks of frustration, compounded by debacle after fiasco, success was at hand.

Peng smiled as he pulled up a chair and sat down at the table. He was in the *Emerald Sea*'s officers' wardroom, located aft of the bridge deck. It was 7:15 P.M. As he settled in, he reached into a coat pocket and pulled out a half-full pack of cigarettes. He offered one to his "visitor."

Jennifer Richmond shook her head. "No, thanks," she said. "I don't smoke."

Jenny was sitting at the table directly across from Peng. Her hands were neatly clasped together on top of the solid oak surface. She exhibited no outward signs of emotion; it was as if she were attending a boring business meeting.

Although Jenny's body language radiated confidence, with a slight hint of arrogance, it was a facade. Her stomach flip-flopped while her legs trembled. She was so scared that she was on the verge of losing bladder control.

Peng lit up and took a long drag. When he exhaled, he deliberately aimed the plume at his prisoner.

Jenny raised her right hand, brushing away the stink. The foul fumes had already penetrated her nostrils and she coughed. And then her eyes began to water.

Peng ignored her discomfort, blowing another cloud her way. It was a test.

Finally, Jenny protested. "Please, could you not do that?"

Good, he thought, *she's not so tough. She'll crack right away.*

Peng used an ashtray to crush out the cigarette.

"Thank you."

Peng made eye contact. Hers were brown, like his own He then glanced down at a set of color photographs on the table, briefly studying the images. He looked back up. *No wonder they had a hard time finding you,* he concluded as he stared at the new Jenny.

Even with the rather drab disguise, she was attractive. The photos they had used during the hunt did not do her justice For a fleeting moment, Peng wondered what she would be like in bed.

"Tell me," he finally said, "when did you first learn about your father's discovery?"

Oh, damn, here it comes.

After another meeting with the secretary of defense and then a teleconference with the president and his National Security Council, the chairman of the Joint Chiefs of Staff once again returned to the National Military Command Center. He was now being briefed by the watch commander.

The brigadier general said, "Operation Deliverance is proceeding on schedule. The *Bellingham* should be in range within minutes."

"What about that Canadian ship?"

"The *Regina* continues to shadow the target vessel. Its helo is currently on standby and the CO guarantees that it can be airborne with two minutes' notice."

"How about that replacement Orion from NAS Whidbey?"

"It's currently orbiting Graham Island, waiting for the go code."

The CJC nodded. "Okay, good. Now, what about that FBI agent? Is he ready to take charge of the ship once it's secure?"

Official U.S. jurisdiction over the *Emerald Sea* had just been obtained. The Bahamian government, in cooperation with the cruise ship's American owners, had just faxed the necessary legal documents to the Pentagon, reflagging the *Emerald Sea* as a U.S.-registered vessel.

"Yes, sir. He's ready. As soon as the helo lands on the ship, he'll coordinate directly with the SEALs. If the woma is still aboard, they'll find her. Agent Molina will then place her under protective custody."

"The president wants her out ASAP. How will you handle that?"

"Once we have her, she'll be airlifted to Ketchikan. We've got a Gulfstream standing by. It'll head straight to Nellis."

"We don't want the Canadians flying her off that ship," the CJC said. "The president was adamant about that. Once we've got her, she has to remain in U.S. jurisdiction at all times. No exceptions."

"Understood, sir. A Coast Guard cutter from Ketchikan is now under way. It has—"

"That the one that had the turbine problem?" interrupted the chairman.

"Yes, sir. It's been repaired. She's under way now. She carries a Seahawk equipped with long-range fuel tanks. Once we have the woman, it'll launch and pick her up. Depending on how far offshore the *Emerald Sea* is at that time, the helo will either fly straight back to Ketchikan or land on the cutter for refueling."

"Okay, General, I guess you've got things pretty well covered." The CJC paused. "Let's just hope that God blesses us with a little luck. We're going to need all the help we can get to pull this off."

"Amen, sir."

"We're ten minutes away," reported the caller.

"Very good. Cut the power and coast in the rest of the way." There was a slight pause. "Are your people ready with the device?"

"Yes, sir. As soon as we slow up, they will deploy."

"Good, I'll be there in a few minutes. Carry on."

Allen Peng hung up the intercom phone without waiting for a final reply from Major Wu. He was too preoccupied with his present work to concern himself with navigational matters. Wu would take care of it.

Peng glanced across the wardroom table. Jennifer Richmond remained seated on the opposite side but had turned away. She was not cooperative at the moment, but he didn't care. Twelve minutes earlier, after a preliminary round of questioning, she had pointed to the duffel bag resting on the tile deck near the end of the table. She informed him that the answers to all of his questions were inside it.

At first, Peng was convinced that she was bluffing, trying to gain time or attempting to trick him. But when she finally picked up the canvas bag, set it on the tabletop, and then unzipped it, his heart skipped a beat. Inside was literally a gold mine of high technology.

He began removing the treasure. The code words *Top Secret, Eyes Only, NSA, DARPA,* and finally the magic words that he had been searching for, *Project MERLIN,* were stamped in brilliant red ink all over the cover sheets of the reports. There were also dozens of pages of complex handwritten calculations on green engineering sheets followed up by reams of computer printouts packed solid with numerical and graphical data. But most intriguing of all was the thermos-sized cylinder. Inside was a computer circuit board. He had studied the strange device for several minutes before resealing it. *That's got to be it,* he had concluded.

Peng was not a scientist, but he had taken several courses in physics and chemistry as an undergraduate. Consequently, he had sufficient basic technical skills to convince himself that the items he was reviewing were legitimate.

Just before Major Wu had interrupted him, Peng had discovered more booty: two VHS tape cassettes labeled "VORTEX-Run 21" and "VORTEX-Run 32." He was trying to figure out how the VCR worked when Major Wu called in the ten-minute warning.

Peng walked back over to the console television and its companion videocassette recorder. He lit up, ignoring Jennifer. All thoughts of mission details and contingency plans had been relegated to the back burner. He had about five minutes before he would have to return to the bridge. So, once again, he studied the VCR's controls. His curiosity was inflamed. He had to know: *What the hell is a VORTEX?*

"Sonar, Conn. What do you have now?"
"Conn, Sonar. Sir, we're still not picking up any propeller turns. She must be coasting."

"What about the power plant? Is it still operating?"

"Can't tell at our speed, sir. We'd have to slow up; maybe then we'd be able to hear it."

"What's our range?"

"Coming up on twenty-four thousand yards."

"Very well, stand by."

"Aye, aye, sir."

Commander Jack Black returned the handheld intercom microphone to its receptacle on an overhead console. He had been speaking with the senior sonar operator, who was seated inside a compartment located just forward of the captain's position.

Black, the *Bellingham*'s commanding officer, was in the control room, standing in front of the periscope pedestal. A dozen other officers and enlisted personnel were inside the compartment.

The control room, or attack center, was located directly under the sail, near the forward end of the pressure casing. It was the nerve center for the ship. Nearly every mechanical/electrical device aboard the $1 billion vessel was monitored and/or controlled from the twenty-by-thirty-foot space.

The captain turned to face his second in command. The executive officer was standing near the periscope pedestal. "XO, what do you think is going on?"

The lieutenant commander shook his head. "I don't know, skipper. Maybe they're getting ready to do something with those hostages. The EAM said they were threatening to blow the ship up."

"Yeah, you might be right. No telling what those pirates will do next."

Black paused to check one of the control room's clocks; it read 2010 hours, local time. They had just completed a four-hour speed run—after retrieving the SEALs. He then looked back at the XO. "We're ahead of schedule so let's reduce turns to one-third and let sonar have a good listen."

"Reduce turns to one-third. Aye, sir."

The XO repeated the command, addressing the diving officer, and within just a few minutes, the *Bellingham* shed almost thirty knots. The Los Angeles–class attack submarine now moved through the inky depths with the stealth of a tiger on a night hunt. Its prey was just a few miles ahead.

As Commander Black and the control room crew carefully maneuvered the boat into position, they were unaware that the *Bellingham* was no longer alone. There was another hunter on the prowl and it was stalking them.

"Mayday! Mayday! Mayday! Any station, please respond. Mayday! Mayday! Mayday! Over."

Tim Carpenter released his thumb from the transmit switch. He had no idea what the proper protocol was for making an emergency call on the radio. All he could remember from his brief flying career was how to slip on the headset with its companion boom mike. Years earlier, he had taken a few introductory lessons in a tiny Cessna. But he never completed the course and he knew next to nothing about how to pilot a helo.

Tim was still inside the Defender, sitting in the pilot's seat. He had been in the aircraft for over half an hour. At first his goal had been simple: find the helo's emergency life raft and then use it to escape in with Jenny.

The four-man rubber raft was in the aft cabin, deflated and compressed into an aluminum box. The box was strapped to a bulkhead. After removing the raft, Tim was just about to deplane when he discovered the helicopter's transceiver. While examining the device, a new thought had jelled: *Maybe, just maybe I can do something with this thing!*

Unlike with his satphone, he guessed—hoped—that the aircraft's radio signals were not jammed. It would be too dangerous to fly without a com system.

It had taken Tim nearly an hour to figure out how to activate the instrument panel, and then activate the radio. The master key that unlocked the controls was missing, forcing Tim to bypass the security device. He ended up hot-wiring the radio with a separate lead from the Defender's battery compartment.

He had allowed himself just a few more minutes to call for help and then he'd have to vacate the helo. More of the bad guys could show up any second.

Tim repeated the SOS, using the helicopter's emergency air to air radio preset frequency. His voice remained strong, but there was an undertone of apprehension. He increased the radio's speaker volume. The faint trickle of static in the earphones continued. *Dammit! Isn't there anyone out there?*

Tim had no way of knowing if anyone was listening or, for that matter, if the radio was even working. The *Emerald Sea* was far offshore and the likelihood that any aircraft were close enough to hear it was remote. Besides, the helicopter was surrounded by tons of steel. The *Emerald Sea*'s hull and superstructure were capable of reflecting and diffracting radio waves, resulting in a jumbled mishmash of incomprehensive words and static.

For a moment, Tim thought about randomly dialing in other frequencies, praying that someone might be listening. But he rejected that plan. He might accidentally activate one of the marine radio channels that the cruise ship monitored.

Tim pressed the transmit key again. "Mayday! Mayday! Mayday! Is anyone out there? Over."

Tim was about to hit the transmit switch again when his earphones came to life: "Aircraft in distress, this is U.S. Coast Guard One Four Five One. Identify yourself and state your emergency. Over."

Sweet Jesus, Tim thought, *it worked!*

40 MISSING IN ACTION

"How many are aboard? Over."

"I counted eighteen, but I'm sure there are more than that. Over."

Ricardo Molina and Tim Carpenter were using the 500MD's radio to communicate. After the U.S. Coast Guard patrol aircraft responded to Tim's Mayday, it handed off the call to the Canadian warship. The *Regina* continued to shadow the *Emerald Sea*, maintaining a twenty-five-mile separation. The Hercules was five miles east of the *Regina*, orbiting the frigate at twenty thousand feet.

"Where's Jennifer?" Ricardo asked, calling from the bridge.

"She's safe. You don't have to worry about that. Over."

Thank God! Ricardo thought. "Okay, but what about you? Over."

Tim glanced through the Plexiglas windscreen of the helicopter. The open deck in front of the 500MD was bathed in light from a bank of bulkhead-mounted floods. Other than the raindrops that pounded the steel plates, it remained empty.

Tim keyed the microphone. "I'm okay for the moment, but I can't stay here much longer. Someone's bound to come along. Over."

"Any chance you can yank that radio set out and take it along?"

Tim eyed the compact console housing the aircraft's communication and navigational electronics. He unconsciously shook his head. "No way. This stuff's all built in. I'd just screw it up. Over."

Shit, Ricardo thought. *If we could just remain in radio contact, it would make things so much easier.* He was about to hit the transmit key on his handheld mike when Tim broke in again.

"You know, Ricky, I've got a combo satphone and cell phone back where Jenny's hiding. The satellite receiever's not working but I'm not sure about the cell mode. Over."

"They're just jamming sat frequencies," offered Molina.

"Hmmm. Well, I know we're too far out for the cellular net to work with the shore-based system. But maybe you guys can still do something with it."

"Stand by, Tim. We'll check it out."

Ricardo briefly consulted with the officer of the deck who, in turn, called the CIC. A minute later Molina had an answer.

"Tim, we might be able to rig up something, but we'll have to call you to make it work. What's your number? Over."

Tim hesitated—for a long moment. He never called his own number. Finally, he remembered.

"Okay, got it," Ricardo said after Tim read off the digits.

Ricardo continued: "It's going to take a while to check this out so we better get our jawboning done right now. Over."

"Right. Let's do it. I need to get back and check on Jenny."

"Yeah, okay, but just hang on a sec. I need to check something else out. Over."

Ricardo heard two quick clicks from the speaker. He then turned to his right, facing the *Regina*'s CO. Captain Mark MacKenzie was standing next to one of the bridge radar consoles, monitoring Ricardo's conversation.

"Do you think the hijackers can hear us?" Ricardo asked.

MacKenzie shrugged. "It's unlikely. Most ships aren't set up to monitor aircraft frequencies, just ship-to-ship channels." He paused. "But then again, they brought that helo aboard, so who knows?"

Ricardo turned away, now looking forward through the bridge windscreen. Ominous gray-black clouds stretched across the horizon, blocking out what little sunlight remained. Soon, it would be totally dark. He took in a deep breath. *If they're monitoring, they'll know everything, and Tim will get nailed for sure. But if they aren't, then we've got a golden opportunity. Shit, what should I do?*

Ricardo finally pulled up the microphone and depressed the transmit switch. "Okay, Tim, here's what I want you to do. . . ."

"Are we getting close?" Peng asked. He was now on the bridge, standing next to the chart table. Major Wu was monitoring the ship's position with a GPS receiver.

"Almost," Wu said. "We're about half a kilometer away."

Peng glanced out the windscreen. The foredeck was lit up with an army of floodlights, but beyond the bow he couldn't see much. The sea-sky interface was nearly blacked out. And it continued to rain like hell.

Peng turned to face the other commando manning the helm. "I can't tell—are we still moving?" he asked.

The soldier moved to a nearby instrument-laden console. A moment later he responded: "Sir, this says we're still making way—about a knot or so."

Eighteen minutes earlier the ship's power plant was throttled back and the propellers disengaged. The thirty-thousand-
ton vessel was still being carried forward by its momentum.

"All right, Major," Peng said, addressing Wu, "I think
we're close enough, so give the signal."

"Yes, sir." Wu slipped on a headset with a boom mike.
He keyed the microphone and spoke a few words in his na-
tive tongue. A few seconds later he looked back at Peng.
"They're lowering it now," he said.

Peng nodded.

Wu reached up with his left hand and touched the head-
phone. He held the speaker as if he were having difficulty
hearing. Twenty seconds passed and he again made eye contact with Peng. "It's in the water," he reported.

Peng waited.

A full minute went by and then the Chinese military officer smiled. "The message has been broadcast."

"What about the reply?"

"Nothing yet."

Peng was not surprised. "It'll probably take them a little
time to get ready."

"Yes, sir."

Ten more minutes passed. Peng was now pacing next to the
windscreen, wearing a racetrack pattern in the deck. His spirits
had plummeted. "Anything?" he asked as he passed Wu.

"No, sir. They've heard nothing so far."

"Then you'd better get down there and find out what's
happening. We should have heard back by now."

"Yes, sir."

Peng continued pacing for a few more minutes then stopped
beside the starboard end of the windscreen. He glanced downward at a lower deck. He could see Major Wu. The commando
leader was standing beside the MSS technicians. There was a
dark fiberglass case sitting on the deck near their feet. It was
about the size of a small sewing machine. One man was wearing a set of earphones connected to the case. Another wire
from the case was draped over the rail.

Peng keyed his handheld radio. "Are they sure the damn
thing is working?" he asked.

Wu looked up at the bridge while keying his own radio, "Yes, sir. They claim it is properly calibrated and that all of the self-diagnostics are in the green."

"Shit, where is it?" Peng said.

Major Wu didn't bother to reply. His thoughts were the same as Peng's: *Where the hell is it?*

The *Emerald Sea*'s signal came in loud and clear in the sonar compartment of the *Yangtze*. The PRC nuclear attack submarine had been monitoring the frequency band for several hours now. It had arrived on station long before the *Emerald Sea*.

The cleverly disguised message was broadcast into the ocean depths by means of a portable hydrophone. The watermelon-size cylinder dangled fifty feet under the cruise ship's keel. The carrier frequency of the signal mimicked the cry from a humpback whale. Currently, there were several hundred of the mammoth *Megaptera novaeangliae* patrolling the offshore waters of southeast Alaska. They had arrived a month earlier, swimming two thousand miles from their home waters off the Hawaiian Islands. Each summer they migrated to Alaska in order to gorge themselves on the rich feeding grounds of the North Pacific.

The biological code had been specifically designed so as not to arouse undue suspicion from the computers and the technicians that monitored the U.S. Navy's Integrated Underseas Surveillance System (IUSS), particularly those stationed at NavFac Whidbey Island.

Although the ultrasecret monitoring facility was located hundreds of miles to the south in Washington State, the underwater network of Sound Surveillance System (SOSUS) sensors that it monitored covered hundreds of thousands of square miles across the Pacific. And many of the submerged listening devices were deployed off the coastlines of British Columbia and Alaska.

The captain and crew of the *Yangtze* were acquainted with the U.S. Navy's NavFac installation at the Whidbey Naval Air Station. For the past two weeks, the People's Liberation Army Navy (PLAN) fast-attack boat had been patrolling off

the Washington coast, near the mouth of the Strait of Juan
de Fuca. It was monitoring Trident missile submarines as
they exited and returned to the Bangor sub base in Hood
Canal. Some thirty hours earlier it had received new orders.

The route to the new rendezvous point was serpentine,
designed to avoid known SOSUS sensors and to evade any
hostile vessels, aircraft, or submarines that might try to follow. Although capable of racing at thirty-five-plus knots, the
Yangtze's speed had been deliberately throttled back to
stealth mode. Its radiated soundprint barely exceeded the
ocean's natural background noise.

The *Yangtze* was Russian-built. The PRC had purchased
the Bars–class submarine two years earlier, paying Moscow
the equivalent of a quarter of a billion U.S. dollars in trade
credits. After refitting the ship with a suite of state-of-the-art
Japanese-manufactured sonar and communication gear, and
then installing a battery of the latest Chinese torpedoes and
antisubmarine missiles—developed in part from dual technology sold to China by friends of the Clinton Administration, the *Yangtze* joined China's ever-expanding undersea
fleet. She had just one mission: kill U.S. Navy subs.

Once again, the racket of the bellowing whale flooded the
Yangtze's attack center. The captain should have responded
to the first signal with his own coded message, another
humpback cry. Instead, he elected to remain silent. There was
just too much traffic on the sonar screens to risk it.

Besides the clamor from the *Emerald Sea*'s idling engines,
the *Yangtze*'s sonar compartment was actively tracking two
additional targets: a distant surface target, positively identified as a Halifax-class frigate, and a subsurface target, ten-
tatively classified as a Los Angeles–class fast-attack sub.

The frigate was not an immediate threat. The submarine
was. They had been tracking it for over an hour as it raced
northward at flank. And about fifty minutes earlier, when it
had closed to within ten miles of the cruise ship, it slowed
up. Eventually, it dropped off the *Yangtze*'s sonar screens.
The newcomer was now out there, silently probing the waters
with its own high-tech ears, listening, waiting.

"Sonar, Captain," called out the *Yangtze*'s commander, using a handheld microphone.

"Captain, Sonar," reported an unseen voice.

"What's the status on Yankee Three?"

"Nothing so far, sir," reported the chief sonarman. He was located one deck below and two compartments forward of the attack center. "We've had no acoustic output from the target since it reduced speed."

"Are you still certain that it's an American?"

"Yes, sir. We now have a positive match on the soundprint." The technician paused. "Los Angeles–class for sure, probably an 'Improved' version of the 688 hull. Very quiet. We won't hear its plant or its screw again unless it exceeds twelve to fourteen knots."

"Very well, stand by."

"Yes, sir."

Soundwise, the American had vanished. But it was still out there, now probably near the motionless cruise ship. The *Yangtze*'s CO had anticipated the 688's tactics and had planned accordingly.

The twenty-four-foot-long probe had been launched twenty minutes before the American finally reduced power. It was now about a mile east of the *Yangtze*. It was drifting with the current, six hundred feet below the surface. A tiny fiber-optic wire led back to the mother submarine, linking the probe's onboard computer with *Yangtze*'s attack computer.

The probe's array of minihydrophones scanned the cold ocean depths. It was listening for a special sound signature that had been programmed into its electronic brain just before it swam out of the torpedo tube.

The captain returned the mike to its bulkhead mounting and then turned to face his executive officer. "Number one," he said, "prepare the probe for immediate release. They'll be coming up soon for a look. I want to be ready."

"Yes, Captain. Switching to preattack mode."

The USS *Bellingham* was now running at eight knots. It was cemetery quiet. There was no propeller cavitation, no reactor pump noise, no boundary layer turbulence from the hull. It was a hole in the ocean.

SSN 775 had just started to ascend from its five-hundred-foot depth. It was 9:14 P.M. Blackjack had ordered periscope depth. He wanted to make a visual observation. There was no way he was going to deploy the SEALs without first verifying with his own eyes that the vessel he had been pursuing was, indeed, the *Emerald Sea*.

The remote-controlled probe registered the first metallic popping noise. It was faint, almost at background level. But that was all it took.

As the *Bellingham* rose through the depths, the enormous hydraulic pressure on the hull relaxed. This allowed the hull's cylindrical casing to expand. And one of the casing's curved steel sheets had just "popped" as the compressive load was diminished.

The probe relayed the acoustic observation to the *Yangtze*'s attack computer. Within a few seconds, new instructions were directed back to the probe. It then began moving.

"Up periscope!"

"Up periscope, aye, sir."

The *Bellingham*'s captain waited a few seconds for his order to be carried out. He then flipped down the twin hand grips on the port periscope and pressed his head against the rubber eyepiece. The Mark 18 search scope was rigged for night conditions; its low-light optics were calibrated for maximum resolution.

Commander Black peered through the eyepiece. He then rotated the scope a few degrees to his right. *Right on the money!* he thought. He didn't need the special optics. The *Emerald Sea* was an island of brilliance sitting atop an ebony sea.

"Target," he called out, "bearing, zero zero five. Range, thirty-two hundred yards."

The executive officer repeated Blackjack's observation. He was standing in the OOD watch station forward of the periscopes.

The captain rotated the Mark 18 clockwise, taking about half a minute to make the 360-degree sweep. After completing the observation, he stepped away from the tube, flipping up the hand grips. "Down scope," he ordered.

"Down scope, aye, sir," answered the quartermaster of the watch.

Black faced his XO. "Looks real good, Jim. She's just sitting there nice and quiet."

"What about that whale?"

"Didn't see it, but it has to be close by with all that racket it's making."

The XO nodded and then glanced at a nearby bulkhead, checking a clock. "We've still got about thirty minutes. Should we get a little closer? Might make it easier for the SEALs."

"Yeah, why not. Take her in another five hundred yards."

Tim Carpenter was absolutely drenched. Although the rain had just let up, he had been forced to endure the last cloudburst without any cover at all. He was chilled to the bone. The ten-knot breeze cut through his soggy clothing as if he were naked.

As miserable as the conditions were, Tim ignored his woe. He was too busy to notice. For the past ten minutes he had been struggling to open the inspection port. He was kneeling on the steel grating, next to the mast. He had managed to back off three of the stainless steel screws, using as a crude screwdriver the knife he had liberated from the helicopter guard. But the fourth screw refused to cooperate.

Once again Tim inserted the stainless steel blade into the screw head slot and cranked the handle counterclockwise. "Come on, you son of a bitch," he mumbled, "get the fuck off there!"

Nothing. No movement.

Tim leaned back on his haunches, taking a break and removing some of the pressure from his bad knee. The bead of moisture on his brow was perspiration, not precipitation.

He took a deep breath and then carefully placed the knife on the steel deck next to his right knee. And then, without thinking, he reached into his shirt pocket and pulled out a quarter-full pack of Marlboros. Somehow they were still dry. He slipped one into his mouth, his saliva already flowing in anticipation. He then flipped open his Zippo and struck the flint. Before the flame managed to leap from its base, he slammed the cover shut. "Dammit," he mumbled, "what the hell are you doing?"

The light could have given his position away—the sun had finally disappeared.

Tim looked down, scanning the foredeck area forward of his perch. At last count, there were four gunmen down there. He froze in place, his heart stuck in his mouth.

None of the bad buys looked up.

You lucky bastard, he thought, *you could have just bought it.* He stared at the cigarette, now cupped in his left hand. *I figured these damn things would kill me someday, but not like this!*

Tim slipped the cigarette and lighter back into his coat pocket. His nicotine addiction had been temporarily placated by the fear-induced burst of body drugs that were now surging through his arteries.

Time to get back to work. He picked up the knife and once again started on the stubborn screw.

Tim was a little over a hundred feet above the ocean surface, about midway up the main radar mast. The eighty-foot steel spire was mounted to the top of the bridgehouse. It looked like a giant flagpole.

The mast housed three separate radar antennas, one stacked on top of another. The nearest unit was about ten feet above Tim's head. He could hear the dull hum of its electric motor as it revolved in endless orbits.

Tim had ignored the warning sign at the base of the mast, next to the access ladder. It cautioned that no personnel were allowed aloft while any radar units were operating. The word *radiation* had been emphasized.

As long as I stay out of the direct beam, Tim had argued to himself while climbing upward, *I should be okay.*

But now he wasn't so sure. Every minute or so, the hair on the back of his head thickened, almost standing straight up. It was unsettling, to say the least. *Just ignore it,* he told himself, *Ricardo's counting on me!*

Tim's current assignment was, indeed, pivotal. If he could pull it off, then the odds that the rescue mission would succeed improved dramatically. And that meant he had a chance of getting Jennifer back.

Tim didn't have a hint as to Jenny's whereabouts. After talking with Ricardo Molina and then disabling the helicopter's flight controls—the Defender would not fly again without a major overhaul—Tim had returned to the cabin hideout. He wanted to retrieve his cell phone and check on Jenny before carrying out Ricardo's directive.

But he hadn't counted on having to deal with the passengers. Twenty minutes prior to when Tim headed below, hordes of passengers had flooded the companionways, stairways, and elevators, all eager to take sanctuary in their cabins. And the couple from Minneapolis would have nothing to do with him when he knocked on the cabin door.

"Jenny," he had said, "it's Tim. Let me in."

"Go away. We don't want any trouble," replied the male voice, partially muffled by the dead-bolted door.

Tim didn't hesitate. He blew the lock apart with a two-round burst from the sound-suppressed MP5. He then tore the door open and stormed in.

The late-middle-age woman was sitting on the side of one of the twin beds, her PFD still wrapped around her torso; her husband stood in the hallway near the bathroom, half dressed in a white T-shirt and boxer shorts. He was holding Tim's Glock like it was infected.

"Drop it, right now!" Tim ordered.

It thunked onto the deck.

Tim picked up the pistol, keeping the SMG trained on the man's gut. "Where's Jennifer?" he finally demanded.

"Don't kill us!" the pot-bellied and nearly bald man said. "Please, just leave us alone—we don't know anything."

"The woman who was staying here—where is she?"

The man shook his head.

By now, however, his wife had it figured out. "The cabin

was vacant when we came back," she said, "but we found
this." She pointed to Tim's briefcase. "It was resting on the
deck near the TV. The gun was on top of it. John was just
looking at it."

"The woman I was with, Jennifer, where'd she go?"

"If you check the bathroom, I think you'll find what you're
looking for."

When Tim opened the bathroom door, his heart shuddered.
It was printed on the mirror over the sink, smeared in ruby
red lipstick:

> *Tim, I've got to stop the killing. I'm giving them the
> MERLIN documents. Maybe they'll let me go if I do
> that. Anyway, my grandmother's legacy is yours now.
> You'll know where to find it, just like we talked about
> the other night over drinks. Just remember Dad's rid-
> dle in the video. Use it as you see fit. Thanks for trying.
> Jenny.*

To say Tim was stunned was an understatement. *He*
grandmother's legacy? Over drinks? What the hell is she
talking about?

Tim's spirits sank even deeper when he finally open his
attaché case, expecting to retrieve his portable phone. It
wasn't there. He then took a long moment to scan the cabin's
interior. Nothing.

Just when he was about to reinterrogate the cabin's occupants, he finally remembered. *Ah, shit!*

After the unsuccessful attempt to use the phone's satellite
mode he'd dumped the phone back inside the duffel bag
instead of his briefcase. And Jenny had taken the bag with
her.

Now what?

"Any luck?" asked the watch officer. He was in the *Regina's*
CIC, standing next to the radio tech.

"Ah, no, sir. It's ringing, but there's no answer."

"You check the number?"

"Yes, sir." The technician then handed over a sheet of

paper to the officer. It had Tim Carpenter's cell phone number printed on it.

The officer checked the number against the one Ricardo Molina had given him earlier. They were identical. "Keep calling until you hear otherwise."

"Aye, aye, sir."

41   BUSHWHACKED

"Just how reliable is this man, anyway?" asked Captain MacKenzie.

Ricardo Molina grinned. "Tim's solid gold. If he says he can do it—he'll do it, come hell or high water."

The American federal agent and the commanding officer of the Canadian warship were seated at the dining table in the officers' wardroom. They were alone—Ricardo had insisted on privacy—and for the past ten minutes he and MacKenzie had been going over last-minute details of Operation Deliverance. As part of that process, Ricardo had openly discussed the mission's prime goal. The hostages were important all right, but the rescue of Jennifer Richmond was paramount. She came first; the other fourteen-hundred-plus passengers and crew were secondary.

MacKenzie took a sip from his mug. He had just refilled it with steaming brew. "But isn't Carpenter the one you've been chasing? I mean, I thought he was some kind of fugitive—along with that woman. Your people have been hunting them down like dogs."

Ricardo shook his head. "It's the proverbial long story. It'd take all night to go over everything, but, in a nutshell, Tim was forced underground to protect Ms. Richmond. We had a helluva security leak on our end, and we lost some fine people because of it. As a result, we couldn't guarantee her safety. So, by default, Tim took over." Ricardo paused to stretch out his arms and then he yawned. He was running on caffeine and not much else. "I don't blame Tim for doing what he did. He's kept her alive so far. We almost got her killed."

MacKenzie was confused. *All of this enormous effort for just one woman? Who is she—what makes her so special?* "The woman, Jennifer," he said, "is she some kind of spy or something like that? I mean she must be pretty damn important for all of this."

Ricardo had been waiting for this question. MacKenzie wasn't cleared for MERLIN. No one aboard the *Regina* was, so telling him the truth was out. "Captain, I'm not at liberty to tell you who or what Ms. Richmond is about. All I can say is that it is in the vital interests of *both* our nations that she be rescued." He paused, choosing his next words with care. "We simply cannot let the Chinese Communists get away with kidnapping her. It'll be an unmitigated disaster for the United States and Canada if she slips through our hands."

MacKenzie's thoughts cascaded in rapid-fire order: *Our hands? You mean your bloody hands. You and your FBI already lost her. We're just here to help you.*

MacKenzie's actual response was more controlled: "Well, I'm sure we'll all do our best, but you know all of this is risky as hell. I mean that sub, the SEALs, this ship, and your private detective friend, Carpenter. For all of it to come together is asking an awful lot."

"I know, Captain, but we're committed now." Ricardo checked his wristwatch. "In fact, things are going to start happening soon so I'd like to head back to your helicopter and get set up."

MacKenzie nodded. "Right, let's go."

Once again Tim cranked on the blade, giving it everything he had. *Come on, you bugger!* His heart pounded; more sweat beaded on his forehead. And then he heard a muffled metallic "crack."

Hot damn, it moved!

A minute later, the twelve-by-twelve-inch inspection hatch was open. The interior of the hollow mast was packed with half a dozen inch-thick steel conduits.

Now what should I do? Tim thought as he peered into the opening.

"Still no response?" Peng asked as he stared down at the lower deck, the phone handset glued to the side of his head.

"Nothing, sir. We've heard no signal." The MSS man stood next to the guardrail. He then looked back up toward the bridge. The glare from floodlights near the base of the superstructure concealed his commanding officer.

"Are you still sending the message?" Peng asked.

"Yes, sir. The computer's continuing the broadcast."

The secret message embedded within the humpback's song was linked to software that varied the timing, amplitude, and quality of the underwater broadcast. The system was designed to disguise the message. American SOSUS computers looked for any type of consistent acoustic pattern. Nature rarely produces sounds that are uniform and repetitive.

"All right, but call me the instant you hear anything."

"Yes, sir."

Peng turned to face Major Wu. The second in command had returned to the bridge ten minutes earlier. He was smoking another cigarette—a powerful Chinese brand. The pilot-house reeked.

"Major, I don't like this. It should have been here by now."

The commando shook his head. "Does it really surprise you—this mission's been fucked up since the start."

"But if it doesn't show up, what then?"

"We keep steaming west—what else can we do?"

Peng shook his head. "They will never let us go." He turned to look through the port bridge windows. "In fact, they're probably out there, right now, getting ready."

The major stepped up to the nearby radar unit, looking down at the fluorescent display. "Well, except for that one ship that continues to track us, we still appear to be alone."

Peng joined Wu, examining the screen. "Yes, but you know they'll probably come in by helicopter. None of these radar units will detect aircraft. They could be all over us in a matter of seconds."

"True, but we're also one hell of a long way out. Any helicopters sent out to find us are going to be sucking on fumes by the time they get here." Major Wu paused, taking a final drag. "That's why I think we should fire up the engines and keep heading west. It'll make any kind of assault that much more difficult for them." He dropped the spent butt onto the deck, crushing it with the heel of his boot. "We can send a SATCOM message back to headquarters telling them that we've now got the woman and all of her records. You can be sure that Beijing will see to it that the submarine finds us."

Peng didn't reply at first. Instead, his mind was racing. *He's right, we should keep going. We're too damned exposed out here right now.*

Peng checked his wristwatch. "Okay, Major, I agree. If we haven't heard from the *Yangtze* in twenty minutes, we're leaving. Go ahead and start coding a message to headquarters. If the submarine doesn't answer by then, we'll send it and get under way."

"Yes, sir."

Water flooded into the forward escape trunk with the force of a fire hydrant. It was icy cold and its salty scent pungent. But the four men crammed inside the five-foot-diameter air lock hardly noticed. Thick wet suits encased their bodies and diving masks covered their faces.

The thought of leaving the submarine while still submerged sixty feet under the ocean surface would have been incomprehensible to most. But to the SEALs it was strictly routine. They had all been through the procedure dozens of times before.

As the chamber filled, a similar operation was under way in the aft escape trunk. Although there were only two men inside that chamber, they were just as cramped as their four companions in the forward air lock. Two giant sausage-shaped rubber containers filled up the remaining space. It was the job of the two occupants to make sure that the team's equipment made it to the surface. Once topside, they would inflate the two rafts and fire up the compact but powerful outboard motors.

Each cycle of flooding the air lock, deploying the swimmers, and then pumping out the seawater to prepare for the next group took several minutes. By cramming in twice the number of men as normal in each escape trunk, the entire fourteen-man deployment operation would take about twenty minutes to complete.

"Both chambers are flooding, Captain," reported the chief of the boat. The COB was standing over the ship control station, monitoring a series of ballast tanks and high-pressure air tanks.

"Very well; let me know when they're out."

"Aye, aye, sir."

Commander Black turned to face the diving officer and asked, "How's our position holding?"

"We're maintaining our depth, sir, but there's a slight eastward current, about half a knot. We may need to compensate for it if we start drifting too far off."

In order to deploy the commandos, the *Bellingham* had come to a full stop. Otherwise, after multiple deployments, the divers would have been strung out across the ocean surface. It was black topside and even if they all popped up in the same general vicinity, the SEAL platoon would still have a tough time finding each other.

Maintaining an even depth without forward motion is difficult for a submarine. Hovering requires constant monitoring of the boat's trim tanks and continuous adjustment of the ballast controls. And the repeated flooding and then evacuating of the two escape trunks severely complicates the process. Already sensitive to changes in ambient buoyancy resulting from varying water temperature and salinity, the tons of seawater flowing into and then out of the transfer chambers upset the boat's delicate balance between sinking and rising.

"Very well; keep monitoring," Blackjack said. "I don't want to engage the screw unless absolutely necessary. The SEALs have enough problems as it is now. I don't want them to have to worry about getting chewed up with our prop."

"Aye, aye, sir."

Despite the ease with which the operation was currently going, launching SEALs was not a routine function for the *Bellingham* or, for that matter, any of its sister ships. The Los Angeles–class submarines were designed to kill other subs and surface vessels. They were never intended to serve as platforms for launching special operation forces. Other submarines in the U.S. Navy's fleet were specially designed for that mission. However, because of unusual circumstances, the *Bellingham* had been directed to undertake the nonstandard mission. And that change in mission profile had now placed SSN 775 in mortal jeopardy.

Ordinarily, the *Bellingham* would have been acoustically invisible as it drifted. With the propeller disengaged and the nuclear power plant on idle, the well-insulated pressure casing radiated virtually no sound at all. However, the flooding of the escape trunks was a noisy process, and some of that energy was now being transmitted into the surrounding water column. It didn't produce much of a soundprint, but it was enough.

"Sir, we're definitely picking up flooding. They must be deploying."

The captain of the *Yangtze* smiled as he faced his second in command. "Then we have them, Number One."

"Yes, sir," replied the officer. He paused. "Should we proceed?"

"In a moment. Let them commit themselves a little more."

"Skipper, forward hatch open to the sea," reported the COB.

The *Bellingham*'s CO nodded.

Twenty seconds later, the COB made another report: "Aft hatch open, sir."

"Very well."

"Execute," ordered the *Yangtze*'s commander.

"Execute," repeated the executive officer. He then flipped

a single toggle switch on the weapons control console. A tiny surge of electrical current flowed from the panel, energizing a wire that led to another control panel in the weapons compartment of the former NATO-designated Akula-class Russian submarine. That command activated a fiberoptic circuit that linked the submarine to its remote probe, now about a mile and a half east of the *Yangtze*.

A microsecond after receiving the light impulse, the forward end of the probe separated from the main body of the probe. The fourteen-foot-long torpedo accelerated like a thoroughbred out of its starting gate.

"Conn, Sonar!" screamed the voice over the control room intercom. "I've got a new contact. High-speed propeller. Bearing one five five."

The *Bellingham*'s captain grabbed a microphone, "What?" he yelled, startled by the sonar report.

"It's a torpedo, sir. And it's coming up on our stern fast, fifty-plus knots."

"How far, man?"

"About twelve thousand yards."

Commander Black turned to face the COB. His face transmitted the shock that they both felt. There was another submarine nearby and it had just fired a torpedo. "The SEALs out yet?"

"No, skipper, both hatches are still open to the sea."

Dear God, thought the captain, *we're sitting ducks!* His ship was horribly vulnerable. Until the divers were clear of the escape trunks, his options were severely limited. If he aborted the deployment and took emergency evasive action, the SEALs already in the water might be sucked into the propeller. But if he waited, the remaining 137 men inside the vessel were doomed.

I can't wait, the captain concluded. He turned to face the XO. He was just about to issue new orders when the COB made a new report.

"Forward hatch secure," he announced, followed two seconds later with, "aft hatch secured. They're all out, sir."

"XO, ahead flank. Prepare for a snapshot."

* * *

"Should be any minute now," commented Ricardo Molina, speaking into his helmet microphone. He was now aboard the *Regina*'s helicopter, Air One. The Sea King remained secured to the warship's flight deck but its five-bladed, sixty-two-foot-diameter rotor was at high idle.

"Right," acknowledged Captain MacKenzie. He was in the CIC, using a handheld radio mike. "We're monitoring the transmissions. As soon as the radars stop, we'll let you know and then you'll be free to launch."

"Understand, Captain."

Captain MacKenzie returned the mike to its overhead mounting. He was standing next to a console manned by an electronic countermeasures technician. The seaman was monitoring the radar transmissions from the *Emerald Sea*. All three of the cruise ship's search bands were radiating.

MacKenzie was about to issue an order to the tech when he was preempted by the *Regina*'s chief sonarman.

"Captain, I'm picking up high-speed propellers—sounds like a torpedo."

"What!" shouted MacKenzie as he moved to the sonar watch station, just a few meters away. The rating manning the console was wearing a pair of Bose headphones.

"I don't think it's a threat to us, sir. Too far away. The signal's faint—I'm working on bearing. I'll have it in . . . wait a second." The tech looked up at the captain, eyes saucer wide. "I've got a sub, too. Jesus, she's moving gangbusters. Cavitating like mad."

"Let me listen."

Captain MacKenzie slipped on another set of headphones. The tones were muted. Nevertheless, they were chilling. *What the hell's going on?*

Tim continued to whack away at the steel conduits. But the combat knife wasn't doing the job. He needed a hacksaw to cut through the tough steel. Better yet, an acetylene torch.

Tim checked his watch. *Shit, I'm never going to get through this thing in time.* He then looked up. All three antennas continued to whirl above his head, one on top of the other. For just a moment he considered raising the H & K and spraying the radar transmitters. But that would be an invitation to a quick death. Even with the suppressor, the ensuing racket of the lead rounds shattering the units would alert the MSS commandos below. One quick burst from any one of the gunmen and he would be blasted from his perch.

Tim again started sawing the electrical conduit. *I'm running out of time.* And then, as he continued to saw away, a new thought popped out. *Yes!* he thought, *that just might work.*

The *Bellingham* was charging through the water at 43.5 knots—fifty miles per hour. She was three hundred feet below the surface. The reactor was redlined to the max—110 percent—there was nothing left.

The tension inside the control room was electric. No one knew what to expect.

"Sonar, Conn," called out Commander Black over the intercom, "where's that fish?"

"Still coming hard, sir. Range thirty-one hundred yards and closing."

Blackjack turned to face the XO. "Jim, launch another decoy."

"Launching decoy, aye, sir."

A third cylinder was then ejected from the hull. As soon as it sheared away from the hull, it began flooding the surrounding water column with millions of bubbles.

The captain waited a few seconds for his sub to speed away from the decoy. He then ordered, "Come right ninety degrees."

The desperate maneuver was designed to confuse the weapon. The burst of noise from the decoy, in combination with the sudden turn, would temporarily mask the huge soundprint from the *Bellingham*'s churning propeller. By causing the torpedo to lose acoustic lock, even for a few seconds, it provided the *Bellingham* with a chance.

However, like the two previous decoys and companion course changes, the weapon hardly noticed. It continued to home in on the American submarine like a bloodhound. Its computer brain was solidly locked onto the SSN 775's churning propeller.

Tim was now standing on top of the bridgehouse, about forty feet below his earlier perch. He held the tail end of an eighth-inch-diameter Dacron line in his right hand. The rest of the line streamed upward, to the inspection port in the mast. He had liberated the rope from a nearby ensign lanyard.

Tim took one last look at his watch. He was four minutes behind schedule. *Better late than never.* He yanked on the line.

A second later the opposite end of the rope slipped free of the inspection port, a tiny steel ring tied to its free end.

As the falling line snaked around him, Tim ducked his head and, without thinking, pushed his body next to the base of the towering radar mast—that was a mistake.

And then a terrific explosion rang out.

The shock wave raced down the spire, generated from the near simultaneous detonation of the grenade and five pounds of plastic explosive that Tim had stuffed inside the radar mast inspection port. The ensuing "clang" rattled Tim's skull. It was like getting punched in the face by a heavyweight slugger.

Tim shook his head, fighting off the blast's concussion. He then looked up, just in time to see the top part of the mast rotating aft. The explosion had severed about half of the mast's hollow core. And then, with its already backward-leaning rake, gravity did the rest. The remaining section of the steel tube buckled under the strain.

Two tons of steel mast and radar antennas crashed into the top of the pilothouse with the impact of a mountain avalanche.

"Holy shit!" Tim cursed under his breath, "now you've done it!"

"What the hell was that?" Peng asked, staring up at the overhead.

"That sounded like some kind of explosion," answered

Major Wu. He then glanced down at one of the radar displays. It had gone blank. He checked the other units—both dead.

The two men had the same reaction: *The Americans are attacking!*

Wow, there they go! thought the ECM technician. He turned away from his console, facing the CO. Captain MacKenzie was still standing next to the nearby sonar console. "Sir, all three units on the *Emerald Sea* just switched off."

MacKenzie nodded but did not respond. He was preoccupied at the moment. He held a hand pressed against each side of the headphones. The sounds from the distant underwater race were diminishing but the drama that they represented intensified. *Who the hell fired that torpedo?*

"Major, what do you think happened here?" Peng asked. He and the *zhongdui* leader were now standing on top of the pilothouse, examining the remains of the radar mast.

Major Wu gestured toward the twisted rubble. "Someone's trying to blind us, sir, electronically. We've lost all the radars, and at least half of the radio antennas."

"What about the communication gear your men brought— can we still talk with Beijing?"

"Yes, that's not a problem. We don't need the ships' antennas to operate it. Besides, we've already disabled the ship's transceivers . . . but the radars, that could be a problem."

"Why?"

"We can't keep track of that ship that was following us."

"How far away was it?"

"Around forty kilometers."

Peng paused. "Then that's what they've got planned! They're going to attack from that ship . . . maybe they've already sent an advance force and they did this."

"Yes, but we've been watching for just that. As near as I can tell, no hostile forces have approached, let alone boarded, the ship."

"So who did this?" Peng asked, pointing to the wreckage at their feet.

"It's got to be one of the passengers."

There was a long pause as Peng considered Wu's comment. Finally, he had the connection: "Could this be the work of that American, you know, Carpenter?"

"Yes. From what little we know about him . . . his military training . . . and his detective work . . . he may have pulled this off."

Peng nodded. "I think you might be right." He then glanced at his watch, remembering something else. "We still haven't heard from the submarine yet. We'll hold here for a few more minutes, but then we've got to get under way. I want to put as much distance between us and that ship as we can. Beijing will direct us to a new rendezvous point."

"I agree, sir, but what about Carpenter?"

"We'll keep an eye out for him. But he's not worth pursuing at this point. He can't do anything to stop us now."

"I don't know, sir. I have a bad feeling about all of this." He again surveyed the remains of the radar mast.

"Major, do you have any spare men to start another ship-wide search?"

"No, not really. They've all got their hands full at the moment. Besides, with all of the passengers now inside, it'll just complicate any kind of search."

"Then I rest my case."

42   GRAY LADY DOWN

"Sonar, Conn, where's that fish?"

"Range's twenty-four hundred yards, sir." The voice paused. "It's still got ten-plus knots on us."

Captain Black made a flash mental calculation. *We've got maybe seven minutes and then that sucker's going to nail us.*

The *Bellingham*'s only hope was to keep running. Just

maybe the torpedo would run out of fuel before closing the final distance.

Black still had no hint as to where the attacking boat was located. All he could count on was that it was still out there.

During the first minute of flight, before reaching flank speed, he had ordered a snapshot. The Mark 48 torpedo was fired down the bearing of the approaching weapon. There was always a small chance that the 48 would intercept the enemy torpedo, destroying it. The real purpose of the counterattack, however, was to shake up the other sub's skipper. If he too had to implement evasion tactics, then he wouldn't be able to continue the attack.

The Mark 48 found nothing. By the time it reached the probe's original firing position, the probe had already retreated to the mother sub, over a mile and a half to the west.

Blackjack again keyed the intercom, this time connecting with the engine compartment. "EO, I need every turn you can give us."

"We're maxed out, skipper. Balls to the walls. We've got nothing left."

Shit! thought the captain, *we're dead.*

Jennifer Richmond still wondered what all the commotion had been about. When the radar mast smashed onto the topside deck ten minutes earlier, the ensuing racket resonated throughout the plush officers' wardroom.

The MSS operative that had just been assigned the task of creating a videotape record of the contents of Jenny's duffel bag jumped up from his chair, startled by the unexpected clamor.

The other Chinese invader, however, hardly glanced up. Half an hour earlier, the *zhongdui* had replaced Peng at the interrogation table. He first removed the remaining items from the duffel bag, piling them on the tabletop. That's when he discovered Carpenter's portable phone. After switching the unit on he verified that the satphone mode was jammed. He then set it aside, knowing Peng would want to personally examine it when he returned. And then, after questioning Jenny for several minutes, he began examining the MERLIN documents. Like Jennifer, he was trained as an engineer, and what he was reading was spellbinding. He couldn't put it down.

The Sea King was now airborne. It had just cleared the *Regina*'s flight deck. The pilot and copilot manned the cockpit while the two passengers occupied the cargo bay.

The ASW specialist sat in his bucket seat, but he ignored the high-tech console in the foreground. The helicopter's prime mission was hunting submarines, and it was his job to operate the aircraft's sonar and weapons systems. Today, however, he had a new task: rifleman. Cradled on his lap was an assault rifle.

Ricardo Molina sat next to the sensor operator. Like the rest of the helo's crew, he was dressed in a cumbersome survival suit, the same one he had used earlier. He had also donned a helmet with built-in headphones and boom mike. His 9 mm Beretta remained in its shoulder holster, buried deep inside the nylon and rubber garment. But he wouldn't need it right away. Resting on the floor near his feet was something far more effective. The twelve-gauge Benelli M1 Super 90 semiautomatic shotgun, on loan from Captain MacKenzie, was sudden death in close-quarters combat.

"Time," shouted the *Bellingham*'s CO, jamming his thumb on the intercom mike key. Commander Black was now visibly shaken. His cool demeanor was eroding by the second.

"Forty-five seconds, Captain," the chief sonar operator's voice announced over the intercom speaker.

Blackjack turned, his face now ashen as he looked into the XO's eyes. He was not alone in his terror. "Jim," he said, "we're not going to make it."

"I know."

Raging fear gripped everyone in the control room. None of the *Bellingham*'s countermeasures had fooled the torpedo. It was like a charging lion, about to rip into its prey.

"Thirty seconds!" screamed the sonar tech's voice.

For a moment the captain felt as if his legs were going to buckle. But it passed as suddenly as it came. He prayed silently, taking a few precious seconds to make final amends. And then he was ready.

"Quartermaster," he said, "One MC. Rig for collision."

Almost instantly, an obnoxious tone began broadcasting from the ship's master intercom system.

"Fifteen seconds," announced the chief sonar operator.

Black's next set of orders came in rapid-fire order: "Emergency blow. Full upward angle on the planes."

Six seconds later the torpedo launched from the *Yangtze*'s remote probe impaled itself on the *Bellingham*'s propeller. The seven-bladed, eighteen-foot-diameter wheel tore apart when the two hundred-kilogram warhead detonated. The entire rudder assembly and the port horizontal plane were similarly knocked out of commission. And shrapnel from the explosion pierced the thin steel plates of the aft main ballast tank.

As bad as the direct impact was, it was the collateral damage that was now the greatest threat to the *Bellingham*'s survival. The massive thrust blocking that surrounded the propeller shaft was failing. The fitting was designed to allow the shaft to rotate while maintaining a watertight seal. But the force of the explosion had warped the steel shaft, upsetting its precise alignment. For the first few seconds after impact, the entire hull vibrated as if it were running on an out-of-balance tire. The drive shaft, still under maximum revolutions, chewed up the special alloy bushing like it was made of clay. Frigid seawater streamed along the length of the steel shaft, gushing into the main pressure casing with the force of a mountain waterfall.

Captain MacKenzie and the sonar tech both heard the impact—a sharp thud followed by several seconds of metallic screeches. And then nothing—just ambient sea tones.

MacKenzie and the sonarman removed their headphones, both stunned by what they had heard.

"Sir, was that what I think it was?"

"Yes, I'm afraid so."

"But who's shooting at who? I thought there was just the one sub out there—the *Bellingham*."

"I know—there's something wrong."

Several minutes passed. MacKenzie had just returned to the bridge. He was still mulling over the consequences of the sonar broadcast when the *Regina*'s communications officer made a startling announcement over the bridge intercom. "Captain, I'm picking up distress signals from the *Bellingham*—simultaneous transmissions on UHF, VHF, SSB, and SATCOM."

Good Lord, thought MacKenzie, *it really did happen.*

The emergency radio system would only be triggered if the submarine were in severe distress. The automated multiband SOS transmissions would identify the boat in peril and its current earth coordinates.

MacKenzie reached for a nearby mike. He keyed it. "CIC, this is the captain. Advise Air One to abort its mission. I want it to divert to the sub's location for SAR duty."

"Yes, sir."

MacKenzie then ordered General Quarters and directed his ship to the broadcast coordinates.

As the *Regina* changed course and crewmen rushed to their assigned battle stations, MacKenzie stared blindly through the windscreen. The Pentagon's carefully orchestrated mission was now an utter failure. *What the hell went wrong?*

At first, Ricardo Molina was furious. "What do you mean we're aborting the mission?" he had yelled over the helo's intercom.

"Sorry, sir," the pilot replied, "but the captain has just ordered us on a SAR mission." He paused for a moment. "There's been some kind of accident with your sub."

"The *Bellingham*—an accident?"

"Affirmative, sir."

Jesus! What happened! "What about the SEALs—did they deploy?"

"Unknown, sir."

All six of the SEALs that exited the *Bellingham* during the first lockout made it to the surface. The two inflatables were deployed and the outboards fired up. Rafted together, they waited for their companions to join them. But they never showed.

After standing by for nearly fifteen minutes, the SEAL leader reluctantly pulled out his portable radio. The mission had called for radio silence until the actual assault.

"Eagle Eye, Baker One, come in."

He repeated the call three times before the replacement Orion from NAS Whidbey answered: "Baker One, Eagle Eye, Over."

"Eagle Eye, I've only got part of my team here. Do you have any info on the delay?"

"Negative, Baker One."

Shit! The platoon leader had a tough decision to make: Continue with the mission, but with less than half of the planned strike force, or abort it. On the other hand, shortly after his group had surfaced, a muffled blast had echoed across the sea surface. The *Emerald Sea*'s radars were knocked out, almost on schedule, blinding the hijackers' electronic eyes and helping to ensure the stealth of the runabouts when they approached the ship.

Fuck it. We should go anyway.

The lieutenant was just about to issue new orders when, once again, Mr. Murphy struck. Far off toward the east, rocket after rocket roared into the night sky, exploding into brilliant flowers of flame. It was like the Fourth of July.

"What the hell?" shouted one of the men.

They had expected flares, from the P-3C. The diversion had been part of the ambush plan—to draw the hijackers out. And then, with night vision gun scopes, the SEALs had expected to kill at least half of the bad guys. But that could only happen *after* they boarded the ship.

The lieutenant keyed his radio. "Eagle Eye, what are you doing with flares? We're not in position yet. Over."

"Baker One, those are *not* our flares, I say again, they're not ours. Over."

The newest SEAL of the group was the first to figure it out: "Skipper," he said, "those things can't be coming from the P-3. They're shooting upwards before exploding." And then another commando joined in. "Yeah, he's right! They look like distress flares to me—like from a ship, not a plane!"

The lieutenant watched another projectile streak into the heavens. He shook his head. *Something's fucked.*

"What do you want to do, skipper?" asked one of the men.

The officer glanced toward the *Emerald Sea*. It was just sitting there, waiting. *Shit! What should I do?* Before he could decide, he was preempted.

"Baker One, Eagle Eye. We've just been notified by *Regina* that the *Bellingham*'s in some kind of trouble. Abort your mission and divert to the flare sightings. Over."

"Roger, we're on the way."

Within seconds, both inflatables were under way.

"They finally answered?" Peng said, facing Major Wu.

"Yes, sir. The hydrophone just picked up their response." The commando had just returned to the bridge. He was slightly winded from running up a series of steep ladder wells.

"It's about fucking time. Where's it going to surface?"

"Ah, it's not—at least not yet. We've been ordered to steam northwest for thirty kilometers."

"What?"

"They don't want to rendezvous out here—there's another . . ."

Wu never finished. The horizon to the east exploded into fountains of phosphorus white and fluorescent orange.

Both men were now standing on the port bridge wing looking aft. The pyrotechnic spectacle continued to illuminate the eastern sky.

"Are those flares?" Peng asked.

"Look's like it." Wu was peering through a pair of binoculars. "Probably distress signals."

"They must be up to something on that ship that's following us—I don't like this."

"I agree, sir," Wu said, lowering the binoculars. "We must conclude this mission immediately. We have no time left."

"I know. Call the engine room and tell them to get us moving."

"Yes, sir."

43 COMPLICATIONS

The Sea King was hovering over the _Bellingham_, using its brilliant xenon searchlight to illuminate the sea surface. It was 11:18 P.M. The bullet-shaped bow of the submarine projected unnaturally high out of the water. The stern was completely submerged.

The ship's crew, every man wearing an inflatable PFD, poured out of the hull. They exited through the forward escape trunk and from the weapons loading hatch located just forward of the towering sail. The aft escape trunk was awash and not usable. The half-dozen men crowded atop the sail used portable lights and bullhorns to choreograph the Abandon Ship drill. But it wasn't a drill. The _Bellingham_ was sinking. Seawater streaming down the propeller shaft continued to flood the engineering spaces, slowly dragging the boat down by her stern. The aft ballast chamber was completely flooded, holed by shrapnel. High-pressure air pumped into the tank roared to the surface in furious torrents.

Dozens of inflatable life rafts had already been deployed and about half the crew were in them.

As Ricardo stared down at the organized chaos, his thoughts wandered, first to the _Regina_—_What about that cell phone patch?_ And then back to the cruise ship—_What's happening out there?_

Tim was waiting. He was on the fantail, crouched down behind a mooring capstan next to the railing. He could hear the hiss of the ship's wake as it surged through the black waters. It had started moving ten minutes earlier. But he could no longer see the wake.

The half-dozen floodlights that ringed the stern were out of commission. He was responsible. He'd used the MP5, switching the selector switch from burst to semiauto. It took seven rounds to knock out the lights. Not bad.

Other than the muffled crack of the lead slugs shattering the glass, there was no noise. Even the dull "splat" of the bullets exiting through the suppressor were swallowed up by the ambient sea sounds.

Tim pressed his head next to a rail, looking straight down the hull. A narrow cone of yellowish light diffracted seaward from a below-deck porthole. He then checked his watch. *Okay, guys, where the hell are you?*

The NMCC watch commander could hardly believe what he was being told. "You mean there's another submarine out there?"

"Yes, sir," replied the U.S. Navy commander. She was speaking via satellite to the Pentagon from NavFac Whidbey Island. "We've confirmed that the *Bellingham* walked into a trap. She was hit with a torpedo—we tracked it with our sensors. She's broached and the skipper reports he has ordered the crew to abandon ship."

"Son of a bitch! Where'd this damn sub come from?"

"Unknown, sir. We were unaware of its presence."

"Well, whose is it?"

"We don't know. We still haven't picked it up."

"But it fired a torpedo—didn't you hear that?"

"Yes, sir. But nothing else. It just suddenly appeared on our hydrophones. I don't have an explanation yet."

"Well, Commander, what do you recommend? Should I have that Canadian frigate go after it?"

"Until we know what we're dealing with, sir, I recommend that the *Regina* not try to pursue the contact. That sub is clearly very quiet and the *Regina* could be walking right into another ambush." She paused. "Besides, sir, she's the only platform we've got out there that can help rescue the *Bellingham*'s crew."

"All right, but I don't want that bastard to get away."

"Understood, sir." She hesitated before continuing. "Ah, sir, you still have that P-3 orbiting over Graham Island, don't you?"

"Yes. We've been holding it in reserve."

"Well, I recommend that NMCC hand off control to

NavFac. We'll link up directly with the aircraft and start a coordinated search. With the P-3's sonobuoys and our fixed sensors, we'll have a much better chance of finding the boat than working independently."

"Yeah, that's what IUSS was set up for. Go ahead and set it up." The one-star paused. "Might as well send some more of your birds to assist."

"Yes, sir, I'll get right on it."

The NavFac commander had anticipated her new orders and had already alerted Whidbey NAS's CO about a possible combat mission. As a result, three more Orion P-3Cs were now in various stages of preflight. Within an hour they would all be airborne.

With four ASW aircraft under her control plus the vast North Pacific SOSUS network as a backup, she was ready for battle. It was now personal. The *Bellingham* had been ambushed on her watch. She wanted payback. *First, I'm going to find that son of a bitch,* she had promised herself, *and then I'm going to kill it!*

After ambushing the *Bellingham*, the *Yangtze* promptly va-cated the kill zone. Another probe was left in its place. The twenty-six-inch-diameter, twenty-five-foot-long cylinder was presently drifting with the current, about five hundred feet below the surface. The autonomous underwater vehicle (AUV) had a very special function.

Tiny transducers along the hull transmitted faint tones into the surrounding waters. The sounds mimicked the noise of circulation pumps from an idling nuclear reactor. In about twenty minutes, the probe would begin moving, heading southwestward at fifteen knots.

The AUV would run for twenty minutes and then stop. After waiting ten minutes, it would once again begin moving, but this time at deeper depth and a different heading. The same stop-and-go pattern, with preprogrammed variations in depth, speed, direction, and duration, would be repeated until the probe ran out of fuel. There was enough fuel aboard for thirty hours of operation.

Although the AUV's own propeller was, for all practical

purposes, soundless, each time the probe sprinted forward, it would broadcast the propeller soundprint of a real submarine. The wheel wash would be faint but, nevertheless, detectable with the right equipment. And after what had just happened to the *Bellingham,* the Americans would saturate the surrounding waters with an armada of underwater listening devices.

The PLAN mission planners could have chosen from a vast array of submarine recordings. At first, a Russian Victor III was considered. And then one of the new Japanese SSNs. But in the end, they had chosen an Améthyst. It was sweet revenge.

The soundprint of the French attack submarine would clearly shake up the Americans.

"What do you mean we can't use the helicopter?" Peng said, yelling into the hand mike.

"It's been wrecked—the cockpit controls are screwed up. Someone cut every wire and cable in sight. This thing will make a nice anchor, but that's about it."

Shit! thought Peng. *What next?*

Peng had just returned to the officers' wardroom. He was sitting at the dining table. His second in command was on the other end of the intercom line. Peng had ordered Wu to prepare the MD500 for imminent departure. The mission was almost over. Ten minutes earlier the *Emerald Sea*'s propellers had been disengaged from the turbine drives; she was still coasting, but barely.

"Major, are you sure it can't be repaired?"

"I asked the pilot that same question. He did some quick checking and he can't even fire up the turbine, let alone test any of the actual flight controls. Believe me, sir, salvaging this thing is a lost cause."

"Carpenter—he's the one behind this—and the radar mast, too."

"Yes, sir."

Although Peng and Wu were speaking in Mandarin, Peng's phonetic pronunciation of the word *Carpenter* brought an instant response from one of the occupants sitting at the opposite end of the table.

Jennifer Richmond looked up from one of the MERLIN reports she was holding. The engineer-trained *zhongdui* remained seated at her side. It was his task to verify their authenticity. He had just pointed to a diagram in the report and had asked Jennifer a question when she abruptly turned away.

Peng's and Jenny's eyes met for an instant. He couldn't help himself: *God, but she's attractive.*

Jenny's thoughts might as well have originated from the other end of the galaxy from his: *You bastard, what have you done to Tim?*

Jenny broke the eye contact, turning to carry on her conversation with the commando-engineer. Peng pressed the mike.

"All right, Major," Peng said, "we're going to have to find another way to make the transfer. What do you suggest?"

"Well, sir, under normal circumstances, that would have been rather easy to accomplish. However, since *we* jettisoned all of the lifeboats and shot up the rest of the life rafts, *we* do have a bit of a problem."

Wu's tone was barely civil. He had warned Peng against launching all of the lifesaving gear. He recommended that at least two of the motorboats be kept in reserve. Peng vetoed that plan, electing instead to dump every launch overboard and pepper all of the life raft canisters with bullet holes.

"There's nothing left that we can use?" Peng asked, strained.

"Nothing." Wu hesitated for a moment. "I suggest that we radio the *Yangtze* and tell them our predicament. Maybe they can come up with something."

You must just love this, Wu, Peng thought. "Very well, Major, make it so."

Dammit to hell. Now what am I going to do?

Tim Carpenter was still hiding near the fantail. He had been waiting for almost fifty minutes. His job was to secure the boarding area. But the SEALs were a no-show. *Some-*

thing must have gone wrong. Maybe that's what all those flares were about.

Earlier, before the *Emerald Sea* restarted its seaward trek, Tim had watched the fireworks in the eastern sky. At first he thought it was some type of distraction, designed to throw the terrorists off guard. He had been certain the SEALs would come alongside the ship any second in their high-powered inflatables. They would then extend the hooked ends of the titanium caving ladders over the rails and scramble up the high sheer of the vessel's hull. But it never happened. Instead, the cruise ship throttled up its engines and began heading further into the ocean.

Only minutes earlier, the *Emerald Sea* had finally slowed up. It was now drifting, both propellers silent.

If I just had some way of talking with Ricardo again, then maybe we could work out a new plan.

Tim silently cursed, disgusted with himself for misplacing his portable phone.

Several minutes had passed by. Tim now wished that he had tried harder—a lot harder—to remove the helicopter's radio.

"Okay," he finally muttered, "I've got to try it again."

Allen Peng was still in the wardroom, half listening to the cross-talk between Jennifer Richmond and the commando-engineer. What really held Peng's attention was the portable phone. Like the *zhongdui* that had found it, Peng had just verified that the satellite mode was still jammed. And then, out of curiosity, he activated the cell mode. Two seconds later the unit broadcast a shrill ring.

Peng almost dropped the phone. It rang again. Jennifer and the commando were now both staring at him. Peng hit the send button and then placed the phone next to his right ear.

"Mr. Carpenter, this is the *Regina* . . . are you there?"

"Shit!" yelled Peng as he propelled the phone at a nearby steel bulkhead. It shattered on impact.

He peered through the view port of the search periscope.
The *Emerald Sea* was about 500 meters away, dead in the
water. It shimmered like a mirage; a crystal city on a sea of
velvet.

The *Yangtze*'s commanding officer smiled as he rotated
the stainless steel tube. He was pleased, very pleased. He had
just executed a textbook evasion maneuver.

After bushwhacking the American submarine, the *Yangtze*
finally answered the *Emerald Sea*'s underwater call. Using a
similar coded humpback whale cry, the PLAN submarine
directed the cruise ship to steam northwestward to new, safer
rendezvous coordinates.

When the *Emerald Sea* began charging through the ocean,
heading for its new meeting place, the *Yangtze* followed.
Within just a few minutes it had slid under the 712-foot-long
hull. The top of its fin was just twenty meters below the
ship's keel.

The cruise ship's thrashing propellers filled the surrounding ocean waters with a shroud of noise. The sound output
from the *Yangtze*'s own propeller, a mere whisper even at
twenty-one knots, was swallowed up by the racket. The result
was a perfect acoustic shield. Soundwise, the *Yangtze* was
invisible. It was an old trick, but it still worked.

The *Yangtze*'s captain completed his first 360-degree observation, and once again focused on the cruise ship. "It's
just sitting there, Number One, all by itself." He paused,
zooming in on the ship's bridgehouse. "What have you got?"

"Working on it, sir," answered the executive officer. He
was sitting at one of the attack center's dozen consoles, just
aft of the periscope platform. The fiberglass console housed
a suite of electronic instruments. They were all wired to a
slender, antennalike tube that projected out of the sail, about
a meter aft of the main periscope. The rubber-coated steel

cylinder extended four feet above the ocean surface. The sensors lining the exposed portion of the tube were designed to detect a myriad of electronic transmissions, from radar to shortwave radio.

The executive officer looked up, facing the captain; the sub commander's forehead remained glued to the periscope view port. He was slowly rotating the scope, working on a second observation.

"Captain, I'm not picking up any radar emissions from the target, but there's a weak trace from another distant unit. It's probably from that Canadian frigate." He paused. "Do you want me to take a quick scan with our radar?"

"Negative. I don't want to take a chance. It might pick up our signal."

"Yes, sir."

"Pick up anything else?"

"Peng just repeated the earlier radio message, about the problem with the helicopter."

"We'll deal with that shortly. Anything else?"

"No, sir."

The captain completed the observation. "Retract the tube," he ordered, directing his command to a nearby crewman. He then picked up a hand microphone and keyed it.

"Sonar, this is the captain. Give me a status report."

"Sonar, Captain. No change, sir. The American continues to flood. Lots of pump noises and high-pressure air venting. It's hard to be sure, but it sounds like they're not going to be able to save it."

"Anything from that frigate?"

"No, sir. No active sonars anywhere."

"Very well, keep monitoring."

"Yes, sir."

The captain moved toward the first officer's console. "Well, Number One, it looks like we're alone out here."

"I agree, sir. Are we going in now?"

"Not yet. We're going to sit here for a few more minutes and monitor things." The captain hesitated, remembering. "But while we wait, let's go ahead and install the limpet. We may not get a better chance."

"Yes, sir. I'll order it now."

While the *Yangtze*'s second in command issued the order, the captain reached into his shirt pocket to retrieve a cigarette. Five minutes later, while the sub's CO puffed away on the Panda, the first officer looked up from his console. "Sir, the ROV's deployed. The unit should be in place within ten minutes."

"Very well."

The first officer swiveled in his chair, now directly facing the captain. "I expect that Peng and the others must be getting pretty upset with all that's happened, especially the delay."

"Yes, I'm sure they're uneasy but we've been lucky so far, and I want to keep it that way. During the transfer, we'll be terribly exposed. I want to make certain that it takes place undetected."

"Satellites?"

"Yes. The Yanks have excellent equipment, and even with the darkness and heavy cloud cover, their radar-equipped birds might see us." The captain paused, inhaling one last, deep drag. "Anyway, I'm more concerned with their aircraft and that ship that's out there. They've got to have at least one Orion in the area by now plus a helo may have launched from the ship. You know what that means."

The first officer nodded, his stomach turning a notch.

Equipped with the latest antisubmarine warfare detection gear, the P-3Cs were armed with a formidable array of weapons, all designed to kill submarines: air-launched torpedoes, antiship/sub missiles, and a vast array of depth charges, some even equipped with nuclear warheads. ASW helos were nearly as lethal, too.

"Well, sir," the first officer offered, "we haven't picked up any aircraft radar transmissions yet, so, hopefully, our probe is keeping them occupied."

The CO sighed. "Yes, Quon, it does appear to be working. Let's just hope that it continues until we are finished here."

"Yes, sir."

* * *

Ricardo Molina couldn't quite fathom what he was viewing.
It was like something out of *The Twilight Zone.*

For the past hour he had remained aboard Air One, orbiting over the *Bellingham.* It was now 12:14 A.M. From an
altitude of two hundred feet, the helicopter directed its powerful spotlight onto the waters around the stricken submarine.
And now the *Regina* had just arrived on scene. It too was
beaming spotlights onto the *Bellingham.* But there wasn't a
lot to see.

The top of the sail was about to flood; only the bow remained afloat, angling unnaturally high out of the water. The
exposed hull looked like an immense prehistoric behemoth,
taking its last gasp of breath before its final submergence
into the abyss.

All of the crew that could get out were out. The last to
abandon ship were the two officers on top of the sail. Ricardo
had just watched them slip overboard.

The waters surrounding the sinking hulk were littered with
over a hundred survivors. At the moment, there were about
a dozen men bobbing about. A few wore PFDs, but most
were wet-suited SEALs. Unable to continue with their mission, the commandos had been trapped aboard the *Bellingham* when it was ambushed.

The majority of the survivors had managed to climb into
the sub's emergency lifeboats. But there wasn't room for
everyone. Several of the rafts failed to inflate. The precarious
situation was partially mitigated when the assault inflatables
showed up. The six SEALs, who earlier had swum out of
the *Bellingham*'s escape trunks before the mission was
aborted, pulled seventeen waterlogged and half-frozen sailors
into their boats. Their fellow SEALs elected to remain wet
until more help arrived.

Ricardo watched as the *Regina* gingerly maneuvered
alongside the submarine, preparing to haul the survivors
aboard. *It won't be long now,* he thought, knowing that the
Bellingham was doomed.

Ricardo looked up from the chaos, glancing westward
through his window. The distant night sky was pewter black.
But out there, some twenty miles away, was the *Emerald*

Sea. The Sea King's radar had just painted it. Ten minutes earlier the ship had stopped fleeing and was now adrift. *What the hell's going on out there?*

Finally, he couldn't stand it any longer.

Ricardo keyed his helmet intercom. "Pilot, I need to speak with Captain MacKenzie; can you patch me through to him?"

"Affirmative, sir. Stand by."

It took about a minute.

"MacKenzie here."

"Captain, any idea on when we'll be able to head out to the cruise ship?"

"It'll be a while yet, Rick. I can't take a chance on releasing Air One until we've got everyone aboard."

Ricardo was not surprised. "How about the cell phone. Your people have any luck rigging something up?"

"The techs got a clone up and running. They've been calling that number you gave us. They thought they had a response once—but nothing came of it."

"You sure it's working right? I mean Tim said he had his own phone aboard."

"Affirmative. My people tell me it's no big deal to set up, especially with our gear. But for whatever reason, Carpenter's not answering."

"Okay, thanks for the update. Please let me know when you think we'll be able to check out the ship."

"I will."

As Ricardo once again peered through the Sea King's cabin window, viewing the ongoing SAR operation, his thoughts lingered. *Tim, old boy, I hope you can handle it on your own because the cavalry sure ain't going to show up like you were expecting.*

Tim was astonished at how easy it had been to make it back to the helicopter. He no longer had to divert around the lifeboat decks; all of the passengers had been sent below, confined to their cabins. And there were no roving patrols to worry about. But most important, there were no guards posted around the 500MD. *I wonder where they all went,* he thought as he climbed back into the cockpit.

The helicopter's flight deck was as he had left it, except for a few telltale clues. A thick maintenance manual was laid open on the copilot's seat, and on the floor was a small metal box full of tools. *Well,* Tim thought as he leafed through the book, *so you guys finally discovered my handiwork.* He smiled. *I bet it didn't take you long to figure out that this baby's grounded.*

Tim next turned to the aircraft's radio. Without his cellular phone, the Defender's radio was his only hope.

He reconnected his hot-wire lead and flipped on the power switch, praying that it still worked. The light emitting diode flashed on. *Hallelujah!*

Tim slipped on a headset and then keyed the microphone switch. His heart raced as he spoke into the lip mike. "Ricky, this is Tim, can you read me? Over."

Nothing.

Tim repeated the call—a dozen times.

No response, just a steady tone of static from the headphones.

And then Tim discovered the problem. "Son of a bitch!" he cursed. In his zeal to disable the craft's flight controls, he had severed the copper wire that linked the transceiver to the exterior antenna. The tiny cable was just one of the dozens within the spaghettilike wire bundle that he had earlier sliced in half with his knife.

"You dumb jerk—now what are you going to do?"

Frustrated, Tim collapsed into the copilot's seat, shaking his head in disgust. He had planned to reactivate the Defender's radio to link up again with Ricardo Molina. He had to find out what had happened to the original rescue operation and when they would try again. But that wasn't going to happen now. So, once again, he was on his own.

Tim was preparing to climb out of the helo when he spotted the movement; it was just a flicker through the cockpit windscreen. He ducked down behind the instrument panel, using it as a shield. He waited a few seconds before inching his head next to the wind screen. He then stole a quick look, scanning the walkway area next to the bulkhead. *Damn!* he thought.

* * *

Allen Peng was in the lead, a *zhongdui* **with a submachine** gun following directly behind. Trailing Peng and the gunman was Jennifer Richmond. Her wrists were bound by plastic cable ties. Her head was bowed in submission. Two more guards, each carrying nasty assault rifles, flanked her. And bringing up the rear, several paces behind the group, was the engineer-commando. Except for the pistol in his hip-mounted holster, he was unarmed. Nevertheless, he carried the most powerful weapon of all. The duffel bag full of the MERLIN documents rested atop his right shoulder.

None of the assembled paid the slightest attention to the helicopter when they passed it. As far as the Chinese invaders were concerned, the Defender 500MD was a piece of junk, useless to their cause.

Had just one of them turned around, he would have spotted Tim Carpenter as he popped open the door and slithered onto the steel deck.

"Raven Three Two, Watchtower. Report. Over."

"Watchtower, Raven Three Two. We've got a possible hostile. The signal's weak and sporadic, but there's definitely something around three hundred feet. No question about it. Over."

"That's got to be the bastard that bushwhacked the *Bellingham.*"

"Affirmative, Watchtower. We concur."

"Can you pinpoint its location? Over."

"Not yet. We're going to set up another datum line and start running on preattack mode. It'll take about twenty minutes to set it up. Over."

"Good, that makes sense." A short pause. "Now, what kind of boat is it?"

"Unknown at this time. We've only picked up a few fragments so far, and none of my people can ID the plant or the screw. I'd like to transmit a recording to you. Maybe your computers can match it up for us." A pause. "I'd sure like to know who I'm shooting at before launching. Over."

"Very well, Raven Three Two, send the recording. But do

not prosecute your attack until you receive *my* permission
Is that clear?"

"Yes, ma'am."

"Watchtower, clear."

"Raven Three Two, clear."

The encrypted radio conversation was between the com
manding officer of SOSUS NavFac Whidbey Island and the
Tactical Coordinator (TACCO) on an Orion, call sign Raven
Three Two. The P-3C was patrolling the coastal waters off
shore of northern British Columbia. Three more Orions were
en route, but until they arrived Raven Three Two was the
only U.S. Navy asset available to hunt down the marauder
that had bushwhacked the *Bellingham*.

Raven Three Two had deployed a string of twenty sono
buoys along a west-to-east track that was about thirty mile
long. Buoy number five made the contact. Its passive hydro
phone barely registered the soft hiss of a propeller and the
faint rumble of a nuclear power plant circulation pump.

Raven Three Two's TACCO and NavFac's CO were both
certain that they would soon have the raider in their sights
It would be hours later, however, before they finally discov
ered the brilliance of the *Yangtze*'s deception.

45   KILL OR BE KILLED

What are they doing? Tim wondered.

He was kneeling, peering around a bulkhead. They were
about forty feet away, lined up against the railing, facing the
sea. Jenny remained flanked by the two guards. Two of the
other Asians were chatting while the man with the duffel bag
listened.

Tim made another quick survey of the surroundings. Ex
cept for Jenny and the five bad guys, the deck was deserted
Dammit, what should I do?

*   *   *

The PRC commando on Jenny's right side was the first to see it. The seascape was as black as ever, but his night vision was exceptional. He pointed with his right hand while shouting in his native tongue, "I see it!"

Peng turned away from the soldiers he was addressing, his eyes following the commando's gesture. At first, nothing registered. But then he too saw it. It was an aberration, a ghostly shadow materializing from an inky environment. He smiled as he reached into a pocket, retrieving the flashlight. *Finally!*

The captain of the *Yangtze* adjusted his night vision binoculars, focusing on a tiny light that blinked from an upper deck. The fluorescent green image of a man holding a flashlight snapped to clarity. He wore jeans and a heavy peacoat. Although there wasn't quite enough background light to make out the man's facial features, he was satisfied. *Must be Peng.* He scanned the others. They wore combat fatigues and several held weapons. *Zhongduis!* He was about to look away when he finally noticed the woman. She was sandwiched between two of the men. *So, they found you after all!*

The captain of the *Yangtze* knew little of Peng's mission. But he had been briefed enough to know that the goal was to kidnap an American woman and then return her to China for interrogation. To accomplish that goal Beijing had directed him to take whatever measures he deemed necessary, even sinking an American warship.

The captain lowered the binoculars. He shook his head. *All of this for one woman? What's so important about her?*

Tim raised the H & K, sliding the butt end of the metal stock into the pocket formed by his right cheek and shoulder. He squinted through the sight, taking a bead on the man standing to Jenny's right. *First him, then the others, one after another. Just like in a shooting gallery.* He held his breath.

Just as he was about to squeeze the trigger, the target moved. *Shit!* Tim lowered the MP5. They were now all in motion, moving forward along the deck. In just a few seconds they were out of view. *Where the hell are they going now?*

Tim slipped around the corner, his back pressed agains the steel wall. He managed to spot the last man as he walke through the doorway, heading back into the ship's interic spaces. It was the commando carrying the duffel bag.

Tim moved across the open deck, peering over the railin *Now, what's so interesting over here?*

The vision took a few seconds to register. "Holy shit! S that's how they're going to do it!"

Tim hobbled forward, heading toward the same doorwa that Jenny and her captors had just passed through.

A boarding ladder had been deployed from the midshir port cargo hatchway. Its lower end was already awash. Nor mally, the heavy steel doors would remain sealed while a sea. Located just twenty feet above the water surface, th hull opening was subject to flooding in rough seas. But th evening the ocean was gentle; the swells low and slow.

Jennifer stood near the opening, looking seaward. She wa shivering. The air was nippy, but it wasn't responsible fc her body tremors. Fear did that. *My God, they're really goin to do it!*

Jenny watched as the submarine crept forward. It was no just two hundred yards away.

The *Yangtze* was semisubmerged. Only the top third of th sail projected above the water surface. The pressure casin remained submerged and the tip of the finlike stern sensc pod was awash. The result was a hull configuration that pro vided minimal exposure to radar.

The *Yangtze* had deliberately surfaced behind the *Emeral Sea,* using the cruise ship's huge structural cross-section a an electronic shield. Like a mini mountain, the towering hu and superstructure blocked radar transmissions from th nearby Canadian warship.

Although the *Regina* could not see the submarine, rada satellites and high-flying aircraft equipped with sea surfac scanning radars could. Consequently, the *Yangtze*'s C played it safe. The sail exposed just a fraction of the surfac area of the main hull. If it were spotted on radar, the refle

on would resemble that of a small tugboat or yacht, not a
0-foot-long nuclear-powered attack submarine.

Allen Peng moved next to the hull opening and looked out-
ard. The *Yangtze* was now parallel with the *Emerald Sea*,
out three hundred feet away. In the reflected light from the
ip, Peng could see the three men standing atop the sail. He
ld his portable radio next to his mouth and keyed it. "Tiger,
agon, over," he said.

The response was immediate, the built-in decoder de-
rambling the incoming encrypted message within micro-
conds. "Dragon, Tiger, go." The voice was flat, devoid of
notion, the result of the encryption process.

"Ah, Captain, we're all set now. Send the raft over."

"Very well, stand by."

Peng watched as one of the men atop the sail inflated the
bber raft. Five minutes later he was paddling toward the
nerald Sea.

Peng eyed the inflatable as it approached. He didn't like
hat he saw. He keyed his radio, "Tiger, that thing's tiny.
can hold maybe four at a time, including your man."

"I know, but that's all we have available."

"I've got twenty-four men plus the woman to transfer—
is is going to take forever."

"Sorry, but that's the best we can do." The captain paused.
can deploy another raft with a man if you want."

"Yes, do it. And make it quick. We're running out of
ne."

Peng turned to the two men guarding Jennifer. "She goes
st; you two escort her. Keep her away from the sub's
ew."

The men nodded in unison.

Peng turned around, scanning the assembled. Most of the
_A commandos and the entire MSS contingent were clus-
red into the holding area. Just Major Wu and two *zhongdui*s
ere topside, all on the bridge. Until the transfer was com-
ete, Peng would retain absolute control of the ship. With
e passengers and crew now confined to their quarters, he
dn't expect any problems from them. But he didn't trust

the ship's officers. They remained locked inside the captain'
stateroom. To ensure that they stayed put, the cabin's onl
door was booby-trapped.

Peng continued surveying his men. He was looking fo
one in particular. He finally gave up. "Where's Liao?" h
asked.

"He had to piss," someone called out. "He went to find
head."

Peng pointed to the speaker, "Go find him and bring hin
back. He's going next. I want both him and those document
onboard the *Yangtze* after the woman is transferred."

"Yes, sir."

Jenny was now sitting on the frigid steel deck near the hu
opening, her back leaning against an equally chilly bulkhead
She hadn't asked to sit down, she had just done it. *The he
with them!*

She ignored the Asians as they milled about her, all jab
bering away in their native tongue. She felt the stares an
knew that some were talking about her. A few leered at he
and one made crude gestures with his tongue. She had see
it all before. Young, horny men, regardless of their race c
nationality, were much alike everywhere.

With her legs bent and her bound wrists resting on he
knees, Jenny bowed her head. Tears streamed down he
cheeks. The nightmare would never end. *I should have li:
tened to Tim!*

Holding the Heckler & Koch with his left hand, his finger o
the trigger guard, Tim Carpenter reached down and graspe
the back of the collar. The rip-stop fabric was strong an
would take the strain. He pulled upward and then took a ste
The load was heavy; it was like dragging a suitcase full c
bricks. His bum knee didn't help matters either.

Tim hauled the corpse across the tile floor. Smeared bloo
marked the path. He stuffed the body into a storage close
next to the purser's office. As he closed the door, his la
image of the man he had just killed was of the eyes. The
were wide open. With the spark of life extinguished, the

were dull, lackluster. Death was forever. He would not forget them.

Tim had not intended to kill the commando. It had all happened in an eyeblink. It was kill or be killed.

Tim had been working his way down an interior flight of stairs, trying to figure out where Jenny had been taken, when the commando suddenly appeared. The man had walked out of the men's room just off a middeck stairway landing.

Both men were equally stunned at the encounter. The *zhongdui* instantly dropped the bag he had been carrying and reached for his holster. Without thinking, Tim leveled the SMG and pulled the trigger. The suppressor coughed three times. The soldier collapsed, his heart minced.

Tim felt no remorse for the vulgar act, at least not yet. There hadn't been time for that. It was just luck that he had fired first. Otherwise, he would be the one with the forever open eyes.

After mopping up the blood trail with paper towels from the rest room, Tim surveyed his surroundings. So far, none of the others had shown up. *But where did they go? Where's Jenny?*

He was prepared to continue downward into the bowels of the ship when he finally made the connection. It was still sitting in front of the doorway to the bathroom. *Damn, but that looks familiar.*

Tim walked over and kneeled down beside the bag the commando had been carrying. He unzipped it. *Wow!*

"What do you mean you can't find Liao?" Peng asked.

"He's not around here, sir," reported the MSS agent. "We've checked all of the toilets in the immediate area, but there's no sign of him."

"What about the documents?"

The man shrugged. "We didn't find them, either."

"Shit," muttered Peng.

The commando-engineer had been instructed to retain possession of the MERLIN documents at all times—and that meant even when relieving himself. But that hadn't been a problem for the man named Liao. The secrets contained within the documents had whetted his curiosity like nothing ever before. He wouldn't rest until he had read every page.

"Well," Peng finally said, "Liao must be around here someplace; he's probably sitting on a toilet as we speak, reading those documents." He raised his hands chest high, gesturing outward. "This damn ship's got shitters everywhere, so keep looking. I'm sure he's in one of them. Find him. We haven't got a lot of time for this."

"Yes, sir."

Peng stepped to the open hatchway. The rubber raft with the woman and the two guards had just reached the submarine. *Good,* he thought, *one less thing to worry about.*

The rubber-coated steel stank of seaweed and algae. It was icy slick. If the hand line had not been available, she would have slipped back into the sea by now.

Jenny paused to catch her breath. She was halfway up the aft turtleback slope of the *Yangtze*'s fin. She glanced upward at the crest. Half a dozen antennae and mastlike cylinders projected upward from the top of the sail. The spires reminded her of a church cathedral. But that wasn't what caught her attention. It was the men. There were four of them. They were all staring down at her.

More Asians! Dear God, this really must be a Chinese submarine. The thought of being sealed up in an interrogation center on mainland China now mortified her. *They'll never let me go.*

The horror of Jenny's predicament hadn't fully registered until a few moments earlier, when her memory somehow resurrected the horrible images. It had been a network television news documentary on China—the People's Liberation Army in particular. The story reported on the PLA's horrific practice of selling body parts from executed prisoners.

They actually took orders. With some four thousand executions each year there was plenty to market. The condemned were checked for tissue and blood types as well as screened for HIV and other infectious diseases.

On Death Day those prisoners reserved for "special treat

ment," both males and females, were injected with antico-
agulants. They were then marched onto the public fields with
the others.

Kneeling, heads bowed down, and with their hands lashed
behind their backs, they were each dispatched with a single
rifle shot to the base of the skull. For the "specials" the barrel
was positioned just right to minimize collateral damage.

The organs were harvested in makeshift field surgeries located adjacent to the killing grounds. They excised kidneys,
corneas, hearts, and livers. The body parts were chilled and
then shipped by air to a PLA-owned hospital located near
Hong Kong.

The hospital marketed a variety of transplants but its specialty was kidney grafts. For $30,000 U.S. one could buy a
new kidney.

Most of the condemned were vile: murderers, rapists, child
molesters. But not all. Petty thieves, forgers, and political
dissenters were sometimes executed. And if a particular tissue type was not available from the execution pool, rumors
abounded that the PLA was not above dipping into the general prison population to find just the right match.

Selling body parts was a growth industry in the People's
Republic of China. Each year the PLA raised tens of millions
of dollars, most of which went to the purchase of new weapons.

Tim Carpenter sucked in a deep breath. His heart thundered
away. Sweat beaded on his brow. Adrenaline surged into his
bloodstream. *Gotta do it now!* he finally said to himself.

He pulled the MP5 to his right shoulder and rushed forward, finger on the trigger.

It was all over in just a few seconds. They never had a
chance.

Allen Peng watched as a raft docked with the *Yangtze*. It
was completing its third round-trip. The first raft, the one
that had transported Jennifer, was now tied up to the base of
the *Emerald Sea*'s boarding ladder and three more commandos were climbing into it. So far, two-thirds of his contingent

had been transferred to the submarine. They were slightly ahead of schedule. But there was still a problem—a big one. Engineer Liao had yet to be located.

Where the hell are you? Peng wondered.

A minute later he finally got his answer. It came from the remote speaker of his handheld radio that was now clipped to the collar of his coat. The voice was pure American.

"Attention on deck, motherfuckers!" There was a short pause. "I say again, attention on deck, you motherfuckers!"

What the hell? Peng asked himself. He reached down to his belt and keyed the transmit switch. "Who is this?"

Tim Carpenter was on the starboard bridge wing, looking aft. He could see the *Yangtze*. Another raft had reached the submarine. The occupants were now climbing up the steep-angled back slope of the sail.

Once again, Tim Carpenter keyed the transmit switch. He had liberated the portable PLA radio from one of the commandos assigned to guard the bridge. That soldier, along with his two companions, was dead.

"Hello there, motherfucker," Tim said, deliberately cursing for its shock value. "Time's getting short, so listen up."

Tim released his thumb from the transmit switch and turned to his side. He grinned at Captain Demetriou.

The master of the *Emerald Sea* was standing just a few feet away. A waterproof telephone handset was glued to his right ear. It was plugged into one of the bridge wing's remote ports.

"Your boys got that camera gear set up?" Tim asked.

Captain Demetriou nodded. "They're ready, just like you wanted."

"Good, tell 'em to stand by. It won't be long."

"Okay."

Tim again thumbed the microphone key. "Okay, here's the lowdown of the situation. As you might have figured out by now, the men you left in the pilothouse are no longer in control." He paused for effect. "Captain Demetriou and his officers now have the conn. You no longer own this ship."

Tim was responsible. After recovering the bag full o

MERLIN documents he headed forward. His destination was the radio shack—to call Ricardo. But to get there required passing near the bridge deck. That meant dealing with the guards.

From an interior aft companionway, he had rushed into the wheelhouse, the MP5 blazing. He caught the three commandos completely off guard. Major Wu was sitting in the captain's pedestal chair, his weapon lying on the deck. The others were standing by the helm, smoking. They all went down without returning a round.

Tim continued with his monologue: "Don't even think of trying to take the pilothouse back. We've got plenty of protection, thanks to *your* well-armed people. Besides, we've been watching you from up here and we know that a good part of your force has already been transferred over to your sub." *And I know Jenny's already on that thing,* he wanted to say, but didn't.

Tim hadn't actually observed the raft that had transported Jenny. One of Demetriou's men had.

After the ambush, during his search for the ship's radio room, Tim discovered the captain's stateroom. The grenades wired to the door handle caught his attention. He disarmed the booby trap and freed the occupants.

While Captain Demetriou and his senior officers took control of the bridge, Tim and the ship's communications officer headed for the radio room. That's when the officer told Tim about Jenny.

Through a porthole in the captain's stateroom he had spotted Jennifer just as she climbed over the sail's cowling and disappeared into an interior hatchway.

Tim keyed the microphone once again: "And don't even think of trying to send your men back to this ship." He turned to his left, nodding to one of Demetriou's men.

The cruise ship's chief engineer, a former Greek naval officer, stood next to the guardrail at the aft end of the bridge wing. He held one of the commandeered assault rifles. An expert with firearms, he aimed and then fired.

Tim watched as a dozen rounds splattered the water about

twenty yards in front of the ship's boarding ladder. *That ought to get their attention!*

Peng heard the dull thuds of the bullets thumping into the water. He had turned toward the opening just in time to see the last few waterspouts.

He had heard enough. He keyed the microphone. "Who am I speaking with?"

"You know."

"Fucking Carpenter!" Peng muttered.

46 BLIND MAN'S BLUFF

"All right, Carpenter," Peng said, "I get your point. How do you want to resolve this situation?"

Tim smiled. *Good,* he thought. "What we have here is a Mexican standoff. . . ." He laughed. "Or should I say a Chinese standoff. Do you know what I mean?"

Peng didn't reply. Instead, he just double-clicked his microphone.

"Good," Tim replied. "Now it's really simple. All you guys have to do is send Ms. Richmond back and then we'll let you go. You can all climb back in that pig boat and disappear."

"No deal," Peng said.

Tim had been expecting the resistance. Whoever these people were, they had gone to enormous efforts to find Jenny. It was time to up the ante.

"Well, you really don't have much time to screw around. They're coming."

"What are you talking about?"

"Oh, roughly half of the U.S. Navy's fleet is about forty minutes away."

Tim was bluffing. Big time. He hadn't a hint as to what the U.S. military was doing. All he knew was what Ricardo Molina had told him hours ago. And just twelve minutes earlier Tim had tried to get an update. But when he and the ship's communications officer walked into the radio room that hope evaporated. Major Wu's men had been very thorough when it came to destroying the ship's sophisticated communication equipment. It had all been smashed, from the SATCOM system to the portable bridge wing radios. Even the handheld radio Tim was now using, liberated from one of the dead commandos, was virtually useless. It was restricted to just two frequencies, both of which were automatically encrypted.

"Ha!" Peng said. "You expect me to believe that? Your navy has no clue as to what we're doing right now!" He paused, looking across the water toward the *Yangtze*. "Do you see any ships or aircraft around? No, you don't, because they're busy elsewhere."

Tim keyed his microphone. "Yeah, that was all true, but they know now because I just told 'em."

Impossible, Peng thought. *We destroyed the radio room— and your own portable phone.* "You're bluffing, Carpenter."

Tim was ready. A sense of urgency was pivotal to his plan. "You didn't find all of the radios." Tim hesitated for a few seconds. "The purser's office is equipped with a single-sideband high-seas radio. I'm now in contact with the Canadian warship that's been following you—the *Regina*. She's not far away now."

Shit! thought Peng. *He must be telling the truth, otherwise how would he know about that ship?* "All right, Carpenter, let's cut the bullshit. What is it you really want?"

Progress, Tim concluded. "Just return Jennifer and we'll call it a day."

Peng shook his head. It was time to call the bet. "You must know that we've accomplished our mission. We have Richmond—she's aboard the submarine. The rest of us here are expendable." He hesitated. "Just one radio call from me and it will submerge. And then the real show will start."

Tim frowned, surprised at the man's statement. "What do you mean?"

"You'd better warn your military people to back off. We've mined the ship."

"What?"

"A robot from the submarine installed the charge. It's attached to the bottom of this ship. A simple coded underwater signal from the submarine and the *Emerald Sea* will cease to exist." He paused. "Oh, and don't think about trying to send a diver down to disarm it. It's loaded with antitamper devices." Again he paused. "One other thing, Carpenter, it doesn't like vibration. So don't engage the propellers."

Damn, Tim cursed to himself. He remembered what his cabin had been like when the starboard screw churned away. "How do I know you're not bluffing?"

"You don't," Peng answered, "but think about it."

Peng wasn't bluffing. The charge had been set before the *Yangtze* ever surfaced. While the sub hovered near the cruise ship, the remotely operated vehicle quietly swam out of torpedo tube four. A technician inside the attack center piloted the ROV, eventually planting the neutrally buoyant device under the *Emerald Sea*'s fuel bunkers. Powerful magnets secured the shaped charge to the steel bottom plates. The thousand kilos of plastic explosive molded inside the mine casing was more than enough to break the ship's back.

All along, the contingency plan had been in place. It was designed to ensure the *Yangtze*'s ultimate escape. If the other diversion tactics failed, then the U.S. military would have to balance the risk of killing fourteen hundred people in order to hunt down one renegade sub. The PRC mission planners had calculated that there was an 88 percent probability that the Americans would not take such a risk.

Tim delayed his response. He was taken aback by the threat.

At first, he was convinced it was a bluff. But the more he thought about it, the more it made sense. *Dammit! These buggers aren't screwing around.*

Tim leaned against the top railing, looking aft. He surveyed the distance between the ship and the submarine. It would be an easy swim for a diver, probably easier for an underwater robotic device. He finally keyed the mike.

"Well, aren't you full of surprises." He paused, knowing

it was time to again raise the stakes. "But I've got one for you, too."

Peng expected the volley from the American: "Enlighten me."

"Jenny wasn't in on the development of MERLIN—her father kept it a secret from her. Her knowledge is limited to what she's been able to read in those documents." Tim hesitated. He was about to pull out his ace. "Now, you've no doubt discovered that the man who was entrusted with the documents is missing. You can stop looking—he's dead. I waxed him." Tim paused for impact. "Oh, and, by the way, I've got all that secret stuff he had."

Tim released the transmit switch, facing Captain Demetriou. "Go ahead and tell 'em to roll it." He then keyed the microphone again. "To prove my point, find a television set and tune it to channel three. You'll see what I'm talking about. Oh, and one last thing. You'd better hurry. Time's getting short."

Bastard, Peng thought, *what's he up to?*

Peng stared at the TV screen. The empty canvas duffel bag was neatly folded at one end of the table. All of its contents were displayed on the tabletop. And one of the ship's crewmen was sitting in a chair, fanning through a bound report. The Greek crewman couldn't read a word of English, but from the camera's point of view it was impossible to tell. The sailor eventually held up the cover, directing it toward the cameraman.

The lens zoomed in on the cover. The words *Top Secret— Project MERLIN,* snapped into focus.

Shit, Peng thought, *they really have the documents.*

The crewman next reached for the plastic cylinder sitting on the tabletop near his right side. It was about the size of a lunch box thermos. He unscrewed the top and then extracted the computer circuit board. It was the device that commando-engineer Liao had shown Peng earlier. Liao had told Peng that it was the one and only "key" that made the MERLIN device work. It was beyond priceless.

Tim Carpenter, watching the same closed-circuit broadcast

from inside the bridgehouse, once again keyed his microphone. "As you can see, we've really got the stuff."

Peng responded: "All right, Carpenter, what's the deal?"

"You can have all that MERLIN stuff. I don't give a crap
about it. All I want in return is Jenny, and your word that
you won't blow this ship up. It's that simple."

"And what about your navy? What am I supposed to do
about that?"

"I'll tell 'em the truth. If they fire on you, you'll blow the
ship. Isn't that how you planned it?"

He's still up to something, Peng guessed. "All right. How
do you want to do this?"

"First," Tim said, "you need to . . ."

The USS *Bellingham* ceased to exist as a United States naval
combat vessel at 0201 hours, local time. It was a simple
matter of physics. The bubble of high-pressure air inside the
forward ballast tank no longer countered the seawater flooding through the propeller shaft. SSN 775's glass-reinforced
plastic bow sonar dome slipped below the ocean with hardly
a ripple.

Ricardo Molina and Captain MacKenzie watched the end
from *Regina*'s fantail. The rain had finally stopped but the
air remained thick with a night mist.

Air One was now on the flight deck, just behind them. It
was being refueled. A half-dozen red-shirted sailors were
also maneuvering a pair of eight-and-a-half-foot-long silver
cylinders next to the helo's starboard side.

Just as the *Bellingham* disappeared Ricardo turned to face
the *Regina*'s CO. "All the men in the water get out?" he asked.

"We think so. We've recovered one hundred fifteen crew
plus all the SEALs." He paused. "We're missing twelve."

"They're still inside?"

"The sub's skipper thinks so. Most were in the engine
compartment. Apparently, there wasn't time to get them all
out before it flooded."

Ricardo shook his head. *What a frigging disaster.*

MacKenzie leaned on the safety rail, silently staring at the
empty ocean, still illuminated by an army of floodlights.

Finally, Ricardo spoke. "So," he said, "what's next?"

MacKenzie turned to face Molina. "We'll maintain station here and continue to search with the ship. I'm also sending Air One up for one last look around."

"After that, can we go?" Ricardo asked. "I've got to find out what's happening on the *Emerald Sea*."

"Yes. We'll take you out for a quick look. But then I've got to turn Air One loose on a new mission."

"New mission?"

"Right. Apparently your ASW people at NAS Whidbey have a lead on the bugger that ambushed the *Bellingham*." He pointed landward. "Our bird's been assigned to assist one of your Orions that's hunting the bastard. We're loading up right now."

Ricardo turned around, now eyeing the Sea King. He spotted the men working with the cylinders.

"Are those what I think they are?"

"Right. If we get a shot, we're going to nail that bugger."

47 ACCELERATION

The exchange point was in neutral water, halfway between the *Emerald Sea* and the *Yangtze*. Only the principals were invited.

Tim Carpenter occupied one raft. The canvas duffel bag stuffed full of the MERLIN documents was wedged between his feet. Peng was in the other raft. Jenny sat behind him.

Marksmen from both sides trained their weapons on the rendezvous point.

All of Peng's men were now aboard the *Yangtze*. Three of the commandos with sniper experience occupied the crest of the submarine's fin, their weapons at the ready. The *Emerald Sea*'s engineering officer and two other armed men watched from concealed positions aboard the ship.

The tension was volcanic. Just one wrong move from ei-

ther side and the tranquil encounter could erupt into chaos
and death.

The two rafts kissed. Tim grabbed the other one. Peng did
likewise. The two men locked eyes.

"So, Carpenter," Peng said, "we finally meet."

Tim ignored the Asian. He surveyed Jenny. Other than her
disheveled hair, she appeared unharmed. "You okay, kiddo?"
he asked, smiling.

She nodded.

"Just hang in there a little longer. It's almost over."

She cracked a weak smile.

Tim turned back to the spy. "All right, how do you want
to do this?"

"You know the routine," Peng said. "I just showed you
mine, now you show me yours."

Tim picked up the duffel bag, resting it on his lap. He then
unzipped it, displaying the contents for Peng's view.

"And the computer device?" Peng asked.

Tim reached into the back of the bag and removed the
container. He handed it to Peng.

Peng opened the lid and briefly examined the circuit board.

"Well," he said, "it appears that you have met your side
of the bargain. But let me tell you something you don't
know." Peng smiled. "We videotaped the contents of the
bag." He turned to face Jenny. "Correct, Miss Richmond?"

Jenny nodded.

Peng continued: "As soon as I return to the submarine,
we're going to check every item you have given us against
what's on the tape. If anything is missing or has been exchanged, and I mean anything, our little transaction will be
considered null and void. You know what will happen then."
He paused, his face neutral. "Now, before we consummate
this deal, is there anything else you want to tell me about?"

Shit! Tim thought. *These bastards are slick.* He hesitated,
his mind racing with options. *What do I do? Maybe they
won't notice. But what if they do?*

In the end, Tim gave in—it was far too risky to continue.

Twenty minutes earlier, he had removed a perfectly intact
circuit board from one of the sabotaged transceivers in the

Emerald Sea's radio room. He then used his lighter to singe the edges of the plastic backing. At first glance, the circuit board looked convincing. But a close inspection would reveal the deception.

Tim reached into his coat pocket and removed a Ziploc plastic bag. It was about the size of a paperback novel. He dangled it in front of Peng.

"Well," Tim said, "then I guess you'll want this." He tossed the bag to the MSS operative.

Allen Peng opened the baggy, examining the microprocessor. He then looked back, frowning at Carpenter. "I take it then that this is the real key for the MERLIN device," he said.

Tim nodded and then he shrugged his shoulders, silently signaling: *I had to try it!*

Peng read the gesture. "We would have figured it out, Carpenter."

"I know; that's why I gave it to you now."

Peng sighed. He had expected Carpenter to pull something. "Anything else you want to come clean on? This is your last chance."

There was no hesitation on Tim's part. "No. You've got it all."

Peng nodded, satisfied. "Very well, let's do it."

By the time Tim and Jenny had climbed up the steep board-ing ladder, the *Yangtze*'s sail was sealed up and it was just getting under way, shearing off to the north.

Once Jenny finally stepped into the *Emerald Sea*'s interior, she collapsed into Tim's arms.

"Oh, thank you," she moaned. Tears flowed. Her legs were Jell-O.

Tim smiled. "It's finally over, Jen." He cradled her head against his chest. She wrapped her arms around his waist.

"I was so scared. They were going to take me away in that thing . . . to God only knows where."

"I know but it's okay now. They can't hurt you. You're safe."

They held each other for half a minute and then Jenny

looked up, meeting Tim's gaze. "Tim, about what happened earlier . . . I'm so sorry. I shouldn't have . . ."

"Don't worry about that. We were both stressed out. I think it's best for everyone if we just let it go . . . like it never happened."

Jenny nodded, reluctantly releasing her security hold. She then started to wipe the tears away with the back of her hand.

Tim removed a handkerchief from his pants pocket and completed the job, tenderly soaking up the wetness. "Whaddaya say we go round up a cup of hot chocolate?" he asked, another beaming smile broadcasting from his movie star–handsome face.

"That sounds great." *What an awesome guy . . . Laura's so lucky!*

They had taken just a few steps when Tim heard it. The tone was more of a vibration than a sound. He stopped and turned around.

"What's wrong?" Jenny asked.

Tim cocked his head toward the hull opening. The noise level increased. *Chopper!*

He sprinted toward the hatchway. Jenny followed.

"Oh, shit!" Tim yelled as he watched the Sea King. It was barely fifty feet above the water surface. Its searchlight was locked on to the now submerging submarine. The water surface was just a few feet from the top of the sail.

"*Regina, Regina,* this is Air One. Forget about that Orion contact. We've definitely got a sub here. We caught her on the surface. She's diving now. Over."

Captain MacKenzie grabbed a hand mike. He was inside the CIC.

"You have a positive visual," MacKenzie said, astonished at the helicopter pilot's radio report.

"Affirmative, sir. From the little we could see of the sail and stern sensor pod, I'd say she was a Victor or maybe an Akula. Definitely Russian. Over."

A Russian, MacKenzie thought. He had been told to expect a Chinese boat. He keyed the microphone. "Air One, stand by for orders."

"Roger."

MacKenzie turned to his XO. "Number One, check the computer—does the PRC have any Victors or Akulas?"

"Just a second, skipper." The man attacked his keyboard with lightning strokes. He had the answer in twenty seconds. "No Victors, sir. But they did buy one Akula. Renamed the *Yangtze.*"

That's got to be it! MacKenzie thought. "Thanks." He keyed his microphone again. "Okay, Air One, do you think you were spotted?"

"Maybe, but I doubt it. We came up from behind. All of the masts were down except for one tube. If they happened to be looking aft, our searchlight might have been visible."

"All right, prepare to take it out."

"Roger, initiating preattack mode."

Ricardo Molina listened to the continuous cross-talk be-tween the cockpit flight crew and his companion in the helo's cabin. The ASW sensor operator had just used an electric winch to lower a hydrophone into the water.

"Probe is wet," called out the technician. He waited a few seconds before continuing. "I've got a propeller. Recording now."

For the next two minutes, the helo continued to hover over the ocean, listening, recording.

"She's on a heading of two nine five, range eight hundred twenty-one meters. Speed twelve knots."

"Okay," the pilot said, "let's set it up."

"Yes, sir. Switching to attack."

I'll be damned, Ricardo thought, *they're really going after that turkey.*

Tim was now on the bridge, Jenny at his side. They were both out of breath.

"Captain," he said, facing Markos Demetriou. "If we don't stop that helicopter, we're all going to die."

"What do you mean?"

"Look at it, on the side of the fuselage, by the float. See it?"

Demetriou pulled up his binoculars. The Sea King was a hundred yards away, hovering. There was just enough reflected light from his ship to see one of the cylinders attached to the helo's fuselage. It had been loaded aboard just minutes earlier during refueling. Its twin was on the opposite side of the craft.

Demetriou lowered the binoculars, locking on to Tim's eyes. "Is that a torpedo?"

"Damn right. And I'll give you ten-to-one odds those guys are getting ready to launch the thing. You know what that'll mean."

Demetriou cursed in his native tongue as he thought about the mine attached to the bottom of his ship. "What can we do?" he finally asked.

"We've got to get their attention—tell 'em to stop."

"But we don't have any radios—did you try the one those pirates had?"

"Yes, but it must be encrypted. None of our people hear it."

How can we communicate with them? the master wondered, now staring at the steel deck. At first he consider firing off flares. *That'll get their attention but we still won't be able to warn them about the bomb.* And then a new idea flashed into focus. *That just might work!*

"Quick," he said, now facing Tim, "follow me!"

Ricardo Molina watched with fascination as the attack progressed. It was all handled by computers. The minicomputer in the aircraft; the mainframe aboard the *Regina,* now directly air-linked to the Air One via a coded microwave circuit, and the microcomputer inside the Mark 44 torpedo— all three were communicating, sharing information, preparing for the kill.

Earlier, Ricardo had asked the pilots to once again try to contact the *Emerald Sea* with the helo's radio. But he had been turned down, temporarily. They were too busy. Besides, after prior attempts, the flight crew was convinced that the cruise ship's communications were out. The fact that the radar mast lay across the pilothouse roof just reinforced that opinion.

Tim and Jenny worked in tandem. She pushed the five-gallon bucket along the deck while he worked the push broom.

"Do you think this stuff will show up?" she asked.

"I hope so," he said, working the broom handle back and forth like a racing locomotive piston.

"Are they done yet?" asked Captain Demetriou. He had just returned to the starboard bridge wing. One of his men was leaning over the guardrail, observing Tim and Jenny's work. They were two levels below.

"I can't tell for sure, but it looks like part of it is up."

"That's good enough. We can't wait."

Captain Demetriou turned to face the bridge interior. The first officer was watching his every move from inside. Demetriou jerked his right hand up and down, like pumping a hand well.

"Stand by for release," the sensor operator said.

"Okay, give us a countdown," replied the pilot.

"Twenty . . . nineteen . . ."

BLAHHHHHHHHH!

"What the hell is that?" shouted the pilot.

The *Emerald Sea*'s massive foghorn blasted once again.

BLAHHHHHHHHH!

The sensor operator ignored the racket. He was totally engrossed in the mechanics of the attack. Not since World War II had anyone in the Canadian navy sunk an enemy submarine, let alone a real-live nuke. He was going into the record books!

". . . twelve . . . eleven . . ."

Ricardo spotted it first. "Holy shit!" he yelled out over the intercom. "Look at the frigging ship."

Both pilots turned in unison. Dozens of flashlights and spotlights were blinking, half directed at the aircraft, the others trained on a small section of the bulkhead just below the bridge. They could see two people working frantically, painting a message in gray on the steel white wall. It was just big enough to see with the naked eye:

THEY LEFT BOMB DONT ATTAC

". . . six . . . five . . ." continued the sensor operator,

Ricardo didn't wait for the pilot—there wasn't time. "Stop!" he yelled, commanding the sensor operator to abort the torpedo attack. The man ignored him.

Ricardo pulled up the Benelli and then jammed the barrel of the twelve-gauge shotgun onto the man's face, an inch below his right eye. "Stop!" he screamed, "or I'll blow your fuckin' head off!"

That worked.

48 REUNION

Ricardo Molina stepped off the Sea King, automatically ducking his head because of the whirling blades. As soon as he had cleared the landing zone, the helo lifted off. Its rotor wash blasted everything.

Tim Carpenter watched as Ricardo made his way across the open deck. He had removed the helmet. His mahogany skin contrasted sharply with the survival suit's fluorescent orange.

Ricardo didn't have any trouble spotting Tim. Although there were dozens standing next to the landing site, Tim Carpenter stood out like the proverbial sore thumb. From head to toe, he was coated with sticky deck paint.

Tim hobbled toward his friend, his bad knee now like an anchor.

The two men embraced; Tim smeared gray onto Ricardo. But the FBI agent didn't care.

"Good to see you again, buddy," Ricardo said.

"About frigging time you showed up," replied Tim, a grin breaking out.

"You're walking like an old fart—are you hurt?"

"Banged up my knee—same one again, you know."

Ricardo nodded.

The two men talked for another minute and then Tim abruptly stopped, turning to his side. "Jenny," he called out, nodding for her to approach. She had been standing in the background, watching the reunion.

"Rick, this is Jenny. Jenny, meet Rick."

Agent Molina smiled as he eyed the pretty woman. "I'm sorry you had to go through all of this. We should have . . ." He paused, finally noticing the droves of passengers and crew that were silently observing the reunion. "We need to talk—in private—is there somewhere we can go?"

"Yeah, sure," Tim said. "Follow me."

"So they have all the documents?" Ricardo said, his tone signaling defeat.

Tim nodded while sipping from his mug. The aroma of the fresh coffee, mixed with the lingering stink of his last cigarette and the ever-present metallic scent of fresh paint, permeated the compartment. They were inside a tiny conference room next to the hotel manager's office.

"Yeah," Tim said, "I had no choice. What was I supposed to do? Let the bastards blow up the ship?" Tim hesitated, taking another sip. He then took a moment to adjust the bag of ice resting on top of his left knee. "And by the way, what the hell are you doing about the bomb? Those bastards could still set it off—they said something about using an underwater signal to do it."

"We're working on it. A naval explosives ordinance disposal team is on the way. In the interim, we're going to transfer everyone off this thing. The *Regina* will be here shortly."

"Is it big enough?" Jenny asked, gesturing with her hands. She sat beside Tim. "I think the captain said there are over fourteen hundred passengers and crew aboard."

Ricardo nodded. "I'm sure it can handle most everyone,

even with the *Bellingham*'s crew aboard. It's got a lot of open deck space." He paused to sip from his coffee mug. "The rest will be loaded onto a Coast Guard cutter out of Ketchikan. It'll be here in a couple of hours."

"So," Tim said, "until then, this thing remains a powder keg."

"Yes."

"Well, I sure hope you got the word out to everyone—don't screw around with that Chinese sub until the damn thing's been neutralized."

"Loud and clear, Tim. No one's going to do anything until the ship's been vacated."

"Good," Tim replied, satisfied. And then he remembered. "Do you think we might be able to make some calls out from that Canadian frigate? I'd like to check on my family."

Ricardo leaned back in his chair. "Where the heck did you stash them, anyway? We've been trying to contact Laura for days."

Tim grinned. He was about to answer when Jenny interrupted.

"Wait a minute, you guys!" She turned to face Molina. "I want to talk to Chris—he probably thinks I'm dead."

Ricardo smiled. "As soon as we take care of business, I'll see to it that you both make those calls. And by the way, your Chris is just fine. They just shook him up a little."

Jenny's eyes bulged. "They hurt Chris?"

Oh, damn, Ricardo thought, *now you've stepped in it.* "He was interrogated for a day, but he's safe now. Don't worry."

Jenny grimaced and then sank back into her chair. *Sweet Chris! I miss you so much . . . thank God you're okay . . . please forgive me!*

Ricardo took another sip. He was about to start the portion of the interrogation he had dreaded the most. He looked Tim straight in the eye. "Now, back to the documents, whatever happened to the original MERLIN CPU?"

"The what?" Tim asked.

"The secret circuit board that Dr. Richmond had. You know what I'm talking about."

"Oh, yeah," Tim said, almost as an afterthought, "they got that, too."

Ricardo's eyes rolled back. "Oh, no," he groaned. The pain was real.

"No, they didn't," Jenny interjected, her spirits suddenly surging.

"Jenny," Tim said, turning to face her, "I tried to fake 'em out, but that guy figured it out. That's what we were talking about in the raft."

"What raft?" Ricardo asked.

He was ignored.

"They didn't get it, Tim. I switched the thing."

"You did what?" Tim asked, a tinge of hope in his voice.

"Before I gave myself up I switched it. Didn't you see my note on the mirror?"

"Yes, but . . ." His voice trailed off as he remembered. He had been so preoccupied with finding Jenny that he had forgotten her cryptic lipstick message.

Jenny picked up the conversation. "Remember the TV you shot up in that cabin?" she asked.

"Yeah."

"Well, I went back there and took out one of the circuit boards from the back of the set—it was kind of cooked like Dad's. And then I stuck it inside the container. It wasn't even a close match, but how would they know?"

Tim shook his head in wonderment.

Ricardo couldn't wait. "So where's the real one?" he asked.

"In the Golden Grotto—the nightclub. I stuck the darn thing back inside the console radio we saw there. That was the solution to my riddle." She turned to face Tim. "Remember? Like what my father did in the storage locker—hiding the damaged circuit board inside Grandma's RCA radio." She paused, now smiling. "You would have eventually figured it out."

Tim didn't respond. Instead, he turned to face Ricardo. Their thoughts were identical: "Let's go!"

* * *

Jenny used the same Swiss Army knife to remove the screws from the back cover of the ancient radio. She then reached inside, being careful to avoid the vast collection of tubes and wires—the receiver still worked. She removed the MERLIN device, holding it up for view.

"That's it?" Tim asked.

"Yep," Jenny answered.

Ricardo took a deep breath. "Ms. Richmond, I know that was your father's property and that . . ."

Jenny shook her head. "It's yours. . . . I don't want anything more to do with it."

She started to hand it to the FBI agent.

"Just a second," interrupted Tim. "Let's get something clear first." He turned toward Ricardo, now stone-faced. "Agent Molina, as the sole inheritor of her father's estate, my client is not relinquishing any of her rights to the MERLIN technology. Understood?"

"What?" Ricardo asked, confused.

Tim turned to face Jenny, and out of Ricardo's view he winked. "Am I right, Jennifer, in assuming that by turning over your father's device to Agent Molina, you are simply entrusting the federal government to protect the device? You still do intend to benefit from your father's contract with the government?"

Jenny smiled back. Tim Carpenter, P.I., would have made a good attorney. "Oh, of course, Tim. That's exactly my intention."

"Good," Tim replied. He turned back to face his friend. "Now, Agent Molina, Ms. Richmond would like an official receipt from the government of the United States of America for the transfer of one MERLIN gadget."

Ricardo shook his head as reached into his shirt pocket. He removed a small notepad with companion ballpoint pen. He faced Jenny.

"I assume you'll want this made out to Jennifer Richmond as executrix of Dr. Jeffrey Richmond's estate."

"Yes," Jenny said. "And don't forget to leave a spot for Tim to sign as my official witness to your signature."

"Details," Ricardo muttered.

AFTERMATH

49 PAYBACK

They nailed it in the Philippine Sea, 155 miles east of the Ryukyu Trench. It didn't have a chance.

The Mark 46 Mod 5 would not stop. The *Yangtze*'s captain tried everything: a barrage of decoys, high-speed turns, surfing the thermocline, and in one last desperate act he even launched one of the special robot probes, hoping it would intercept the weapon. But the countermeasures were useless.

The torpedo's computer brain had been programmed to follow just one sound signature. The underwater recording provided by the *Regina*'s ASW helicopter was all it took.

Hundreds of Captor torpedo mines had been deployed—every one in the U.S. Navy's Pacific Fleet arsenal. The half-million-dollar units were air-dropped by transport planes, launched from subs, and released from surface vessels. Every known PRC sub route and choke point was covered.

The monitoring hydrophone for each mine mooring ignored all other sounds—surface and subsurface. It was interested only in the *Yangtze*'s unique soundprint.

Preprogrammed into the Captor's computer brain was a digital blueprint of the Akula-class submarine's hull. All of the sub's vulnerable structural points were flagged. Depending upon the angle of attack, the torpedo's sonar-controlled computer would select the impact point.

The Mark 46 hit the crown of the hull just forward of the sail's leading edge. The ninety-six-pound directional warhead punctured the hull's outer skin and then angled downward to the base of the hatchway that linked the top of the sail to the sub's internal nerve center—the control room. The warhead detonated on the hatch, cracking the thick steel as if it were plate glass. An instant later, the pressure casing imploded. The *Yangtze* sank in 9,400 feet of water.

There had been no attempt to send a message. No last-second transmissions of any kind. There just hadn't been time for that. And there was no emergency buoy that would pop to the surface and electronically broadcast the grave-site's earth coordinates. It, too, had been obliterated by the implosion.

No one heard the attack, not even the U.S. Navy's vast Pacific Ocean SOSUS system. But within just a few days the truth was known. When the mines were checked, the monitoring teams discovered that Unit No. 135 had deployed. The tiny recorder built into the mine's mooring capsule replayed the kill to a select few back in the Pentagon.

Weeks later, the PLAN Command in Shanghai quietly struck the *Yangtze*'s name from its official register of combat vessels. Nothing was said about the vessel's fate, only that she had failed to return to port from a routine patrol and was presumed to have sunk with all hands.

The official goal of Operation Linebacker had been to intercept the Chinese submarine before it could transfer the MERLIN documents. Anyway, that's what was written in the mission planning documents. But to the flag officers that directed the covert operation, Linebacker was payback, pure and simple.

No one bushwhacks an American submarine or knocks down an innocent patrol aircraft and gets away with it.

EPILOGUE   TOP GUN

The challenge was tantalizing: the U.S. Air Force vs. the U.S. Navy. On Navy turf. Southern California. Fightertown U.S.A.

The best of the Navy's best were up: six brand-new F/A-18E Super Hornets as primary interceptors, each piloted by a Top Gun trophy winner. Two vintage F-14 Tomcats, with two-man crews, served as backup. The fighters were loaded with electronic simulations of the latest versions of the Sparrow, AMRAAM, Sidewinder, and/or Phoenix air-to-air missiles, plus assorted cannon fire.

The battle boundary covered some four million acres of the Mojave Desert. The ceiling ranged from a cap of sixty thousand feet down to cactus level.

For the past fifty minutes a chorus of sonic booms, accompanied by a pulsating deep-toned beat—thud! . . . thud! . . . thud!—reverberated over the desert valley. Multiple jet contrails, thin sinuous streaks, crisscrossed the heavens. And intertwined with the jet wash was a peculiar, pufflike exhaust stream: doughnuts on a string.

It was eight against one.

The NAS LeMoore battle control center was overflowing with Navy and Air Force brass: four-star admirals and generals to lowly ensigns and second lieutenants. There was a near equal mix between pilots and technical staff. Also in attendance were a dozen civilian engineers and scientists from the Pentagon.

It was the studs vs. the nerds.

The duel was almost over. Two against one now.

All eyes were glued to the master display. Radar icons flashed across the movie-size screen, tracking the aerial combat taking place several hundred miles to the east. Unseen speakers broadcast the pilots' frantic chatter.

"Get out of there, Snake!" yelled the F-14 Tomcat pilot. His surviving F-18E teammate was a mile ahead, racing east at Mach 1.2.

"Where's that little prick? I can't see it!"

"It's below you, coming up on your six. Break left, now!"

The F-18E Super Hornet was halfway through the evasion maneuver when its icon on the LeMoore radar display screen pulsed in intensity and then began blinking on and off.

"Kill number seven," called out one of the referees.

Each pilot in attendance, Navy and Air Force alike, including four Top Gun instructors, let out a collective groan. The DARPA engineers and DIA reps, however, grinned from ear to ear. A few even high-fived each other.

It was now one on one.

The F-14 Tomcat was on afterburners, its variable geometry wings fully swept back. "I see the bastard!" screamed the Navy pilot.

"Let's kill it!" roared the backseated RIO.

Twenty minutes earlier the F-14's radar intercept officer had given up any hope of using the interceptor's electronic eyes to track their opponent. He could never achieve radar lock, just occasional traces that flashed onto his screen for a second or two. The Air Force's experimental unmanned combat aerial vehicle, code name VORTEX, had the radar cross-section of a butterfly.

The black dart was now just half a mile ahead of the Tomcat.

"Switching to Sidewinders," announced the Tomcat pilot. The Navy commander was preparing to launch the electronic equivalent of a heat-seeking missile. He was just about to fire when it happened. His quarry bolted to the right in an eye blink.

"Where'd it go?" he screamed.

"What?" yelled the RIO.

"It was just there and then it disappeared."

"Oh, shit! Skipper, you better get us outta here ASAP."

The pilot managed to bank right and was roaring downward at a forty-degree angle, heading for the hard deck at 1,100-plus mph. But it wasn't near enough.

The wobbling tone now blaring away inside the helmets of the F-14's flight crew broadcast their electronic erasure.

"Damn!" the RIO blurted, disgusted.

The pilot said nothing. He was too overwhelmed to speak.

GLOSSARY

AI: Artificial intelligence
ASW: Antisubmarine warfare
AUV: Autonomous underwater vehicle
BND: Bundesnachrichtendienst (West Germany's Federal Intelligence Service)
CAPTOR: En CAPsulated Torpedo mine that can be moored in deep water and is designed to sink submarines (U.S. Navy)
Chen di yu: PRC deep-cover intelligence agent (spy)
CIA: Central Intelligence Agency
CIC: Combat Information Center
CID: Criminal Investigation Division (U.S. Army)
CJC: Chairman of the Joint Chiefs of Staff (top U.S. military officer)
CO: Commanding officer
COB: Chief of the boat (senior chief on a U.S. submarine)
CPC: Chinese Communist Party
CPU: Central Processing Unit (CPU)
CSIS: Canadian Security Intelligence Service
DARPA: Defense Advanced Research Projects Agency
DCI: Director of Central Intelligence (CIA boss)
Deuxième Bureau: French Military Intelligence Agency
DGSE: Direction Générale de la Sécurité Extérieur (French intelligence agency responsible for foreign espionage; successor of the SDECE)
DIA: Defense Intelligence Agency (U.S.A.)
DOD: Department of Defense
DOE: Department of Energy
ECM: Electronic countermeasures
ELF: Extremely low frequency (radio frequency received by submarines at depth)
EO: Engineering officer

FAA: Federal Aviation Agency

FBI: Federal Bureau of Investigation

500MD: Light military helicopter manufactured by McDonnell Douglas

G's: Multiples of the gravity force

G-lock: Point at which a fighter pilot loses consciousness due to gravity effects resulting from extreme maneuvering

Glock 26: Nine-millimeter semiautomatic pistol manufactured by Glock of Austria

GPS: Global Positioning System (satellite navigation system)

H & K: Heckler & Koch (*see* MP5)

HMCS: Her Majesty's Canadian Ship

INSCOM: Intelligence and Security Command (U.S. Army)

IUSS: Integrated Underwater Surveillance System (*see* SOSUS)

MARK 48: U.S. Navy heavyweight torpedo

MP5: Nine-millimeter submachine gun manufactured by Heckler & Koch of Germany

MSS: Ministry of State Security (People's Republic of China's equivalent of the CIA, and then some!)

NAS: Naval Air Station

NATO: North Atlantic Treaty Organization

NavFac: Naval Facility (U.S. Navy)

NCIC: National Crime Information Center (FBI)

NMCC: National Military Command Center (located at the Pentagon)

NORAD: North American Aerospace Defense Command

NRO: National Reconnaissance Office (coordinates satellite operations for U.S. intelligence agencies; located near Washington, D.C.)

NSA: National Security Agency (U.S.A.)

NTSB: National Transportation Safety Board

NV or NVD: Night vision or night vision device (see-in-the-dark optics)

OOD: Officer of the deck (ship driver)

ORION: *See* P-3C

PFD: Personal flotation device (life vest)

PLA: People's Liberation Army (PRC military)

PLAN: People's Liberation Army Navy

PRC: People's Republic of China (Communist China)

P-3C: U.S. Navy long-range patrol aircraft (submarine hunter)

RCMP: Royal Canadian Mounted Police

REM: Rapid eye movement (dream state)

RF: Radio frequency

ROV: Remotely operated vehicle

SAC: Special agent in charge (FBI)

SAM: Surface-to-air missile

SAR: Search and rescue

SAS: Special Air Service (British commandos)

SATCOM: Satellite communications

SDECE: Service de Documentation Extérieure et de Contre-Espionnage (French counterespionage service, replaced by the DGSE in 1981)

SEAL: Sea/Air/Land (U.S. Navy special warfare unit)

Second Department: PRC's military intelligence department

Semtex: Plastic explosive

SIGINT: Signals intelligence (the interception, decryption and analysis of hostile communications)

SMG: Submachine gun

SOP: Standard operating procedure

SOSUS: Sound Surveillance System (U.S. Navy network of underwater listening devices; designed to track submarines)

SSN: Nuclear-powered attack submarine (U.S. Navy)

SUBCOMPAC: Commander, Submarine Forces Pacific (U.S. Navy)

TOP GUN: U.S. Navy Fighter Weapon School (responsible for training Navy pilots in air combat)

UAV: Unmanned aerial vehicle

UCAV: Unmanned combat aerial vehicle

UW: University of Washington

VHF: Very high frequency (radio frequency)

VLF: Very low frequency (radio frequency used to communicate with submarines located near the surface)

XO: Executive officer

Zhongdui: PLA's seaborne special forces (naval commandos)